He collected his wits. 'What I don't understand,' he said, 'is how anyone could pay attention to the opera when you were in the place.'

'They're French,' she said. 'They take art seriously.'

'And you're not French?'

She smiled. 'That's th̶ ̶...'

'French,' he said. 'Yo̶ ̶...ch.'

'You're so sure,' she sa̶ ̶...

'I'm merely a thickhea̶ ̶...he said. 'But even I can tell French ̶ ̶...omen apart. One might dress an Englishwoman in French fashion from head to toe and she'll still look English. You…'

He trailed off, letting his gaze skim over her. Only consider her hair. It was as stylish as the precise coifs of other Frenchwomen…yet, no, not the same. She was…different.

'You're French, through and through,' he said. 'If I'm wrong, the stickpin is yours.'

'And if you're right?' she said.

He thought quickly. 'If I'm right, you'll do me the honour of riding with me in the Bois de Boulogne tomorrow,' he said.

'That's all?' she said, in French this time.

'It's a great deal to me.'

She rose abruptly in a rustle of silk. Surprised—*again*—he was slow coming to his feet.

'I need air,' she said. 'It grows warm in here.'

He opened the door to the corridor and she swept past him. He followed her out, his pulse racing.

THE DRESSMAKERS SERIES

Loretta
CHASE

Silk
is for
Seduction

Published in Great Britain 2014
by Mills & Boon, an imprint of Harlequin (UK) Limited,
Eton House, 18-24 Paradise Road, Richmond, Surrey, TW9 1SR

© 2011 Loretta Chekani

Excerpt from *Wicked in Your Arms* © 2011 Sharie Kohler

ISBN: 978 0 263 24571 4

009-0214

Harlequin (UK) Limited's policy is to use papers that are natural, renewable and recyclable products and made from wood grown in sustainable forests. The logging and manufacturing processes conform to the legal environmental regulations of the country of origin.

Printed and bound by
CPI Group (UK) Ltd, Croydon, CR0 4YY

Loretta Chase has worked in academe, retail and the visual arts, as well as on the streets—as a meter maid (aka traffic warden)—and in video, as a scriptwriter. She might have developed an excitingly chequered career had her spouse not nagged her into writing fiction. Her bestselling historical romances, set in the Regency and Romantic eras of the early nineteenth century, have won a number of awards, including the Romance Writers of America's RITA®.

Website: www.LorettaChase.com.

In Memory of Princess Irelynn

ACKNOWLEDGEMENTS

Thanks to:

The milliners and tailors of Colonial Williamsburg's Margaret Hunter Shop, with special thanks to mantua-maker and mistress of the shop Janea Whitacre and tailor Mark Hutter, for helping me with numerous details of the art of dress, and for so generously sharing their expertise and enthusiasm

Chris Woodyard, for her invaluable help with dolls and demolished houses and every other pesky question I could think to ask her

Susan Hollowy Scott for storms at sea, as well as her usual wit, wisdom and moral support

My husband Walter for his cinematic eye, unceasing supply of encouragement and inspiration, and numerous acts of undaunted courage

Cynthia, Nancy, and Sherrie for what they always do

and, of course,

Trinny and Susannah

In the summer of 1810, Mr. Edward Noirot eloped to Gretna Greene with Miss Catherine DeLucey.

Mr. Noirot had been led to believe he was eloping with an English heiress whose fortune, as a result of this rash act, would become his exclusively. An elopement cut out all the tiresome meddling, in the form of marriage settlements, by parents and lawyers. In running off with a blue-blooded English lady of fortune, Edward Noirot was carrying on an ancient family tradition: His mother and grandmother were English.

Unfortunately, he'd been misled by his intended, who was as accomplished in lying and cheating, in the most charming manner possible, as her lover was. There had indeed been a fortune. Past tense. It had belonged to her mother, whom John DeLucey had seduced and taken to Scotland in the time-honored fashion of his own family.

The alleged fortune by this time was long gone. Miss DeLucey had intended to improve her financial circumstances in the way women of her family usually did, by luring into matrimony an unsuspecting blue-blooded gentleman with deep pockets and a lusting heart.

She, too, had been misled, because Edward Noirot had no more fortune than she did. He was, as he claimed, the offspring of a French count. But the family fortune had been swept away, along with the heads of various relatives, years before, during the Revolution.

Thanks to this comedy of errors, the most disreputable branch of one of France's noble families was united with its English counterpart, better known—and loathed—in the British Isles as the Dreadful DeLuceys.

The reader will easily imagine the couple's chagrin when the truth came out shortly after they'd made their vows.

The reader will undoubtedly expect the screaming, crying, and recriminations usual on such occasions. The reader, however, would be mistaken. Being the knaves they were—and furthermore quite truly in love—they laughed themselves sick. Then they joined forces. They set about seducing and swindling every dupe who crossed their path.

It was a long and convoluted path. It took them back and forth between England and the Continent, depending on when a location became too hot for comfort.

In the course of their wanderings, Catherine and Edward Noirot produced three daughters.

Chapter One

THE LADIES' DRESS-MAKER. Under this head
we shall include not only the business of a Mantua
Maker, but also of a Milliner . . . In the Milliner,
taste and fancy are required; with a quickness
in discerning, imitating, and improving upon
various fashions, which are perpetually changing
among the higher circles.

The Book of English Trades,
and Library of the Useful Arts, 1818

London
March 1835

Marcelline, Sophia, and Leonie Noirot, sisters and
proprietresses of Maison Noirot, Fleet Street,
West Chancery Lane, were all present when Lady Renfrew, wife of Sir Joseph Renfrew, dropped her bombshell.

Dark-haired Marcelline was shaping a papillon bow
meant to entice her ladyship into purchasing Marcelline's
latest creation. Fair-haired Sophia was restoring to order
one of the drawers ransacked earlier for one of their more
demanding customers. Leonie, the redhead, was adjust-
ing the hem of the lady's intimate friend, Mrs. Sharp.

Though it was merely a piece of gossip dropped casually into the conversation, Mrs. Sharp shrieked—quite as though a bomb *had* gone off—and stumbled and stepped on Leonie's hand.

Leonie did not swear aloud, but Marcelline saw her lips form a word she doubted their patrons were accustomed to hearing.

Oblivious to any bodily injury done to insignificant dressmakers, Mrs. Sharp said, "The Duke of Clevedon is *returning*?"

"Yes," said Lady Renfrew, looking smug.

"To London?"

"Yes," said Lady Renfrew. "I have it on the very best authority."

"What happened? Did Lord Longmore threaten to shoot him?"

Any dressmaker aspiring to clothe ladies of the upper orders stayed au courant with the latter's doings. Consequently, Marcelline and her sisters were familiar with all the details of this story. They knew that Gervaise Angier, the seventh Duke of Clevedon, had once been the ward of the Marquess of Warford, the Earl of Longmore's father. They knew that Longmore and Clevedon were the best of friends. They knew that Clevedon and Lady Clara Fairfax, the eldest of Longmore's three sisters, had been intended for each other since birth. Clevedon had doted on her since they were children. He'd never shown any inclination to court anyone else, though he'd certainly had liaisons aplenty of the other sort, especially during his three years on the Continent.

While the pair had never been officially engaged, that was regarded as a mere technicality. All the world had assumed the duke would marry her as soon as he returned with Longmore from their Grand Tour. All the world had been shocked when Longmore came back alone a year ago, and Clevedon continued his life of dissipation on the Continent.

Apparently, someone in the family had run out of patience, because Lord Longmore had traveled to Paris a fortnight ago. Rumor agreed he'd done so specifically to confront his friend about the long-delayed nuptials.

"I believe he threatened to horsewhip him, but of that one cannot be certain," said Lady Renfrew. "I was told only that Lord Longmore went to Paris, that he said or threatened something, with the result that his grace promised to return to London before the King's Birthday."

Though His Majesty had been born in August, his birthday was to be celebrated this year on the 28th of May.

Since none of the Noirot sisters did anything so obvious as shriek or stumble or even raise an eyebrow, no onlooker would have guessed they regarded this news as momentous.

They went on about their business, attending to the two ladies and the others who entered their establishment. That evening, they sent the seamstresses home at the usual hour and closed the shop. They went upstairs to their snug lodgings and ate their usual light supper. Marcelline told her six-year-old daughter, Lucie Cordelia, a story before putting her to bed at her usual bedtime.

Lucie was sleeping the sleep of the innocent—or as innocent as was possible for any child born into their ramshackle family—when the three sisters crept down the stairs to the workroom of their shop.

Everyday, a grubby little boy delivered the latest set of scandal sheets as soon as they were printed—usually before the ink was dry—to the shop's back door. Leonie collected today's lot and spread them out on the worktable. The sisters began to scan the columns.

"Here it is," Marcelline said after a moment. " 'Earl of L___ returned from Paris last night . . . We're informed that a certain duke, currently residing in the French capital, has been told in no uncertain terms that Lady C___ was done awaiting his pleasure . . . his grace expected to return to London in time for the King's Birthday . . . engagement to be announced at a ball at Warford House at the end of the Season . . . wedding before summer's end.' "

She passed the report to Leonie, who read, " 'Should the gentleman fail to keep his appointment, the lady will consider their 'understanding' a *misunderstanding*.' " She laughed. "Then follow some interesting surmises regarding which gentleman will be favored in his place."

She pushed the periodical toward Sophia, who was shaking her head. "She'd be a fool to give him up," she said. "A dukedom, for heaven's sake. How many are there? And an unmarried duke who's young, handsome, and healthy? I can count them on one finger." She stabbed her index finger at the column. "Him."

"I wonder what the hurry is about," Marcelline said. "She's only one and twenty."

"And what's she got to do but go to plays, operas, balls, dinners, routs, and so on?" said Leonie. "An aristocratic girl who's got looks, rank, and a respectable dowry wouldn't ever have to worry about attracting suitors. This girl . . ."

She didn't have to complete the sentence.

They'd seen Lady Clara Fairfax on several occasions. She was stunningly beautiful: fair-haired and blue-eyed in the classic English rose mode. Since her numerous endowments included high rank, impeccable lineage, and a splendid dowry, men threw themselves at her, right and left.

"Never again in her life will that girl wield so much power over men," Marcelline said. "I say she might wait until her late twenties to settle down."

"I reckon Lord Warford never expected the duke to stay away for so long," said Sophy.

"He always was under the marquess's thumb, they say," Leonie said. "Ever since his father drank himself to death. One can't blame his grace for bolting."

"I wonder if Lady Clara was growing restless," Sophy said. "No one seemed worried about Clevedon's absence, even when Longmore came home without him."

"Why worry?" said Marcelline. "To all intents and purposes, they're betrothed. Breaking with Lady Clara would mean breaking with the whole family."

"Maybe another beau appeared on the scene—one Lord Warford doesn't care for," said Leonie.

"More likely Lady Warford doesn't care for other beaux," said Sophy. "She wouldn't want to let a dukedom slip through her hands."

"I wonder what threat Longmore used," Sophy said. "They're both reputed to be wild and violent. He couldn't have threatened pistols at dawn. Killing the duke would be antithetical to his purpose. Maybe he simply offered to pummel his grace into oblivion."

"That I should like to see," Marcelline said.

"And I," said Sophy.

"And I," said Leonie.

"A pair of good-looking aristocratic men fighting," Marcelline said, grinning. Since Clevedon had left London several weeks before she and her sisters had arrived from Paris, they hadn't, to date, clapped eyes on him. They were aware, though, that all the world deemed him a handsome man. "There's a sight not to be missed. Too bad we shan't see it."

"On the other hand, a duke's wedding doesn't happen every day—and I'd begun to think this one wouldn't happen in our lifetime," Sophy said.

"It'll be the wedding of the year, if not the decade," Leonie said. "The bridal dress is only the beginning. She'll want a trousseau and a completely new wardrobe befitting her position. Everything will be of superior quality. Reams of blond lace. The finest silks. Muslin as light as air. She'll spend thousands upon thousands."

For a moment, the three sisters sat quietly contemplating this vision, in the way pious souls contemplated Paradise.

Marcelline knew Leonie was calculating those thousands down to the last farthing. Under the untamable mane of red hair was a hardheaded businesswoman. She had a fierce love of money and all the machinations involving it. She labored lovingly over her ledgers and accounts and such. Marcelline would rather clean privies than look at a column of figures.

But each sister had her strengths. Marcelline, the eldest, was the only one who physically resembled her father. For all she knew, she was the only one of them who truly was his daughter. She had certainly inherited his fashion sense, imagination, and skill in drawing. She'd inherited as well his passion for fine things, but thanks to the years spent in Paris learning the dressmaking trade from Cousin Emma, hers and her sisters' feelings in this regard went deeper. What had begun as drudgery—a trade learned in childhood, purely for survival—had become Marcelline's life and her love. She was not only Maison Noirot's designer but its soul.

Sophia, meanwhile, had a flair for drama, which she turned to profitable account. A fair-haired, blue-eyed innocent on the outside and a shark on the inside, Sophy could sell sand to Bedouins. She made stonyhearted moneylenders weep and stingy matrons buy the shop's most expensive creations.

"Only think of the prestige," Sophy said. "The Duchess of Clevedon will be a leader of fashion. Where she goes, everyone will follow."

"She'll be a leader of fashion in the right hands," Marcelline said. "At present . . ."

A chorus of sighs filled the pause.

"Her taste is unfortunate," said Leonie.

"Her mother," said Sophy.

"Her mother's dressmaker, to be precise," said Leonie.

"Hortense the Horrible," they said in grim unison.

Hortense Downes was the proprietress of Downes's, the single greatest obstacle to their planned domination of the London dressmaking trade.

At Maison Noirot, the hated rival's shop was known as *Dowdy's*.

"Stealing her from Dowdy's would be an act of charity, really," said Marcelline.

Silence followed while they dreamed their dreams.

Once they stole one customer, others would follow.

The women of the beau monde were sheep. That could work to one's advantage, if only one could get the sheep moving in the right direction. The trouble was, not nearly enough high-ranking women patronized Maison Noirot because none of their friends did. Very few were ready to try something new.

In the course of the shop's nearly three-year existence, they'd lured a number of ladies, like Lady Renfrew. But she was merely the wife of a recently knighted gentleman, and the others of their customers were, like her, gentry or newly rich. The highest echelons of the ton—the duchesses and marchionesses and countesses and such—still went to more established shops like Dowdy's.

Though their work was superior to anything their London rivals produced, Maison Noirot still lacked the prestige to draw the ladies at the top of the list of precedence.

"It took ten months to pry Lady Renfrew out of Dowdy's clutches," said Sophy.

They'd succeeded because her ladyship had overheard Dowdy's forewoman, Miss Oakes, say the eldest daughter's bodices were difficult to fit correctly, because her breasts were shockingly mismatched.

An indignant Lady Renfrew had canceled a huge order for mourning and come straight to Maison Noirot, which her friend Lady Sharp had recommended.

During the fitting, Sophy had told the weeping eldest daughter that no woman in the world had perfectly matching breasts. She also told Miss Renfrew that her skin was like satin, and half the ladies of the beau monde would envy her décolleté. When the Noirot sisters were done dressing the young lady, she nearly swooned with happiness. It was reported that her handsomely displayed figure caused several young men to exhibit signs of swooning, too.

"We don't have ten months this time, " Leonie said. "And we can't rely on that vicious cat at Dowdy's to insult Lady Warford. She's a marchioness, after all, not the lowly wife of a mere knight."

"We have to catch her quickly, or the chance is gone forever," said Sophy. "If Dowdy's get the Duchess of Clevedon's wedding dress, they'll get everything else."

"Not if I get there first," Marcelline said.

Chapter Two

ITALIAN OPERA, PLACE DES ITALIENS. The lovers of the Italian language and music will here be delighted by singers of the most eminent talents, as its name indicates; this theatre is devoted exclusively to the performance of Italian comic operas; it is supported by Government, and is attached to the grand French opera. The performances take place on Tuesdays, Thursdays, and Saturdays.

Francis Coghlan,
*A Guide to France, Explaining Every Form
and Expense from London to Paris*, 1830

*Paris, Italian Opera
14 April 1835*

Clevedon tried to ignore her.

The striking brunette had made sure she'd attract attention. She'd appeared with her actress friend in the box opposite his at the last possible moment.

Her timing was inconvenient.

He had promised to write Clara a detailed description of tonight's performance of *The Barber of Seville*.

He knew Clara longed to visit Paris, though she made do with his letters. In a month or so he'd return to London and resume the life he'd abandoned. He'd made up his mind, for Clara's sake, to be good. He wouldn't be the kind of husband and father his own father had been. After they were wed, he would take her abroad. For now they corresponded, as they'd been doing from the time she could hold a pen.

For the present, however, he intended to make the most of every minute of these last weeks of freedom. Thus, the letter to Clara wasn't his only business for the night.

He'd come in pursuit of Madame St. Pierre, who sat in a nearby box with her friends, occasionally casting not-unfriendly glances his way. He'd wagered Gaspard Aronduille two hundred pounds that Madame would invite him to her post-opera soirée whence Clevedon fully expected to make his way to her bed.

But the mysterious brunette . . .

Every man in the opera house was aware of her.

None of them was paying the slightest attention to the opera.

French audiences, unlike the English or Italians, attended performances in respectful silence. But his companions were whispering frantically, demanding to know who she was, "that magnificent creature" sitting with the actress Sylvie Fontenay.

He glanced at Madame St. Pierre, then across the opera house at the brunette.

Shortly thereafter, while his friends continued to speculate and argue, the Duke of Clevedon left his seat and went out.

"That was quick work," Sylvie murmured behind her fan.

"Reconnaissance pays," Marcelline said. She'd spent a

week learning the Duke of Clevedon's habits and haunts. Invisible to him and everyone else, though she stood in plain sight, she'd followed him about Paris, day and night.

Like the rest of her misbegotten family, she could make herself noticed or not noticed.

Tonight she'd stepped out of the background. Tonight every eye in the theater was on her. This was unfortunate for the performers, but they had not earned her sympathy. Unlike her, they had not put forth their best effort. Rosina was wobbling on the high notes, and Figaro lacked joie de vivre.

"He wastes not a moment," said Sylvie, her gaze ostensibly upon the doings on stage. "He wants an introduction, so what does he do? Straight he goes to the box of Paris's greatest gossips, my old friend the Comte d'Orefeur and his mistress, Madame Ironde. That, my dear, is an expert hunter of women."

Marcelline was well aware of this. His grace was not only an expert seducer but one of refined taste. He did not chase every attractive woman who crossed his path. He did not slink into brothels—even the finest—as so many visiting foreigners did. He didn't run after maids and milliners. For all his wild reputation, he was not a typical libertine. He hunted only Paris's greatest aristocratic beauties and the crème de la crème of the demimonde.

While this meant her virtue—such as it was—was safe from him, it did present the challenge of keeping his attention long enough for her purposes. And so her heart beat faster, the way it did when she watched the roulette wheel go round. This time, though, the stakes were much higher than mere money. The outcome of this game would determine her family's future.

Outwardly, she was calm and confident. "How much will you wager that he and monsieur le comte enter this box at precisely the moment the interval begins?" she said.

"I know better than to wager with you," said Sylvie.

The instant the interval began—and before the other audience members had risen from their seats—Clevedon entered Mademoiselle Fontenay's opera box with the Comte d'Orefeur.

The first thing he saw was the rear view of the brunette: smooth shoulders and back exposed a fraction of an inch beyond what most Parisian women dared, and the skin, pure cream. Disorderly dark curls dangled enticingly against the nape of her neck.

He looked at her neck and forgot about Clara and Madame St. Pierre and every other woman in the world.

A lifetime seemed to pass before he was standing in front of her, looking down into brilliant dark eyes, where laughter glinted . . . looking down at the ripe curve of her mouth, laughter, again, lurking at its corners. Then she moved a little, and it was only a little—the slightest shift of her shoulders—but she did it in the way of a lover turning in bed, or so his body believed, his groin tightening.

The light caught her hair and gilded her skin and danced in those laughing eyes. His gaze drifted lower, to the silken swell of her breasts . . . the sleek curve to her waist . . .

He was vaguely aware of the people about him talking, but he couldn't concentrate on anyone else. Her voice was low, a contralto shaded with a slight huskiness.

Her name, he learned, was Noirot.

Fitting.

Having said to Mademoiselle Fontenay all that good manners required, he turned to the woman who'd disrupted the opera house. Heart racing, he bent over her gloved hand.

"*Madame Noirot,*" he said. "*Enchanté.*" He touched his lips to the soft kid. A light but exotic scent swam into his nostrils. Jasmine?

He lifted his head and met a gaze as deep as midnight. For a long, pulsing moment, their gazes held.

Then she waved her fan at the empty seat nearby. "It's uncomfortable to converse with my head tipped back, your grace," she said.

"Forgive me." He sat. "How rude of me to loom over you in that way. But the view from above was . . ."

He trailed off as it belatedly dawned on him: She'd spoken in English, in the accents of his own class, no less. He'd answered automatically, taught from childhood to show his conversational partner the courtesy of responding in the latter's language.

"But this is diabolical," he said. "I should have wagered anything that you were French." French, and a commoner. She had to be. He'd heard her speak to Orefeur in flawless Parisian French, superior to Clevedon's, certainly. The accent was refined, but her friend—forty if she was a day—was an actress. Ladies of the upper ranks did not consort with actresses. He'd assumed she was an actress or courtesan.

Yet if he closed his eyes, he'd swear he conversed at present with an English aristocrat.

"You'd wager *anything*?" she said. Her dark gaze lifted to his head and slid down slowly, leaving a heat trail in its wake, and coming to rest at his neckcloth. "That pretty pin, for instance?"

The scent and the voice and the body were slowing his brain. "A wager?" he said blankly.

"Or we could discuss the merits of the present Figaro, or debate whether Rosina ought properly to be a contralto or a mezzo-soprano," she said. "But I think you were not paying attention to the opera." She plied her fan slowly. "Why should I think that, I wonder?"

He collected his wits. "What I don't understand," he said, "is how anyone could pay attention to the opera when you were in the place."

"They're French," she said. "They take art seriously."

"And you're not French?"

She smiled. "That's the question, it seems."

"French," he said. "You're a brilliant mimic, but you're French."

"You're so sure," she said.

"I'm merely a thickheaded Englishman, I know," he said. "But even I can tell French and English women apart. One might dress an Englishwoman in French fashion from head to toe and she'll still look English. You . . ."

He trailed off, letting his gaze skim over her. Only consider her hair. It was as stylish as the precise coifs of other Frenchwomen . . . yet, no, not the same. Hers was more . . . something. It was as though she'd flung out of bed and thrown herself together in a hurry. Yet she wasn't disheveled. She was . . . different.

"You're French, through and through," he said. "If I'm wrong, the stickpin is yours."

"And if you're right?" she said.

He thought quickly. "If I'm right, you'll do me the honor of riding with me in the Bois de Boulogne tomorrow," he said.

"That's all?" she said, in French this time.

"It's a great deal to me."

She rose abruptly in a rustle of silk. Surprised— *again*—he was slow coming to his feet.

"I need air," she said. "It grows warm in here."

He opened the door to the corridor and she swept past him. He followed her out, his pulse racing.

* * *

Marcelline had seen him countless times, from as little as a few yards away. She'd observed a handsome, expensively elegant English aristocrat.

At close quarters . . .

She was still reeling.

The body first. She'd surreptitiously studied that while he made polite chitchat with Sylvie. The splendid physique was not, as she'd assumed, created or even assisted by fine tailoring, though the tailoring was exquisite. His broad shoulders were not padded, and his tapering torso wasn't cinched in by anything but muscle.

Muscle everywhere—the arms, the long legs. And no tailor could create the lithe power emanating from that tall frame.

It's hot in here, was her first coherent thought.

Then he was standing in front of her, bending over her hand, and the place grew hotter still.

She was aware of his hair, black curls gleaming like silk and artfully tousled.

He lifted his head.

She saw a mouth that should have been a woman's, so full and sensuous it was. But it was pure male, purely carnal.

An instant later she was looking up into eyes of a rare color—a green like jade—while a low masculine voice caressed her ear and seemed to be caressing parts of her not publicly visible.

Good grief.

She walked quickly as they left the box, thinking quickly, too, as she went. She was aware of the clusters of opera-goers in the corridor making way for her. That amused her, even while she pondered the unexpected problem walking alongside.

She'd known the Duke of Clevedon was a handful.

She'd vastly underestimated.

Still, she was a Noirot, and the risks only excited her.

She came to rest at last in a quieter part of the corridor, near a window. For a time, she gazed out of the window. It showed her only her own reflection: a magnificently dressed, alluring woman, a walking advertisement for what would one day—soon, with a little help from him—be London's foremost dressmaking establishment. Once they had the Duchess of Clevedon, royal patronage was sure to follow: the moon and the stars, almost within her grasp.

"I hope you're not unwell, madame," he said in his English-accented French.

"No, but it occurs to me that I've been absurd," she said. "What a ridiculous wager it is!"

He smiled. "You're not backing down? Is riding with me in the Bois de Boulogne so dreadful a fate?"

It was a boyish smile, and he spoke with a self-deprecating charm that must have slain the morals of hundreds of women.

She said, "As I see it, either way I win. No matter how I look at it, this wager is silly. Only think, when I tell you whether you're right or wrong, how will you know I'm telling the truth?"

"Did you think I'd demand your passport?" he said.

"Were you planning to take my word for it?" she said.

"Of course."

"That may be gallant or it may be naïve," she said. "I can't decide which."

"You won't lie to me," he said.

Had her sisters been present, they would have fallen down laughing.

"That's an exceptionally fine diamond," she said. "If

you think a woman wouldn't lie to have it, you're catastrophically innocent."

The arresting green gaze searched her face. In English he said, "I was wrong, completely wrong. I see it now. You're English."

She smiled. "What gave me away? The plain speaking?"

"More or less," he said. "If you were French, we should be debating what truth is. They can't let anything alone. They must always put it under the microscope of philosophy. It's rather endearing, but they're so predictable in that regard. Everything must be anatomized and sorted. Rules. They need rules. They make so many."

"That wouldn't be a wise speech, were I a Frenchwoman," she said.

"But you're not. We've settled it."

"Have we?"

He nodded.

"You wagered in haste," she said. "Are you always so rash?"

"Sometimes, yes," he said. "But you had me at a disadvantage. You're like no one I've ever met before."

"Yet in some ways I am," she said. "My parents were English."

"And a little French?" he said. Humor danced in his green eyes, and her cold, calculating heart gave a little skip in response.

Damn, but he was good.

"A very little," she said. "One purely French great-grandfather. But he and his sons fancied Englishwomen."

"One great-grandfather is too little to count," he said. "I'm stuck all over with French names, but I'm hopelessly English—and typically slow, except to jump to wrong conclusions. Ah, well. Farewell, my little pin." He brought his hands up to remove it.

He wore gloves, but she knew they didn't hide calluses or broken nails. His hands would be typical of his class: smooth and neatly manicured. They were larger than was fashionable, though, the fingers long and graceful.

Well, not so graceful at the moment. His valet had placed the pin firmly and precisely among the folds of his neckcloth, and he was struggling with it.

Or seeming to.

"You'd better let me," she said. "You can't see what you're doing."

She moved his hands away, hers lightly brushing his. Glove against glove, that was all. Yet she felt the shock of contact as though skin had touched skin, and the sensation traveled the length of her body.

She was acutely aware of the broad chest under the expensive layers of neckcloth and waistcoat and shirt. All the same, her hands neither faltered nor trembled. She'd had years of practice. Years of holding cards steady while her heart pounded. Years of bluffing, never letting so much as a flicker of an eye, a twitch of a facial muscle, betray her.

The pin came free, winking in the light. She regarded the snowy linen she'd wrinkled.

"How naked it looks," she said. "Your neckcloth."

"What is this?" he said. "Remorse?"

"Never," she said, and that was pristine truth. "But the empty place offends my aesthetic sensibilities."

"In that case, I shall hasten to my hotel and have my valet replace it."

"You're strangely eager to please," she said.

"There's nothing strange about it."

"Be calm, your grace," she said. "I have an exquisite solution."

She took a pin from her bodice and set his in its place.

She set her pin into the neckcloth. Hers was nothing so magnificent as his, merely a smallish pearl. But it was a pretty one, of a fine luster. Softly it glowed in its snug place among the folds of his linen.

She was aware of his gaze, so intent, and of the utter stillness with which he waited.

She lightly smoothed the surrounding fabric, then stepped back and eyed her work critically. "That will do very well," she said.

"Will it?" He was looking at her, not the pearl.

"Let the window be your looking glass," she said.

He was still watching her.

"The glass, your grace. You might at least admire my handiwork."

"I do," he said. "Very much."

But he turned away, wearing the faintest smile, and studied himself in the glass.

"I see," he said. "Your eye is as good as my valet's—and that's a compliment I don't give lightly."

"My eye ought to be good," she said. "I'm the greatest modiste in all the world."

His heart beat erratically.

With excitement, what else? And why not?

Truly, she was like no one he'd ever met before.

Paris was another world from London, and French women were another species from English. Even so, he'd grown accustomed to the sophistication of Parisian women, sufficiently accustomed to predict the turn of a wrist, the movement of a fan, the angle of the head in almost any situation. Rules, as he'd told her. The French lived by rules.

This woman made her own rules.

"And so modest a modiste she is," he said.

She laughed, but hers was not the silvery laughter he was accustomed to. It was low and intimate, not meant for others to hear. She was not trying to make heads turn her way, as other women did. Only his head was required.

And he did turn away from the window to look at her.

"Perhaps, unlike everyone else in the opera house, you failed to notice," she said. She swept her closed fan over her dress.

He let his gaze travel from the slightly disheveled coiffure down. Before, he'd taken only the most superficial notice of what she wore. His awareness was mainly of her physicality: the lushly curved body, the clarity of her skin, the brilliance of her eyes, the soft disorder of her hair.

Now he took in the way that enticing body was adorned: the black lace cloak or tunic or whatever it was meant to be, over rich pink silk—the dashing arrangement of color and trim and jewelry, the—the—

"Style," she said.

Within him was a pause, a doubt, a moment's uneasiness. His mind, it seemed, was a book to her, and she'd already gone beyond the table of contents and the introduction, straight to the first chapter.

But what did it matter? She, clearly no innocent, knew what he wanted.

"No, madame. I didn't notice," he said. "All I saw was you."

"That is exactly the right thing to say to a woman," she said. "And exactly the wrong thing to say to a dressmaker."

"I beg you to be a woman for the present," he said. "As a dressmaker, you waste your talents on me."

"Not at all," she said. "Had I been badly dressed, you would not have entered Mademoiselle Fontenay's box.

Even had you been so rash as to disregard the dictates of taste, the Comte d'Orefeur would have saved you from a suicidal error, and declined to make the introduction."

"*Suicidal?* I detect a tendency to exaggerate."

"Regarding taste? May I remind you, we're in *Paris*."

"At the moment, I don't care where I am," he said.

Again, the low laughter. He felt the sound, as though her breath touched the back of his neck.

"I'd better watch out," she said. "You're determined to sweep me off my feet."

"You started it," he said. "You swept me off mine."

"If you're trying to turn me up sweet, to get back your diamond, it won't work," she said.

"If you think I'll give back your pearl, I recommend you think again," he said.

"Don't be absurd," she said. "You may be too romantic to care that your diamond is worth fifty such pearls, but I'm not. You may keep the pearl, with my blessing. But I must return to Mademoiselle Fontenay—and here is your friend monsieur le comte, who has come to prevent your committing the faux pas of returning with me. I know you are enchanted, devastated, your grace, and yes, I am *desolée* to lose your company—it is so refreshing to meet a man with a brain—but it won't do. I cannot be seen to favor a gentleman. It's bad for business. I shall simply hope to see you at another time. Perhaps tomorrow at Longchamp where, naturally, I shall display my wares."

Orefeur joined them as the signal came for the end of the interval. A young woman waved to her, and Madame Noirot took her leave, with a quick, graceful curtsey and—for Clevedon's eyes only—a teasing look over her fan.

As soon as she was out of hearing range, Orefeur said, "Have a care. That one is dangerous."

"Yes," said Clevedon, watching her make her way

through the throng. The crowd gave way to her, as though she were royalty, when she was nothing remotely approaching it. She was a shopkeeper, nothing more. She'd said so, unselfconsciously and unashamedly, yet he couldn't quite believe it. He watched the way she moved, and the way her French friend moved, so unlike that they did not even seem to belong to the same species.

"Yes," he said, "I know."

Meanwhile, in London, Lady Clara Fairfax was longing to throw a china vase at her brother's thick head. But the noise would attract attention, and the last thing she wanted was her mother bursting into the library.

She'd dragged him into the library because it was a room Mama rarely entered.

"Harry, how could you?" she cried. "They're all talking about it. I'm *mortified*."

The Earl of Longmore folded himself gingerly onto the sofa and shut his eyes. "There's no need to shriek. My head—"

"I can guess how you came by the headache," she said. "And I have no sympathy, none at all."

Shadows ringed Harry's eyes and pallor dulled his skin. Creases and wrinkles indicated he hadn't changed his clothes since last night, and the wild state of his black hair made it clear that no comb had touched it during the same interval. He'd spent the night in the bed of one of his amours, no doubt, and hadn't bothered to change when his sister sent for him.

"Your note said the matter was urgent," he said. "I came because I thought you needed help. I did not come to hear you ring a peal over me."

"Racing to Paris to give Clevedon an ultimatum," she

said. " 'Marry my sister or else.' Was that your idea of helping, too?"

He opened his eyes and looked up at her. "Who told you that?"

"All the world has been talking of it," she said. "For weeks, it seems. I was bound to hear eventually."

"All the world is insane," he said. "Ultimatum, indeed. There was nothing like it. I only asked him whether he wanted you or not."

"Oh, no." She sank into a nearby chair and put her hand over her mouth. Her face was on fire. How *could he*? But what a question. Of course he could. Harry had never been known for his tact and sensitivity.

"Better me than Father," he said.

She closed her eyes. He was right. Papa would write a letter. It would be much more discreet and far more devastating to Clevedon than anything Harry could say. Father would have the duke tied up in knots of guilt and obligation—and that, she suspected, was probably what had driven his grace to the Continent in the first place.

She took her hand from her mouth and opened her eyes and met her brother's gaze. "You truly think it's come to that?"

"My dear girl, Mother is driving *me* mad, and I don't have to live with her. I came to dread stopping at home because I knew she'd harp on it. It was only a matter of time before Father gave up trying to ignore her. You know he never wanted us to go away in the first place. Well, not Clevedon, at any rate. Me, he was only too happy to see the back of."

It was true that Mama had grown increasingly strident in the last few months. Her friends' daughters, who'd come out at the same time Clara had, were wed, most of them. Meanwhile Mama was terrified that Clara would forget Clevedon and become infatuated with someone unsuitable—meaning someone who wasn't a duke.

Why do you encourage Lord Adderley, when you know he's practically bankrupt? And there is that dreadful Mr. Bates, who hasn't a prayer of inheriting, with two men standing between him and the title. You know that Lord Geddings's country place is falling to pieces. And Sir Henry Jaspers—my daughter—encouraging the attentions of a baronet? Are you trying to kill me by inches, Clara? What is wrong with you, that you cannot attach a man who has loved you practically since birth and could buy and sell all the others a dozen times over?

How many times had Clara heard that rant, or one like it, since they'd returned to London for the Season? "I know you meant well," she said. "But I wish you hadn't."

"He's been abroad for three years," Harry said. "The situation begins to look a little ridiculous, even to me. Either he means to marry you or he doesn't. Either he wants to live abroad or he wants to live in England. I think he's had time enough to make up his mind."

She blinked. Three years? It hadn't seemed so long. She'd spent the first of those years grieving for her grandmother, whom she'd adored. She hadn't had the heart to make her debut then. And that year and those following had been filled with Clevedon's wonderful letters.

"I didn't realize it was so long," she said. "He writes so faithfully, it seems as though he's here." She'd been writing to him since she first learned to scrawl such inanities as "I hope this finds you well. How do you like school? I am learning French. It is difficult. What are you learning?" Even as a boy, he'd been a delightful correspondent. He was a keen observer, and he had a natural gift for description as well as a wicked wit. She knew him very well, better than most knew him, but that was mainly through letters.

It dawned on her now that they hadn't spent much time together. While she'd been in the schoolroom, he'd been away at school, then university. By the time she'd entered Society, he'd gone abroad.

"I daresay he didn't realize it, either," Harry said. "When I asked him straight out what he was about, he laughed, and said I did well to come. He said he supposed he might have returned sooner, but your letters told him you were enjoying being the most sought-after girl in London Society, and he didn't like to spoil your fun."

She hadn't wanted to spoil his, either. His had not been a pleasant childhood. He'd lost father, mother, and sister in the course of a year. Papa meant to be a kind guardian, but he had very strict ideas about Duty and Responsibility, and Clevedon, unlike Clara's brothers, had tried to live up to his standards.

When Clevedon and Harry had decided to go abroad, she'd been glad for them. Harry would acquire some culture, and Clevedon, away from Papa, would find himself.

"He ought not to come home before he's quite ready," she said.

Harry's black eyebrows went up. "Are *you* not quite ready?"

"Don't be absurd." Of course she'd be happy to have Clevedon back. She loved him. She'd loved him since she was a little girl.

"You needn't worry about being hurried to the altar," Harry said. "I suggested he wait until the end of May. That will give your beaux plenty of time to kill themselves or go into exile in Italy or some such or quietly expire of despair. Then I recommended he give you another month to get used to having his hulking great carcass about. That will take you to the end of the Season, at which point I suggested a beautifully worded formal offer of marriage, with many protestations of undying affection, accompanied by a prodigious great diamond ring."

"Harry, you're ridiculous."

"Am I? He thought it was an excellent idea—and we celebrated with three or four or five or six bottles of champagne, as I recollect."

Paris
15 April

Seduction was a game Clevedon very much enjoyed. He relished the pursuit as much—and lately, more—than the conquest. Chasing Madame Noirot promised to be a more amusing game than usual.

That would make for a change and a pleasant finish to his sojourn abroad. He wasn't looking forward to returning to England and his responsibilities, but it was time. Paris had begun to lose its luster, and without Longmore's entertaining company, he foresaw no joy in wandering the Continent again.

He'd planned to go to Longchamp, in any event, to observe, in order to write Clara an entertaining account of it. He still owed her an account of the opera—but never mind. Longchamp would provide richer fodder for his wit.

The annual promenade in the Champs Élysées and the Bois de Boulogne occurred on the Wednesday, Thursday, and Friday of the week preceding Easter. The weather, which had promised so well earlier in the week, had turned, bringing a chill wind. Nonetheless, all of Paris's haut ton appeared, all dressed in the latest fashions, and showing off their fine horses and carriages. These went up the road on one side and down on the other. The center belonged to royal carriages and others of the highest ranks. But a great many attending, of both high and lower degree, traversed the parade on foot, as Clevedon had chosen to do, the better to study and eavesdrop on the audience as well as the participants.

He'd forgotten how dense a crowd it was, far greater than Hyde Park at the fashionable hour. For a time he wondered how the devil he was supposed to find Madame Noirot. Everyone and her grandmother came to Longchamp.

Mere minutes later, he was wondering how it would have been possible to miss her.

She made a commotion, exactly as she'd done at the opera. Only more so. All he had to do was turn his gaze in the direction where the accidents happened, and there she was.

People craned their necks to see her. Men drove their carriages into other carriages. Those on foot walked into lamp posts and each other.

And she was enjoying herself thoroughly, of that he had no doubt.

This time, because he viewed her from a distance, undistracted by the brilliant dark eyes and beckoning voice, he could take in the complete picture: the dress, the hat . . . and the way she walked. From a distance, he could pay attention to the ensemble: the straw bonnet trimmed with pale green ribbons and white lace, and the lilac coat that opened below the waist to display a pale green fluttery concoction underneath.

He watched one fellow after another approach her. She would pause briefly, smile, say a few words, then walk on, leaving the men staring after her, all wearing the same dazed expression.

He supposed that was what he'd looked like last night, after she'd taken her leave of him.

He made his way through the crowd to her side. "Madame Noirot."

"Ah, there you are," she said. "Exactly the man I wished to see."

"I should hope so," he said, "considering you invited me."

"Was it an invitation?" she said. "I thought it was a broad hint."

"I wonder if you hinted the same to everyone at the Italian Opera. They all seem to be here."

"Oh, no," she said. "I only wanted you. They're here because it's the place to be seen. Longchamp. Passion Week. Everyone comes on holy pilgrimage to see and be seen. And here am I, on display."

"A pretty display it is," he said. "And exceedingly modish it must be, judging by the envious expressions on the women's faces. The men are dazzled, naturally—but they're no use to you, I daresay."

"It's a delicate balance," she said. "I must be agreeable to the men, who pay the bills. But it's the ladies who wear my clothes. They won't be eager to patronize my shop if they see me as a rival for the attentions of their beaux."

"Yet you dropped me a broad hint to come today and seek you out in this mob," he said.

"So I did," she said. "I want you to pay some bills."

It was, yet *again,* the last thing he expected. This time he was not amused. His body tensed, and his temperature climbed and it had nothing to do with desire. "Whose bills?"

"The ladies of your family," she said.

He could hardly believe his ears. He said, his jaw taut, "My aunts owe you money, and you came to Paris to dun me?"

"Their ladyships your aunts have never set foot in my shop," she said. "That's the problem. Well, one of the problems. But they're not the main issue. The main issue is your wife."

"I don't have a wife," he said.

"But you will," she said. "And I ought to be the one to dress her. I hope that's obvious to you by now."

He needed a moment to take this in. Then he needed another moment to tamp down his outrage. "Are you telling me you came all the way to Paris to persuade me to let you dress the future Duchess of Clevedon?"

"Certainly not. I come to Paris twice a year, for two reasons." She held up one gloved index finger. "One, to attract the attention of the correspondents who supply the ladies' magazines with the latest fashion news from Paris. It was an admiring description of a promenade dress I wore last spring that drew Mrs. Sharp to Maison Noirot. She in turn recommended us to her dear friend Lady Renfrew. By degrees, their friends will soon join our illustrious clientele."

"And the second reason?" he said impatiently. "You needn't put up your fingers. I am perfectly able to count."

"The second reason is inspiration," she said. "Fashion's heart beats in Paris. I go where the fashionable people go, and they give me ideas."

"I see," he said, though he didn't, really. But this was his payment, he told himself, for consorting with a shopkeeper, a vulgar, money-grubbing person. He could have bedded Madame St. Pierre last night—and he was running out of time for bedding anybody—but he'd spoiled his chance by chasing this—this creature. "I am merely incidental."

"I'd hoped you'd be intelligent enough *not* to take it that way," she said. "My great desire is to be of service to you."

He narrowed his eyes. She thought she could play him

for a fool. Because she'd lured him across an opera house and into the Longchamp mob, she imagined she'd enslaved him.

She wouldn't be the first or the last woman to let her imagination run away with her in that way.

"I only ask you to consider," she said. "Do you want your lady wife to be the best-dressed woman in London? Do you want her to be a leader of fashion? Do you want her to stop wearing those unfortunate dresses? Of course you do."

"I don't give a damn what Clara wears," he said tautly. "I like her for herself."

"That's sweet," she said, "but you fail to consider her position. People ought to look up to and admire the Duchess of Clevedon, and people, generally, judge the book by the cover. If that were not the case, we'd all go about in tunics and blankets and animal hides, as our ancestors did. And it's silly for you of all men to make out that clothes are not important. Only look at you."

He was all but dancing with rage. How dare she speak of Clara in that way? How dare she patronize him? He wanted to pick her up and—and—

Devil confound her. He couldn't remember when last he'd let a woman—a *shopkeeper*, no less—ignite his temper.

He said, "Look about you. I'm in Paris. Where fashion's heart beats, as you said."

"And do you wear any old thing in London?" she said.

He was so busy trying not to strangle her that he couldn't think of a proper retort. All he could do was glare at her.

"It's no use scowling at me," she said. "If I were easily intimidated, I should never have got into this business in the first place."

"Madame Noirot," he said, "you seem to have mistaken me for someone else. A fool, I believe. Good day." He started to turn away.

"Yes, yes." She gave a lazy wave of her hand. "You're going to storm off. Go ahead. I'll see you at Frascati's, I daresay."

Chapter Three

HOTEL FRASCATI, *No.* 108, rue *de Richelieu.* This is a gaming-house, which may be considered the second in Paris in point of *respectability,* as the company is *select. Ladies* are admitted.

Galignani's New Paris Guide, 1830

Clevedon stopped, turned back, and looked at her.

His eyes were green slits. His sensuous mouth was set. A muscle worked at his jaw near his right ear.

He was a large, powerful man.

He was an English duke, a species known for its tendency to crush any small, annoying thing that got in its way.

His stance and expression would have terrified the average person.

Marcelline was not an average person.

She knew she'd waved a red cape in front of a bull. She'd done it as deliberately as an experienced matador might. Now, like the bull, he was aware of no one else but her.

"Confound you," he said. "Now I can't storm away."

"I shouldn't blame you if you did," she said. "You've been greatly provoked. But I warn you, your grace, I am the most determined woman you'll ever meet, and I am determined to dress your duchess."

"I'm tempted to say, 'Over my dead body,' " he said, "but I have the harrowing suspicion that you will answer, 'If necessary.' "

She smiled.

His countenance smoothed a degree and a wicked gleam came into his eyes. "Does this mean you'll do *whatever* is necessary?"

"I know what you're thinking," she said, "and *that* will not be necessary. Pray consider, your grace. What self-respecting lady would patronize a dressmaker who specializes in seducing the lady's menfolk?"

"Ah, it's a specialty, is it?"

"You of all men must know that seduction is an art, and some practitioners are more skilled than others," she said. "I've chosen to apply my talents to dressing ladies beautifully. Women are capricious and difficult to please, yes. Men are easy to please but far more capricious."

To a discerning woman, his beautiful face was wonderfully expressive. She watched, fascinated, while a speculative expression gradually erased the lingering signs of temper. He was puzzling over her, revising his original estimation and, therefore, his tactics.

This was an intelligent man. She had better be very careful.

"Frascati's," he said. "You're a gambler."

"The game of chance is my favorite sport," she said. Gambling—with money, with people, with their futures—was a way of life for her family. "Roulette, especially. Pure chance."

"This explains the risks you take with men you don't know," he said.

"Dressmaking is not a trade for the faint of heart," she said.

The humor came back into his green eyes and the corners of his mouth quirked up. On any other man that look would have been charming. On him it was devastating. The eyes, the sweet little smile—it stabbed a girl to the heart and then lower down.

"So it would seem," he said. "A more dangerous trade than I'd supposed."

"You've no idea," she said.

"This promises to be interesting," he said. "I'll see you at Frascati's."

He made her a bow, and it was pure masculine grace, the smooth and confident movement of a man completely at ease in his powerful body.

He took his leave, and she watched him saunter away. She watched scores of elegant hats and bonnets change direction as other women watched him pass.

She'd thrown down the gauntlet and he'd taken it up, as she'd known he would.

Now all she had to do was not end up on her back with that splendid body between her legs.

That was not going to be easy.

But then, if it were easy, it wouldn't be much fun.

London
Wednesday night

Mrs. Downes waited in a carriage a short distance from the seamstress's lodgings. Shortly after half-past nine, the seamstress passed the carriage. She glanced up but didn't stop walking. A moment later, Mrs. Downes stepped down from the carriage, continued down the street, and greeted the young woman as though theirs was an accidental encounter of two old acquaintances. They asked after each other's health. Then they walked a few steps to the door of the house where the seamstress lived. After a moment of conversation, the seamstress withdrew from her pocket a folded piece of paper.

Mrs. Downes reached for it.

"The money first," the seamstress said.

"Let me see what it is first," Mrs. Downes said. "For all I know, it's nothing out of the way."

The seamstress stepped closer to the street lamp and opened the folded sheet of paper.

Mrs. Downes gave a little gasp, and hastily covered it up with a disdainful sniff. "Is that all? My girls can run up something like that in an hour. It's hardly worth half a crown, let alone a sovereign."

The seamstress folded up the paper. "Well, then, let them do it if they can," she said. "I've made notes on the back about how it's done, but I'm sure your clever girls don't need any help working out how to keep those folds the way she has them, or how to make those bows. And you don't need to know which ribbon she uses and who she gets it from. No, indeed, you don't want any of that. So I'll take this in with me, shall I, and throw it on the fire. *I* know how it's done, and Madame knows how it's done, and one or two of our less clumsy girls know the trick."

This particular seamstress spoke dismissively of the others, deeming herself superior to them and not half-properly appreciated. Otherwise, she wouldn't have been standing in the street, late at night, when she was hungry for her supper. She certainly wouldn't be talking to the competition if Some People valued her as they ought to do.

"No, madam, you don't need a bit of it," she said, "and

I wonder at your coming out at this hour, wasting your valuable time."

"Yes, I've wasted quite enough," Mrs. Downes reached into her reticule. "Here's your money. But if you want more, you'd better bring me something better."

"How much more?" the seamstress said as she pocketed the money.

"One can't do much with scraps. One dress at a time. The book of sketches, now that would be worth something."

"It certainly would," said the seamstress. "It would be worth my place. It's one thing to copy a pattern. But the book of sketches? She'd miss it right away, and they're sharp, those three, you know."

"If she lost her book of sketches, she'd lose everything," Mrs. Downes said. "You'd have to find another place then. And I daresay seeking new employment would be a more agreeable experience, were you to have twenty guineas to ease the way."

A lady's maid in a noble household might earn twenty guineas per annum. That was a great deal more than an experienced seamstress was paid.

"Fifty," the seamstress. "It's worth fifty to you, I know, to have her out of your way, and I won't risk it for less."

Mrs. Downes drew in a long, slow breath while she did some quick calculations. "Fifty, then. But it must be everything. You'd better note every last detail. I'll know right away, and if I can't make an exact copy, you shan't have a penny." She stalked away.

The seamstress watched her retreating back and said, under her breath, "As if you could make any kind of copy, you stupid hag, if I didn't tell you every last detail."

She chinked the coins in her pocket and went into the house.

Paris, the same night

Since the Italian Opera was closed on Wednesdays, Clévedon took himself to the Théâtre des Varieties, where he could count on being amused as well as treated to a superior performance. Perhaps, too, he might find Madame Noirot there.

When she failed to appear, he grew bored with the entertainment, and debated whether to cut his stay short and proceed directly to Frascati's.

But Clara looked forward to his reports, and he'd failed to give her an account of Tuesday's performance of *The Barber of Seville,* one of her favorites. Now he recalled that he'd come away from Longchamps with nothing as well—nothing, that is, he chose to describe to Clara.

He stayed, and dutifully made notes in his little pocket notebook.

Its pages held none of Madame Noirot's remarks about Clara's style—or lack thereof. At the time, he'd dismissed them from his mind. Or so he'd thought. Yet he found them waiting, as though the curst dressmaker had sewn them onto his brain.

When last he'd seen Clara, she'd been in mourning for her grandmother. Perhaps grief's colors did not become her. The style . . . Confound it, she was grieving! What did she care whether she wore the latest mode? She was a beautiful girl, he told himself, and a beautiful girl could wear anything—not that it mattered to him, because he loved her for herself, and had done so for as long as he could remember.

Still, if Clara were to dress as that provoking dressmaker did . . .

The thought came and hung in his mind through the last scenes of the performance. He saw Clara, magnificently garbed, making men's heads turn. He saw himself proudly in possession of this masterpiece, the envy of every other man.

Then he realized what he was thinking. "Devil take her," he said under his breath. "She's poisoned my mind, the witch."

"What is it, my friend?"

Clevedon turned to find Gaspard Aronduille regarding him with concern.

"Does it truly matter what a woman wears?" Clevedon said.

The Frenchman's eyes widened and his head went back, as though Clevedon had slapped him. "Is this a joke?" he said.

"I want to know," Clevedon said. "Does it really matter?"

Aronduille looked about him in disbelief. "Only an Englishman would ask such a question."

"Does it?"

"But of course."

"Only a Frenchman would say so," said Clevedon.

"We are right, and I will tell you why."

The opera ended, but the debate didn't. Aronduille called in reinforcements from their circle of acquaintance. The Frenchmen debated the subject from every possible philosophical viewpoint, all the way to the Hotel Frascati.

There the group separated, its members drifting to their favorite tables.

The roulette table was crowded, as usual, men standing three deep about it. Clevedon saw no signs of any women. But as he slowly circled it, the wall of men at the table thinned.

And the world shifted.

Revealed to his view was a ravishingly familiar back. Again, her coiffure was slightly disarranged, as though she'd been in a lover's embrace only minutes ago. A bit was coming undone, a dark curl falling to the nape of her neck. The wayward curl drew one's gaze there and down over the smooth slope of her shoulders and down to where her sleeves puffed out. The dress was ruby red, shockingly simple and daringly low cut. He wished, for a moment, he could have her captured like that, in a painting.

He'd title it *Sin Incarnate*.

He was tempted to stand beside her, close enough to inhale her scent and feel the silk of her gown brush his legs. But a roulette table was no place for dalliance—and by the looks of things, she was as engrossed in the turn of the wheel as everybody else.

He moved to a place opposite her. That was when he recognized the man standing next to her: the Marquis d'Émilien, a famous libertine.

"21—Red—Odd—Passed," one of the bankers said.

With his rake another banker pushed a heap of coins toward her.

Émilien bent his head to say something to her.

Clevedon's jaw tightened. He let his gaze drop to the table. Before her stood piles of gold coins.

"Gentlemen, settle your play," the banker called. He threw in the ivory ball, and set the wheel spinning. Round and round it went, gradually slowing.

That time she lost. Though the rake took away a large amount of gold, she appeared not at all troubled. She laughed and bet again.

Next time Clevedon bet, too, on red. Round the ball went. Black—Even—Missed.

She won. He watched the rakes push his coins and others toward her.

The marquis laughed, and bent his head to say something to her, his mouth close to her ear. She answered with a smile.

Clevedon left the roulette table for Rouge et Noir. He told himself he would have come whether or not she was here. He told himself she was on the hunt for other men's wives and mistresses and he wasn't the only well-to-do bill payer in Paris. Émilien had deep pockets, too, not to mention a wife, a longtime mistress, and three favorite courtesans.

For about half an hour Clevedon played. He won more than he lost, and maybe that was why he became bored so quickly. He left the table, found Aronduille, and said, "This place is dull tonight. I'm going to the Palais Royal."

"I'll go with you," said Aronduille. "Let's see if the others wish to join us."

The others had moved to the roulette table.

She was there still, in the crimson silk one could not ignore. The marquis remained at her side. In the same moment Clevedon was telling himself to look away, she looked up. Her gaze locked with his. An endless time seemed to pass before she beckoned with her fan.

He would have come whether or not he'd expected to find her here, he assured himself. He'd come, and found another man glued to her side. It was nothing to him. Paris abounded in fascinating women. He could have simply nodded or bowed or smiled an acknowledgment and left the hotel.

But there, she was, Sin Incarnate, daring him.

And there was Émilien.

The Duke of Clevedon had never yet yielded a woman he wanted to another man.

He joined them.

"Ah, Clevedon, you know Madame Noirot, I understand," said Émilien.

"I have that honor, yes," Clevedon said, sending her his sweetest smile.

"She has emptied my pockets," said Émilien.

"The roulette wheel emptied your pockets," she said.

"No, it is you. You look at the wheel, and it stops where you choose."

She dismissed this with a wave of her fan. "It's no use arguing with him," she said to Clevedon. "I've promised to give him a chance to win back his money. We go to play cards."

"Perhaps you will be so good as to join us," said Émilien. "And your friends as well?"

They went to one of Paris's more discreet and exclusive card salons, in a private house. When Clevedon arrived with the marquis's party, several games were in progress in the large room.

By three o'clock in the morning, the greater part of the company had departed. In the small but luxurious antechamber to which the marquis eventually retired with a select group of friends, the players had dwindled to Émilien, a handsome blonde named Madame Jolivel, Madame Noirot, and Clevedon.

About them lay the bodies of those who'd succumbed to drink and fatigue. Some had been playing for days and nights on end.

At roulette, where skill and experience meant nothing, Noirot had won more often than not. At cards, where skill made a difference, her luck, oddly enough, was not nearly as good. The marquis's luck had run out in the last half hour, and he was sinking in his chair. Clevedon was on a winning streak.

"This is enough for me," said Madame Jolivel. She rose, and the men did as well.

"For me, too," Émilien muttered. He pushed his cards to the center of the table and dragged himself out of the room after the blonde.

Clevedon remained standing, waiting for the dressmaker to rise. He had her to himself at last, and he was looking forward to escorting her elsewhere. Any elsewhere.

"It seems the party is over," he said.

Noirot gazed up at him, dark eyes gleaming. "I thought it was only beginning," she said. She took up the cards and shuffled.

He sat down again.

They played the basic game of Vingt et Un, without variations.

It was one of his favorite card games. He liked its simplicity. With two people, he found, it was a good deal more interesting than with several.

For one thing, he could no longer read her. No wry curve of her mouth when her cards displeased her. No agitated tap of her fingers when she'd drawn a strong card. When they'd played with the others, she'd exhibited all these little cues, and her play had struck him as reckless besides. This time was altogether different. By the time they'd played through the deck twice, he felt as though he played with another woman entirely.

He won the first deal and the second and the third.

After that, she won steadily, the pile of coins in front of her growing while his diminished.

As she passed the cards to him to deal, he said, "My luck seems to be turning."

"So it does," she said.

"Or perhaps you've been playing with me, madame, in more ways than one."

"I'm paying closer attention to the game," she said. "You won a great deal from me before. My resources, unlike yours, are limited. I only want to win my money back."

He dealt. She looked at her card and pushed a stack of coins to one side of it.

He looked at his card. Nine of hearts. "Double," he said.

She nodded for another card, glanced at it.

Nothing. No visible sign of whether the card was good or bad. He'd had to practice to conceal his small give-away signs. How had she learned to reveal or conceal them at will? Or had Dame Fortune simply smiled on her this night? She'd won at roulette, a game, as she'd said, of pure chance, though men never gave up trying to devise systems for winning.

She won again.

And again.

This time, when they'd gone through the pack, she swept her coins toward her. "I'm not used to such late hours," she said. "It's time for me to go."

"You play differently with me than you did with the others," he said.

"Do I?" She brushed a stray curl back from her eyebrow.

"I can't decide whether you've the devil's own luck or there's something more to you than meets the eye," he said.

She settled back in her chair and smiled at him. "I'm observant," she said. "I watched you play before."

"Yet you lost."

"Your beauty must have distracted me," she said. "Now I've grown used to it. Now I can discern the ways you signal whether it's going well or badly for you."

"I thought I gave no signals," he said.

She waved a hand. "You nearly don't. It was very hard for me to decipher you—and I've been playing cards since I was a child."

"Have you, indeed?" he said. "I've always thought of shopkeepers as respectable citizens, not much given to vices, especially gambling."

"Then you haven't been paying attention," she said. "Frascati's teemed with ordinary citizen-clerks and tradesmen. But to men like you and Émilien, they're invisible."

"The one thing you are not is invisible."

"There you're wrong," she said. "I've passed within a few yards of you, on more than one occasion, and you didn't look twice."

He sat up straighter. "That's impossible."

She took up the cards and shuffled them, her hands quick, smooth, expert. "Let me see. On Sunday at about four o'clock, you were riding with a handsome lady in the Bois de Boulogne. On Monday at seven o'clock, you were in one of the latticed boxes at the Académie Royale de Musique. On Tuesday shortly after noon, you were strolling through the galleries of the Palais Royal."

"You said I wasn't your sole purpose for coming to Paris," he said. "Yet you've been following me. Or should I say *stalking* me?"

"I've been stalking fashionable people. They all go to the same places. And you're hard to miss."

"So are you."

"That depends on whether I wish to be noticed or not," she said. "When I don't wish to be noticed, I don't dress this way." One graceful hand indicated the low bodice of the crimson gown. His diamond stickpin twinkled at him from the center of the V to which the bodice dipped. She lay the cards, precisely stacked now, on the table in front of her, and folded her hands.

"A good dressmaker can dress anybody," she said. "Sometimes we're required to dress women who prefer not to call attention to themselves, for one reason or another." She brought her folded hands up and rested her elbows on the table and her chin on her entwined fingers. "That you failed to notice me in any of those places ought to prove to you that I'm the greatest dressmaker in the world."

"Is it always business with you?" he said.

"I work for a living," she said. She turned her head, and he watched her gaze sweep over the various bodies draped over furniture and sprawled on the floor. The look spoke the volumes she left unsaid.

He was nettled, more than he ought to be. Otherwise he would have pretended not to understand. But these were the people with whom he customarily associated, and her mocking half smile was extremely irritating. Provoked, he said it for her before he could catch himself: "Unlike me and these other dissolute aristocrats, you mean. The bourgeoisie is so tediously self-righteous."

She shrugged, calling his attention to her smooth shoulders, and unfolded her hands. "Yes, we're great bores, always thinking about money and success." She took out her purse and scooped her winnings into it, a clear signal that the evening was over for her.

He rose and came round the table to move her chair. He gathered up her shawl, which had slid down her arm. As he did so, he let his fingers graze her bare shoulder.

He heard the faint hitch in her breath, and a bolt of pleasure wiped out his irritation. The feeling was fierce— fiercer than it ought to have been after so slight a touch and so obvious a ploy. But then, she gave so little away that to achieve this much was a great deal.

Though no one about them was conscious, he bent his head close to her ear and said, in a low voice, "You haven't told me when I'll see you again. Longchamp, the first time. Frascati's this night. Where next?"

"I'm not sure," she said, moving a little away. "Tomorrow—tonight, rather—I must attend the Comtesse de Chirac's ball. I suspect that gathering will be too staid for you."

For a moment he could only stare at her, his eyes wide and his mouth open. Then he realized he was gaping at her like a yokel watching a circus. But he'd no sooner erased all signs of surprise than he wondered why he bothered. What was the use, with her, of pretending that nothing surprised him when everything did? She was the least predictable woman he'd ever met. And at this moment he felt like one of the men who'd walked into a lamp post.

He said, slowly and carefully, because surely he'd misunderstood, "You've been invited to Madame de Chirac's ball?"

She made a small adjustment to her shawl. "I did not say I was invited."

"But you're going. Uninvited."

She looked up at him, and the dark eyes flashed. "How else?"

"How about *not* going where you're not invited?"

"Don't be silly," she said. "It's the most important event of the social season."

"It's also the most *exclusive* event of the social season," he said. "The *king* will be there. People negotiate and plot and blackmail each other for months in advance to get an invitation. Did it not occur to you that an uninvited guest is very liable to be noticed?"

"Didn't I pass by you a dozen times undetected?" she said. "Do you think I can't attend a ball without calling attention to myself?"

"Not this ball," he said. "Unless you were planning to go disguised as a servant?"

"Where's the fun in that?" she said.

"You'll never get through the door," he said. "If you do, you'll be discovered immediately thereafter. If you're lucky, they'll merely throw you into the street. Madame de Chirac is not a woman to trifle with. If she's not amused—and she rarely is—she'll claim you're an assassin." The accusation might well be taken seriously, for France was unsettled, and one heard rumblings of another revolution. "At best you'll end up in jail, and she'll make sure no one remembers you're there. At worst, you'll make the personal acquaintance of Madame Guillotine. I don't see the fun in that."

"I won't be discovered," she said.

"You're mad," he said.

"The richest women in Paris will be there," she said. "They'll be wearing creations by Paris's greatest modistes. It's the greatest fashion competition of the year—a notch above Longchamp. I must see those dresses."

"You can't stand outside with the rest of the crowd and watch them go in?"

Her chin went up and her eyes narrowed. Emotion flashed in those dark depths, but when she spoke, her voice was as cool and as haughty as the comtesse's. "Like the child with her nose pressed to the bakery shop window? I think not. I mean to examine those gowns closely as well as study the jewelry and coiffures. Such opportunities do not come along every day. I've been planning for it for weeks."

She'd said she was a determined woman. He'd understood—to a point—her wishing to dress Clara. Dressing a duchess would be highly profitable. But to run this risk—she, an English nobody—with the Comtesse de Chirac, stupendously high in the instep and one of the most formidable women in Paris? And to do so at a time like this, when the city was in a state of ferment on account of an impending trial of some alleged traitors, and nobles like the comtesse saw assassins lurking in every shadowy corner?

It was a mad chance to take, merely for a little shop.

Yet Madame Noirot had announced her lunatic intention as cool as you please, with a gleam in her eye. And why should this surprise him? She was a gambler. This gamble, clearly, was of vast importance to her.

"You may have slipped into other parties unnoticed but you won't get into this one," he said.

"You think they'll know I'm a nobody shopkeeper?" she said. "You think I can't fool them? You think I can't make them see what I want them to see?"

"Others, perhaps. Not Madame de Chirac. You haven't a prayer."

He thought perhaps she did have a prayer, but he was goading her, wanting to know what else she'd reveal of herself.

"Then I reckon you'll simply have to see for yourself," she said. "That is, I presume you've been invited?"

He glanced down at his diamond stickpin, winking up at him from the deep neckline of her red dress. Her bosom was rising and falling more rapidly than before.

"Oddly enough, I have," he said. "In her view, we English are an inferior species, but for some reason, she makes an exception of me. It must be all my deceitful French names."

"Then I'll see you there." She started to turn away.

"I hope not," he said. "It would pain me to see you manhandled by the gendarmes, even if that would enliven an exceedingly dull evening."

"You have a dramatic imagination," she said. "In the unlikely event they don't let me inside, they'll merely send me away. They won't want to make a scene with a mob outside. The mob, after all, might take my side."

"It's a silly risk to take," he said. "All for your little shop."

"Silly," she repeated quietly. "My little shop." She looked up at the leering demigods and satyrs cavorting on the ceiling. When her gaze returned to him it was cool and steady, belying the swift in-and-out of her breathing. She was angry but she controlled it wonderfully.

He wondered what that anger would be like, let loose.

"That *little shop* is my livelihood," she said. "And not only mine. You haven't the remotest idea what it took to gain a foothold in London. You haven't the least notion what it's taken to make headway against the established shops. You've no inkling of what we contend with: not merely other dressmakers—and they're a treacherous lot—but the conservatism of your class. French grandmothers dress with more taste than do your countrywomen. It's like a war, sometimes—and so, yes, that's all I think about, and yes, I'll do whatever is necessary to raise the reputation of my shop. And if I'm thrown into the street or into jail, all I'll think about is how to take advantage of the publicity."

"For clothes," he said. "Does it not strike you as absurd, to go to such lengths, when English women, as you say, are oblivious to style? Why not give them what they want?"

"Because I can make them more than what they want," she said. "I can make them *unforgettable*. Have you drifted so far beyond the everyday concerns of life that you can't understand? Is nothing in this world truly important to you, important enough to make you stick to it, in spite of obstacles? But what a silly question. If you had a purpose in life, you would give yourself to it, instead of frittering away your days in Paris."

He should have realized she'd strike back, but he'd been so caught up in her passion for her dreary work that she took him unawares. An image flashed in his mind of the world he'd fled—the little, dull world and his empty days and nights and the pointless amusements he'd tried to fill them with. He recalled Lord Warford telling him, *You seem determined to fritter away your life.*

He felt an instant's shame, then anger, because she'd stung him.

Reacting unthinkingly to the sting, he said, "Indeed, it's all sport to me. So much so that I'll make you a wager. Another round of cards, madame. Vingt et Un—with or without variations, as you choose. This time, if you win, I shall take you myself to the Comtesse de Chirac's ball."

Her eyes sparked—with anger or pride or perhaps simple dislike. He couldn't tell and, at the moment, didn't care.

"Sport, indeed," she said. "One rash wager after another. I wonder what you think you'll prove. But you don't think, do you? Certainly you haven't stopped to ask yourself what your friends will think."

He hardly heard what she was saying. He was drinking in the signs of emotion—the color coming and going in her face, and the sparks in her eyes, and the rise and fall of her bosom. And all the while he was keenly aware of the place where her sharp little needle had stabbed him.

"Nothing to prove," he said. "I only want you to *lose.* And when you lose, you'll admit defeat with a kiss."

"A kiss!" She laughed. "A mere kiss from a shop-keeper. That's paltry stakes, indeed, compared to your dignity."

"A proper kiss would not be *mere*, madame, or paltry," he said. "You may not pay with a peck on the cheek. You'll pay with the sort of kiss you'd give a man to whom you've *surrendered*." And if he couldn't make her surrender with a kiss, he might as well go back to London this night. "Considering your precious respectability, that's high stakes for you, I know."

One flash from her dark eyes before her face turned into a beautiful mask, cool, impervious. But he'd had a glimpse of the turbulence within, and now he couldn't walk away if his life depended on it.

"It's nothing to me," she said. "Haven't you been paying attention, your grace? You haven't a prayer of winning against me."

"Then you've everything to gain," he said. "Easy entrée into the most exclusive, most boring ball in Paris."

She shook her head pityingly. "Very well. Never say I didn't warn you."

She returned to her chair and sat.

He sat opposite.

"Any game you like," she said. "In any way you like. It won't matter. I'll win—and it will be most amusing."

She pushed the cards toward him.

"Deal," she said.

At the time of the French Revolution, Marcelline's aristocratic grandfather had kept his head by keeping his head. Generations of Noirots—the name he'd taken after fleeing France—had inherited the same cool self-containment and ruthless practicality.

True, her passions ran dark and deep, as was typical

of her family, on both sides. Like them, though, she was quite good at hiding what she felt. She'd had to teach her sisters the skill. She, apparently, had been born with it.

But the casually disparaging way Clevedon referred to her shop and her profession made her blood boil.

That was noble blood, too, running in her veins—no matter that hers was the most corrupt blue blood in all of Europe. But Noirot was a common name, as common as dirt, which was why Grandpapa had chosen it. Now, most of the family was gone, taking their infamy with them.

Notorious or not, her family was as old as Clevedon's—and she doubted all his ancestors had been saints. The *only* difference at the moment was that he was rich without having to work for it and she had to work for every farthing.

She knew it was absurd to let him provoke her. She knew her customers looked down on her. They all behaved the way Lady Renfrew and Mrs. Sharp did, speaking as though she and her sisters were invisible. To the upper orders, shopkeepers were simply another variety of servants. She'd always found that useful, and sometimes amusing.

But he . . .

Never mind. The question now was whether to let him win or lose.

Her pride couldn't let him win. She wanted to crush him, his vanity, his casual superiority.

But his losing meant a serious inconvenience. She could hardly enter a ball on the Duke of Clevedon's arm without setting off a firestorm of gossip—exactly what she didn't want to do.

Yet she couldn't let him win.

"We play the deck," he said. "We play each deal, but

with one difference: We don't show our cards until the end. Then, whoever has won the most deals wins the game."

Not being able to see the cards as they played through would make it harder to calculate the odds.

But she could read him, and he couldn't read her. Moreover, the game he proposed could be played quickly. Soon enough she'd be able to tell whether he was playing recklessly.

The first deal. Two cards to each. He dealt her a natural—ace of diamonds and knave of hearts. But he stood at two cards as well, which he never did if they totaled less than seventeen. Next deal she had the ace of hearts, a four, and a three. The next time she stood at seventeen, with clubs. Then another natural—ace of spades and king of hearts. And next the queen of hearts and nine of diamonds.

On it went. He often drew three cards to her two. But he was intent, as he hadn't been previously, and by this time, she could no longer detect the flicker in his green eyes that told her he didn't like his cards.

She was aware of her heart beating faster with every deal, though her cards were good for the most part. Twenty-one once, twice, thrice. Most of the other hands were good. But he played calmly, for all his concentration, and she couldn't be absolutely sure his luck was worse.

Ten deals played it out.

Then they turned their cards over, slapping them down smartly, smiling coolly at each other across the table as they did so, each of them confident.

A glance at the spread-out cards told her she'd beat him all but four times, and one of those was a tie.

Not that she needed to see the cards laid out to know

who'd won. She had only to observe his stillness, and the blank way he regarded the cards. He looked utterly flummoxed.

It lasted but an instant before he became the jaded man of the world again; but in that look she glimpsed the boy he used to be, and for a moment she regretted everything: that they'd met in the way they'd done, that they were worlds apart, that she hadn't known him before he lost his innocence . . .

Then he looked up and met her gaze, and in his green eyes she saw awareness dawn—at last—of the problem he'd created for himself.

Once again, he recovered in an instant. If he was at a loss—as surely he must be—there was no further sign. Like her, he was used to covering up. She should have covered up, too. He ought to have second thoughts. It was no more than she expected. His consternation, however faintly evidenced, rankled all the same, and more than it ought to have done.

"You've been rash, your grace," she taunted. "Again. Another silly wager. But this time a great deal more is at stake."

His pride, a gentleman's most tender part.

He shrugged and gathered up the cards.

But she knew what the shrug masked.

His friends had seen him at the opera in the box of an aging actress, seeking an introduction to the actress's friend. Émilien knew she was a London dressmaker, and by tomorrow night, at least half of Paris would know she was a nobody: no exciting foreign actress or courtesan, and certainly not a lady of any nationality.

What would his friends think, when they saw him enter a party he wouldn't normally attend, bringing a most unwelcome guest, a shopkeeper?

"What hypocrites you aristos are," she said. "It's all well enough to chase women who are beneath you, merely to get them beneath you—but to attempt to bring them into good company? Unthinkable. Your friends will believe you've taken leave of your senses. They'll believe you've let me make a fool of you. Enslaved, they'll say. The great English duke is enslaved by a showy little bourgeoise."

He shrugged. "Will they? Well, then, watching their jaws drop should prove entertaining. Will you wear red?"

She rose, and he did, too, manners perfect, no matter what.

"You put on a brave show," she said. "I'll give you credit for that. But I know you're having second thoughts. And because I'm a generous woman—and all I want, foolish man, is to dress your wife—I'll release you from a wager you never should have made. I do this because you're a man, and I know that there are times when men use an organ other than their brains to think with."

She gathered her reticule, arranged her shawl—and instantly recalled the brush of his fingers upon her skin.

Crushing the recollection, she swept to the door.

"Adieu," she said. "I hope a few hours' sleep will restore your good sense, and you'll let us be friends. In that case, I'll look forward to seeing you on Friday. Perhaps we'll meet on the Quai Voltaire."

He followed her to the door. "You're the most damnable female," he said. "I'm not accustomed to having women order me about."

"We bourgeoise are like that," she said. "No finesse or tact. So *managing*."

She walked on, into the deserted corridor. From one room she heard low murmurs. Some were still at their gaming. From elsewhere came snores.

Mainly, though, she was aware of his footsteps, behind her at first, then alongside.

"I've hurt your feelings," he said.

"I'm a dressmaker," she said. "My customers are women. If you wish to hurt my feelings, you'll need to exert yourself to a degree you may find both mentally and physically debilitating."

"I hurt *something*," he said. "You're determined to dress my duchess, and you'll stop at nothing, but you've stopped. You're quite prepared to give up."

"You underestimate me," she said. "I never give up."

"Then why are you telling me to go to the devil?"

"I've done no such thing," she said. "I've forgiven the wager, as it is the winner's prerogative to do. If you'd been thinking clearly, you would never have proposed it. If I hadn't allowed you to provoke me, I should never have agreed. There. We were both in the wrong. Now go find your friends and arrange to have them carried home. I have a long day ahead of me, and unlike you, I can't spend most of it recovering from this night."

"You're afraid," he said.

She stopped short and looked up at him. He was smiling, a self-satisfied curve of his too-sensuous mouth. "I'm *what*?" she said quietly.

"You're afraid," he said. "You're the one who's afraid of what people will say—of you—and how they'll behave—toward you. You're quite ready to sneak in like a thief, hoping nobody notices, but you're terrified to enter with me, with everybody looking at you."

"It distresses me to shatter you illusions, your grace," she said, "but what you and your friends think and say is not as important to other people as it is to you. I hope no one will notice me for the same reason a spy prefers not to be noticed. And it seems to escape you that the thrill of

going where one isn't wanted and hasn't been invited—
and getting away with it—will make the party more fun
for me than it will be for anyone else."

She walked on, her breath coming and going too fast,
her temper too close to the surface. Her self-control was
formidable, even for her kind, yet she'd let him provoke
her. She only wanted to dress his wife-to-be, but somehow she'd been drawn into the wrong game altogether.
And now she wondered if she'd bollixed it up, if he'd got
her into a muddle with his beautiful face and falsely innocent smiles and his fingers brushing her skin.

His voice came from behind her.

"Coward," he said.

The word seemed to echo in the empty passage.

Coward. She, who at scarce one and twenty had gone
to London with a handful of coins in her purse and overwhelming responsibilities on her shoulders: a sick child
and two younger sisters—and staked everything on a
dream and her courage to pursue it.

She stopped and turned and marched back to him.

"Coward," he said softly.

She dropped her reticule, grasped his neckcloth, and
pulled. He bent his head. She reached up, cupped his face,
dragged his mouth to hers, and kissed him.

Chapter Four

Mrs. Clark is as usual constantly receiving Models from some of the first Milliners in Paris, which enables her to produce the earliest Fashions for each Month, and trust that her general mode of doing business will give decided approbation to those Ladies who will honour her with a preference.

La Belle Assemblée,
or Bell's Court and Fashionable Magazine,
Advertisements for June 1807

It was no surrender, but a slap in the face of a kiss.

Her mouth struck and opened boldly against his, and the collision rocked him on his heels. It was as though they'd been lovers a long time ago and hated each other now, and the two passions had melded into one: They could fight or love, and it was all the same.

She held his jaw with a powerful grip. If she'd dug her nails into his face, that would have seemed fitting: It was that kind of kiss.

Instead she damaged him with her soft mouth, the press of her lips, the play of her tongue, like a duel. She damaged him, above all with the taste of her. She tasted like brandy, rich and deep and dark. She tasted like forbidden fruit.

She tasted, in short, like trouble.

For a moment he reacted instinctively, returning the assault in the same spirit, even while his body tensed and melted at the same time, his knees giving way and his insides tightening. But she was wondrously warm and shapely, and while his mind dissolved, his physical awareness grew more ferociously acute: the taste of her mouth, the scent of her skin, the weight of her breasts on his coat, and the sound of her dress brushing his trousers.

His heart beat too fast and hard, heat flooding through his veins and racing downward. He wrapped his arms about her and splayed his hands over her back, over silk and the neckline's lace edging and the velvety skin above.

He slid his hands lower, down the line of her back and along the curve from her waist to her bottom. Layers of clothing thwarted him there, but he pulled her hard against his groin, and she made a noise deep in her throat that sounded like pleasure.

Her hands came away from his face and slid between them, down over his neckcloth and down over his waistcoat and down further.

His breath caught and his body tensed in anticipation.

She thrust him away, and she put muscle into it. Even so, the push wouldn't have been enough to move him, ordinarily; but its strength and suddenness startled him, and he loosened his hold. She jerked out of his arms and he stumbled backward, into the wall.

She gave a short laugh, then bent and collected her reticule. She brushed a stray curl back from her face, and with an easy, careless grace, rearranged her shawl.

"This is going to be so much fun," she said. "I can hardly wait. Yes, now that I think about it, I should like nothing better, your grace, than to have your escort to the Comtesse de Chirac's ball. You may collect me at the Hotel Fontaine at nine o'clock sharp. Adieu."

She strolled away, as cool as you please, down the passage and through the door.

He didn't follow her.

It was a splendid exit, and he didn't want to spoil it.

So he told himself.

Yet he stood for a moment, collecting his mind and his poise, and trying to ignore the shakiness within, as though he'd run to the edge of a precipice and stopped only inches short of stepping into midair.

But of course there was no precipice, no void to fall into. That was absurd. She was merely a woman, the tempestuous type, and he was a trifle . . . puzzled . . . because it had been a while since he'd encountered her kind.

He went the other way, to find his friends—or the bodies of the fallen, rather. While he arranged for their transport to their respective lodgings and domiciles, he was aware, in a corner of his mind, of a derisive voice pointing out that he had nothing more important to do at present than collect and sort a lot of dead-drunk aristocrats.

Later, though, when he was alone in his hotel and starting a letter to Clara because he couldn't sleep, he found he couldn't write. He could scarcely remember the performance. It seemed a lifetime ago that he'd sat in the theater, anticipating his next encounter with Madame Noirot. His notes about the performance became gibberish swimming before his eyes.

The only clear, focused thought he had was of Madame de Chirac's ball looming mere hours away, and the fool's bargain he'd made, and the impossible riddle he'd insisted on solving: how to get the accursed dressmaker in without sacrificing his dignity, vanity, or reputation.

* * *

When Marcelline returned to her hotel, she found Selina Jeffreys drowsing in a chair by the fire. Though the slender blonde was their youngest seamstress, recently brought in from a charitable establishment for "unfortunate females," she was the most sensible of the lot. That was why Marcelline had chosen her to play lady's maid on the journey. A woman traveling with a maid was treated more respectfully than one traveling alone.

Frances Pritchett, the senior of their seamstresses, was probably still sulking about being left behind. But she'd come last time, and she hadn't taken at all to playing lady's maid. She wouldn't have sat up waiting for her employer to return, unless it was to complain about the French in general and the hotel staff in particular.

Jeffreys awoke with a start when Marcelline lightly tapped her shoulder. "You silly girl," Marcelline said. "I told you not to wait up."

"But who will help you out of your dress, madame?"

"I could sleep in it," Marcelline said. "It wouldn't be the first time."

"Oh, no, madame! That beautiful dress!"

"Not so beautiful now," Marcelline said. "Not only wrinkled, but it smells of cigar smoke and other people's perfumes and colognes."

"Let's get it off, then. You must be so weary. The promenade—and then to be out all night."

She had accompanied Marcelline on the Longchamp promenade and obligingly faded out of sight when Marcelline gave the signal. Unlike Pritchett, Selina Jeffreys never minded in the least making herself inconspicuous. She'd been happy simply to drink in the sight of so many rich people wearing fine clothes, riding their beautiful horses or driving their elegant carriages.

"One must go where the aristocrats go," Marcelline said. "I don't know how they do it, night after night."

"They're not obliged to be at work at nine o'clock every morning."

The girl laughed. "That's true enough."

While she was quick, it was efficiency rather than hurry. In a trice she had Marcelline out of the red dress. She soon had hot water ready, too. A full bath would have to wait until after she'd slept—later in the day, when the hotel's staff were fully awake. Meanwhile Marcelline needed to scrub away the smell of the gambling houses. That was easy enough.

The taste and smell of one gentleman wouldn't be eradicated so easily. She could wash her face and clean her teeth but her body and mind remembered: Clevedon's surprise, his quick heat, the bold response of his mouth and tongue, and the thrumming need he'd awakened with the simple motion of his hand sliding down her back.

Kissing him had not been the wisest move a woman could make, but really, what was the alternative? Slap him? A cliché. Punch him? That hard body? That stubborn jaw? She'd only hurt her hand—and make him laugh.

She doubted he was laughing now.

He was thinking, and he would need to be thinking very hard. Harder, probably, than he'd done before in all his life.

She felt certain he wouldn't back down from the challenge. He was too proud and too determined to have the upper hand—of her, certainly, and probably the world.

It would be entertaining, indeed, to see how he managed her entrée into the comtesse's party. If it ended in humiliation for him, maybe he'd learn from the experience. On the other hand, he might come to hate Marcelline instead, and forbid his wife to darken the door of Maison Noirot.

But Marcelline's instincts told her otherwise. Whatever his faults—and they were not few—this was not a mean-spirited man or the sort who held grudges.

"Go to bed," she told Jeffreys. "We've a busy time ahead of us, preparing for the party. Everything must be *perfect*."

And it would be. She'd make sure of it, one way or another.

Awaiting her was a once-in-a-lifetime opportunity, nearly as important as stealing the about-to-be Duchess of Clevedon from Dowdy's.

Clevedon had complicated what ought to have been a straightforward business. On her own, getting in would have merely demanded expert camouflage, evasive maneuvers, and, of course, thorough self-assurance. But no matter. Life had a way of wrecking her careful plans, again and again. Roulette was more predictable than life. Small wonder she was so lucky at it.

Life was not a wheel going round and round. It never, ever, returned to the same place. It didn't stick to simple red and black and a certain array of numbers. It laughed at logic.

Beneath its pretty overdress of man-imposed order, life was anarchy.

All the same, every time life had knocked her plans awry, she'd made a new plan and salvaged something. Sometimes she even triumphed. She was nothing if not resilient.

Whatever happened this night, she'd make the most of it.

That night

It would have served the insolent dressmaker right had
Clevedon made her wait. He was not accustomed to
taking orders from anybody, let alone a conceited little
shopkeeper. *Nine o'clock sharp*, she'd said, as though he
was her lackey.

But that was a childish reaction, and he preferred she
not add childishness to the list of character flaws she
seemed to be compiling. She was sure to ascribe any
delays to cowardly heel-dragging. She'd already as much
as called him a coward, in offering to release him from
the wager.

He arrived promptly at nine o'clock. When the carriage door opened, he saw her outside at one of the tables
under the portico. A gentleman, whose manner and dress
proclaimed him English, was bent over her, talking.

Clevedon had planned so carefully: what to wear to the
ball and what to say to his hostess and what expression to
wear when he said it. He had taken up and discarded half
a dozen waistcoats and left his valet, Saunders, a heap of
crumpled neckcloths to tend to. He had composed and rejected scores of clever speeches. He was, in short, wound
up exceedingly tight.

She, on the other hand, could not have appeared more
at ease, lounging under the portico, flirting with any
fellow who happened along. One would think she'd no
more on her mind than an idle conversation with yet another potential payer of dressmakers' bills.

And why should she consider anything else? It wasn't
her friends who'd be whispering behind her back and
shaking their heads in pity.

He could easily imagine what his friends would
whisper: Cupid's arrow had at last struck the Duke of

Clevedon—and not on account of Paris's greatest beauty, not on account of its most irresistible courtesan, not on account of its most fashionable, sought-after titled lady.

No, it was a nobody of an English shopkeeper who'd slain his grace.

He silently cursed his friends and his own stupidity, stepped down from the carriage, and strolled to her table.

As he approached, her dark glance slanted his way. She said something to the talkative fellow. He nodded at her and, without taking any notice of Clevedon, bowed and went into the hotel.

When Clevedon came to the table, she looked up at him. To his very great surprise, she smiled: a warm, luscious upturn of the mouth that had nearly brought him to his knees.

But he was not slain, not by half.

"You're prompt," she said.

"I never keep a lady waiting," he said.

"But I'm not a lady," she said.

"Are you not? Well, then, you're a conundrum. Are you ready? Or would you prefer a glass of something first, to fortify yourself for the ordeal?"

"I'm as fortified as I need to be," she said. She rose and made a sweeping arc with her hand, drawing his attention to her attire.

He supposed a woman would have a name for it. To him it was a dress. He knew that the sleeves would have their own special name—*à la Taglioni* or *à la Clotilde* or some equally nonsensical epithet, comprehensible only to women. Their dresses were all the same to him: swelling in the sleeves, billowing out in the skirts, and tight in the middle. It was the style women had been wearing throughout his adulthood.

Her dress was made of silk, in an odd, sandy color he

would have thought bland had he seen the cloth in a shop. But it was trimmed with puffy red bows, and they seemed like flowers blooming in a desert. Then there was black lace, yards of it, dripping like a waterfall over her smooth shoulders and down the front, under a sash, down over her belly.

He made a twirling gesture with his finger. Obligingly she turned in a complete circle. She moved as effortlessly and gracefully as water, and the lace about her shoulders floated in the air with the movement.

When she finished the turn, though, she didn't pause but walked on toward the carriage. He walked on with her.

"What is that dreadful color?" he said.

"Poussière," she said.

"Dust," he said. "I congratulate you, madame. You've made dust alluring."

"It's not an easy color to wear," she said. "Especially for one of my complexion. True *poussière* would make me appear to be suffering from a liver disease. But this silk has a pink undertone, you see."

"How can I make you understand?" he said. "I don't see these things."

"You do," she said. "What you lack is the vocabulary. You said it's alluring. That is the pink undertone, which flatters my complexion, and the magnificent blond lace, close to my face, is even more flattering as well as adding drama."

"It's black," he said. *"Noir,* not *blond."*

"Blond lace is a superior silk lace," she said. "It doesn't mean the color."

This exchange took them to the carriage. He had braced himself for a continuation of last night's battle, but she behaved as though they were old friends, which disarmed and bothered him at the same time. Too, he was so preoccupied with the nonsense of *blond* referring to every color under the sun that he almost forgot to look at her ankles.

But instinct saved him, and he came to his senses in the nick of time. As she went up the steps and took her seat, she gave him a fine view of some six inches of stockinged, elegantly curving limb, from the lower part of her calf down.

Last night came back in a dark surge of recollection, more feeling than thought, that sent heat pumping through him. He saw himself bending and grasping one slim ankle and bringing her foot onto his lap and sliding his gloved hand up her leg, up and up and up . . .

Later, he promised himself, and climbed into the carriage.

A short time later

"I hope you will do me the kindness of allowing me to present Madame Noirot, a London dressmaker of my acquaintance," the Duke of Clevedon said to his hostess.

For a time, the noise about them continued. But about the instant the Comtesse de Chirac realized she hadn't misunderstood the duke's less-than-perfect French and that he had actually uttered the words *London dressmaker* in her presence and referring to the uninvited person beside him, the news was traveling the ballroom, and a silence spread out like ripples from the place where a large rock had landed in a small pond.

Madame de Chirac's posture grew even tighter and stiffer—though that seemed anatomically impossible—and her chilly grey gaze hardened to steel. "I do not understand English humor," she said. "Is this a joke?"

"By no means," Clevedon said. "I bring you a curiosity, in the way that, once upon a time, the savants brought back remarkable objects from their travels in Egypt. I met this exotic creature the other night at the opera, and she was the talk of the promenade yesterday. I beg you will forgive me, and in the interests of scientific inquiry, overlook this so-great imposition upon your good nature. You see, madame, I feel like a naturalist who has discovered a new species of orchid, and who has carried it out of the hidden places of its native habitat and into the world, for other naturalists to observe."

He glanced at Noirot, whose stormy eyes told him she was not amused. The tan and black she wore made her look like a tigress, and the bursts of red might have been her victims' blood.

"Perhaps, on second thought, a flower is not the most apt analogy," he added. "And all things considered, I might have done better to put her on a leash."

The tigress slanted him a smile promising trouble later. Then she bowed her head to the countess and sank into a curtsey so graceful and beautiful—the lace wafting gently in the air, the butterfly bows fluttering, the fabric shimmering—that it took his breath away.

All about him, he heard people gasp. They were French, and couldn't help but see: Here were grace and beauty and style combined in one unforgettable, tempestuous masterpiece.

The comtesse heard the onlookers' reactions, too. She glanced about her. Everyone in the room was riveted on the tableau, all of them holding their breath. This scene would be talked about for days, her every word and gesture anatomized. It would be the most exciting thing that had ever happened at her annual ball. She knew this as well as Clevedon did.

The question was whether she would break tradition and allow excitement.

She paused, with the air of a judge about to deliver sentence.

The room was quite, quite still.

Then, *"Jolie,"* she said, precisely as though Clevedon *had* presented an orchid. With a condescending little nod, and the slightest motion of her hand, she gave the modiste leave to rise. Which Noirot did with the same dancer's grace, eliciting another collective intake of breath.

That was all. One word—*pretty*—and the room began to breathe again. Clevedon and his "discovery" were permitted to move on, along the short reception line and thence into the party proper.

"A dressmaker? From London? But it is impossible. You cannot be English."

The men had attempted to surround her, but the ladies elbowed them aside and were now interrogating her.

Marcelline's dress had awakened both curiosity and envy. The colors were not unusual. They were fashionable colors. The style was not so very different from the latest fashions displayed at Longchamp. But the way she combined style and color and the little touches she added—all this was distinctively Noirot. Being French, these ladies noticed the touches, and were sufficiently intrigued to approach her, though she was a social anomaly—not a person but an exotic pet.

Clevedon's exotic pet.

She was still seething over that, though a part of her couldn't help but admire his cleverness. It was the sort of brazen nonsense members of her family typically employed when they found themselves in a tight spot.

But she'd deal with His Arrogance later.

"I am English and a dressmaker," said Marcelline. She opened her reticule and produced a pretty silver case. From the case she withdrew her business cards: simple and elegant, like a gentleman's calling card. "I come to Paris for inspiration."

"But it is here you should have your shop," said one lady.

Marcelline let her gaze move slowly over their attire. "You don't need me," she said. "The English ladies need me." She paused and added in a stage whisper, *"Desperately."*

The ladies smiled and went away, all of them mollified, and some of them charmed.

Then the men swarmed in.

"This is a mystery," said Aronduille.

"All women are mysteries," Clevedon said.

They stood at the fringes of the dance floor, watching the Marquis d'Émilien waltz with Madame Noirot.

"No, that is not what I mean," said Aronduille. "Where does a dressmaker find time to learn to dance so beautifully? How does an English shopkeeper learn to speak French indistinguishable from that of the comtesse? And what of the curtsey she made to our hostess?" He lifted his gaze heavenward, and kissed the tips of his fingers. "I will never forget that sight."

I'm not a lady, she'd said.

"I admit she's a bit of a riddle," Clevedon said. "But that's what makes her so . . . amusing."

"The ladies went to her," said Aronduille. "Did you see?"

"I saw." Clevedon hadn't imagined they'd approach her. The men, yes, of course.

But the ladies? It was one thing for the hostess to admit her, politely overlooking a high-ranking guest's bad man-

ners or eccentricity. It was quite another matter for her
lady guests to approach his "pet" and converse with her.
Had Noirot been an actress or courtesan or any other
dressmaker, for that matter, they would have snubbed her.

Instead, they'd pushed men aside to get to her. The
encounter was brief, but when the women left, they all
looked pleased with themselves.

"She's a dressmaker," he said. "That's her profession:
making women happy."

But the curtsey he couldn't explain.

He couldn't explain the way she talked and the way
she walked.

And the way she danced.

How many times had Émilien danced with her?

It was nothing to Clevedon. He'd never do anything so
gauche as dance with her all night.

But considering he'd risked humiliation for her, he was
entitled to one dance, certainly.

Though Marcelline appeared to heed only the partner
of the moment, she always knew where Clevedon was.
It was easy enough, his grace standing a head taller than
most of the other men, and that head being so distinctive:
the profile that would have made ancient Greece's finest
sculptors weep, the gleaming black hair with its boyish
mass of tousled curls. Then there were the shoulders. No
one else had such shoulders. But then, no one else had that
body. Very likely he could have spouted any nonsense he
pleased at their hostess, and she would have accepted
whatever he said, for aesthetic reasons alone. Well, pruri-
ent ones, too, possibly. The countess was old and cold but
she wasn't dead.

For a time he'd danced, and now and again, the steps
took them within inches of each other. But he always ap-

peared as attentive to his partner as Marcelline did to hers. One might have believed he was completely indifferent to what she did. He'd got her into the party, and anything after that was her affair.

But one must be an extremely stupid or naïve woman to believe such a thing, and she was neither.

She knew he was watching her, though he excelled at seeming not to. In the last hour, though, he'd shed the pretense. He'd been prowling the ballroom, his friend trailing him like a shadow—a talkative one, by the looks of it.

Then at last the Duke of Clevedon's seemingly casual wanderings brought him to her.

Men crowded about her, as they had from the instant she'd satisfied the ladies' curiosity. He seemed not to notice the other men. He simply walked toward her, and it was as though a great ship sailed into port. The pack of men offered no resistance. They simply gave way, as though they were mere water under his hull.

She wondered if that was what it had been like, once upon a time, for her grandfather, when he was young and handsome, a powerful nobleman of an ancient family. Had the world given way before him, and had it likewise never occurred to him that the world would do anything else?

"Ah, there you are," Clevedon said, as though he'd stumbled upon her by accident.

"As you see," she said. "I have not shredded the curtains, or scratched the furniture."

"No, I reckon you're saving your claws for me," he said. "Well, then, shall we dance?"

"But Madame has promised this next dance to me," said Monsieur Tournadre.

Clevedon turned his head and looked at him.

"Or perhaps I misunderstood," said Monsieur Tournadre. "Perhaps it was another dance."

He backed away, as a lesser wolf would have withdrawn before the leader of the wolf pack.

Oh, she ought not to be thrilled. Only a giddy schoolgirl would thrill at a man's snarling over her, the way a wolf snarled when another wolf dared to approach his bitch.

Still, this was the most desirable man in the ballroom, and his little show of possessiveness would have excited any woman in the room. Whatever else she was, she was still a woman, and a young one, and for all her worldly experience, she'd never had a peer of the realm warn another man away from her.

Before she could tell herself not to be a ninny, he led her out into the dancing. Then his hand clasped her waist, and hers settled on his shoulder.

And the world stopped.

Her gaze shot to his and she saw in his green eyes the same shock that made her draw in her breath and stop moving. She'd danced with a dozen other men. They'd held her in the same way.

This time, though, the touch of his hand was an awareness so keen it hummed over her skin. She felt it deep within, too, a strange stillness. Then her heart lurched into beating again, and she gathered her wits.

Her face smoothed into a social mask and his did, too. Their free hands clasped in the next same instant, and he swung her into the dance.

They danced for a time in silence.

He wasn't ready to speak. He was still shaken by whatever it was that had happened at the start of the dance.

He knew she'd felt it, too—though he couldn't say what *it* was.

At the moment, her attention was elsewhere, not on him. She was looking past his shoulder, and he could look down and study her. She was not, truly, a great beauty, yet she gave that impression. She was handsome and striking and absolutely different.

Her dark hair was modishly arranged, yet in a slightly disarranged way. Had they been elsewhere, he would have dragged his fingers through it, scattering the pins over the floor. The slight turn of her head showed a small, perfect ear from whose lower lobe dangled a garnet earring. In that other place, elsewhere, he would have bent and slid his tongue along the delicate little curve.

But they were not in another place, and so they danced, round and round, and with every turn the familiar waltz grew darker and stranger and hotter.

With every turn he grew more intensely aware of the warmth of her waist under his gloved hand, of the way the heat made her creamy skin glow a tantalizing pink under the dewy sheen, and the way the heat enhanced her scent: the fragrance of her skin mingled with the jasmine she wore so lightly. It was a mere hint of scent in a warm and crowded room thick with them, but he was aware, keenly aware, only of hers.

In the same way he was distantly cognizant of dancers moving about them, a whirl of colors set off by the blacks and greys and whites of the men's dress. But all this glorious color faded to a blur, while below him and about him was a swirl of pale gold, pink-tinged like desert sands at dawn, dotted with red bows trembling like poppies in a summer breeze. Nearer still was the black lace, wafting in the air with every movement.

At last she looked up at him. He saw the heat glow-ing in her face, the throb of the pulse at her neck, and he was aware, without needing to look precisely there, of the rapid rise and fall of her bosom.

"I'll give you credit," she said, her husky voice slightly breathless. "Of all the ruses you might have tried, that was one I never considered. But then, I've never thought of myself as anybody's *pet*."

"I presented you as an *exotic*," he said.

"I take exception to the part about the leash," she said.

"It would be an elegant leash, I assure you," he said. "Studded with diamonds."

"No, thank you," she said. "I take exception as well to your behaving as though you won me in a wager, when in fact you *lost*—and not for the first time." Her dark gaze swept up to the top of his head and down, pausing at his neckcloth, and leaving a wash of heat behind. "That's a pretty emerald."

"Which you shall not have," he said. "No wagers with you this night. We may yet be cast out. The Vicomtesse de Montpellier showed me the business card you gave her. Did no one ever point out to you the difference between a social function and a business function? This is not an institutional banquet of the Merchant Taylors' Company."

"I noticed that. The tailors would be better dressed."

"Are you blind?" he said. "Look about you."

She threw a bored glance about the room. "I saw it all before."

"We're in *Paris*."

"I'm talking about the men, not the women." Her gaze came back to him. "Of all the men here, you are the only one a London tailor would not be ashamed to acknowledge as his client."

"How relieved I am to have your approval," he said.

"I did not say I approve of you altogether," she said.

"That's right. I forgot. I'm a useless aristocrat."

"You have some uses," she said. "Otherwise I should not be courting you."

"Is that what you call it?"

"You keep forgetting," she said. "This party. You. This is all business to me."

He had forgotten. She'd wanted to come to this ball to observe. She would have come without him but for their wager—though that had been less a wager than a war of wills.

"How could I forget?" he said. "I could scarcely believe my eyes when my friends showed me the business cards you handed out as though they were party favors."

"Has your exotic pet embarrassed you, monsieur le duc? Does the odor of the shop offend your nostrils? How curious. As I recall, you were the one who insisted on bringing me. You taunted me with cowardice. Yet you—"

"It would be vulgar to strangle you on the dance floor," he said. "Yet I am sorely tempted."

"Don't be silly," she said. "You haven't had this much fun in an age. You told me, did you not, of the machinations the high and mighty employ to be invited to this exceedingly dull ball. You've done what scores of Parisians would give a vital organ to accomplish. You've achieved the social coup of the decade. In escorting me, you've broken a host of ancient, unbreakable rules. You're thumbing your nose at Society, French and English. And you're dancing with the most exciting woman in the room."

His heart was thudding. It was the dance, the furious dance, and talking, and trying to keep up with her, matching wits. Yet he was aware of an uneasiness inside, the same he'd felt with her before—because it was true, all true, and he hadn't known the truth himself until she uttered it.

"You have a mighty high opinion of yourself," he said.

"My dear duke, only look at the competition."

"I would," he said, "but you're so aggravating, I can't tear my gaze away."

They were turning, turning, both breathless from dancing and talking at the same time. She was looking up at him, her dark eyes brilliant, her mouth—the mouth that had knocked him on his pins—hinting at laughter.

"Fascinating," she said. "You mean *fascinating*."

"You've certainly fascinated my friend Aronduille. He wonders where you learned to curtsey and dance and speak so well."

There was the barest pause before she answered. "Like a lady, you mean? But I'm only aping my betters."

"And where did you learn to ape them, I wonder?" he said. "Do you not work from dawn till dusk? Are dressmakers not apprenticed at an early age?"

"Nine years old," she said. "How knowledgeable you are, suddenly, of my trade."

"I asked my valet," he said.

She laughed. "Your valet," she said. "Oh, that's rich. Literally."

"But you have a maid," he said. "A slight girl with fair hair."

Instantly the laughter in her eyes vanished. "You noticed my maid?"

"At the promenade, yes."

"You're above-average observant."

"Madame, I notice everything about you, purely in the interests of self-preservation."

"Call me cynical, but I suspect there's nothing pure about it," she said.

The dance was drawing to a close. He was distantly aware of the music subsiding, but more immediately aware of her: the heat between them, physical and mental, and the turbulence she made.

"And yet you court me," he said.

"Solely in the interests of commerce," she said.

"Interesting," he said. "I wonder at your methods for attracting business. You say you wish to dress my duchess—and you start by making off with my stickpin."

"I won it fair and square," she said.

The dance ended, but still he held her. "You tease and provoke and dare and infuriate me," he said.

"Oh, *that* I do for fun," she said.

"For fun," he said. "You like to play with fire, madame."

"As do you," she said.

Tense seconds ticked by before he noticed that the music had fully stopped, and people were watching them while pretending not to. He let go of her, making a show of smoothing her lace—tidying her up, as one might a child. He smiled a patronizing little smile he knew would infuriate her, then bowed politely.

She made him an equally polite curtsey, then opened her fan and lifted it to her face, hiding all but her mocking dark eyes. "If you'd wanted a tame pet, your grace, you should have picked another woman."

She slipped away into the crowd, the black lace and red bows fluttering about the shimmering pink-tinged gold of her gown.

Chapter Five

Masked balls are over for the season, but dress balls are as frequent as they were in the beginning of the winter. Some of the most novel dancing dresses are of gauze figured in a different colour from the ground, as jonquille and lilac, white and emerald green, or rose, écre and cherry-colour.

Costume of Paris by a Parisian correspondent,
The Court Magazine and Belle Assemblée, 1835

*M*arcelline swiftly made her way out of the ballroom and into the corridor. She started toward the stairway.

"I picked *you*?" came a familiar, low voice from close behind her.

Startled, she spun around—and collided with Clevedon. She stumbled, and he caught hold of her shoulders and righted her.

"Delicious exit line," he said. "But we're not quite done."

"Oh, I think we are," she said. "I've looked my fill tonight. My card will be in the hands of at least one reporter by tomorrow, along with a detailed description of my dress. Several ladies will be writing to their friends and family in London about my shop. And you and I have caused more talk than is altogether desirable. At the moment, I'm not absolutely certain I can turn the talk to account. Your grasping me in this primitive fashion doesn't improve matters. May I point out as well that you're wrinkling my lace."

He released her, and for one demented instant, she missed the warmth and the pressure of his hands.

"I did not *pick* you," he said. "You came to the theater and flaunted yourself and did your damndest to rivet my attention."

"If you think that was my damndest, you're sadly inexperienced," she said.

He studied her face for a moment, his green eyes glittering.

If he took hold of her again and shook her until her teeth rattled, she wouldn't be surprised. She was provoking him, and it wasn't the wisest thing to do, but she was provoked, too, frustrated on any number of counts, mainly the obvious one.

"I brought you," he said tightly. "I'll take you back to your hotel."

"There's no reason for you to leave the party," she said. "I'll find a fiacre to take me back."

"The party is boring," he said. "You're the only interesting thing in it. You'd scarcely left before it deflated, audibly, like a punctured hot-air balloon. I heard the sigh of escaping excitement behind me as I stepped into the corridor."

"It didn't occur to you that the deflation was on account of your departure?" she said.

"No," he said. "And don't try flattery. It sits ill on you. In fact, it turns your face slightly green. I do wonder how you get on with your clients. Surely you're obliged to flatter and cajole."

"I flatter in the same way I do everything else," she said. "Beautifully. If I turned green it was due to shock at your flattering *me*."

"Then collect your wits before we descend the stairs. If you take a tumble and crack your head, suspicion will instantly fall on me."

She needed to collect her wits, and not for fear of tumbling down the stairs. She hadn't yet recovered from the waltz with him: the heat, the giddiness, the almost overpowering physical awareness—and most alarming, the yearning coursing through her, racing in her veins, beating in her heart, and weakening her mind as though she'd drunk some kind of poison.

She started down the stairs.

As the buzz of the party grew more distant, she became aware of his light footfall behind her, and of the deserted atmosphere of the lower part of the house.

Risk-taking was in her blood, and conventional morality had not been part of her upbringing. If this had been another man, she wouldn't have hesitated. She would have led him to a dark corner or under the stairs and had him. She would have lifted her skirts and taken her pleasure—against a wall or a door or on a windowsill—and got it out of her system.

But this wasn't another man, and she'd already let temper and pride get the better of her judgment.

Leonie had warned her, before she left: "We'll never have another chance like this. Don't bugger it up."

The hell of it was, Marcelline wouldn't know whether or not she'd botched it until it was too late.

He said nothing for a time, and she wondered if he, too, was pondering the stories shortly to fly about London, and deciding how best to deal with them.

But why should he fret about gossip? He was a man, and

men were expected to chase women, especially in Paris. It was practically his patriotic duty. Lady Clara certainly hadn't made any fuss about his affairs. It would have been common knowledge if she had. Since Longmore behaved much the same as his friend did, Marcelline doubted it had even dawned on the earl to mention the subject when issuing the ultimatum, whatever that was.

Still, all the duke's other liaisons in Paris had been ladies or sought-after members of the demimonde. Those sorts of conquests were prestigious.

But a dressmaker—a common shopkeeper—wasn't Clevedon's usual thing, and anything unusual could set the ton on its ear.

These cogitations took her to the ground floor. They did nothing to quiet her agitation.

She waited while he told the porter to summon his carriage.

When Clevedon turned back to her, she said, "How do you propose to explain this evening to Lady Clara? Or do you never explain yourself to her?"

"Don't speak of her," he said.

"You're ridiculous," she said. "You say it as though my uttering her name will somehow contaminate her. That must be your guilty conscience speaking, because it most assuredly isn't your intellect. You know that she's the one I want. She's the one I came to Paris for. 'Don't speak of her,' indeed." She imitated his haughty tone. "Is that what you do with everything uncomfortable? Pretend it isn't there? She's there, you stubborn man. The woman you're going to marry by summer's end. You ought to speak of her. You ought to be reminding me of her vast superiority to me—except as regards dress, that is."

"I had originally planned," he said levelly, "to write to Clara as I always do. I had planned to repeat the most fatuous conversations to which I was subjected in the course of the evening. I had planned to give my impressions of the company. I had planned to describe my sufferings from boredom—a boredom endured entirely on her account, in order provide her entertainment."

"How noble of you."

Something flickered in his eyes, and it was like the flash of a lighthouse, seen through a storm.

She knew she approached dangerous waters, but if she didn't get him under control, she risked smashing her business to pieces.

"And you'd completely disregard my part in events?" Marcelline said. "Stupid question. It's tactless to mention the women of dubious character you encounter in the course of your travels and entertainments. On the present occasion, however, I'd recommend against that approach. News of our exciting arrival at the party will soon be racing across the Channel, to arrive in London as early as Tuesday. I suggest you tackle the subject straight on. Tell her you brought me to win a wager. Or you did it for a joke."

"By God, you're the most managing female," he said.

"I'm trying to manage my future," she said. She heard the slight wobble in her voice. Alarmed, she took a calming breath. His gaze became heavy-lidded and shifted to her neckline. Her reaction to that little attention was the opposite of calming.

Devil take him! He was the one who belonged on a leash.

She started for the gate. The porter hastily opened it.

"The carriage hasn't arrived yet," Clevedon said. "Do you mean to wait on the street for it, like a clerk waiting for the omnibus?"

"I am not traveling in that or any other carriage with you," she said. "We'll go our separate ways this night."

"I cannot allow you to travel alone," he said. "That's asking for trouble."

And traveling with him in a closed carriage, in the dead of night, in her state of mind—or not mind—wasn't? She needed to get away from him, not simply for appearances' sake, but to think. There had to be a way to salvage this situation.

"I'm not a sheltered miss," she said. "I've traveled Paris on my own for years."

"Without a servant?"

She wished she had something heavy to throw at his thick head.

She'd grown up on the streets of Paris and London and other cities. She came from a family that lived by its wits. The stupid or naïve did not survive. The only enemy they hadn't been able to outwit or outrun was the cholera.

"Yes, without a servant," she said. "Shocking, I know. To do anything without servants is unthinkable to you."

"Not true," he said. "I can think of several things to do that do not require servants."

"How inventive of you," she said.

"In any event, the point is moot," he said. "Here's my carriage."

While she'd been trying *not* to think of the several activities one might perform without servants' assistance, the carriage had drawn up to the entrance.

"Adieu, then," she said. "I'll find a fiacre in the next street."

"It's raining," he said.

"It is not . . ."

She felt a wet *plop* on her shoulder. Another on her head.

A footman leapt down from the back of the carriage, opened an umbrella, and hurried toward them. By the time he reached them, the occasional *plop* had already built to a rapid patter. She felt Clevedon's hand at her back, nudging her under the umbrella, and guiding her to the carriage steps.

It was the touch of his hand, the possessive, protective gesture. That was what undid her.

She told herself she wasn't made of sugar and wouldn't melt. She told herself she'd walked in the rain many times. Her self didn't listen.

Her self was trapped in feelings: the big hand at her back, the big body close by. The night was growing darker and colder while the rain beat down harder. She was strong and independent and she'd lived on the streets, yet she'd always craved, as any animal does, shelter and protection.

She was weak in that way. Self-denial wasn't instinctive.

She couldn't break way from him or turn away from the open carriage door where shelter waited. She didn't want to be cold and wet, walking alone in the dark in Paris.

And so she climbed the steps and sank gratefully onto the well-cushioned seat, and told herself that catching a fatal chill or being attacked and raped in a dirty alley would not do her daughter or her sisters any good.

He sat opposite.

The door closed.

She felt the slight bounce as the footman returned to his perch. She heard his rap on the roof, signaling the coachman to start.

The carriage moved forward gently enough, but the streets here were far from smooth, and despite springs and well-cushioned seats, she felt the motion. The silence within was like the silence before a thunderstorm. She became acutely conscious of the wheels rattling over the stones and the rain drumming on the roof . . . and, within, the too-fierce pounding of her heart.

"Going to find a fiacre," he said. "Really, you are ridiculous."

She was. She should have risked the dark and cold and rain. It would be for only a few minutes. In a fiacre, at least, she might have been able to think.

The night was dark, the sheeting rain blotting out what little light the street and carriage lamps shed. Within the carriage was darker yet. She could barely make out his form on the seat opposite. But she was suffocatingly aware of the long legs stretched out over the space between them. He seemed to have his arm stretched out over the top of the seat cushions, too. The relaxed pose didn't fool her. He lounged in the seat in the way a panther might lie on its belly in a tree, watching its prey move along the forest floor below. If he'd owned a tail, it would have twitched.

"I was an idiot to attend this event with you," she said.

"You seemed to be having a fine time. You certainly did not lack for dance partners," he said.

"Yes, I was doing quite well, thank you, until you had to turn medieval—"

"Medieval?"

"Out of my way, peasants. The wench belongs to me." She mimicked the Duke of Clevedon at his haughty best. "I thought Monsieur Tournadre would wet himself when you bared your fangs at him."

"What a grotesque imagination you have."

"You're big and arrogant, and I think you know exactly how intimidating you can be."

"Alas, not to you."

"Still, perhaps all is not lost," she said. "That sort of possessive behavior is typical of your kind. Furthermore, I am your pet. You brought me to the party for your amusement. And I did make it abundantly clear to the company that I'd come to drum up business and was using you for that purpose."

"But that isn't what happened," he said.

"That is exactly what happened," she said.

"What happened was, we waltzed, and it was plain to everyone what we were doing even though we had our clothes on," he said.

"Oh, that," she said. "I have the same effect on every man I dance with."

"Don't pretend you weren't affected as well."

"Of course I was affected," she said. "I never danced with a duke before. It was the most exciting thing that's ever happened in my mediocre little bourgeois life."

"A pity I am not medieval," he said. "In that case, I shouldn't hesitate to make your mediocre little life even more exciting, and a good deal littler."

"Perhaps I ought to put it in an advertisement," she said. "Ladies of distinction and fashion are invited to the showrooms of Mrs. Noirot, Fleet Street, West Chancery Lane, to inspect an assemblage of such elegant and truly nouvelle articles of dresses, mantles, and millinery, as in point of excellence, taste, and splendor, cannot be matched in any other house whatever. Often imitated but never surpassed, Mrs. Noirot alone can claim the distinction of having danced with a duke."

The carriage stopped.

"Have we reached the hotel already?" she said. "How quickly the time flies in your company, your grace." She started to rise.

"We're nowhere near your hotel," he said. "We've stopped for an accident or a drunk in the street or some such. Everyone's stopped."

She leaned forward, to look out of the window. It was hard to make out anything but the sheen of the rain where the lamp lights caught it.

"I don't see—"

She felt rather than saw him move, but it was so quick and smooth that he took her off guard. At one moment she was leaning forward toward the door's window. In the next, his hands were under her arms, and he was lifting her, as easily as if she'd been a hatbox, out of her seat and onto his lap.

For an instant, she was too startled to react. It was only the briefest of moments, scarcely the blink of an eye. But when she started to push away from him, he caught one hand in the hair at the back of her head and brought her face close to his.

"Speaking of business, which you do incessantly, we have some of our own," he said, his voice low and dangerous. "That isn't finished, madame. It hasn't even begun."

"Don't be stupid," she said. Her voice was shaky. Her heart pumped wildly, as though she dangled from a ledge over an abyss.

She told herself he was only a man, and she understood men through and through. But her reasoning self hadn't a prayer of being listened to.

He was strong and solid and warm. His size excited her. His beauty excited her. His power and arrogance excited her. That was the danger. She was weak in this way, her will and mind easily beaten down by the wantonness in her blood.

She felt the heat of his muscled thighs through the layers of her dress and petticoats, and the heat sped through her, upward and downward, stirring cravings she was hopeless at stifling. "I don't want you," she lied. "I want your duch—"

His mouth cut her off.

It was warm and firm and determined. Centuries earlier, his ancestors had taken what they wanted: lands, riches, women. Called it "mine," and it was.

His mouth took hers in the same way, a siege of a kiss, single-minded, insistent, potent.

His mouth was a hedonist's dream, luscious carnal sin. The feel of it, the unyielding pressure—a saint might have withstood it, but she hadn't a saintly bone in her body. She gave way instantly. Her mouth parted to take him in, to find the taste of him on her tongue and to relish it, as she hadn't let herself do the last time. He tasted of a thousand sins, and those sins were like honey to her.

Her hands, still braced on his chest to push away from him, now slid up, over the hard angles of the emerald and the crisp linen of his neckcloth and up. She pushed off his hat and let her fingers tangle in the thick curls, as they'd itched to do from the moment he'd bent over her hand in the Italian Opera House.

It was as stormy a kiss as the last time, but different. He was angry with her; she was angry with him. But far more than anger was at work between them. This time she wasn't in control. She was drowning in feeling, in the taste of him, and the scent of his skin and the feel of his hard body under hers, and his hand so tight in her hair, possessive.

A lifetime had passed since a man had held her like this.

She knew—a part of her mind knew—she needed to break away from him. But first . . . oh, a little more. She rubbed her body against his, reveling in the heat and hardness of his, and feeling a jolt of triumph because his arousal was obvious even through the layers of her dress and petticoats. As that hard part pressed against her hip, heat and pleasure coursed through her, like a madness.

He made a sound deep in his throat, and broke the kiss.

She should have pulled away then, but she wasn't yet ready to stop. Then his mouth slid to her throat, trailing down and over her collarbone and up to her shoulder. She let out a little moan of pleasure and her head fell back, and she gave herself up to sensation: his big hands sliding over her, stirring up wants she'd shut away for years . . . his mouth on her, making a trail of kisses like little fires. They burned her skin and set fire to her inside, too, deep inside.

She wasn't the only one inflamed. She heard his breathing grow harsher, and when his hand closed over her breast, she gasped and he growled again, deep in his throat. The low sounds they made mingled in the darkness, and she thought of panthers coupling in the shadows. She could have laughed, because the image fit so well.

He was a predator. So was she.

His mouth found hers once more, and he was moving his hands over her, taking possession. She was claiming him as well, running her hands over his muscled arms and taut torso. She thrilled as his body tensed under her touch. Every sign of his slipping control elated her, even while hers slipped, too.

She changed position and moved her hand down, to the front of his trousers, and spread her hand wide there, feeling the throb and heat of his phallus—and a great ducal one it was—and that wicked thought made her head swim—and, ye gods, how she wanted him! Her drunken mind filled with images: naked, sweating bodies . . . herself impaled and shrieking with pleasure.

Without breaking the kiss but deepening it instead, her tongue thrusting against his, she lifted herself up and turned to straddle him. In the closed space of the carriage, her skirt's and petticoats' rustling sounded like thunder.

He moved his hands over her shoulders, tugging down the dress. She heard—or felt—the silk rip. She didn't care.

He dragged the dress down, and pushed down the top of her corset. She felt the air on her exposed breasts before he broke the kiss to bring his mouth there. His tongue grazed her nipple and she groaned, and when he suckled, she gasped, and threw her head back, and laughed, and caught her hands in his hair and kissed the top of his head, again and again. But the tug on her breast tugged deep inside as well, low in her belly, making her impatient, squirming.

She let go of him to grasp her skirts and petticoats. She pulled them up, and his big hand slid over her thigh—

Light exploded, filling the carriage's interior. It lasted only an instant, but it was an instant's too-bright daylight, and it shocked and woke her from the mad dream she'd fallen into, even before the deafening *crack* shook the carriage.

She pushed his hand away, pushed down her skirt, and pulled up her bodice. She climbed down from his lap.

"Damnation," he said thickly. "Just when it was getting interesting."

Another blinding flash of light. A pause. More thunder.

She returned to her seat and tried to put her dress to rights. "It wasn't supposed to get *interesting*, devil take me. I *knew* I oughtn't to get into a vehicle with you, not when we were so wrought up. Stop the carriage. You must let me out."

Lightning crackled again. And again. Thunder boomed, and it sounded like a war.

"You're not going out in that," he said.

"I most certainly am," she said. She got up to wrestle with the window. She had to get it down to reach the door handle outside. Before she could do so, the carriage lurched to a stop, and she stumbled. He caught her, but she dug her nails into his hands.

He didn't let go. "It was only a kiss," he said.

"It was more than *only*," she said. "If not for the lightning, we should have done exactly what I told you I absolutely will not, must not, cannot do."

"That isn't what you told me."

"Were you even listening?"

"You didn't say you would not must not cannot do it," he said. "Not precisely. What you said, in so many words, was that your prospective London patrons mustn't get wind of it."

She wrenched away from him, and the carriage lurched into motion at the same time. This time she fell onto him. She wanted to stay, oh, how she wanted to stay. She wanted to climb onto his lap and wallow in his warmth and his strength and his touch. She made herself scramble away, pushing away his hands, and she flung herself onto her seat. It was the work of a few seconds, but it felt like a lifetime's labor to her.

Resisting temptation was *horrible*.

"You split your hairs exceedingly fine," she said breathlessly.

"And you thought I wasn't listening," he said.

"You chose to hear what a man would choose to hear," she said.

"I'm a man," he said.

That ought not to strike her as the understatement of the decade, but it did.

A man, only a man, she told herself—but look at what he'd done, what she'd done.

Nothing ought to have happened as it had: the incendiary kiss, the speed with which reason and self-control had disintegrated—even for her, that was extreme. She had underestimated him or overestimated herself, and now she wanted to kill somebody because she couldn't think of a way to have him without ruining everything.

If she hadn't done that already.

Think. Think. Think.

The carriage stopped and she wanted to scream. Would this journey never end?

The door opened. An umbrella appeared, attached to the gloved hand of a drenched footman.

Clevedon started up from his seat.

"Don't," she said.

"I'm not accustomed to tossing women from the carriage and allowing them to make their own way to their doors."

"I don't doubt there's a good deal you're not accustomed to," she said.

But he was already moving down the steps, and arguing with him wouldn't make the footman any drier.

Ignoring the hand Clevedon offered, she stepped down quickly from the carriage and ran through the rain for the haven of the hotel's portico. He ran after her. His legs were longer. He caught up in no time, and threw a sheltering arm about her for the last few feet.

"We need to talk," he said.

"Not now," she said. "Your footmen will catch their death."

He glanced back, and there was enough light at the hotel entrance for her to make out the puzzled look on his handsome face.

"You can't leave them standing in a downpour while we argue," she said.

No doubt he did it all the time. To him, servants were merely animated furniture.

"I wasn't intending to argue," he said, "but I forgot. Talking with you is most usually an argument."

"We can talk on Sunday," she said.

"Later today," he said.

"I'm engaged with Sylvie," she said.

"Break the engagement."

"I'm not free until Sunday," she said. "You may take me riding in the Bois de Boulogne when it isn't teeming with aristocrats showing off their finery. After Longchamp, the place will be relatively quiet."

"I was thinking of a place not so public," he said.

"I wasn't," she said. "But let's not debate now. Send me a message on Saturday, and I'll meet you on Sunday, wherever you choose, as long as it isn't too disreputable. There are places even a lowly dressmaker shuns."

"Wherever I choose," he repeated.

"To *talk*," she said.

"Yes, of course," he said. "We have business to discuss."

She was well aware that the business he wanted to discuss was not her shop and Lady Clara's patronage thereof. She'd been a fool to imagine she could manage this man. She should have realized that a duke is used to getting his own way, to a degree common folk could scarcely imagine. She should have realized that getting his way all his life would affect his brain and make him not altogether like other men.

In short, she would have done better to keep out of his way and send Sophy after his bride-to-be.

But she hadn't realized, and now she had to salvage the situation as best she could. She knew only one way to do that.

"I know your footmen are mere mechanical devices to you," she said. "But I can only think that one or both of them is sure to take a chill, and develop a putrid sore throat or affection of the lungs. So bourgeois of me, I know, but I can't help it."

Again he glanced back. One footman stood at a discreet distance, holding the umbrella, awaiting his grace's pleasure. The other stood on his perch at the back of the carriage. They'd both donned cloaks, which by now must be soaked through, in spite of their umbrellas.

"Until Sunday, then," she said.

His gaze came back to her, unreadable. "Sunday it is."

She smiled and said good night, and made herself stroll calmly through the door the hotel porter held open for her.

Clevedon strode briskly back to the coach, under the umbrella Joseph held.

He had to get her out of his mind. He had to regain his sanity.

He made himself speak. "Filthy night," he said.

"Yes, your grace."

"Paris isn't pretty in the rain," Clevedon said.

"No, your grace. The gutters are disgraceful."

"What took us so long?"

"An accident, your grace," Joseph said. "A pair of vehicles collided. It didn't look serious to me, but the drivers were shouting at each other, then others got into it, and there was a bit of a riot. But when the lightning struck, they all scattered. Otherwise we might be boxed in there yet."

The way Noirot had fussed about his poor, drenched footmen, Clevedon had expected to find them slumped on the ground, clutching their chests.

But when he'd looked back, Thomas was talking animatedly over the top of the carriage to Hayes, the coachman. And here was Joseph, full of youthful energy, though it must be close to two o'clock in the morning.

All three servants would have vastly enjoyed watching the Parisians pummel one another. They would have laughed uproariously when the lightning sent the combatants scurrying.

Hayes was a tough old bird who cared only how circumstances affected his horses, and he'd kept them calm. The footmen were young, and youth cared nothing for a bit of damp.

All of Clevedon's servants were well paid and well dressed and well fed. They were doctored when they were ill and pensioned generously when they retired.

That wasn't the case in every household, he knew, and a shopkeeper would have no way of knowing how well or ill his servants were treated. Being in the service line herself, Noirot was liable to attacks of sympathy.

Even so . . .

He climbed into the carriage. The door closed after him.

He didn't trust her.

He didn't trust her as far as he could throw her.

She cheated at cards—he was sure of it—or if she didn't cheat, she shaved honesty mighty close.

She said she did not seduce her patron's menfolk, but she'd—

"By God," he muttered. "By God." Her scent lingered in the carriage, and he could almost taste her still. He could almost feel her skin under his fingertips.

Only a kiss.

He'd gone from desire to madness in a single pulse beat.

He was still . . . not right.

And no wonder.

They would have to finish it. Then he could put her out of his mind and complete in peace his remaining weeks of freedom.

Chasing a provoking woman about Paris was not part of his plans, and certainly not in his style. He was accustomed to games with women, yes. He liked play as well as foreplay. But it was an altogether different matter, dancing to the tune of an impudent dressmaker who would not stop talking about her curst business—even if she made him want to laugh at the exact instant he wanted to choke her—and even if she kissed like Satan's own mistress, trained specially by Mephistopheles, who'd helped design her body . . . her perfect breasts . . . the smooth arc of her neck . . . the exquisite curve of her ears . . .

Her wicked tongue.

Her lying tongue.

What engagement had she with Sylvie Fontenay that would occupy all of Friday and Saturday?

Meanwhile, at the Hotel Fontaine

"Pack?" Jeffreys repeated. Expecting Marcelline to come back late, she'd napped. She was brightly alert at the moment.

So was Marcelline. She was alert with panic. "We need to leave as early as possible tomorrow. Today, I mean," she said.

It was only two o'clock in the morning on Friday. If they could get seats on a steam packet to London on Saturday, they could be home as early as Sunday. The guests at the ball would not be writing their letters until later today, which meant they mightn't be posted until Saturday. And the London post was closed on Sundays.

With any luck, she and Jeffreys would be in London before any letters arrived from Paris. That would give Sophy time to devise a way to capitalize on any rumors about Mrs. Noirot and the Duke of Clevedon.

"We haven't a minute to lose," she said. "By Tuesday or Wednesday, the rumors will be flying. We have to manage them."

Jeffreys didn't say, "What rumors?" She was not naïve

and she was not stupid. She knew Marcelline had attended the ball with the Duke of Clevedon. She'd noticed the torn dress. She'd even raised an eyebrow. But it was an interested eyebrow, not a shocked or censorious one. Jeffreys was no innocent lamb. She'd had dealings with the upper orders, especially its male contingent. That was how she'd ended up as "an unfortunate female."

No one had to tell her how the dress had come to be damaged. Her concern was whether the damage was reparable.

"It's all a matter of interpretation," Marcelline said. "We simply reinterpret. Something like—let me see— 'Duke of C captivated by Mrs. Noirot's gown of *poussière* silk displayed to magnificent advantage in the course of a waltz,'" Marcelline said, thinking aloud. "No, it wants more detail. 'Gown of *poussière* silk, dotted with crimson papillon bows, a black lace pelerine completing the ensemble . . . met with the approval of one of the highest ranking members of the peerage.' Yes, that could do it."

"I can mend it easily," said Jeffreys. "Everyone will want to see it."

"They will see it, if we manage this properly," Marcelline said. "But that means taking charge of the tale before anyone else gets it. Sophy can give her contact at *Foxe's Morning Spectacle* an exclusive, early report. She'll tell him the Duke of Clevedon took me to the party as one of his jokes. Or to win a wager."

"Wouldn't a joke be better?" said Jeffreys. "To some people, a wager might sound disreputable."

"You're right. My being there started out as a joke, but the dress captured the other guests' attention—"

"Something ought to be put in about 'the effect of the color arrangement while in motion—'"

"Exactly," said Marcelline. "Then something about a

waltz as the perfect showcase for the dress's unique effects. Struck by my appearance, even the Duke of Clevedon danced with me."

"Madame, how I wish I had been there," said Jeffreys. "Any lady who reads a story like that will feel the same. They'll all be wild to see the dress—and the shop it came from—and the women who made it."

"We'll have time enough to work out the details while we're on the boat," Marcelline said. "But we have to catch it first. Pack as if your life depended on it."

And, *I've done that more times than I can count,* she thought.

"Certainly, madame. But the passports?"

"What about them?"

"You recall that the ambassador's secretary told us that before leaving, we must send him our passports to be countersigned. Then we must take them to the prefecture of police. Then to—"

"We don't have time," Marcelline said.

"But, madame—"

"It will take all day, even two days," Marcelline said. She ran this gauntlet twice a year, spring and autumn, when she visited Paris. She knew the entire tedious routine by heart. "The different offices are open at different hours. The British ambassador only deigns to put his name to the passports between the hours of eleven and one. Then one must wait upon the prefecture of police. After that comes the nonsense with the foreign minister—again who allows only two hours, and demands ten francs to take up his pen. You know it's ridiculous."

They need rules. They make so many.

She could hear Clevedon's low voice, the tone implying a shared joke about the French and their rules. The first night, at the opera, came back in a rush of sensation:

her hand on the costly neckcloth, exchanging his pin for hers . . . the way he'd watched her, so still, like a cat: the panther lying in wait.

She pushed him from her mind. She hadn't time to brood about him.

"I know it's silly, madame, but the secretary said we were liable to be detained if our papers are not perfectly in order."

"You see to the packing," Marcelline said. "Leave the passports and the officials to me."

Saturday evening

"I can't believe it," Jeffreys said as she looked about the tiny cabin. They had been unable to obtain a chief cabin—but then, they were lucky to have been allowed aboard the steam packet at all, considering all the rules they'd disregarded. "You did it."

"Where there's a will, there's a way," said Marcelline. Especially, she thought, when the will belonged to a Noirot. It was amazing how much could be accomplished with a little forgery, a little bribery, a little charm, and a good deal of décolleté.

Not amazing, actually, considering that all the officials were men.

While Jeffreys was unaware of some of the details— Marcelline's forgery skills, for instance, had best go unmentioned—she'd caught on to the other methods, and had even assisted. As the ambassador's secretary had warned, several attempts had been made to detain them. The last bit, with the customs officials, was the most difficult.

"We did it," Marcelline said. "And with time to spare, thanks to your clever gambit with your shoe ties."

"I vow, I was frantic, madame," Jeffreys said. "It would have been horrible to be within sight of the packet and not be allowed aboard."

"And I was about one minute from losing my temper and ruining everything," Marcelline said.

"You were tired, madame. I don't believe you slept a wink, all the way from Paris."

"A wink here and there," Marcelline said. The French roads were improving, but they remained far from smooth. Between the jolting of the carriage and the plotting how to get through the next phase of bureaucracy and Clevedon's thrusting himself into her overworked brain when she most needed to be logical, her fitful dozes had provided precious little rest. She'd made herself eat, but they hadn't time to wait for a proper meal. They'd snatched what they could, and it wasn't the best she'd ever eaten. Dyspepsia did not aid the thinking process.

Jeffreys had come to her rescue, however. She'd broken a shoe tie accidentally on purpose, and burst into tears. Two officials had assisted her with the repairs. It was hard to say whether her pretty ankles had softened their hearts or they'd feared another weeping fit or they were feeling hurried and harassed, too, thanks to the tumult behind them of another late arrival. Whatever the reason was, the men had waved them on.

Had Marcelline brought Frances Pritchett with her, they'd still be in Paris.

She examined her pendant watch. "We should depart soon," she said. "I'm going up to take a turn about the deck."

"I should have thought you'd want to fall into bed," Jeffreys said. "I certainly do, and I had a great deal more sleep than you did."

"I need to breathe the salt air and calm myself first,"

Marcelline said. "It's very pretty at night, watching the lights of the town retreat. You ought to come. We arrived from London in broad day. It's so different at night."

Jeffreys gave a little shiver. "You're a better sea traveler than I," she said. "I hope to be asleep before we set sail. I was sick most of the way coming here. I should rather not be sick on the way back."

"Poor girl," Marcelline said. "I'd forgotten. It was dreadful for you."

"It was worth it, madame," Jeffreys said firmly. "And I should do it again. I shall *pray*, in fact, to do it again." She laughed. "But you go, and enjoy yourself."

Marcelline left her, and made her way to the deck. The officers and crew were preparing to set out, and the passengers were settling down after the flurry of finding their places and seeing about their belongings. There was a good deal of noise, and a great many people. Night had fallen but the stars were out en masse, along with a bright half moon.

She had no trouble making out the tall figure at the rail, and even before he turned, and the moonlight and starlight traced his features, her heart was racing.

Chapter Six

Between the first week in April, and the last in November, Steam-Packets run daily, weather permitting, from their Moorings off the Tower of London to Calais, in about twelve hours; and likewise from Calais to London, in about the same time. Carriages, horses, and luggage, conveyed by Steam-Packets, are shipped and relanded free of expense.

Mariana Starke, *Travels in Europe*, 1833

She stood completely still, but for the feathers and lace of her bonnet shuddering in the wind. Outwardly Clevedon was as still as she was, while his heart leapt with an excitement growing all too familiar.

He strode toward her. "Surprise," he said.

Her eyes narrowed. They were deeply shadowed, and he doubted that was merely the moonlight's effect. She was fatigued, and no wonder. He was amazed at the speed with which she'd quit Paris. She couldn't have slept at all after the party. Then, to reach Calais so soon, she couldn't have stopped for more than the change of horses on the way.

He wondered how she'd done it. Getting all her papers signed in the middle of the night must have cost a fortune in bribes—paid, no doubt, from the money she'd won at roulette and cards.

Even he, for all his great rank, had not had an easy time getting through officialdom, and he'd set out hours after she did, when the bureaucrats were awake at least, though not all of the offices had been open.

Had he not been the Duke of Clevedon, and furthermore, had he not thrown his full ducal weight about, the packet would have sailed an hour ago, and he'd be in Calais watching it retreat across the Channel while he cursed himself for a fool.

He was a fool, and he was cursing himself now, but to little effect.

In any event, she was angry enough for the two of them.

"Surprise?" she said. "There's an understatement. Have you taken leave of your senses?"

Yes.

"I was worried about you," he said. "When you left Paris so suddenly, I thought a catastrophe had occurred. Or a murder. Have you murdered anybody, by the way? Not that I would dream of criticizing, but—"

"I lcft Paris to gct away from you," she said.

"Well, that didn't work."

"How in blazes did you do it?" she said. "How did you know? How did you—but no, I won't ask how you got through French officialdom. You're a duke, and they haven't cut off any noble heads this age. Still, one would have thought they'd learned how useless aristos are, not remotely worth indulging."

He smiled. "But you need my noble head, Madame Noirot. You need me to pay the bills."

"How did you know I was leaving?" she said.

"You are single-minded, I notice," he said.

"How did you know?" she demanded, hands clenched.

Though he felt his face heat, he answered carelessly, "I sent my porter to spy on you. He was loitering about your hotel in the small hours of the morning when you and your maid departed from it, in a fiacre. At first he assumed you'd merely set a shockingly early hour for meeting Mademoiselle Fontenay. Then, when he counted the number of portmanteaux being stowed in the vehicle, he grew curious. From one of the inn servants, he learned that you had quit the hotel. Your destination, he discovered, was the posting office, and you were traveling to 'visit a relative.' In point of fact, I should be asking how you contrived to get out of France. You left hours before any of the officials who must approve your exit were even awake."

"It didn't occur to you that I might have made my arrangements previously?" she said.

"Did you?" he said.

"Ah, your spying porter didn't find that out," she said. "What a pity, because I'm not going to satisfy your curiosity. I've been traveling for a day and a half over wretched French roads, and I'm tired. Good night, your grace."

She dipped the barest of curtseys and walked away from him.

He fought the urge to follow her. He'd behaved absurdly enough as it was. For what? What did he think he'd achieve aboard a steam packet mobbed with travelers? He was lucky this was an English boat, or they would not have delayed its departure for him. As it was, he'd paid massive bribes to change places with other passengers. Even so, had he been a man of lesser rank, he'd be waiting in Calais for the next vessel.

Staying in Calais was what he ought to have done. No, he ought not to have left Paris at all. Six more weeks of freedom, and he'd thrown them away—for what?

But he'd done it, and having spent a day and a half racing over abominable roads, he was hardly likely to stand tamely on the dock, watching the packet sail away.

His behavior was lunatic—but never mind. In truth, Paris was growing wearisome, and a mad race to Calais was better excitement than anything he'd done in recent weeks, perhaps months. Certainly it had been worth it, simply to see Noirot's shocked expression when she caught sight of him.

Surprise, indeed. He doubted anybody or anything had surprised her in a very long time.

He stayed on deck until the packet had sailed out of the harbor and out into the Channel. He noticed the clouds drifting across the heavens, dimming the starlight and moonlight, but he thought nothing of it. The sky over the English Channel was never perfectly clear.

He went below, where he let Saunders peel off his coat and relieve him of his neckcloth, waistcoat, and boots. Then his grace fell into bed and instantly asleep.

Not an hour later, the storm struck.

Marcelline staggered out into the narrow passage. The smell was foul: scores of panicked passengers being sick. Her own stomach, usually reliable even in rough seas, heaved. She paused for a moment, breathing through her mouth, willing her insides to quiet.

The ship lurched hard to her right, and she fell against a door. From behind it came shrieks and shouts, the same she'd heard from other cabins. The vessel screamed more loudly, its timbers groaning as the waves knocked it about.

She walked on unsteadily, telling herself that this was normal, the ropes and timbers protesting the sea's pummeling. Her heart thudded all the same, with fear. It was hard not to imagine death when every lurch threatened to overturn them, and the vessel itself seemed to be screaming.

The crew had closed the hatches, but water washed in. Under her feet, the deck was wet and slippery.

Nearby, someone was crying.

"Repent!" a man shouted. "Thy time is nigh."

"Go to the devil," she muttered. Yes, she was afraid, as any sane person would be. But her time was *not* nigh and she was *not* going to die. She was not going to drown. The ship was not going down. She had a daughter and sisters waiting for her in London.

She trembled all the same, and her stomach churned. She was never sick. She couldn't be sick. She hadn't time. Jeffreys was ill, desperately so, and needed Marcelline's help.

But oh, she did not feel well at all.

Later. Later she could be as sick as she wanted.

One thing at a time.

She came to the door she thought was the right one, the one where she'd seen the liveried servants loitering earlier. She'd heard, on her way back to her cabin, that the Duke of Clevedon had commandeered the best cabin for himself and two lesser ones for his retinue.

She pounded on the door. It opened abruptly at the same moment the ship gave an almighty lurch. She slid, stumbled, and fell straight into the cabin. Two big hands caught her and pulled her upright.

"Dammit, Noirot. You might have broken your neck."

The hands bracing her were warm and firm, and she wanted to lean into him. He was big and strong and so was his personality. An image rushed into her mind of medieval knights protecting their castles, their women— and for one mad moment she wanted nothing but to put herself in his hands.

But she couldn't. She daren't lean on him.

She certainly daren't look up. She did not feel well at all, at all.

"Had . . . to . . . come," she managed to say.

"I was on my way out to find you, to see if you needed—Noirot, are you all right?"

She was looking down at his feet and thinking that any minute now she was going to be sick on his costly slippers. But the sea had ruined them already. Pity. Such fine slippers. He had big feet. Funny.

"Quite well," she said, gagging.

"Saunders, brandy! Quick!"

Yes, that was it. Brandy. Why she'd come. Brandy. Jeffreys needed it.

So, heaven help her, did she.

"My . . . my s-seamstress," she began. "Sh-she—"

"Here." He put a flask to her lips. "Drink."

"I'm n-never sick," she said.

"Drink," he said.

She drank, welcoming the fire sliding down her throat. If it scoured her insides, so much the better.

For a moment she thought she'd be well again.

Then the deck tilted and she slid and stumbled. This time his arms were about her, though. "Don't," she said. "Going to be . . . going to be—"

"Saunders!"

Something was thrust in front of her. A bucket. Good.

Then she was retching, doubled over, so sick she couldn't see straight. Her head pounded and her knees gave way.

Sick, so sick.

Someone was holding her. Men talked above her head. His voice. Another's. She was shifted onto something soft. A bed. Oh, that felt good. To lie down. She would simply lie here for a moment while the boat rose and fell, rocked this way and that.

But no. She hadn't time for this.

Someone slid a pillow under her head, then drew a blanket over her. That felt so good. But she wasn't supposed to feel good. She had to get up. It was Jeffreys who needed help. But if she moved, she'd be sick again.

Must lie very quietly.

Impossible, with the ship pitching so. Slowly it tilted up, then slowly down again, and all the while, the horrible noises, ropes and timbers grinding and creaking and groaning as though all the souls of the drowned were rising to meet them. From a distance came the sounds of passengers crying and screaming. And somewhere above all the noise of the ship, she heard the storm's fury, the wailing wind.

Hell, she thought. Dante's Inferno. Or that other thing. Not a poem but a picture of Hell, of the damned. Curse it, what was wrong with her? She couldn't lie here, wondering about paintings.

"No." She could barely form the words. "Not me. My—my— s-seamstress."

"Your maid?" His voice was so calm. So reassuring.

"Jeffreys. She's badly ill. Brandy. I came for . . . brandy."

More talking, over her, around her. She heard screaming and shouting, too, but far away. The world went up, then down, and down, and down.

Don't let me be sick again. Don't let me be sick again.

Something cool and wet touched her face. "Saunders will see about your maid," the familiar voice said.

"Don't let her die," she said. Or did she? Her voice

sounded far away, so small against the infernal clamor about them. Hell, she thought. This was like the Hell the righteous ranted about. The Hell in the pictures.

"People almost never die of seasickness," he said.

"They only wish they might," she said.

An odd sound. A chuckle? It was his voice, low and close. Behind it, around it, above it were horrible sounds, like death. A long, drawn-out moan, a terrible grinding, then a *crack*.

The ship . . . cracking open . . .

"We can't go down," someone said. Had she spoken? *Don't talk. Lie quietly. Don't move. Don't breathe.*

"We won't go down," he said. "It's bad, but we won't go down. Here, swallow this."

She moved her head from side to side. That was a mistake. Bile rose. "Can't."

"Only a drop," he coaxed. "Laudanum. It will help. I promise."

She couldn't raise her head, couldn't even open her eyes. The world was spinning round and round, leaping up and down, throwing itself from side to side.

Where am I?

He lifted her head, so gently. Was it he? Or was it she, spooning medicine into Lucie? *Lucie, Lucie.*

But she was away from this. She was safe in London with her doting aunts, who spoiled her appallingly. Lucie was safe because her mother and aunts had turned into three witches, brewing potions to keep her alive.

They had not fought so hard only to leave Lucie an orphan, because her mother had made a foolish mistake. A man-mistake. More than six feet tall and beastly arrogant and . . . oh, those big, beautiful hands.

"A little more," he said. "Another drop."

Take your medicine. Get better. Get back to Lucie.

She swallowed it. So bitter.

"Vile," she said. "Vile."

"I know, but it helps. Trust me. I know."

"Trust you," she said. "Hah."

"Clearly you're not dying."

"No. Devil won't take me."

The low chuckle again. "Then we're all safe."

She wasn't safe. The storm raged and the ship moaned and rose and fell and flung itself from wave to wave. She'd been in rough seas before. She knew this was very bad, and she wasn't remotely safe. Yet while her mind knew this, her heart understood matters altogether differently: his voice, his surprisingly gentle touch, and the calm of his presence. Reassuring. How ironic!

"Ah, you're smiling," he said. "The opium is starting to take hold already."

Already? Had she fallen asleep? She'd lost track of time.

"No, it's you," she said. How far away her voice sounded, as though it had traveled to London already, ahead of her. "Your ducal self-assurance. Everything will give way to you. Even Satan's own storm."

"You're definitely improving," he said. "Full, mocking sentences."

"Yes. Better." Her insides seemed to be quieting. But her head was so heavy. She opened her eyes, and that was hard work. He was leaning over her. The light was too dim to make out details, and nothing would stay put. His eyes were deep shadows in his face. But she knew they were green. Jade green. Or was it sea green? A color not many women could wear successfully. A color not many women could withstand . . . in a man's eyes.

She closed her eyes again.

She felt the cool cloth on her forehead. So gentle. A

feeling she had trouble naming washed over her. Then she realized: She was protected. Sheltered. Safe.

What a joke!

"Strange," she said.

"Yes," he said.

"Yes," she said.

The world grew heavy and dark, then everything went away.

Clevedon had no idea long the storm lasted. He'd long since lost all sense of time. He'd awoken in a room heaving this way and that, to a clamor of panicked voices, a roaring storm, and the creaking and groaning vessel. He'd been sick, a bit. But his was a strong stomach—as numerous drunken entertainments testified—and the first thing in his mind was Noirot, somewhere on this boat. He'd been about to go to her cabin, medicine box in hand, when she fell through his door.

Since then, he hadn't time to be sick or to worry about anybody else. Her pearly skin was dull and drawn. That much one could see even in the dim light. She'd been shockingly ill, and delirious. That was so unlike her. She was strong, strong to a fault, and the change had him halfway into a panic before his frantic mind sorted it out.

This was no more than seasickness, reason told him. The delirium must be part of it—or due to her having little sleep and hurried meals, thanks to her mad haste to get away from him.

Whatever caused the alarming symptoms, she was too ill to be left on her own. He left his servants to look after themselves while he tended to her and tried to stay calm. He knew what to do, he told himself. He worried all the same.

He was no physician and he wasn't used to playing

nursemaid. He told himself that he and Longmore had lived through the cholera epidemic on the Continent, and he'd learned a few basic principles from the doctors who'd had any success with the disease. They hadn't much success, and they argued about what worked and what didn't, but this wasn't the cholera. This was seasickness, and there was nothing to worry about, he told himself. When the storm passed, she'd be better.

If the ship didn't go down.

But it wouldn't.

Meanwhile, he knew he needed to make sure she took in nourishment, and especially liquids—not easy when she couldn't keep anything down. The brandy might have helped a little, but the laudanum proved more effective. It took a while, and she was out of her head for part of the time, muttering about witches and Macbeth and angels and devils, but eventually she quieted. When at last she fell asleep, he let himself draw a breath of relief.

He sat on the edge of his bunk and gently bathed her face now and again with a wet cloth. He didn't know that it did any good, but he needed to do something. Saunders undoubtedly would know what to do, but Saunders was attending the maid—or seamstress—or whatever she was.

Gad, the facts about Madame Noirot were as slippery as the deck under his feet.

Deception, thy name is Noirot.

Manipulative and elusive and not to be trusted.

If he had trusted her, he wouldn't have set a spy on her, he wouldn't have pursued her from Paris, and he wouldn't be on this curst vessel in this hellish storm.

Yet not trusting was no excuse for his deranged behavior. He had no excuse. She wasn't even beautiful, especially not now. In the murky light, she looked like a ghost. He found it hard to believe that this was the same vibrant, passionate creature who'd straddled him in the carriage and kissed him witless.

He smoothed the damp hair back from her forehead.

Dreadful, dreadful woman.

Marcelline awoke to a watery light.

At first she thought she'd died and was floating in another realm.

By degrees she realized that the ship was rocking, but not in the deranged way it had done before. The clamor had quieted.

It was over.

The storm had passed.

They'd survived.

Then she became aware of the weight and warmth pressing against her back. Her eyes flew open. In front of her was only blank wood. She remembered: her desperate visit to Clevedon's cabin, the vicious seasickness that seized her . . . brandy . . . laudanum . . . his hands.

This wasn't her cabin, her bed.

She was in his bed.

And judging by the size of the body squeezed alongside her in the narrow bunk, Clevedon was in it with her.

Oh, perfect.

She tried to turn over, but he was lying on the skirt of her dress, pinning her down.

"Clevedon," she said.

He mumbled and moved, flinging his arm over her.

"Your grace."

His arm tightened, pulling her closer.

How she wished she might snuggle there, her back curved against the front of his hard, warm body, his strong arm holding her safe.

But she wasn't safe. When he woke up, he'd be in the

state men usually were in when they woke, and she had no confidence in her powers to resist so much temptation.

She shoved her elbow into his ribs.

"What?" His voice was low, thick with sleep.

"You're crushing me."

"Yes," he said. He nuzzled her neck.

She was desperately aware of his arousal, the great ducal phallus awake well before his brain was.

"Get off," she said. "Get off. *Now.*"

Before it's too late, and I decide to celebrate a narrow escape from death in the traditional manner of our species.

"Noirot?"

"Yes."

"Then it wasn't a dream."

"No. *Get off.*"

He muttered something too low for her to hear, but he moved away. She turned over. Her head spun. She had to struggle to focus.

He stood at the side of the bunk, looking down at her. The shadow of a beard darkened his face, and he was scowling.

She started up from the bed.

Then fell back onto it, clutching her head.

"That wasn't wise," he said. "You've been sick. All you've had to eat was cold gruel and a little wine."

"I ate?"

"You don't remember."

She shook her head. "I don't know what's real and what isn't," she said. "I'm having trouble sorting out what I dreamed and what happened. I dreamed I was in London. Then I wasn't. I was at the bottom of the sea, looking up at the bottom of the boat." For a moment she saw the dream clearly in her mind's eye, and for that moment she felt the despair she'd felt then. *I've drowned. I'll never see Lucie again. Why did I leave London?* "People hung over the rail, looking down at me. They were gesturing and seemed to be saying something, but I couldn't make out what it was. You were there. You were very angry." And that, strangely enough, had been the most reassuring part of the dream.

"That much was real enough," he said. "You've tried my patience past all endurance. I'm not accustomed to playing nursemaid, and you didn't make it easy, thrashing about like a lunatic."

"Was that why you were lying on top of me?"

"I was not lying on top of you," he said. "Not on purpose. I fell asleep. I was tired. I'd had very little sleep before the storm broke. Then you burst in and decided to be sick in my cabin."

"I didn't *decide* to be sick—though now I consider, it was a good idea," she said. "I wish I had thought of it. But I didn't. I came for help—for Jeffreys. I was only a bit queasy—but then . . . something happened." She shook her head. "I'm never sick. I should not have been sick."

"You're very lucky I was here," he said. "You're very lucky I'm a patient man. You're a deuced difficult patient. I would have thrown you overboard, but the crew had closed the hatches."

She made herself sit up, but more slowly and carefully this time. Her head pounded. She clutched it.

"You'd better not get up," he said.

She remembered his patience, his gentle touch. She remembered the feeling, so rare that she'd had trouble recognizing it: the feeling of being sheltered and protected and being looked after. When last had anybody looked after her? Not her parents, certainly. They'd never hesitated to abandon their children when the children became inconvenient. Then they'd turn up, months and months later, expecting those children to run into their open arms.

And we did, Marcelline thought. *Naïve fools that we were, we did.* Whether Mama and Papa were about or not, it was always Marcelline, the eldest, who looked after everybody, because one couldn't rely on anyone else. Even after she was wed. But what could she expect when she wed her own kind? Poor, feckless Charlie!

Clevedon wasn't her kind. He was another species altogether. She remembered his hand at her back, guiding her to the shelter of his well-appointed carriage. A woman could be spoiled so easily by a rich, privileged man. So many women were.

She couldn't afford it.

"I . . . truly, I thank you for enduring the ghastliness of nursing me," she said. "But I must get back, before anyone realizes where I've been."

"Who do you think will notice or care?" he said. "We sailed into the devil's own storm. People have been running about screaming and puking and generally making nuisances of themselves for hours. I doubt most of them even know where they've been this night." He looked about him. "Morning, rather. Since most of them were sick, they'll be starved by now, and the only thing they'll think about is getting something to eat. Your head is aching because you're hungry." He scowled again. "Or perhaps I gave you too much laudanum. I wasn't sure what was the proper dose for a woman. You're lucky I didn't poison you."

"Clevedon." She winced. It hurt to speak.

"Don't move," he said. "You'll make yourself sick again, and I'm tired of that." He moved away from the bunk. "I'll have one of the servants fetch you something to eat."

"Stop taking care of me!"

He turned back to look at her. "Stop being childish," he said. "Are you afraid I'll ply you with food in order to seduce you? Think again. Have you looked in a mirror lately? And may I remind you that I was the one holding your head while you were sick last night. Not exactly the most arousing sight I've ever seen. In fact, I can't remember what I ever saw in you. I only want to feed you so you'll be well and get out of my cabin and out of my life."

"I want to be out of your life, too," she said.

"Right," he said. "Until it's time to pay my duchess's dressmaking bills."

"Yes," she said. "Exactly."

"Good," he said. "That suits me very well."

He went to the door, opened it, went out, and slammed it behind him.

By the time the packet docked at the Tower Stairs, Marcelline wanted to scream. The storm had blown the ship off course, and a trip that in good weather took about twelve hours had taken more than twenty. The advertised "refreshments" had run out, the ship's servants were limp with fatigue, and the mood of the hungry passengers was vile, as was their smell. Even above deck, in the brisk sea air, it was impossible to escape the evidence of too many people confined with one another in too small an area for too long. Couples quarreled with each other and scolded their whiny children, who picked fights with their siblings.

Naturally, nobody could wait to get off the boat, and they all tried to disembark simultaneously, shoving and shouting and even kicking.

Though she longed desperately get off the vessel as well, Marcelline decided to wait. She fended off the packet's servants, eager to help her with her belongings, telling them to come back later. While she felt a good deal better, she didn't feel quite herself. Too, Jeffreys was still weak from her own far worse bout with sickness. It made no sense to endure the pushing and hurrying and ill temper—and above all, the whiny children.

Marcelline wanted her own child. Lucie was no angel, but she did not whine. And when her mama surprised her by returning home a week early, that mama would be smiling and happy.

She *would* be smiling and happy, Marcelline assured herself, once the crowd dissipated, and she could have a moment's peace, to sort herself out.

Clevedon must be long gone by now. He wouldn't have to shove people out of his way. His servants could do that for him—not that it would be necessary. Clevedon appeared, and people simply made way for him.

"Make way, make way!"

She looked up. A tall, burly footman was bearing down on her, another footman behind him. The livery was all too familiar.

The first one elbowed an indignant packet servant aside, strode to her, and bowed. "His grace's compliments, Mrs. Noirot, and would you be so good as to let him see you and Miss Jeffreys home. He understands Miss Jeffreys was dire ill, and he dislikes to leave her to the public conveyances, let alone being jostled by this infern—this crowd. If you ladies would come with us, me and Joseph will take you along to the Customs officers and then in a trice we'll have you in the carriage, which is only around the corner."

Even as he spoke, he was collecting their things, hoisting one portmanteau under one arm and another under the other. His counterpart made easy work of the remaining bags, ignoring the protests of the packet servants they'd displaced and deprived of their tips.

It all happened so quickly that Marcelline had no time even to decide whether to object. She'd hardly taken in what they were about when Thomas and Joseph marched away with her luggage.

The drive to the shop on Fleet Street, silent for the most part, seemed interminable.

The first thing Jeffreys did when she settled into her seat, next to Marcelline and opposite the duke, was thank him for sending Saunders to look after her when she was ill.

He shrugged. "Saunders dotes on playing physician," he said. "He likes nothing better than to make disgusting potions to cure the effects of overindulgence. It's his subtle way of punishing us, no doubt, for getting wine stains on our linen."

"He was very kind," Jeffreys said.

"That would make for a change," said Clevedon. "He isn't, usually."

And that was all he said, all the way from the Tower to Jeffreys's lodgings.

From there it was an easy walk to the shop. The drive was not so easy.

Marcelline's mind was working as always, looking for a way to turn matters to her account. He'd said . . . what had he said before he slammed out of his cabin?

He'd said something about paying the dressmaking bills. That it suited him very well.

But he'd been so angry, and he hadn't come back.

His valet had appeared, though, with a bottle of wine and assorted cold meats and cheese that must have cost a king's ransom in bribes.

A woman could, too easily, get used to such luxury.

She couldn't afford to get used to it.

"I can't decide," she said, "whether you're exercising forbearance or merely indulging your curiosity to see my lair."

"Why should I do either?" he said. Seeming to make himself perfectly at ease, he stretched out his long legs, as he hadn't been able to do when Jeffreys shared the seat with her. He rested one arm along the back of the richly appointed seat and looked out of the louvered panel, open at present to let him see out while shielding him from others trying to look in. Not that it was any secret who he was, when the crest emblazoned on the door shouted his identity to all the world.

The late afternoon light traced the smoothly sculpted lines of his profile.

Longing welled up. To touch his beautiful face. To feel that arm curl about her shoulders. To tuck herself into that big, warm body.

She crushed it. "Or perhaps you took pity on us," she said.

"It was your maid or seamstress or whatever she is upon whom I took pity," he said. "You can take care of yourself, I've no doubt. But Saunders told me the girl was prodigious ill. For a time, he said, he wasn't sure she'd survive the voyage. She did not look well just now." He paused briefly. "She doesn't lodge with you?"

"She did, but that was only temporary. I can hardly lodge my seamstresses. For one thing, it isn't good for them to do nothing but eat, drink, and live nothing but shop. For another, there isn't room. Not that I should want half a dozen seamstresses about all day and all night. The working hours can be trying enough, what with their little jealousies and—"

"Half a dozen?" he said. He leaned forward. *"Half a dozen?"*

He was too astonished to pretend he wasn't.

Yes, of course she'd babbled that advertisement for the corner of Fleet Street at Chancery Lane, and it was the direction she'd given the coachman. That didn't mean her shop wasn't squeezed into a passage or a cellar.

"Half a dozen girls at present," she said. "But I'll certainly be hiring more in the near future. As it is, we're shorthanded."

"Half a— Devil take you, what is wrong with you?"

"You've already pointed out any number of my character flaws," she said. "To which do you now refer?"

"I thought . . . Noirot, you're the damndest woman. Your dogged pursuit of me led me to believe you were in desperate straits."

"How on earth did you come by that idea?" she said. "I told you I was the greatest modiste in the world. You've seen my work."

"I imagined a dark little shop in a basement, drat you," he said. "I did wonder how you contrived to make such extravagant-looking dresses in such a place."

"I'm sure you didn't wonder about it overlong," she said. "You were mainly occupied with bedding me."

"Yes, but I'm done with that now."

He was. He truly was. He'd had enough of her. He'd had enough of himself, chasing her. Like a puppy, like the veriest schoolboy.

"I'm very glad to hear it," she said.

"It's only Clara I'm thinking of," he said. "Much as it pains me to contribute to your vainglory, it was clear, even to me, that the women of Paris were besotted with your work. You're the most aggravating woman I've ever met, but you make yourself agreeable to women, I noticed, and that and beautiful, fashionable clothes are what matter, I daresay. I should not hold a grudge, merely because I long to shake you until your teeth rattle."

Her weary face lit up, her eyes most brilliantly of all. "I knew it," she said. "I knew you'd see."

"Still, I don't trust you."

Something flickered in her eyes, but she said nothing, only waited, her attention riveted.

She was riveted on him—for her business. He was merely the means to an end.

But he scorned to hold grudges, especially on such a petty account—his vanity, of all things!

"I wanted to see the place for myself," he said. "To make sure it truly existed, for one thing—and to see what sort of place it was. For all I knew, you were toiling alone in a dark room in a cellar."

"Good grief, what a mind a man has," she said. "How could you imagine I should produce such creations in— But never mind. Maison Noirot is an elegant shop. Everything is of the first stare, exceedingly neat and clean and airy. It's much more neat and elegant, I promise you, than the den of that dull-witted incompetent—but no, I will not foul the air with her name."

He was done with her. He needed to be done with her. But now, when she spoke of her shop, she was so animated. So passionate.

"I smell a rival," he said.

She sat straighter. "Certainly not. I have no rivals, your grace. I am the greatest modiste in the world." She leaned forward to look out of the door window. "We're nearly there. You'll soon see for yourself."

It wasn't as soon as it might have been, the street being a tangle of carriages, riders, and pedestrians. But eventually they came to the place, and there it was, a handsome modern shop, with a bow window and the name in gold lettering over the door: Noirot.

The carriage stopped. The door opened. The steps were folded down.

Clevedon stepped out first, and put out his hand to steady her.

As she took his hand, he heard a cry behind him.

She looked up, looked past him, and the light he'd seen in her face before was nothing to this. Her countenance was the sun, shedding happiness and setting the world aglow.

"Mama!" the voice cried.

Noirot practically leapt from the last step, past him, forgetting him entirely.

She crouched down on the pavement and opened her arms, and a little girl, a little dark-haired girl, ran into them.

"Mama!" the child cried. "You're home!"

Chapter Seven

The Dress-Maker must be an expert anatomist; and must, if judiciously chosen, have a name of French termination; she must know how to hide all defects in the proportions of the body, and must be able to mould the shape by the stays, that, while she corrects the body, she may not interfere with the pleasures of the palate.

The Book of English Trades,
and Library of the Useful Arts, 1818

A child.
She had a child.

A little girl with dark, curling hair who ran at her, laughing. Noirot's arms went around her and tightened to hold her close. "My love, my love," she said, and the way she said it made a knot in his chest.

He was distantly aware of other feminine voices, but his attention was locked upon the scene: Noirot crouched on the pavement, crushing the little girl to her, and the child, whose face he could see so clearly over her mother's shoulder, eyes closed, her face alight and dawn-rosy, her happiness radiating in almost visible waves.

He didn't know how long he stood there, oblivious to

all else about him: the busy street, the people detouring round the mother and child on the pavement. He scarcely noticed his own servants, carrying her things into the place, then returning to the carriage. He was only dimly aware of the two women who had come out of the shop behind the little girl.

He stood and watched the mother and child because he couldn't turn away, because he didn't understand and scarcely believed what his senses told him.

After some time, some very short time perhaps, Noirot rose and, taking her daughter's hand, started toward the shop. The child said, "Who is that, Mama?"

Noirot turned around and saw him standing, like a man at the window of a peepshow, entranced by a foreign world, unable to look away.

He collected his wits and took a step toward them. "Mrs. Noirot, perhaps you'd be so kind as to make me known to the young lady."

The child looked up at him, eyes wide. They were not her mother's eyes, but blue, vividly blue. They seemed vaguely familiar, and he tried to remember where he might have seen those eyes before. But where could that have been? Anywhere. Nowhere. It didn't signify.

Noirot looked from the girl to him and back to the girl, who said, "Who is it, Mama? Is it the king?"

"No, it isn't the king."

The child tipped her head to one side, looking past him at the carriage. "That is a very grand carriage," she said. "I should like to drive about in that carriage."

"I don't doubt that," said her mother. "Your grace, may I present my daughter, Miss Lucie Cordelia Noirot."

"I beg your pardon, Mama," the child said. "That isn't my name, you know."

Noirot looked at her. "Is it not?"

"My name is Erroll now. E-R-R-O-L-L."

"I see." Noirot began again. "Your grace, may I present my daughter—" She broke off and looked enquiringly at the child. "You're still my daughter, I take it?"

"Yes," said Erroll. "Of course, Mama."

"I'm relieved to hear it. I had quite grown used to you. Your grace, may I present my daughter Erroll. Erroll, His Grace, the Duke of Clevedon."

"Miss . . . erm . . . Erroll," he said. He bowed gravely.

"Your grace," the girl said. She curtseyed. It was nothing half so stunning as her mother's style of curtsey, but it was gracefully done nonetheless. He wondered at it and at her remarkable self-possession.

Then he recalled whose daughter she was, and wondered why he wondered.

Then he recalled who it was who had a child.

A child, Noirot had a child!

How had she failed to mention such a thing? But what was wrong with him that he was so shocked? She was *Mrs.* Noirot—and while the title "Mrs." was used, cavalierly enough, by unwed shopkeepers, actresses, and whores alike, he needn't have assumed she wasn't a married woman, with a family and . . . a husband . . . who did not seem to be in evidence. Dead? Or perhaps there was no husband, merely a scoundrel who'd fathered and abandoned this child.

"Do you ever take children for a drive in that carriage?" Erroll said, calling him back to the moment. "Not *little* children, I mean, but proper grown-up girls who would sit quietly—not climbing about and spoiling the cushions or putting sticky fingers on the glass. Not them, but well-behaved girls who keep their hands folded in their laps and only look out of the window." The great blue eyes regarded him steadily.

"I—"

"No, he does not," her mother said. "His grace has many claims on his time. In fact, I am sure he has an appointment elsewhere any minute now."

"Do I?"

Noirot gave him a warning look.

"Yes, of course," he said. He took out his pocket watch and stared at it. He had no idea where the hands pointed. He was too conscious of the little girl with the great blue eyes watching him so intently. "I nearly forgot."

He put the watch away. "Well, Erroll, I am pleased to make your acquaintance."

"Yes, I'm glad to meet you, too," she said. "Please come again, when you're not so busy."

He made a polite, non-committal answer, and took his leave.

He climbed into his coach and sat. As the vehicle started to move, he looked out through the louvered panel. That was when he finally took notice of the other two women, a blonde and a redhead. Even through the wooden slats, at this distance, he discerned the family resemblance, most especially in the way they carried themselves.

He had mistaken her. He'd formed an idea that was entirely wrong.

Her shop was not a little hole-in-corner place but a proper, handsome establishment. She had a family. She had a child.

She was not to be trusted. Of that he was quite, quite sure.

As to everything else—he'd misjudged, misunderstood, and now he was at sea again, and it was a rough sea, indeed.

* * *

"Well done," Sophy said, when the shop door had closed behind them. "I know you, of course, and I should never underestimate you—"

"But my dear," said Leonie, "you could have knocked me over with a feather when I saw the crest on the carriage door."

"And then to see him spring out of the carriage—"

"—the prints don't half do him justice—"

"—to see him hand you out—"

"—I thought for a minute I was dreaming—"

"—It was very like a vision—"

"I saw it first, Mama," Lucie/Erroll cut into her aunts' chatter. "I was sitting in the window, reading my lessons, when I heard a noise, and I looked out—and I thought the king was passing by."

"The king, with a paltry two footmen?" Marcelline said. "I think not."

"Oh, yes. It might have been, Mama. Everyone knows King William doesn't like to make a show. I'm sorry, too, because they say the old king, the one before this one . . ." She frowned.

"King George the Fourth," Leonie prompted.

"Yes, that one," Lucie said. "Everyone says he was vastly more splendid, and you always knew who it was when he went by. But a duke is grand, too. I thought he was very handsome, like the prince in the fairy tale. We did not expect you so soon, but I'm glad you came early. Was it very agreeable to travel in that fine carriage? I collect the seat cushions were thick and soft."

"They were, indeed," Marcelline said. Out of the corner of her eye she spotted two women approaching the shop. It would not do for Lucie to be interrogating her about the Duke of Clevedon in front of customers, but it wasn't easy to distract her daughter from a fascinating object, especially a large, expensive fascinating object. "I shall tell you all about it down to the last detail, but I'm perishing for a cup of tea. Shall we go upstairs, and will you make Mama a cup of tea?"

"Yes, yes!" Lucie jumped up and down. "I'll send Millie to the pastry shop. We're so glad you're home, and we shall have a party, a wonderful party, with cakes!"

Hours later, when Lucie was safely abed, the sisters gathered in the workroom.

There they drank champagne, to celebrate Marcelline's return—with her quarry, no less—and while they drank, Marcelline described her experiences with the Duke of Clevedon in all their lurid detail. Though her sisters were virgins, so far as she knew—and she couldn't imagine why they wouldn't tell her if they were not—they were by no means innocent. In any case, one could hardly expect them to help her deal with the complications if they did not fully understand what had happened.

"I'm truly sorry," she said. "I had promised I wouldn't bollix it up—"

"So you did," said Leonie. "Yet none of us expected him to be quite so . . . quite so—"

"Everyone said he was handsome," said Sophy. "But really, he's beautiful. He took my breath away." She patted Marcelline's hand. "I'm so sorry you had to restrain yourself. I'm not sure I could have done it."

"It's not his beauty," Marcelline said.

Both sisters eyed her skeptically.

"It's his curst ducal-ness," she said. "Those fellows are the very devil to manage. They're not merely accustomed to having their way: The alternative simply doesn't enter their heads. They don't think the way normal people do. Then, too, he can *think*. He's quicker-witted than I had allowed for. But what sort of excuse is that? I should have adjusted my methods, but for reasons that still elude me, I didn't. The fact is, I played it very ill, and now Sophy must turn my error to account."

She went on to explain the advertisements she and Jeffreys had devised immediately after the comtesse's party—a lifetime ago, it seemed . . . before the storm . . . when he'd looked after her . . .

His hands, his hands . . .

"I'll plant a story in the *Morning Spectacle*," Sophy said. "But it may be too late to make tomorrow's edition. Confound it, you haven't left us much time."

"I came as quickly as I could. We were nearly ship-wrecked!"

"Sophy, do be reasonable," said Leonie. "And only think, if the storm delayed their packet, others were delayed as well. The mail will be late. That gives you as much as an extra day, if you'll only be quick about it."

"We can't rely on the mail's arriving late," Sophy said. "I'll have to find Tom Foxe tonight. But that might answer very well: a late-night summons . . . a story whispered in the dark. I'll wear a disguise, and let him think I'm Lady So-and-So. He won't be able to resist. We'll have the front of the paper, a prime spot."

"The ladies will flock to see the dress," said Leonie. "We may even see some as early as tomorrow afternoon. I know for a fact that the Countess of Bartham reads the *Spectacle* devotedly."

"The dress had better be on display, then," Marcelline said. "It needs repairs. Jeffreys was able to clean it before the packet sailed, but she was too sick afterward to stitch the bodice. And I lost at least one papillon bow. What else?" She rubbed her head.

"We're perfectly capable of seeing for ourselves what needs to be done," Leonie said. "I'll work on it while Sophy goes out to her clandestine meeting with Tom. You'd better go to bed."

"You'll want to be rested," Sophy said. "We've got a—"

She broke off, and Marcelline looked up in time to catch the look Leonie sent Sophy.

"What?" Marcelline said. "What are you not telling me?"

"Really, Sophy, you might learn to curb your dramatic impulses," Leonie said. "You can see she's weary."

"I did not *say*—"

"What haven't you told me?" Marcelline said.

There was a pause. Her two younger sisters exchanged reproachful looks. Then Sophy said, "Someone is stealing your designs and giving them to Horrible Hortense."

Marcelline looked to Leonie for confirmation.

"It's true," Leonie said. "We've a spy in our midst."

On Monday night, Lady Clara Fairfax received a note from the Duke of Clevedon, informing her of his return to London and of his wish to call on her on Tuesday afternoon, if convenient.

The family were not usually at home to callers on Tuesday, but the usual rules did not apply to the Duke of Clevedon. For one thing, as her father's former ward, his grace was considered a part of the family; for another, he was no better at following rules than her brothers were. Papa had forbidden Clevedon and Harry to go abroad three years ago, citing the raging cholera epidemic. They went anyway, leaving Papa no alternative but to shrug and say Clevedon needed to sow his wild oats, and since

Longmore was bound to do damage somewhere, it might as well be in another country.

The Tuesday appointment was not, in short, inconvenient to anybody else, and Lady Clara told herself it wasn't inconvenient to her, either. She had missed Clevedon, truly, especially when Longmore was behaving in a particularly obnoxious manner and in dire need of one of the duke's crushing setdowns—or, better yet, his powerful left fist.

But Clevedon in person was a different proposition than Clevedon via letter.

Now that he was here, she wasn't sure she was ready for him to be here.

But any doubts or shyness she'd felt vanished the instant he entered the drawing room on Tuesday. He wore the same affectionate smile she knew of old, and she smiled at him in the same way. She loved him dearly, always had, and she knew he loved her.

"Good grief, Clara, you might have warned me you'd grown," he said, stepping back to look her over, quite as he used to do when he came home from school. "You must be two inches taller at least."

He didn't remember, she thought. She'd always been a tall girl. She hadn't grown at all since last he saw her. He was used to French women, she supposed. The observation, which she wouldn't have hesitated to put in a letter, she wouldn't dream of uttering aloud, most certainly not in front of her mother.

"I should hope she is not such a gawky great Amazon as that," said Mama. "Clara is the same as she ever was, only perhaps a little more *womanly* than you recollect."

Mama meant *more shapely*. For a time, she'd claimed that Clevedon had "run away" because Clara was too thin.

A man liked a woman to have some flesh on her—and she would never have a good figure if she would not eat.

It hadn't occurred to Mama at the time that Grandmama Warford had died only a few months earlier, and Clara, still grieving, had no appetite and did not particularly care what Clevedon thought of her figure.

But a great deal did not occur to Mama. She'd ordered tray upon tray of refreshments, and plied Clevedon with cake, which he took politely, though Mama ought to know by now he did not have a sweet tooth. And while she fed him sweets he didn't want, she dropped what she thought were exceedingly subtle hints about Clara's numerous beaux, with the obvious intent of stirring his competitive instincts.

In her mind's eye, Clara saw herself jumping up, covering her mother's mouth, and dragging her from the room. A tiny snort of laughter escaped her. Mama, happily, was too busy talking to hear it. But Clevedon noticed. He shot her a glance, and Clara rolled her eyes. He sent her a small, conspiratorial smile.

"I'm relieved I didn't have to fight my way through hordes of your beaux, Clara," he said. "I'm still a little tired, I confess, after the Channel tried so determinedly to drown me."

"Good heavens!" Mama cried. "I read in the *Times* of a near shipwreck in the Channel. Were you aboard the same vessel?"

"I sincerely hope ours was the only one caught in that storm," he said. "Apparently it took our mariners unawares."

"I would not be too sure of that," said Mama. "They're supposed to know about the wind and that sort of thing. Those steam packets take too many risks, and as I have told Warford any number of times . . ." She went to repeat one of Papa's harangues about the steam trade.

When she paused for breath, Clevedon said, "Indeed, I'm glad to be on English ground again, and to breathe English air. I drove here today because I woke up wishing to take a turn round Hyde Park in an open vehicle. If you would be so kind as to give your permission, perhaps I might persuade Clara to join me."

Mama threw Clara a triumphant glance.

Clara's heart began to pound.

He can't be meaning to propose. Not yet.

But why should he not? And why should she be so alarmed? They'd always been meant to marry, had they not?

"I should like it above all things," Clara said.

"An original design!" Lady Renfrew cried. She pushed the ball gown that lay on the counter at Marcelline. "You assured me it was an *original* design, your own creation. Then how, pray, did Lady Thornhurst come by precisely the same dress? And now what am I to do? You know I meant to wear the dress to Mrs. Sharpe's soirée this very night. You cannot expect me to wear it now. Lady Thornhurst will attend—and she'll recognize it. Everyone will recognize it! I'll be mortified. And I know there isn't time to make up another dress. I'll have to wear the rose, which everyone has seen. But that isn't the point. The point is, you *assured* me—"

A clatter behind her made her break off. She turned an indignant look in that direction. But the irritation vanished in an instant, and wonder took its place. "Good heavens! Is *that* it?"

Clever, clever Sophy. She'd stepped away from the temper tantrum to the other side of the shop. There stood a mannequin, wearing the gown Marcelline had worn to the comtesse's ball. Sophy had knocked over a nearby footstool accidentally on purpose.

"I beg your pardon?" Marcelline said innocently.

She wasn't sure what exactly Sophy had done to or with Tom Foxe. Perhaps it was better not to know. What mattered was, the tale—of Mrs. Noirot's gown and her dancing with the Duke of Clevedon at the most exclusive ball of the Paris Season—had appeared in today's *Morning Spectacle*.

Lady Renfrew was a reader, apparently, because she moved away from the counter to the famous *poussière* gown. When she'd first entered the shop, His Majesty might have been there, telling his favorite sailor jokes, and she wouldn't have noticed. She'd been in too hysterical a state to heed anything but her own grievances and Marcelline, the ostensible cause of them.

"Is this the gown you wore to the ball in Paris, Mrs. Noirot?" her ladyship said.

Marcelline admitted that it was.

Lady Renfrew stared at it.

Marcelline and Sophy exchanged looks. They knew what the lady was thinking. The highest sticklers of the Fashion Capital of the World had admired this gown. Its designer stood, not in Paris, but a few feet away, behind the counter.

They let Lady Renfrew study it. She had a great deal of money, and she had taste—which was not the case with all of their customers. She was socially ambitious, which they understood perfectly well, for they were, too.

After Marcelline reckoned her ladyship's meditations upon the wondrous dress had calmed her sufficiently, she said, "Was it precisely like?"

Lady Renfrew turned back to her, still looking slightly dazed. "I beg your pardon."

"Was the gown Lady Thornhurst wore *precisely* like this one?" Marcelline ran a loving hand over the beautiful green gown lying rejected upon the counter.

Lady Renfrew returned to the counter. She considered the dress. "Not precisely. Now I think of it, her gown was not so—not so . . ." She trailed off, gesturing helplessly.

"If your ladyship would pardon me for speaking plainly, I should suggest that the other was not so well made," Marcelline said. "What you saw was a mere imitation, of inferior construction. I'm sorry to say this is not the first case that has been brought to our attention."

"There's shocking skullduggery at work," Sophy said. "We haven't yet got to the bottom of it—but that is not your ladyship's problem. You must have a magnificent gown for the ball tonight—and it must not be in any way like the other lady's."

"I shall remake this dress," Marcelline said. "I shall remake it myself, in private. When I'm done, no one will see the smallest resemblance to the *thing* Lady Thornhurst wore. I call it a *thing*, your ladyship, because it would shame any proper modiste to call those abominations *dresses*."

The shop bell tinkled.

Neither Marcelline nor Sophy so much as glanced toward the door. Lady Renfrew was their best customer to date. They could not afford to lose her. All their world— their very beings—revolved around her. Or so it must appear.

"I or one of my sisters will personally deliver it to you, at not later than seven o'clock this evening, at which time we shall make any final adjustments you require," Marcelline continued. "The dress will be *perfect*."

"Absolutely perfect," said Sophy.

Lady Renfrew was not listening. Not being a shopkeeper in danger of losing her most profitable and prestigious customer, she did look over her shoulder at the door. And she froze.

"Well, then, here we are," said a familiar, deep voice. "You may see for yourself, my dear. And there is the dress itself, by gad."

And the Duke of Clevedon laughed.

His heart was beating in an embarrassingly erratic way.

He'd opened the door, and tried to keep his attention on Clara, but it was no use. He was talking to her, treating this visit to the shop like the joke he'd made out the entire Noirot Episode to be. Meanwhile, though, he couldn't stop his gaze from sweeping the shop, dismissing everything until he found what he was looking for.

Noirot stood behind the counter, dealing with an apparently troublesome customer, and she did not at first look toward the door. Neither did the blonde standing nearby, who appeared to be a relative.

He quickly looked away from her, past the gaping customer, and spotted the mannequin wearing the dress. How could he forget that infernal dress? Then he had to laugh, because Noirot had done exactly as she'd promised. She'd taken charge of the gossip before it could take hold, and turned it to her own account.

Saunders had brought him a copy of today's *Morning Spectacle*. There it was, impossible to miss on the front page: Noirot's version of events in all its stunning audacity—and not very unlike the mocking advertisement she'd composed when he'd driven her home from the ball. He remembered the tone of her voice when she'd come to the last bit: *Mrs. Noirot alone can claim the distinction of having danced with a duke.*

Mrs. Noirot's dark, silken hair was, as usual, slightly askew and contriving to appear dashing and elegant rather than untidy under a flimsy, fluttery bit of lace apparently passing for a cap. Her dress was a billowy white froth, adorned with intricate green embroidery. A lacy cape sort of thing floated about her neck and shoulders, fastened in front with two bows of the same shade of green as the embroidery.

He'd taken all that in with only a glance before making himself look away—but what was the good of looking away when it wanted only the one glance to etch her image in his mind?

"My goodness," said Clara, calling his attention back to her, back to the dust-colored dress with its red bows and black lace. "This is . . . rather daring, is it not?"

"I know nothing of these matters," he said. "I only know that every lady at the Comtesse de Chirac's ball wanted this dress—and those were the leaders of Parisian Society. I shall not be at all surprised if one of them at least sends to London— Ah, but here she is."

He'd done a creditable job, in the circumstances, of pretending not to be watching Noirot out of the corner of his eye, while all his being was aware of her every movement. He'd been aware of her stepping out from behind the counter and approaching them, seeming not at all in any hurry. She brought with her a light haze of scent, so familiar that he ached with recollection: her scent swarming about him while they waltzed, and when she'd kissed him, and when she'd climbed onto his lap in the carriage. He tried to make his mind call up images of her sick on the boat, but those only made him ache the more. For a time she'd been vulnerable. For a time, she'd needed him. For a time, he'd been important to her—or at least he'd believed himself to be.

Meanwhile, she wore a smile, a professional smile, and her attention was on Clara, not him.

He introduced her to Clara, and at the words "Lady Clara Fairfax," a sharp little gasp emanated from the troublesome customer, who'd evidently been handed off to the blonde.

Noirot curtseyed. It was nothing like the outrageous thing she'd done at the ball, but light and polite and grace-ful, exactly the proper amount of deference in it.

"I thought Lady Clara would like to be among the first to view your ball gown," he said, "before the curious hordes descend upon your shop."

"I've never seen anything like it," Clara said.

"We wonder whether one ought to call the gown 'daring,' " he said.

"It's daring compared to the usual run of English fash-ion, admittedly," said Noirot. "The color combination is not what English ladies are accustomed to. But pray keep in mind that I designed this dress for an event in Paris, not London."

"And you designed it to attract attention," he said.

"What was the point of attending that ball if not to at-tract attention?" she said.

"Indeed, I do wish you had been there, Clara," he said, turning back to her. But she wasn't there. She was circling the dress, warily, as though it were a sleeping tiger. He went on doggedly, "I thought it would be amusing, to discover whether Mrs. Noirot and I should be admitted or ejected. But the joke was on me."

"I've never seen anything like this," Clara said. "How pretty it must have been, when you were dancing." She looked at Clevedon, then Noirot, then quickly looked away, toward the counter. "Oh, what a beautiful shade of green!"

The troublesome customer laid her hand protectively over the dress. "This is mine," she said. "It only wants . . . alterations."

But Clara assured her she simply wanted to look at it, and in a minute or less, three heads were bent over the dress, and a conversation proceeded, in murmurs.

"Thank you," Noirot said in an undertone.

"You hardly needed me to bring her," he said, in the same low tone. He was hot, stupidly hot. "You'll have half the beau monde on your doorstep by tomorrow, thanks to your stunning piece of puffery in the *Morning Spectacle*."

She looked up at him, eyebrows raised. "I didn't know you read the *Spectacle*."

"Saunders does," he said. "He brought it to me with my coffee."

"In any event, while I'm happy to accommodate half the beau monde, your bride-to-be is the prize I covet."

"I promise nothing," he said. "I've only made the introduction—much as I did at the countess's ball. As you see, I hold no grudges, though you've used me abominably."

"I told you I was using you, practically from the beginning," she said. "I told you as soon as I was sure I had your full attention."

She was incorrigible. She was the most hard-hearted, calculating, aggravating . . .

And he was a dog, because he wanted her still, and there was Clara, the innocent, who'd been worried—*worried!*—because he hadn't written to her for a week.

He had meant to get it over with, to put his life in order, and make his offer of marriage in the park, while it was yet quiet, before the ton descended. But they'd hardly left Warford House when she'd said, "What on earth happened to you, Clevedon? A week without a letter? I thought you'd broken your arm—for when do you *not* write?"

And so he'd told her, shaving very near the truth, and instead of driving to Hyde Park, he'd taken her here.

"I thought it best to tell Clara the truth, though not every everlasting detail," he said. "I told her that you'd waylaid me at the opera, determined to use me to further your own mercenary ends, that you were the most provoking woman who ever lived, otherwise I should not have taken leave of my senses and dared you to attend the ball with me. And the rest was more or less as you put it in your clever little piece in the *Morning Spectacle*."

It wasn't the whole truth, but as much as he could tell without hurting Clara. He'd told it in the way he believed would entertain her, the way of his letters. In any event, what he'd told her was no more or less than the truth from Noirot's point of view: All she'd ever wanted him for was to get Clara into her shop.

She'd been right, too, drat her: Clara needed her. He had only to look at Noirot and the blonde relative and even the troublesome customer to realize that Clara was ill dressed. He'd be hard put to explain the difference in words—women's clothes were merely decoration to him—yet he could see that, compared to these women, she looked like a provincial.

He wished he had not been able to see it. The difference made him angry, as though someone had deliberately tried to make a fool of Clara. But it was natural to be angry, he told himself. He'd been protective of her from the moment he'd met her, when she was a little girl, probably younger than Noirot's daughter.

Her daughter!

"I leave the rest to you," he said. "I don't doubt you'll manage matters with your usual aplomb."

More audibly he said, "Clara, my dear girl, I did not bring you to shop. You know I loathe shopping with women above all things. At any rate, it's long past time I took you home. Come away from the fascinating dress. Make Longmore bring you again another day, if you want Mrs. Noirot to dress you." Then, for the troublesome customer's benefit as well as to ease his conscience, he added, "I see no reason you should not, as you won't find a better dressmaker in London—or Paris, for that matter—but do shop without me, pray."

Chapter Eight

Mrs. Thomas takes this opportunity of observing,
that she hopes the inconvenience she has always
sustained by the imposition of Milliners coming
to her Rooms, under assumed characters, to take
her Patterns, will not be repeated.

La Belle Assemblée,
or Bell's Court and Fashionable Magazine,
Advertisements for November 1807

Clevedon had already handed Clara into the carriage.
Resisting the impulse to look back at the shop—as
though he'd gain anything by that—he was about to join
her, when he felt a tug at the hem of his coat. He whipped
round, ready to collar a pickpocket.

At first he saw nothing. Then he looked down.

A pair of enormous blue eyes looked up at him. "Good
afternoon, your grace," said Erroll.

A nursemaid, out of breath, hurried to the carriage.
"Miss, you ought not to—oh, do come away." She took
the child's hand, muttering apologies, and tried to lead
her away.

A hard, stubborn look came over Erroll's face, and she
wrenched her hand from the maid's. "I only wished to say

good day to his grace," she said. "It would be rude to pass by without saying a word."

"Which you was not passing by, only broke away from me and ran halfway down the street, as you know—"

"Good afternoon, Erroll," said Clevedon.

She had turned to regard the nursemaid with a baleful eye. At his greeting, though, the thunderclouds vanished, and she beamed upon him a sunshine so pure and clear that, for a moment, he couldn't bear it.

All those years ago . . . his little sister, Alice, shedding sunshine . . .

"It is a fine day, is it not?" she said. "A fine day to drive in an open carriage. If I had a carriage like that, I should drive in Hyde Park on such a day."

He wrenched himself back to the present.

She was beautifully dressed, as one might expect. A little straw bonnet, adorned with heaps of ribbons and lace, set off prettily a precise miniature of one of those coat-like dresses women wore. What did they call them? The same as a man's type of frock coat, wasn't it? *Redingotes,* that was the term. Erroll's was pink. A long row of black frog fastenings down the front gave it a vaguely— and on her, comically—military look.

"Yes, miss," said the maid, "but the gentleman was getting ready to leave, in case you didn't notice, which he has a lady with him as well."

"I noticed, Millie," said Erroll. "I'm not blind. But I can't speak to the lady, because we haven't been introduced. Don't you know *anything*?"

Millie's face went scarlet. "That's quite enough, Miss Lu— Miss Er— Miss Noirot. I never heard such impertinence, and I'm sure the lady and the gentleman never did, neither. Come along now. Your mama will be vexed with you for pestering customers." She tugged at the little gloved hand. Erroll's countenance changed again: eyes narrowing, mouth tightening into a stubborn line. She refused to budge, and the maid seemed less than eager to try to make her budge.

Clevedon couldn't blame the servant. While he did not approve of children disobeying those in charge of them, he was not entirely sure what one ought to do in such cases. In any event, it was not his place to interfere.

"Oh, Clevedon, don't be obtuse," Clara said. "It's Miss Noirot—the dressmaker's daughter, I take it?"

The maid nodded, biting her lip.

"Yes, it is," he said, and marveled all over again that she was Noirot's daughter, that Noirot was a mother. Where the devil was the father? How could he abandon . . . but men did that all the time. They carelessly brought children into the world and carelessly treated them. It was none of his concern . . . and perhaps, after all, the poor fellow was dead.

"Well, then, Mrs. Noirot knows you," Clara said. "She won't mind your taking her daughter up for a moment, and letting her hold the reins."

She turned to Millie, who was sending panicked looks at the shop door. "You needn't be anxious," Clara said. "Miss Noirot will be perfectly safe. His grace used to let me hold the reins when I was a child. He will not let the carriage run away with her."

For an instant, the old nightmare returned: the lurid scene his imagination had painted in boyhood, of a carriage overturning into a ditch, his mother and sister screaming, then the dreadful silence.

What was wrong with him? Old ghosts. So stupid.

Clara had always been safe with him. His father's recklessness had taught him to be careful.

Even so, this child . . .

Erroll's murderous expression instantly melted into childish eagerness and her eyes widened another degree. "May I, truly, your grace?" she said. "May I hold the reins?"

"Lady Clara says you may, and I dare not contradict her," he said.

He wasn't sure what possessed Clara at present. Still, he knew she was fond of children in general and had some notion how to manage them. In her letters she'd described numerous amusing incidents with young cousins.

He was not used to small children—not anymore, at any rate—and this was no ordinary child. But what choice had he now? His best groom, Ford, held the horses and he could be counted on to control the mettlesome pair.

In any event, how was Clevedon to deny the child the treat, when she was trembling with excitement?

He lifted her up—the small, quivering body weighed a shocking nothing—and set her next to Clara. Then he climbed up into his seat, took the child onto his lap, took up the reins, and showed her how to hold them to go straight. She watched and listened avidly. Soon her trembling abated, and before long she had the reins threaded between her little gloved fingers. She looked up, smiling proudly at him, and he smiled back. He couldn't help it.

"How quick and clever you are," Clara said. "You got the hang of it in no time at all. I thought you would."

Erroll turned from him to send her beatific smile upward to Clara—and melt her ladyship's heart, as was plain enough to see. Not that this was any difficult accomplishment. Clara was soft-hearted, and Erroll, it had become abundantly clear, was a calculating creature. Like her mother.

"How does one make them go?" she said.

He didn't have time to decide what to answer.

Noirot burst from the shop. "Oh, the wretched child," she said. "Has she wheedled you into taking her up? She'll persuade you to drive her to Brighton, if you don't look out. Come down, Erroll. His grace and her ladyship have business elsewhere." She put up her hands. Torn between reluctance and relief, Clevedon yielded the girl to her mother.

He ought to feel relieved—he was no longer used to children and found them tedious, in fact. But she . . . ah, well, she was a cunning little minx.

He noticed that Erroll did not fight with her mother as she'd done with the maid. Docile or not, though, Noirot didn't trust her. She didn't set her down but carried her back into the shop.

He watched them go, Erroll waving goodbye to him over her mother's shoulder.

He waved back, smiling, yet he was watching the sway of Noirot's hips as she moved along, apparently unhampered by her daughter's weight. To him, the weight was nothing, but Noirot was not the great, hulking fellow he was, nor was she built in the Junoesque mold, like Clara . . . whose presence he belatedly recalled.

He turned away hastily and gathered the reins. A moment later, they were on their way.

Clara had watched those swaying hips, too, and she'd watched him watching them.

She'd felt the atmosphere change when she and Clevedon entered the shop. She'd felt him tense, in the way of a hound scenting quarry. When the dressmaker had approached, the tension between them was palpable.

"A fetching little girl," she said. That was the only thing she could safely say. The child was adorable. Clevedon's? But no, she'd discerned no resemblance at all, and the Angier looks were distinctive.

"I dare not come again," he said. "Next time Miss Noirot will wish to drive. And I'll have you to thank. I shouldn't have taken her up—I'm sure her mother wasn't pleased. But she could hardly rebuke me. Shopkeepers must consider their livelihood before their own feelings."

"Mrs. Noirot didn't seem angry. She seemed amused, rather."

"That's her way. It's her business to make herself pleasing. I told you how she had the ladies at the ball eating out of her hand. But never mind. It doesn't signify. I have no reason to come again, in any event. You'll persuade Longmore or one of your other brothers to bring you. Or come on your own, with Davis."

Davis was Clara's bulldog of a maid.

"Or with Mama," she said.

"What a nonsensical thing to say!" he said. "Your mother would never approve of this shop. It's too fashionable, and she seems determined that you should wear the most—" He broke off, his expression taut.

"Determined I should wear the most what?" Clara said.

"Nothing," he said. "I slept ill last night, and I've spent too long in a dressmaker's shop. Women's chatter has addled my wits. What were you three conspiring about, by the way?"

"Clevedon."

"You three were bent over the green dress you admired, talking in whispers," he said.

She glanced up at his face. He was looking straight ahead, his handsome face set in hard lines.

What a state he was in!—a contained fury that made the air about him seem to thrum even while he appeared outwardly calm.

Clevedon wasn't like this—not the Clevedon she knew, the man she'd recognized when he'd entered the drawing room and smiled in his old, fond way. This was a stranger.

She looked away, to gaze blankly at the passing scene while she tried to form an answer. She hardly knew what the other two women had been saying about the green dress. She'd been trying to hear what he was saying to Mrs. Noirot. She'd been trying to watch them without appearing to do so.

"I didn't quite understand," she said. "It was a beautiful dress, I thought, but they seemed to be discussing how to remake it." She tried desperately to remember what exactly they'd said, but she had only half-listened, and now her mind was whirling.

She was not naïve. She knew Clevedon had affairs. Longmore did, too. But she'd never seen her brother in a state anything like Clevedon's when Mrs. Noirot approached them. She'd been trying to make sense of that, when he snapped about Mama and . . . what Clara wore?

"I think . . ." She thought frantically. "I received the impression that something was wrong with the dress, but not wrong with the dress."

"Clara, that makes no sense."

Really, he could be as irritating as any of her brothers. She said goodbye to her patience. "If it's so important to you, you'd better ask Mrs. Noirot," she said. "What did you mean about Mama and what I wear?"

"Damnation," he said.

"You told me I ought to shop there, but you said I must not take Mama."

"I beg your pardon," he said. "I should not have said that."

"Oh, come, Clevedon. When did you ever mince words with me? What makes you so missish all of a sudden?"

"Missish?"

"So delicate. One of the things I have always liked about you is your refusing to treat me like an imbecile female. In your letters, you speak your mind. Or so I thought. Well, perhaps you don't tell me everything."

"Good God, certainly not. And I shall not tell you where to have your dresses made. It's of no concern to me."

"You may be sure that I shall take care not to ask you to accompany me to a dressmaker ever again," she said. "It puts you in the vilest temper."

Some hours later

"The little wretch!" Marcelline said, when they were closing up the shop that evening. "I knew she wouldn't forget his fine carriage or his fine self."

"My dear, she can't help it," said Sophy. "It's in her blood. She can spot a mark at fifty paces."

"He didn't seem to mind," said Leonie. She'd come out into the showroom in time to see Clevedon and Lady Clara leave.

All three sisters had had time to observe Lucie/Erroll's antics through the shop windows. It was clear in an instant that Millie had lost control of her, but it had taken Marcelline precious minutes to extract herself from Lady Renfrew and go out to collect her wayward child.

Sitting on his lap, the schemer, and holding the ribbons! She'd be expecting to drive her own carriage next.

"Of course he didn't mind," Marcelline said. "She was at her winsome best, and even the Duke of Clevedon can't help but succumb." Meanwhile, she, more cynical and calculating than he could ever be, had not been able to steel her heart against the sweet, indulgent smile he bestowed upon her daughter.

"She made sure to shed some winsomeness on Lady Clara, I noticed," said Sophy.

"Yes," Marcelline said.

"He did bring her," Leonie said. "And not a moment too soon."

They hadn't had time until now to talk of the day's events, because the day had been exceedingly eventful.

Marcelline had had her hands full, making the changes to Lady Renfrew's dress. She'd had to do this in secret, of all things—upstairs, away from the seamstresses, as though she were forging passports. Meanwhile Sophy and Leonie, in between trying to calm two other irate customers, had to dance attendance on the steady trickle of curious ladies who'd come mainly to stare at the famous gown.

The curious ladies gaped at the dress and peered into every corner of the shop, looking for Marcelline. They made the sisters show them lengths of fabric and take out of the drawers any number of buttons, ribbons, beads, feathers, fur, and other trim.

They left without buying anything.

At present, Sophy and Marcelline were restoring order to the drawers of trim and accessories. Leonie, as she did every evening, was taking an inventory of the showroom and trying to deduce which of their visitors had made off with a length of black satin ribbon, eleven jet buttons, and three cambric handkerchiefs.

"His timing couldn't have been better," Marcelline said. "If he hadn't turned up while Lady Renfrew was in the shop, I think we might have lost her forever."

She told herself to concentrate on that, and never mind the savage beating of her heart when she'd heard his voice. He'd come in the nick of time, and that was what mattered. It was all very well to offer to remake a dress to appease an irate customer, but customers had no idea of the amount of work involved. Meanwhile, into Lady Renfrew's mind would enter poisonous doubts about Marcelline's advertised ability to create "unique styles, designed for the individual, not the general."

"That doesn't bear thinking of," said Leonie. "Lady Clara is all very well, but we haven't got her yet. At present Lady Renfrew is our best customer. A bird in the hand is worth two in the bush."

Lady Renfrew's gown had been delivered precisely at seven o'clock—a few last, minor alterations had taken not half an hour—and Sophy had left a mollified customer behind her.

"She'll be back," Sophy said. "The whole time I was there, she talked about the duke and Lady Clara. You know that's all she'll talk about tonight at Mrs. Sharp's. She'll be quoting him, you may be sure: 'You won't find a better dressmaker in London—or Paris, for that matter.'" She mimicked Clevedon's bored voice and his accent— the unmistakable sound of the upper reaches of the privileged classes.

"We can only hope she was too busy being impressed with his grandeur to notice the way he looked at Marcelline," said Leonie.

"Like a hungry wolf," said Sophy.

Marcelline went hot all over. She still hadn't shaken off the feelings he'd stirred, And with what? A look. The sound of his voice. She still felt his melting green gaze upon her. She still heard the husky intimacy of his voice. Had she been free to do so, had she nothing and no one else to consider but herself, she would have led his provoking self away into one of the shop's back rooms and had her way with him, and there would be an end of it.

But she wasn't free, on a dozen counts. His beautiful bride-to-be stood a few yards away, across the shop, and the easy way he and she conversed made their mutual affection clear. Marcelline had pointed this out to herself. She'd planted Lucie's image firmly in her mind, too. And her own parents, the living example of what happened to a family when the adults thought only of themselves, their whims and passions.

She had no morals to speak of, but her survival instincts were acute. Succumbing to Clevedon was a mistake that would undermine the respect she'd worked day and night to earn. That would destroy her business and, with it, her family.

Even so, when she'd looked up into his eyes, and felt as much as heard the sound of his voice, her brain clouded over and her willpower ebbed away.

Such a fool she was! She need only recall how Charlie had looked at her, and the husky longing in his voice . . .

And where had that led?

"That's the way Clevedon always looks at women," she said. "That's the look of an expert seducer. Engrave it upon your mind, if you don't want to end up on your back, or against a wall, losing your maidenhead before you'd quite meant to."

"He didn't look at Lady Clara that way," Leonie said.

"Why should he?" Marcelline said. "Everything between them is settled or as good as settled. He takes her for granted, the coxcomb. But that's their problem. If she's wise, she'll find a way to get his full attention. It's not that difficult. Meanwhile, we have a *serious* problem." She glanced at the door leading to the workroom, now empty, the seamstresses having gone home at their usual time.

"Well," said Leonie, "I have my suspicions."

On Tuesday night, Mrs. Downes met with the seamstress at the usual time at the usual place.

The seamstress gave her a pattern she'd copied.

"That's all?" Mrs. Downes said. "You promised me a book of patterns, with details."

"And you'll get it," the seamstress said. "But they were in an uproar over that green dress of Lady Renfrew's, and then we were run ragged, fetching this and that for all the ladies coming to look at the dress Mrs. Noirot wore to that ball."

Mrs. Downes knew about the *poussière* dress, and the excitement it had stirred among the ladies. Her own customers had been talking about it, right in front of her!

But worse even than this indignity was the news of the Duke of Clevedon taking Lady Clara Fairfax to the accursed shop.

"I want those patterns," she said. "And you'd better get them soon."

"I'd better!" the seamstress said. "Or else what? I'm the one doing your dirty work."

"And I'm the one losing customers to that French whore. If you can't do what you promised, I'll tell her how you came to me and offered to spy for me. Then you'll be out on the street. There won't be any fifty pounds. I will give you something, though, like your mistress will: a bad name. And you won't ever get work in any respectable shop again."

* * *

On Wednesday night, the Duke of Clevedon was among the last to arrive at the Earl of Westmoreland's assembly. Had he tried to enter Almack's at that hour, he'd have found the doors firmly shut. But Almack's weekly assemblies had not yet begun, and in spite of this being a much livelier gathering, he danced only once with Lady Clara, then adjourned to the card room for the remainder of the evening.

On Thursday, he spent a quarter hour at the Countess of Eddingham's rout before departing for White's Club, where he played cards until dawn.

On Friday, he dined at Warford House. That night he couldn't escape to play cards. Instead, he pretended to enjoy himself, though it was clear as clear to Clara that he couldn't wait for the evening to be over.

He wasn't unkind to her. He hadn't said a cross word to her since Tuesday. But he was remote and unhappy, and she'd heard he was losing shocking amounts at cards. Even allowing for the usual gossipy exaggerations, he was playing more recklessly than was his custom.

Then, on Saturday, at a ball, Lady Gorrell, pretending not to see Clara standing well within hearing range, described in lurid detail the contents of the letter she'd received that day from her sister-in-law in Paris.

Monday

Two sharp knocks at the closed shop door startled the Noirot sisters. It was scarcely nine o'clock in the morning, and while they and their seamstresses usually toiled from nine to nine, the shop itself usually did not open until late in the forenoon. There wasn't much point in opening the showroom early when few of their customers rose before noon.

The question was whether they'd have any more customers. If they didn't stop their traitor soon, they wouldn't have a shop to open.

While Leonie had her suspicions, so far they hadn't any proof, and various ruses had failed. Early this morning they'd set a trap. If this one worked, they'd discover the culprit by tomorrow. Meanwhile, they could only wait, and seethe, and go about their business in the usual way.

At present that meant Marcelline, Sophy, and Leonie were arranging shawls and lengths of fabric upon the counters in a seemingly careless array meant to entice.

Early hour or not, business was business, and one must put a cheerful face on it.

Leonie went to the door and opened it.

Lady Clara Fairfax, red-faced, sailed over the threshold, a square-jawed maid following close behind. Ignoring Leonie's greeting, her ladyship made straight for Marcelline. Gliding toward her with a smooth greeting and a smoother curtsey, Marcelline asked in what way she might serve her ladyship.

"You might serve me by telling me the truth," Lady Clara said. "On Saturday night, I overheard a most astonishing tale—one I could hardly credit—"

She broke off, belatedly remembering the servant at hand. "Davis, wait in the carriage," she said.

Davis sent a glower round the shop, alighting on each sister in turn, then went out, slamming the door behind her.

Lady Clara took a breath, let it out, and began again. "Mrs. Noirot, I happened to overhear an outrageous story regarding a gentleman of my acquaintance—a gentleman who accompanied me to this shop not a week ago."

Marcelline did not utter a single one of the sarcastic responses, flippant rejoinders, interruptions, distractions, or violent oaths that came to mind. She was a professional. Her expression became one of polite interest.

"Before you leap to any conclusions," Lady Clara went on, "let me assure you that I have not come here in a jealous spirit. That would be absurd, in his case. I'm not blind, and I know— That is, I have brothers, and they think they're more discreet than they are. Oh." She took out a handkerchief, and dabbed her eyes. "Oh."

This was an alarming turn of events. Anger, outrage— perfectly usual and understandable.

Tears— Oh, Gemini!

"My dear—my lady." Marcelline took her by the elbow and led her to a chair. "Sophy, bring her ladyship a glass of wine."

"No," Lady Clara said. "I do not need wine."

"Brandy, then," said Marcelline.

"Well, perhaps," said Lady Clara.

Sophy went out.

Lady Clara gave a little sob, then stiffened, visibly composing herself. "I don't cry. I never cry. I'm not like that. But he's the dearest friend I have." Her blue gaze lifted to Marcelline. "I can't let you hurt him," she said.

Noirots were born unencumbered with consciences. Even if she'd owned one, Marcelline had not done anything so very wrong as to cause it to trouble her.

She told herself she was untroubled, but she couldn't make herself believe it. After all, this was an agreeable young lady, who had not treated Marcelline or her sisters other than politely—which was far from the case with most of their customers. Furthermore, it was clear she truly loved Clevedon, and it was very true that Marcelline felt sorry for her on this count, though she knew that was completely absurd. Lady Clara was the daughter of a marquess. She was on the brink of marrying a duke, and looking forward to an income of at least one hundred thousand pounds a year, perhaps double that.

Marcelline's shop, along with their upstairs living quarters, would easily fit into his London townhouse's servant quarters, and still leave room for his army of servants.

Meanwhile, the Noirots were on the brink of being destroyed by an incompetent competitor.

While Marcelline tried to harden her heart, Leonie—the least sentimental of three unsentimental siblings—said, "Pray, put your mind at rest, my lady. None of us wish to hurt any gentleman except in the pocketbook. In that regard, naturally, we should like to do as much damage as possible."

Lady Clara looked over at her. "That is not what I heard."

"I daresay not," said Leonie. "But I don't think that anyone in your circle quite understands the degree to which we are mercenary."

Ah, yes. Disarming honesty. That was the best tack with this one. Leave it to hardheaded Leonie to strike the right note when her elder sister was temporarily unhinged.

"My sister is right," said Marcelline. "It's completely incomprehensible to persons of rank. You never think of money. We think of little else."

"Well, then, if it is money," said Lady Clara, "I shall give you as much as ever you want, if only you would go away, without letting him find out, to a place where he can't find you."

"This is very dramatic," said Marcelline.

"Brandy is definitely called for," said Sophy, entering with the Noirots' sovereign remedy for all troubles. The brandy glowed within a small crystal decanter that sat, along with a matching glass, on a pretty tray. There she'd set out a delectable offering of biscuits, cakes, and cheese. Some customers spent hours in the shop, and one must be prepared to feed them—and ply them with drink, if necessary.

Lady Clara sipped her brandy without blinking and with obvious appreciation. Given the early hour, this small gesture went a great way in increasing the Noirot sisters' respect for her—which was highly inconvenient, when they were all trying to maintain a coldly professional and mercenary detachment.

"I know these things are always exaggerated," she said. "But I know as well that there's truth in the tales. I've seen with my own eyes. He's changed."

"With respect, your ladyship has not seen the gentleman for three years," Leonie said. "Men change. They're the most changeable creatures."

"He's moody and bored and remote," said her ladyship. "No matter where he is, he's absent. The only time he was present, truly present, was when we came here. I saw." She waved her glass at Marcelline. "I saw the way he looked at you, Mrs. Noirot. And so what must I think, when I hear about a dark adventuress who got her hooks into the D—into a certain gentleman. Or that he had pursued this exotic at the opera, at Longchamp, at the gaming hells—with half the world as witness—before he so far took leave of his reason as to bring this object of his obsession—"

"This sounds like something I could have written," Sophy murmured.

"—bring his *obsession* to the Comtesse de Chirac's annual ball. And this was *not* because his grace thought it a great joke to bring her, but because his—his lover—his *paramour* had threatened to kill herself if he didn't."

"*Kill* herself?" all three sisters echoed. They looked at one another. Their eyebrows went up a barely perceptible degree. This was the only outward sign of their incredulity—this and Leonie's having to bite her lip to keep from laughing.

"Nor was this the first time this woman had made threats," Lady Clara went on. "I heard of violent scenes all over Paris, culminating in a duel with the Marquis d'Émilien. This shocked even the most jaded of jaded Parisians. Shortly after grievously wounding the marquis in the Bois de Boulogne, the love-maddened gentleman pursued the young woman from Paris in the dead of night. In the course of this pursuit, he threatened the British consul and every other official he encountered. He was so deranged, it appears, that he believed they were deliberately obstructing his departure from France."

They were all accustomed to playing cards. This was why Sophy and Leonie did not fall down laughing, and why Marcelline, who was growing increasingly exasperated, had no trouble maintaining her politely interested expression. As though she hadn't enough problems, with Dowdy actively working to destroy her business. Now Marcelline was to be torn to pieces by the scandalmongers, merely because some people had seen what looked like flirtation! It was absurd—but then, the high ranks were not famous for their rationality.

She ought to be amused, but she was alarmed. Rumors alone could destroy her business. Though it wasn't hard to seem unmoved outwardly, she was having trouble deciding what to say.

Leonie, who didn't have her problems, had no such difficulty. "Clearly, members of the higher orders cannot count," she said. "If they would only count the number of days my sister had been in Paris—let alone the date when she first met the gentleman—they'd realize this is utter nonsense. Their first encounter occurred on the fourteenth of this month. I remember the date, because it headed the letter she wrote to us the same night, announcing the fact. That leaves the time from the night of the fourteenth to the early morning of the seventeenth, when my sister left Paris. How, I ask your ladyship, could all these events occur in little more than two full days?"

Leave it to Leonie to reduce emotion to numbers, Marcelline thought. And how little those numbers seemed. A few days. That was all the time Clevedon had needed to damage Marcelline's brain and jab thorns into her heart and plant dreams in her mind, so that she was uneasy by day and by night.

She gathered her wits. "Meanwhile he'd had so many months to live among the Parisians," she said. "They're the ones you ought to blame, if you want scapegoats. You've never been to Paris, I believe?"

"Not yet," said Lady Clara.

"Then you've no notion how different it is from London."

"I know what Paris is like," said Lady Clara. "Cleve— The gentleman wrote to me faithfully—until, that is, he met you. It's no good denying it. When I asked him why he hadn't written—I could see he had not broken his arm—he told me what had happened."

"And what, precisely, was that?" Marcelline said. "It can't have been an incriminating tale. Last week you accompanied him here in cheerful spirits. You didn't look at all as though you wanted to kill him. Or me."

"He told me he'd met a vastly provoking dressmaker," Lady Clara said. "But he's a man, and as articulate as he can be in letters, his vocabulary, in matters of emotion, is less than clear. What he meant—and pray don't confuse me with an idiot, as you know it perfectly well—what he meant was that Mrs. Noirot was *provocative*. What he meant was, he was fixed on her."

As though he did nothing to fix me on him, Marcelline thought. *As though he's a victim of my wiles—or demonic powers, more like it.*

"I asked him directly whether he was infatuated," Lady Clara continued, "and he laughed and said that seemed the likeliest explanation."

Business, Marcelline reminded herself. This was business. This was the customer she'd wanted. It was trying to lure Lady Clara into her shop that had led Marcelline into so much trouble. And here the lady was. In the shop.

She said, "How could he help it? Only look at me."

She gestured in the graceful way she so often did, her hand sweeping downward from her neckline.

Lady Clara looked, truly looked, finally, at what Marcelline was wearing.

Pink and green, one of her favorite color combinations, this time in silk batiste, with a deeply plunging pelerine of the same material, over gossamer puffed sleeves and a delicately pleated chemisette.

"My goodness," said Lady Clara.

Marcelline resisted the temptation to roll her eyes. Lady Clara was as oblivious as Clevedon. They noticed nothing about a dress until one forcibly called their attention to it.

"This isn't half what you would have seen in Paris," Marcelline said. "There I was obliged to exert myself, because I was competing with the most stylish women in the world, who've made a high art of attracting men. *That* is your ladyship's true rival: Paris. I'm nothing. If the gentleman is bored and remote, it's because the women about him at present don't know how to get his attention."

She let her gaze slide from the top of Lady Clara's dull bonnet, over the white crepe dress trimmed in black—mainly ribbon and a little embroidery but not a stitch of lace in sight—and downward, with a small, despairing sigh, to the hem. The style was—well, it hadn't any style. As to the craftsmanship: In a drunken stupor, the least talented of Marcelline's six seamstresses could do better than this.

Sophy and Leonie drew nearer to Marcelline, their gazes moving in the same pitying way over the dress.

"The Court has been wearing mourning for the Emperor of Austria, then the Prince of Portugal," Lady Clara said defensively. "We've only recently changed from black."

"You cannot wear this shade of white," Marcelline said. "It *ruins* your complexion."

"Such a complexion!" Sophy said. "*Translucent*. Women would weep and gnash their teeth in envy, were you not wearing a white that drains away all the vitality."

"The black trim can't be helped," said Leonie. "But must it be so heavy?"

"It isn't required to be crepe, certainly," said Marcelline. "Where is the rule that says one may not use a thinner ribbon, of satin? And perhaps some knots—so. Or a jet lozenge. And a little silver, perhaps here and there, to brighten it. But above all, *never* this shade of white!"

"You're not making the most of your figure," said Sophy.

"I'm big," Lady Clara said.

"You're *statuesque*," said Leonie. "What I should give to have your height. What I should give to be able to look a man in the eye."

"Mainly, I'm looking down at them," said Lady Clara. "Except for my brothers and Cl—the gentleman."

"All the better," said Sophy. "A man ought to look up to a woman, literally or figuratively, because that is the proper mode of worship, and worship is the very least he can do. It doesn't matter what her height is. You're the most beautiful young woman in London—"

"That's doing it too brown," said Lady Clara. She drank more brandy. "You're wicked, the three of you."

She was not wrong.

"Perhaps one might see at the theater a whore who seems prettier," said Sophy. "But that's only because she makes the most of herself and of certain cosmetic aids. *You*, however, have a deep, true English beauty that will only make you handsomer as time passes. It's disgraceful and ungrateful of you not to make the most of the gifts with which you've been blessed."

"You look big," said Marcelline, "because the dress is matronly. You look big because it's carelessly cut and ill sewn. Puckers! My six-year-old daughter can sew better than this. I say nothing of the overall design, which seems to have been adopted from fashions current in Bath among the grandmother set. The analogy is fitting, since so many drink the waters for their health, and this shade of white makes you look bilious. Let me show you the shade of white you ought to wear. Sophy, fetch a hand mirror. Leonie, the soft white organdy."

"I did not come here to buy a dress," Lady Clara said.

"You came because you want to bring the gentleman back from wherever it is he's gone to," said Marcelline. "We're going to show you how to do it."

Chapter Nine

We have seen some robes of white crape prepared
for the change of mourning; the *corsages* drooped,
and retained in the centre of the bosom, and at
the sides by knots of black satin riband, with a jet
lozenge in the centre of each.

La Belle Assemblèe,
fashions for the month of April 1835

Warford House
Tuesday afternoon

"Her ladyship is at home, your grace, but she is engaged," Timms the butler said.

"Engaged?" Clevedon repeated. "Isn't this Tuesday?"

The Warfords were not at home to visitors on Tuesdays. That was why he'd called today rather than yesterday or tomorrow. On Tuesday he need not make his way
through the scrum of Clara's beaux, the infatuated pup-
pies who swarmed about her at social events. Whenever he
approached, he was disagreeably aware of casting a pall
over the activities, whatever they were: fellows composing
odes to her eyes and such, he supposed. Squabbling over
who had which dance. And competing, no doubt, in point

of fashion—which was amusing, since Clara didn't care about fashion. She could not tell one lapel from another, let alone evaluate the quality of a waistcoat.

Still, he might have mistaken the day. He had drunk more than agreed with him last night, and his head still ached. Perhaps it would be better to come back on the correct day. Maybe the damned sun wouldn't be shining so brightly then.

After confirming that this was indeed Tuesday, Timms apologetically led Clevedon to the small drawing room to wait while he sent a footman to inform Lady Clara of his grace's arrival.

Unaccustomed to be made to wait when he called anywhere, least of all at Warford House, Clevedon grew restive.

It was exceedingly odd, Clara being engaged on a Tuesday afternoon. He was sure he'd told her—on Saturday, wasn't it?—he'd take her for a drive today.

He needed to settle this marriage business today. Already a week had passed since he'd decided to put his life in order and make his formal offer. After that, they'd put all in train for a wedding at the earliest opportunity.

The trip to the dressmaker's had thrown him off balance. Seeing Noirot again . . . and the child . . .

He'd been unable to collect his thoughts, let alone remember what he'd meant to say to Clara. The time hadn't felt . . . right. He and Clara needed to get used to each other again, he'd told himself. Hadn't Longmore said so?

But now it seemed they'd have to get used to each other after they were married. Now a formal—and short—engagement seemed the best way to put an end to speculation and gossip.

He'd heard rumors of a mad tale that had traveled from Paris, and would, he knew, reach Warford House before long. Last week he'd confided in Clara—to a point. He knew she was too sensible a girl to fret over idle gossip. In her letters, hadn't she ridiculed one after another piece of scandal making the London rounds? Her mother, though, was another matter altogether.

When Lady Warford heard the rumors, she'd throw one of her fits. She'd say nothing to Clevedon directly. Instead, she'd harass her family, carrying on about the shame of Clara's being ignored in favor of a *dressmaker, a milliner, a common shopkeeper!* She'd grow more and more hysterical until one of the men took Clevedon to task.

In Paris, only last month, he'd borne one awkward visit from Longmore—instigated, no doubt, by Lady Warford. Clevedon doubted his friend was any more eager than he to repeat the experience.

He had nothing to feel anxious or guilty about, he told himself. He'd done nothing improper since he'd returned to London. Before that didn't count.

Dreams, however torrid, were nothing to feel in the least uneasy about. Fantasies were nothing more than that. Men had fantasies regarding women, all sorts of women, suitable and unsuitable. They had them all the time, waking and sleeping.

As to the discontent: That would stop after he was married.

But his mind, not shy in the least, shied away from contemplating his wedding night.

Where the devil was the footman? Why hadn't Timms gone himself? What on earth was Clara about? With whom was she engaged on a Tuesday? Had he not told her he would come? He was sure he had . . . but his mind strayed from time to time—and how could he recollect now, with this vile headache?

He realized he was pacing. He stopped, and told himself he was out of sorts. This was not a suitable humor for a casual call, let alone a momentous one.

She had something else to do. He must have forgotten to tell her about driving today. Or she'd forgotten.

He'd see her tomorrow night at Almack's. When he did, he'd make an appointment to speak to her.

No, he ought to speak to her father first. That was the proper way to go about it. He'd return another day, when Lord Warford was at home. On Tuesdays his lordship customarily visited one of his charities.

Clevedon left the drawing room. Having run tame in this house since boyhood, he knew every inch of it. Best to slip out quietly, before he ran into other family members.

He strode to the antechamber nearby, where he knew he'd find his hat, gloves, and walking stick.

He entered, and his heart began to beat very hard.

It happened before he was fully conscious of what had set it going.

A bonnet. An absurd conglomeration of ribbons and flowers and feathers, it sat on the table where the servants customarily put visitors' hats and such.

He stared at it for a moment, then started for the door.

But there was something . . . in the air.

He paused at the door. Then he turned back and walked to the bonnet. He picked it up, and brought it close to his face. The scent, the familiar, tormenting scent swam about him, as light and as inescapable as a gossamer net: the faint scent of jasmine, mingled with the scent of her hair and her skin.

Noirot.

He set the bonnet down.

He stepped out into the corridor.

A maid passed, carrying a heap of clothing.

He started in the direction she'd come from.

He heard an anguished cry.

Clara.

He ran toward the sound.

He pulled open the door to the music room. Bright sunlight burst upon him, blinding him for a moment and making lightning bolts in his head.

"Clara, are you—"

"Clevedon! What on earth—"

But Clara was gaping at him, astonished, and his gaze shot to the other woman.

Noirot stood, eyes wide and mouth slightly parted. She closed it promptly, and her face closed down into her playing-cards look.

"What are you about?" he said. "What the devil are you doing here?"

"Look at her," Clara cried. "That's my favorite dress—the one I was wearing when Lord Herringstone composed an ode to my eyes."

Look at her. At Noirot. Look at her.

He looked, his gaze sliding down from the slightly disordered coiffure, loose strands of dark, silken hair clinging to her neck . . . down over her dark, brilliant eyes . . . down over her dangerous mouth while he remembered the taste of her, the feel of her mouth against his . . . down over the firm bosom while he remembered the velvet of her skin under his hand and against his mouth . . . and down at last to the dress she was holding.

Clara crossed to her and snatched the dress away.

"She says we must give it away," Lady Clara said. "She objects to everything. Nothing is right—even this, my favorite."

"The dress is jade green," Noirot said. "Your eyes are

blue and very beautiful, and that's what prompted Lord Herringstone to compose an ode. Had you been wearing a more suitable color, you would have inspired him to compose an epic. Very few women can wear this color successfully. You may not wear very many shades of green. I should recommend against it—"

"That woman—Lady Renfrew—you made her a beautiful dress, exactly this color."

"It was not *exactly* this color," Noirot said. "It was an entirely different shade of green—and one that would suit you no better. It would seem that your ladyship cannot distinguish hues. Whether it was your governess or your painting master, whoever failed to train your eye ought to be pilloried. You must give me the dress, my lady."

"Oh, you are horrible, cruel! You've taken all my favorite things!"

Noirot pulled the dress away from her and threw it on the floor and kicked it aside.

Clara clapped her hand over her mouth.

Noirot folded her arms.

A dangerous glint came into Clara's blue eyes.

Noirot regarded her with the same cool lack of expression she would have bestowed on a promising hand of cards.

The fool! She could not treat a marquess's daughter like a temperamental child, even if she was behaving like one. Noirot would lose any hope of a commission—she'd lose Clara forever—and she'd be lucky if Lady Warford didn't have her driven from London.

"If I may interpose a—"

"No, Clevedon, you may not," Clara said. "I told her to come. I *made* her come. She left me no choice. Nothing she's proposed bears the smallest resemblance to what I normally wear, and I can't believe I am such a provincial, so lacking in taste and discernment—but you know I've never cared very much, and Mama always advises me. But now I'm told to throw everything out, and what am I to tell Mama? And I am not to have a green dress!"

She stamped her foot. Clara actually stamped her foot.

"It must be blue-green," Noirot said. She put the tip of her index finger to her chin and regarded Clara with narrowed eyes. "I envision embroidered *poult de soie*, the *corsage* decorated with a mantilla of blond lace." Her finger came away from her chin to lightly glide over her shoulder. As she indicated the fall of the mantilla she imagined, her finger lingered at the place where he'd touched her, on that night when they'd played cards, when he'd helped her with her shawl. He remembered the tiny hitch in her breath and the heated triumph he'd felt, because finally, finally he'd affected her.

"But that is for later," she went on. "For the present, as your ladyship has reminded me *repeatedly,* we are wearing white. And as I have reminded your ladyship repeatedly, it must be a *soft* white. No ivory." She made a dismissive gesture at a dress draped over a chair. "Too yellow. And not that blinding white." She indicated another dress, hanging over the back of a small sofa.

"Speaking of blinding," Clevedon said. "Might we have the curtains drawn? I've the devil of a headache—"

"I wonder where you got it," Clara said. "The same place Longmore gets his, I daresay. Well, you must grin and bear the light. Madame can't work in the dark."

"I thought she could do anything," Clevedon muttered, retreating to the darkest corner of the room. "She told me—more than once—that she's the greatest modiste in the world."

"Beyond a doubt she's the most exacting modiste in the world," Clara said. "She's been showing me how colors affect one's complexion. We came to this room because it has the best light at this time of day." She paused, frowning. "If you have a headache, why are you here?"

"You were screaming," he said.

"It's upsetting when someone takes one's clothes away," Clara said. "I find I'm not as philosophically detached as I had supposed. But why are you here, at the house, I mean? You know Papa is never at home on Tuesdays, and you would never come to see Mama, even if she were at home, which she isn't, else Mrs. Noirot wouldn't be here. She's my dark secret, you know."

"I came to take you for a drive," Clevedon said. Had she always used to be so talkative?

"But you can see I'm not at liberty. Why did you not tell me you meant to come?"

"I did, on Saturday."

"You did not. You did not spare me above five minutes on Saturday, and if you uttered ten words to me, that's all you did. Today, obviously, is inconvenient."

"We're nearly done," Noirot said.

"Hardly," Clara said. "Now we must decide what to tell Mama."

Noirot didn't roll her eyes, which he considered evidence of superhuman self-control. Clara was driving him mad, and he'd only been here for a few minutes. Noirot must be wanting to throttle her.

But her expression only became kindly. "Tell her, my lady, that one can't expect a fashionable gentleman—who has spent time in Paris—to come up to scratch—"

"Come up to *what*?" Clevedon said.

"—when one looks like a dowd and a fright and elderly to boot," Noirot continued past the interruption. "Be sure to hold your head high when you say it, and make it sound like a fact that ought to be obvious to the meanest intelligence. And if there's a difficulty, throw a tantrum. That's what high-bred girls generally do."

"But I never did," Clara said aghast.

"A moment ago you stamped your foot," Clevedon said. "You pouted, too."

"I did not!"

"Your ladyship was too distressed to realize," Noirot said. "However, you must do it with greater force and with absolute confidence in the rightness of your cause. Still, we must remember that a temper fit is simply a way to obtain the audience's notice. Once you have her ladyship's full attention, you will become sweet reason itself, and tell her this anecdote."

Noirot folded her hands and, while Clevedon and Clara watched, astonished, her eyes filled. The tears hung there, glistening, but did not fall. She said, "Dearest Mama, I know you do not wish for me to be *mortified* in front of all my acquaintance. And here," Noirot added in a more normal voice, "be sure to mention somebody your mother loathes. And when her ladyship says this is all nonsense, as she well might, you will tell her about the French gentleman who was mad in love with a married woman—"

"That isn't the sort of thing for Clara to—"

"Pray let her finish," Clara said. "You're the one who brought me to this aggravating person, and I've steeled myself to suffer with her in order to be beautiful."

"Your ladyship is already beautiful," Noirot said. "How many times must I repeat it? That's what's so infuriating. A perfect diamond must have the perfect setting. A masterpiece must have the perfect frame. A—"

"Yes, yes, but we know that argument won't work with Mama. What about the gentleman and the married woman?"

"His friends reasoned with him, pleaded with him—

all in vain," Noirot said. "Then, one night, at an entertainment, the lady asked him to fetch her shawl. He hastened to serve her, imagining the silken softness of a cashmere shawl, the scent of the woman he loved enhancing its perfection . . ."

Clevedon remembered Noirot's scent, the memory reawakened only minutes ago: the scent her bonnet held. He remembered inhaling her, his face in her neck.

". . . a cashmere shawl that would put all the other ladies' cashmeres to shame. He found the garment but— *quelle horreur!*—not cashmere at all. Rabbit hair! Sick with disgust, he fell instantly and permanently out of love, and abandoned her."

Clara stared at her. "You're roasting me," she said.

Clevedon collected himself and said, "You'll find the anecdote in Lady Morgan's book about France. It was published some years ago, but the principle remains. I wish you'd seen my friend Aronduille's face when I asked him whether it mattered what a woman wore. I wish you could have heard him and his friends talking about it, quoting philosophers, arguing about Ingres and Balzac and Stendhal and David, art and fashion, the meaning of beauty, and so on."

Clara glanced at him, then returned to Noirot. "Well, then, I shall try it, and I shall say it is all because Clevedon is so infernally discriminating, worse even than Longmore—"

"Clara would it not be better if you—"

"But what am I to wear to Almack's tomorrow night?" Clara said. "You've rejected *everything.*"

Almack's, he thought. Another dreary evening among the same people. He would have to pluck Clara from her hordes of admirers and dance with her. Whatever she wore, he would know Noirot had touched it.

He said, "Since no one was being murdered, and I seem to be *de trop*—"

"Not at all, your grace," Noirot said. "You've arrived in the nick of time. Her ladyship has been remarkably patient and open-minded, considering that I've upset her universe."

"You have, rather," Clara said.

"But here is his grace, come to take you for a drive. Fresh air, the very thing you need after this trying morning and afternoon."

"But Almack's—"

"I shall send you a dress tomorrow," Noirot said. "I or one of my sisters will personally deliver it to you, at not later than seven o'clock, at which time we shall make any final adjustments you require. The dress will be *perfect*."

"But my mother—"

"You will have already dealt with her, as I suggested," Noirot said.

Clara looked at Clevedon. "She is the most dictatorial creature," she said.

"His grace has been so kind as to mention this character flaw before," Noirot said with nary a glance at Clevedon. "I serve women of fashion all day long, six days a week. One must either dominate or be dominated."

Ah, there it was: the disarming frankness, leavened with a touch of humor.

Gad, she was beyond anything!

"I have had enough of being dominated for the present," Clara said. "Clevedon, pray be patient another few minutes, and I shall be glad to take the air with you. I promise to be back in a trice. Mrs. Noirot has left me a few paltry items she finds not completely abhorrent. My maid shall not have any momentous decisions to make regarding bonnets or anything else."

She started toward the door, and hesitated. Then, with the look of one who'd made up her mind, she went out.

She had exactly what she wanted, Marcelline told herself. More than she'd hoped for. She hadn't even had to wait for the betrothal. She had Lady Clara already, and a large order. Tomorrow night, the crème de la crème of Society would see Lady Clara Fairfax wearing a Noirot creation.

Maison Noirot would soon be the foremost dressmaking establishment in London.

Marcelline had accomplished everything—and more—than she'd planned when she set out for Paris, mere weeks ago.

She could not be happier.

She told herself this while she set about sorting the various rejected items of Lady Clara's wardrobe.

"Are you going to burn them?" came Clevedon's voice from the corner to which he'd withdrawn.

"Certainly not," she said.

"But they have no redeeming qualities," he said. "I should never have noticed the poor choices in color before you poisoned my mind, but even I can discern inferior cut and stitchery."

"They can be taken apart and remade," Marcelline said. "I am a patroness of a charitable establishment for women. Her ladyship was so generous as to allow me to take half the discards for my girls."

"Your girls," he said. "You—*you're* a philanthropist?" He laughed.

She longed to throw something at him.

A chair. Herself.

But that was her shallow Noirot heart speaking. He was beautiful. Watching him move made her mouth go dry. It wasn't fair that she couldn't have him without complications. In bed—or on a carriage seat or against a wall—it wouldn't matter that he was idle and arrogant and oblivious. If only she could simply use him and discard him, the way men used and discarded women.

But she couldn't. And she'd used him already, though not in that way. She'd used him in a more important way. She'd got what she'd wanted.

A maid entered, and Marcelline spent a moment directing her. When she went out again with a heap of clothing, Marcelline did not take up the conversation where it had stopped. She did not take up the conversation at all.

She wouldn't let him disturb her in any way. She was very, very happy. She'd achieved her goals.

"Which set of unfortunate women is it?" he said. "I'll tell my secretary to make a donation. If they can make anything of those dresses, they'll have earned it."

"The Milliners' Society for the Education of Indigent Females." She could have added that she and her sisters had founded it last year. They'd learned at an early age more than they wanted to know about indigence and the difficulties of earning a living.

But her past was a secret under lock and key. "Some of our girls have gone on to become ladies' maids," she said. "The majority find places as seamstresses, for which there's always need, particularly during mourning periods." Luckily for them, the court was frequently in mourning, thanks to the British royal family's penchant for marrying their Continental cousins.

The butler entered, followed by a footman carrying a tray of refreshments to sustain his grace during the wait for her ladyship.

Marcelline was famished. She'd been waiting on Lady Clara since this morning, and had not been offered a bite to eat or anything to drink. But mere tradesmen did not merit feeding.

Oh, would the girl never be dressed? How long did it take to tie on a bonnet and throw a shawl about one's shoulders? One would think, given her anxieties about Marcelline ruining his life, Lady Clara would not leave them alone together for above half a minute.

But they were hardly alone, with servants going to and fro. Not that Lady Clara had anything to worry about, servants or no servants.

The only designs Marcelline had were upon her ladyship's statuesque person—and her father's and future husband's purses.

That was all.

She was very, very happy.

The silence stretched out, broken only by the servants' comings and goings.

Then, at last, at long last, Lady Clara reappeared.

Marcelline stopped sorting for long enough to make an adjustment to her ladyship's bonnet—it was not tilted precisely as it ought to be—and to twitch her cashmere shawl into a more enticing arrangement. Her shawls were very fine. One could not fault her there.

Having arranged Lady Clara to her satisfaction, Marcelline stepped away, made a proper curtsey, and returned to her work.

She was aware of Clevedon's big frame passing not far from her. She was aware of the muffled sound of his boots on the carpet. She heard the low murmur, his voice mingling with Lady Clara's, and the latter's soft laughter.

Marcelline kept busy with her work and did not watch them go.

And when they were gone, she told herself she'd done

a fine job, and she'd done nobody any great wrong—a miracle, considering her bloodline—and she had every reason to be glad.

That evening

The gown Mrs. Whitwood had returned lay on the counter. The enraged customer had come and gone while Marcelline was dancing attendance upon Lady Clara Fairfax at Warford House.

Sophy had soothed Mrs. Whitwood. Sophy could soothe Attila the Hun. The dress would be remade. The cost was mainly in labor, the smallest cost of making a dress. Still, it cost time—time that Marcelline, her sisters, and her seamstresses could be spending on other orders.

If this kept up, they'd be ruined. It wasn't simply that they couldn't afford to keep remaking dresses. They couldn't afford the damage to their reputation.

Marcelline was studying the dress, deciding what to change. "Who worked on it?" she asked Pritchett, her senior seamstress.

"Madame, if there is a fault with the workmanship it must be mine," Pritchett said. "I supervised every stitch of this dress. But madame can see for herself. It is precisely as madame ordered."

"Indeed, and the details, as you know, are of my own design," Marcelline said. "It's very strange that another dress should appear, bearing these same details. The angle and width of the pleats of the bodice was my own invention. How curious that another dressmaker should have precisely the same idea, in the same style of dress."

"Most unfortunate, madame," Pritchett said. "Yet some would think it a miracle we haven't had this problem before, when you consider that we take in all sorts of girls, from the streets, practically. One doesn't wish to be uncharitable. Some of them don't know any better, I daresay. Never taught right from wrong, you know. I shall be happy to work late—as late as needed—to make the dress over, if madame wishes."

"No, I'll want you fresh tomorrow," Marcelline said. "Lady Clara Fairfax's ball dress must be ready to deliver at seven o'clock sharp in the evening. I shall want all my seamstresses well rested and alert. Better to come in early. Let us say eight o'clock in the morning." She glanced at her pendant watch. "It's nearly eight. Send them all home now, Pritchett. Tell them we want them here at precisely eight o'clock tomorrow morning, ready for a very busy day."

She rarely kept her seamstresses past nine o'clock, even when the shop was frantically busy, as it had been when Dr. Farquar's daughter had needed to be married in a hurry—or when Mrs. Whitwood, having quarreled with Dowdy, had come to Maison Noirot to have herself and her five daughters fitted out in mourning for a very rich aunt.

Marcelline's personal experience had taught her that one did better work early in the day. By nightfall, spirits flagged and eyesight failed. The workroom had a skylight, but that was no use after sunset.

"Yes, Madame, but we have not quite completed Mrs. Plumley's redingote."

"It isn't wanted until Thursday," Marcelline said. "Everybody is to go home, and prepare for a long, hard day tomorrow."

"Yes, Madame."

Marcelline watched her go out of the showroom.

The trap she and her sisters had set yesterday morning was simple enough.

Before they went home at the end of the workday, the

seamstresses were required to put everything away. The workroom was to be left neat and tidy. No stray bits of thread or ribbon, buttons or thimbles should remain on the worktable, the chairs, the floor, or anywhere else. The room had been perfectly neat early yesterday morning when Marcelline deliberately dropped a sketch of a dress for Mrs. Sharp on the floor.

The first seamstress arriving in the morning—and that was usually Pritchett—should have noticed the sketch, and turned it over to Marcelline, Sophy, or Leonie. But when Sophy went in, shortly after the girls' workday began, the sketch was gone and nobody said a word about it. It didn't turn up until this morning. Selina Jeffreys found it under her chair when she came to work.

Pritchett had scolded her for hurrying away at night and leaving a mess. She'd made a great fuss about the sketch—Madame's work was never to be carelessly handled.

But Marcelline, Leonie, and Sophy knew there hadn't been a mess, and that Jeffreys's place had been as clean and orderly as the others. Nothing had been lying under her chair or anyone else's.

Well, now they knew. And now they were ready.

The shop door swung open, setting the bell jangling.

She looked up from the dress, and her heart squeezed painfully.

Clevedon stood for a moment, his green gaze sweeping the shop and finally coming to rest on her. He frowned, then quickly smoothed his beautiful face and sauntered toward her. Riveted on that remarkable face, too handsome to be real, it took her a moment to notice the large box he was carrying.

"Your grace," she said, bobbing a quick curtsey.

"Mrs. Noirot," he said. He set the box on the counter.

"That cannot be Lady Clara's new dress," she said. "Sophy said her ladyship was delighted with it."

"Why the devil should I be returning Clara's purchases?" he said. "I'm not her servant. This is for Erroll."

Marcelline's heart beat harder, with rage now. She was aware of her face heating. It probably didn't show, but she didn't care whether it did or not. "Take it back," she said.

"Certainly not," he said. "I went to a good deal of trouble. I know nothing about children anymore, and you will not believe the number and variety of—"

"You may not give my daughter gifts," Marcelline said.

He took the lid off the box, and lifted from it a doll— such a doll! She had black curling hair and vivid blue glass eyes. She was dressed in silver net and lace, trimmed with pearls. "I'm not taking it back," he said. "Burn it, then."

At that moment, Lucie burst through the door from the back. She stopped short at the sight of the doll, which the beast hadn't the grace to return to its box.

She'd been watching the street from the window upstairs, no doubt, as she always did. She'd recognized his fine carriage.

She was six years old. It was too much to expect her to resist the doll. Her eyes widened. Yet she managed a creditable "Good evening, your grace," and a curtsey. All the while, her eyes never left the doll. "My, that's a fine doll," she said. "I think it's the most beautiful doll I've ever seen in all my life."

All six years of it.

"You're going to pay for this," Marcelline said under her breath. "And painfully."

"Is it, indeed?" he said to Lucie. "I'm not a good judge of these matters."

"Oh, yes." Lucie drew a step nearer. "She isn't like ordinary dolls. Her eyes are blue glass, you see. And her face is so lifelike. And her hair is so beautiful, I think it must be *real* hair."

"Perhaps you'd like to hold her," Clevedon said.

"Oh, yes!" She started toward him, then hesitated and looked at Marcelline. "May I, Mama?" she asked in her best Dutiful Child voice.

"Yes," Marceline said, because there was nothing else she could say. She was hardheaded and practical, and any mother would know this was setting a terrible precedent as well as compromising her reputation.

But to deny her child—any child—such a treat, after the child had seen it and had done nothing wrong to be punished for, was wanton cruelty. She was a strict mother. She had to be. But too many cruelties, large and small, had marked her own childhood. That was one legacy she wouldn't pass on.

Folding his large frame, he crouched down to Lucie's level. Solemnly he held out the doll. Equally solemnly, she took it, holding her breath until it was safely in her arms. Then she held it so carefully, as though she believed the thing was magical, and might disappear in a minute. "What is her name?" she asked.

"I have no idea," he said. "I thought you would know."

Oh, the wretched, manipulative man!

Lucie considered. "If she were my doll, I should call her Susannah."

"I think she would like to be your doll," Clevedon said. He slanted a glance upward, at Marcelline. "If she may."

Though she was captivated by the doll, Lucie didn't fail to see whose permission he sought. "Oh, if Mama says she may? Mama, may she? May she be my doll?"

"Yes," Marcelline said. What other answer could she make, curse him!

"Oh, thank you, Mama!" Lucie turned back to Clevedon, and the look she sent him from those great blue eyes was calculated to break his heart, which Marcelline sincerely hoped it did. "Thank you, your grace. I shall take very good care of her."

"I know you will," he said.

"Her limbs move, you see," Lucie said, demonstrating. "She needn't wear only one dress. This one is very beautiful, but she's like a princess, and a princess must have a vast wardrobe. Mama and my aunts will help me cut out and sew dresses for her. I'll make her morning dresses and walking dresses and the most beautiful carriage dress, a blue redingote to match her eyes. The next time you come, you'll see."

The next time you come.

"Why don't you take Susannah upstairs to meet your aunts?" Marcelline said. "I have something to discuss with his grace."

Lucie went out, cradling the doll as though it were a living infant. Clevedon rose and watched her go out, through the door to the back of the shop. He was smiling, and it was a smile Marcelline had never seen before. It was not his charming smile or his seductive one or his winning one.

It was fond and wistful, and she could not withstand it. It won her and weakened her will more effectively than any of his other smiles could have done.

Which only made her angrier.

"Clevedon," she began.

He turned back to her, the smile fading. "You may not rake me over the coals," he said. "She set out to captivate me, much as her mother did—"

"She's six years old!"

"You both succeeded," he said. "What was I to do? She's a little girl. Why should she not have a doll?"

"She has dolls! Does she seem neglected to you? Deprived in any way? She's *my* daughter, and I take care of her. She has nothing to do with you. You've no business buying her dolls. What will Lady Clara think? What do you think your fine friends in the ton will say when they hear you've given my daughter gifts? You know they'll hear of it." Lucie would show the doll to the seamstresses, naturally, and they'd tell everybody they knew, and word would spread through the ton in no time at all. "And do you think their speculations will do my business any good?"

"That's all you think about. Your business."

"It's my life, you great thickhead! This"—she swept her hand to indicate the shop—"This is how I *earn* my living. Can you not grasp this simple concept? Earning a living?"

"I'm not—"

"This is how I feed and clothe and house and educate my daughter," she raged on. "This is how I provide for my sisters. What must I do to make you understand? How can you be so blind, so willfully obtuse, so—"

"You'll make me run mad," he said. "Everywhere I turn, there you are."

"That's monstrous unfair! Everywhere I go, there is your great carcass!"

"You upset everything," he said. "I've been trying for a fortnight to propose to Clara, and every time I steel myself to it—"

"*Steel* yourself?"

"Every time," he went on, unheeding, *"you"*—he waved his hand—"There you are. I went to Warford House today to *come up to scratch,* as you so poetically put it, but you had her worked up into such a state, we couldn't have a proper conversation, and all my speech—

and I spent *half an hour* composing it—went out of my head."

The door to the back of the shop opened again and Leonie came in.

"Oh, your grace," she said, feigning surprise, though she'd probably heard the row from the stairs. Marcelline hoped the seamstresses had followed orders and left early, else they'd have had an earful.

"He was about to leave," Marcelline said.

"No, I wasn't," he said.

"It's closing time," Marcelline said, "and we know you aren't buying anything."

"Perhaps I shall," he said.

"Leonie, please lock up for me," she said. To him she said, "I'm not keeping my shop open all night to pander to your whims."

"Do you plan to throw me out bodily?" he said.

She could knock him unconscious. Then she and her sisters could drag him out into the alley behind the shop. It wouldn't be the first time they'd had to dispose of a troublesome male.

"You're too big, curse you," she said. "But we're going to settle something, once and for all."

Chapter Ten

Approaching Marriages in High Life.—A marriage is on the tapis between Mr Vaughan and Lady Mary Anne Gage, sister of Lord Kenmare. Viscount Palmerston, it is said, will shortly be united to the rich Mrs Thwaites.

The Court Journal, Saturday 25 April 1835

Marcelline stormed through the passage, past the stairs toward the back of the building, and through the open door into the workroom.

She met chaos.

Worktable covered with scraps of fabric, thimbles, thread, pincushions. Floor littered with debris. Chairs left where they'd been pushed out. It looked as though seamstresses had fled or been chased out.

She didn't have time or mind to wonder at it. She didn't have time or mind to put two and two together. The state of the room was one more trial in a long, wearying day of biting her tongue and maintaining an even temper in the face of stupidity, rudeness, and ill-usage. A long day of crushing her own wants and giving all her energy to winning and pleasing.

She'd deal with this latest aggravation later.

Clevedon first.

She turned to face him, bracing her hands against the edge of the disgracefully cluttered worktable.

She took pride in the neatness and order of her shop, a stunning contrast to life in her parents' household, or what had passed for a household. But it didn't matter what he thought of the disarray, she told herself. How would he know the difference between how a workroom ought and ought not to be maintained? And what did he care?

"You're not to come here again," she said. "Ever."

"That suits me," he said. "This is the last place on earth I'd wish to be."

"You're not to buy my daughter any more gifts," she said.

"Why did you think I would?"

"Because she's a conniving little minx who knows how to wrap men about her finger," she said.

"So like her mother," he said.

"Yes, I connived, and I wrapped you about my finger. But now I'm done with that. What did I ever want of you but your betrothed?"

Liar, liar.

"We're not betrothed," he said, "thanks to you."

"Thanks to me?" she said with a mocking laugh. Mocking him. Mocking herself. "You're not betrothed because of *you*. Why didn't you make your so-carefully-rehearsed speech to that beautiful girl? The speech to which you devoted a mere half hour for the most important question of your life—"

"Clara doesn't need—"

"But why should you take any trouble, when you take for granted everything you have? You're used to getting whatever you want and losing interest as soon as you get it."

"I love her," he said. "I've loved her since we were children. But you—"

"It's my fault, is it?" she said. "I'm the demon destroying your happiness? Only look at yourself and listen to yourself. Like every other man, you want what you can't have. Like every other man, you'll stay interested—even obsessed—until you get it. You came here this evening because you can't think straight—because it drives you mad not to have something you want."

His color darkened, and she saw his hands clench. "If you think that something is you, think again," he said. "I don't want you. But you want me, and I feel so sorry for you."

Inwardly, it was as though she'd walked into a wall. Her head pounded and pain shot deep, deep inside.

She wanted him. She wanted to be the heartbreakingly beautiful girl he loved. She wanted to be someone else: a woman who mattered to him and to all those who mattered, instead of a nobody to be used and discarded. She wanted everything her family had taken away: every opportunity they'd squandered and all the damage done to her future long, long ago, generations before she was born.

Outwardly, she didn't blink. "Then send me more customers," she said. "I find money a great comfort in any calamity."

She heard his sharp inhale. "By gad," he said. "By gad, you're a devil."

"And you're an angel?" She laughed.

He crossed the room, and in that instant she knew what would happen. But she was a devil and so was he, and she only stood there, gripping the table, daring him, daring her own destruction.

* * *

He stood over her, looking down into her dark, brilliant eyes. They mocked and taunted, as her voice had mocked and taunted him with the ways he lied to himself and everyone else.

The truth was, he was no angel. Three years ago, he'd abandoned his responsibilities, gone abroad, and found himself. He'd settled in Paris because he could be free there as he could never be in England. In Paris, his hunger for excitement and pleasure could do no damage to those he loved.

She promised nothing but damage, everywhere.

She was wrong for him in every possible way, and especially wrong at this time. Why couldn't he have met her a year ago, three years ago?

But when he looked down into her eyes, right and wrong meant nothing. He and she were two of a kind, and like called to like, and he wanted her. And she, who read him so easily and so well, had spoken one needle-sharp truth after another.

Yes, he'd go on wanting her until he had her.

Then it would be done, and he could be free of her.

He cupped her face and tilted it upward and brought his mouth to hers and kissed her. She turned her head away, breaking the kiss. He trailed his mouth along her cheek, to her ear and down. Her scent rose from her neck, and all the air he breathed then was her and all he knew then was her.

"Fool," she said. "Fool."

"Yes," he said. He wrapped his arms about her and pulled her away from the table and dragged her up against him.

That was right, no matter how desperately wrong it was. It was right, the warmth of her back against his forearm, and the way her supple body fit to his, as though it had been tailored special in some infernal shop where Beelzebub presided.

He was done for, caught. Heat pumped through him, fever-fierce, and scorched his reason.

This was all he'd ever wanted: possession. Images burned in his mind—the cool way she'd taken her leave of him in the opera house . . . men colliding with one another or stumbling over their own feet when she passed . . . the way she had of turning her head . . . the graceful arc of her fan, sweeping over her dress . . . the light movement of her hand touching her shoulder in the place where he'd touched her. All this and more—every moment in her company—all of it was swirling in his mind and racing through his veins when he took her into his arms.

This was what he'd wanted. To hold her. To keep her. *Mine.*

Unthinking, like a brute.

With one arm he swept the table clear. Pieces of cloth, bits of lace and ribbons wafted down, while spools of thread, thimbles, and other bric-a-brac clattered to the floor.

He lifted her onto the table.

She set her hand against his chest, to push him away. He laid his hand over hers, and held hers there, over his pounding heart. He lifted her chin and dared her, his gaze locking with hers. Her eyes were wide and so dark, as dark as night. That was where he wanted to be: lost in the darkness, the unknowable place that was Noirot.

Noirot. That was all he knew. He didn't know if that was truly her name. He didn't know her Christian name. He didn't know whether she'd ever had a husband. It didn't matter.

She brought her hands up and grasped his head and

pulled him to her. She wrapped her legs about his hips and kissed him in that wild way of hers, holding nothing back, and demanding the same *everything* from him.

He gave it, too, in a mad, hungry kiss, while his hands moved greedily over her, wanting and wanting, endlessly wanting. He'd stored it up for so long. Mere weeks had passed since he met her, yet it seemed forever that he'd wanted her. It seemed an eternity he'd lived in dreams and fantasies and the memories that came unbidden, haunting his days and nights. Now he wasn't dreaming. Now he was alive, finally, after sleepwalking for a lifetime.

Under his hands, silk and muslin and lace rustled, the sound so intimate, inviting possession. But everywhere he found obstacles, layer upon layer of her curst *fashion* between his hands and her skin. He slid his hand over her bodice, seeking skin, remembering the velvety miracle of hers, and its warmth. The memory was maddening, because he couldn't touch her in the way he wanted, lingeringly. For all his demented heat, he knew they had little time, no time, only a moment. They'd met at the wrong time and they were not meant for each other and this was all he'd have.

No time.

He dragged up her skirt and petticoats and slid his hand up over the fine muslin drawers. Awareness crackled, electric: of the smooth flesh under his hand . . . its heat warming the thin fabric . . . the sweet fullness of her thighs . . .

But they had no time. He found the opening to the drawers. He heard her sharp inhalation as his fingers slid over the softness there. Then, as he stroked, she gave a little, unwilling cry, which she quickly smothered against his mouth.

He knew what he was doing. A part of him knew where they were and how mad it was. A part of him knew he'd closed the door behind him, but hadn't locked it. A part of him knew this was a room anyone might enter at any moment. All this was in his mind, in the smallest part of his mind. The awareness hovered and nagged, a low, urgent warning: *Make haste, make haste*.

He was a fool and he ought to be mortified. After all this time, to be no more than a schoolboy, wanting a girl, and stealing a moment for a furtive and hurried coupling.

But he couldn't stop.

She reached down and unbuttoned his trousers, and he gasped against her mouth as she touched him, her hand grasping his swollen shaft, and sliding up and down, and his mind went dark, and there was only need and heat.

He pushed her hand away, and pushed into her. She gave another little cry, again quickly stifled, and then there was only the sound of their breathing, ragged and harsh, as he thrust again and again, merely a brute, possessing, mindless.

Mine.

He felt her nails dig into his arms and he felt her body shudder as pleasure caught her, but that was all. She didn't cry out. He heard only the sound of her breath, quick and shallow.

He wanted more, endless more, but he'd waited too long, wanted too long, and when her muscles contracted about him so fiercely at her climax, his control shattered. Pleasure pounded through him like a live thing, dragging him to a precipice, and over. And down he went, in a surge of triumph so ferocious that he never thought of pulling away. It was too late, too late. He felt her spasms as her pleasure peaked again, and he heard her hoarse cry, damning him to hell, and happiness flooded him, and he spilled into her, in a fiery rush of relief and raging joy.

Marcelline did not want to cling to him, but she had to, or she'd slide off the table and slither to the floor in a limp heap. Her heart had slowed from its frenzy, and now beat slow and fierce, a sledgehammer at her ribs.

Oh, she was a fool, the greatest fool there ever was! She could have lived in blissful ignorance. She could have supposed all men were the same and coupling was a relief for strong feeling as well as a great pleasure.

Now she knew that the simple act could be volcanic, and the world could begin and end in a few minutes, leaving everything upended, the universe destroyed and rebuilt, and nothing as it had been before.

But the day had offered one injury after another. What was one more catastrophe?

She'd made a fatal mistake, and it wouldn't be the first time. She'd survived others. She'd survive this.

He held her still, so tightly, his powerful arms bracing her back. She needed to push him away. She should have done it long since, at least at the critical moment. She knew one couldn't rely on a man to remember to withdraw at such a time. But she couldn't be relied on, either. She'd wanted him inside her. She'd wanted him to be *hers* and hers alone, even if it was only for a moment, only for this once. And she hadn't wanted to let go.

Even now.

She let herself wallow for one more moment in the strength and warmth enveloping her. She let herself inhale his scent, purely male and purely his. She let her cheek graze his—and somehow that seemed more intimate than anything they'd done, though he stood between her legs, though she felt his shaft slipping from her and the wetness of his seed . . . the seed he'd spilled inside her because she hadn't the wit or will to prevent it. And that, too—their savage, desperate coupling, for she wouldn't call it lovemaking, never, never—had seemed a greater intimacy than if they'd lain naked in bed, enjoying each other at their leisure.

But she was a fool, and there was the beginning and end of it.

"You must let go," she said. Her voice was thick.

He tightened his hold, his arms like iron bands.

"You must let go," she said.

"Wait," he said. "Wait."

"We haven't time." She kept her voice low. "They'll want me for dinner, and someone will come. You can't stay, in any case. You can't stay," she repeated. "And you must never come back."

She felt him tense.

"We can't leave it like this," he said.

"We shouldn't have begun it."

"Too late for that."

"It's done," she said, "and I'm done with you and you're done with me." She pushed, and this time he let go. She found her handkerchief and made quick work of cleaning herself, then pushed her petticoat and skirt down.

While she attended to herself, he put his clothing in order.

She started to get down from the table, but he must be a glutton for punishment—or, more likely, he truly was done, and touching her again meant nothing to him— because he caught her by the waist and lifted her down in the same easy way he'd lifted her up, as though she weighed nothing.

She remembered how easily and gently he'd lifted

Lucie out of his lap and into her arms. She remembered the wistful smile he'd bent on her child. Her throat tightened and she had all she could do not to weep.

She'd heard, she wasn't sure where or when, that he'd lost a sister at a young age . . .

But what did it matter?

She was starting toward the door, steeling herself to watch him walk out of her life forever, when she heard the thud.

Leonie would have finished locking up the shop long before now, and she would have made sure nobody surprised Marcelline with an interruption. No one ought to be downstairs at present. The family ought all to be upstairs, setting out dinner.

"Wait," she said in an undertone.

She went to the door and pressed her ear to it. Nothing.

"I thought I heard something," he said softly. "Erroll? Would she—"

"No. Not after we close up shop. She's not allowed, but she wouldn't come, in any case. She's afraid of the dark." That had started after she recovered from the cholera. That and other anxieties. "Be quiet, will you?"

Another thump. Someone was out there, stumbling about in the darkness.

He reached for the door handle. "I'll deal with—"

"Don't be stupid," she whispered. *"You can't be here."*

Carefully she opened the door. She looked down the passage in the direction the sound had come from. She saw a faint light in the little office where Leonie kept her ledgers. There, lately, they'd been storing Marcelline's designs, in a locked box. And there, today, they'd set out their bait.

Her heart began to race.

She slipped through the door into the gloomy passage.

She heard his soft footstep behind her. She stopped and gestured at him to stay in the workroom.

"Don't be—"

She put her hand over his mouth. "I have to deal with this," she hissed. "It's business. It's our spy. We've been waiting for her."

He was shattered, still.

That was the only excuse he had for heeding her, and as an excuse, it lasted but a moment.

He ought not to be here, certainly not at this hour, after the shop was closed.

But the shop . . . *A spy?* Had not Clara said something about—

Clara!

With the thought of her, cold shame washed over him. Betrayal. He'd betrayed his friend, his future wife.

My wife, my wife, he told himself. He smoothed his neckcloth as though he could smooth over what he'd done. He tried to imbed her image in his mind, to engrave the picture of his future, the one he'd always supposed was the right, the only possible one. He would wed the sweet, beautiful girl he'd loved since she was a child, the fair, blue-eyed child he'd met when he was still grieving for his sister. She had a sweet innocence like Alice's and she looked up to him the way Alice had looked up to her big brother. He'd always assumed he'd marry Clara and take care of her and protect her forever.

But at the first excuse, and with the slightest encouragement, he'd run away from her and stayed away; and after three years of indulging himself, he still wasn't satisfied. No, he must betray her trust within a few days of returning to her.

But the shame wasn't strong enough to wipe out the

recollection of what had happened minutes ago or the sensation of the earth having shifted on its axis.

Never mind, never mind.

He'd had Noirot and he was done with her.

And here he was, standing like an idiot, while she— What the devil was she about?

"No!" someone shrieked.

He moved noiselessly into the passage. A faint glow a few steps down from the workroom showed an open doorway.

"I hope Mrs. Downes has paid you well for betraying my trust," he heard Noirot say. "Because you'll never work in this trade again. I'll see to it."

"You can't hurt me," the higher-pitched voice answered. "You're finished. Everyone knows you're the duke's whore. Everyone knows you lift your skirts for him, practically under his bride's nose."

"Regardless what anybody knows or doesn't know, I recommend you give me back those patterns, and not make matters worse for yourself. There's only one way in and out, Pritchett. And you won't get past me."

"Won't I?"

Another crash, as of furniture knocked over. A clatter of broken crockery. A screech of rage.

He didn't care what Noirot had said about her dealing with this. He didn't care that he oughtn't to be discovered here. A business problem was none of his affair, but this was getting out of hand. In a minute, the others would hear the noise and come running downstairs. Erroll might well escape her nursemaid and run down with the others, and be hurt by a flying missile.

All this raced through his mind while he moved quietly toward the doorway. An object—a bowl or vase or pot or some such—sailed through the door and crashed against the wall inches from his head. He burst into the room in time to see a woman throw an inkstand at Noirot. As she dodged, Noirot tripped over a toppled chair and fell. He heard another crash. Looking that way, he saw an overturned lantern on the desk and the flames licking over the stacks of papers there. In the blink of an eye, the flames leapt to the window curtains and raced upward.

The woman ran past him. She was carrying something, but he did not try to stop her. Noirot was struggling to get up, and the fire was racing from the window curtains to shelves of books and papers. One corner of the room was in flames already. His mind flashed over the materials he'd seen in the showroom. There would be more materials of their trade elsewhere, in storerooms and workrooms: heaps of highly combustible wrapping papers and boxes as well as cloth of all kinds.

Already the flames were too high for him to smother easily.

He made his decision in a fraction of a heartbeat. He couldn't chance fighting the fire. In minutes they'd be trapped in an inferno.

Clutching the precious portfolio, Pritchett pushed through the rear door into the yard, and ran without once looking back, all the way to Cary Street. Only then did she stop to catch her breath. She saw the smoke rising from the shop, and she felt a pang. She hoped the child wasn't hurt. She'd planned so carefully, then madame had thrown everything into disarray with her abrupt decision to send the seamstresses home early. Pritchett had chased them out, saying she'd tidy the workroom. When the duke came, she'd breathed a prayer of thanks. She'd thought he'd keep madame occupied for a time.

But it had all gone wrong, and now not only madame but his grace knew what she'd done.

Never mind, never mind. She had the patterns, and Mrs. Downes's money would allow her to start fresh elsewhere. Frances Pritchett would take a new name, and nobody would be the wiser.

She glanced upward again. Above the rooftops, against the starry sky, the smoke hovered like a black thundercloud.

Marcelline saw the flames, and stared for a moment in shocked disbelief. Then, "Lucie!" she screamed.

Clevedon was dragging her up from the floor, dragging her to the door. She heard shouts from upstairs. They'd heard the noise or smelled the smoke

"Out!" Clevedon shouted. "Everybody out! *Now!*"

A thumping and clatter from above. More shouting. *"Everybody!"* he roared.

Marcelline started toward the stairs. He pulled her back.

"Lucie!" she cried. She heard more noise from above. "Why don't they come?" Had the fire risen so fast? Were they trapped? *"Lucie!"*

But he was dragging and pushing her down the passage toward the front door. "No!" she cried. "My daughter!"

"They're coming," he said.

Then she heard the footsteps on the stairs and the voices.

Behind her came his voice: "Out, out, everybody. Quickly. Noirot, for God's sake, take them all outside."

In the dark, smoke-filled passage, she couldn't see them. But she heard Lucie's voice, and her sisters' and Millie's.

Clevedon shoved her. *"Out!"* he shouted, his voice savage.

She went out, and it was only then, when they were all out of the smoke and confusion that she discovered Lucie wasn't with them after all.

"Where's Lucie?" Marcelline shouted over the din of panicked neighbors and the clatter of carriages and neighing horses.

"But she was with us."

"She was just here."

"I had her, ma'am," Millie said. "But she broke away— and I thought she was running to you."

No. No. Marcelline's gaze went to the burning building. Her mind shrank from the thought.

"Lucie!" she shouted. Her sisters echoed her. The street was filling with gawkers. Her gaze raced over the crowd but no, there was no sign of her. There wouldn't be. Lucie wasn't brave at night. She wouldn't run into a crowd of strangers.

"The doll!" Sophy cried. "She wanted to take the doll. There wasn't time."

"But she couldn't have gone back," Leonie said, her voice high, panicked.

Marcelline started to run back into the shop. Her sisters grabbed her. She fought.

"Marcelline, *look*," Sophy said in a hard voice.

Flames boiled in the windows. The showroom was a bonfire of garish colors made of silks and satins and laces and cottons.

"Lucie!" Marcelline screamed. *"Lucie!"*

Clevedon had counted heads as they passed through the door. He'd heard their voices outside the building. He was sure they were all safely out.

But he'd scarcely stepped out onto the pavement when he heard Noirot scream for her child.

No. Dear God, no. Don't let her be in there.

He ran back in.

"Lucie!" he shouted. "Erroll!"

The fire was spreading over the ground floor and flowing upward, hissing, crackling. Through the smoke, he could scarcely make out the stairs. He found them mainly by memory, and ran up.

"Lucie! Erroll!"

He kept calling, straining to hear, and at last, as he felt his way along the first-floor passage, he heard the terrified cry.

"Lucie!" he shouted. "Where are you, child?"

"Mama!"

The smoke was thick and choking. He could barely hear her above the fire's noise. He very nearly missed her. Had he passed that spot a moment sooner or later, he wouldn't have caught the muffled cry. But where was it coming from? "Lucie!"

"Mama!"

He searched frantically, and it was partly by sight and partly by sound and partly by moving his hands over the place where the cry seemed to come from that led him to the low door. It was under the stairs leading to the second floor. She might have hidden or played there before, or it simply might have been the first door she found.

He wrenched the door open.

Darkness. Silence.

No, please. Don't let her be dead. Give me a chance, please.

Then he made out the little form, huddled in a corner.

He scooped her up. She had the doll clutched tightly against her chest, and she was shaking. "It's all right," he said, his voice rough—with the smoke, with fear, with relief. She turned her face into his coat and sobbed.

He cradled her head in his hand. "It's all right," he said. "Everything will be all right."

Everything *would* be all right, he promised himself. It had to be. She *would not* die. He wouldn't let her.

Behind him the fire hissed and crackled, racing toward them.

Marcelline fought bitterly, but they wouldn't let her go back for Lucie. Now it was too late.

The fire engine had come quickly, but not quickly enough. The hose poured water into the shop, but the flames had told her how fierce and fast the fire was. With luck, they could keep it from spreading to the adjoining shops.

As to hers . . .

Nothing could have survived that furious fire. She didn't want to survive, either, but they wouldn't let her go back.

She was sick, so sick that her legs would not hold her. She sank to her knees on the pavement, her arms wrapped about her, shivering as though she were naked. She couldn't weep. The pain burned too deep for that. She only rocked there, in a black misery beyond any she'd ever known. Mama, Papa, Charlie, Cousin Emma—what she'd felt, losing them, was mere sorrow.

She was only dimly, distantly aware of her sisters on either side—their touch on her head, her shoulders . . . the sound of their sobs.

Around her was pandemonium and she was in Hell, and Hell was a black eternity where the only sensation was pain, sharp as a knife.

Lucie. Lucie. Lucie.

* * *

Clevedon had to decide in an instant, and he decided against the stairs. The fire seemed to be moving from back to front on the western side of the building. That meant a conflagration might await them at the foot of the stairs. He went the other way, to the back, but keeping to the side of the passage where he'd found Lucie, in hopes that the floor would hold. Above the showroom and workrooms, packed with combustibles, the fire would burn more fiercely.

That was the gamble, at any rate.

"Hold tight," he told Lucie. "And don't look." Her arms tightened about his neck and she buried her face in his neckcloth. She didn't release the doll, and he was aware of one of its limbs tapping his shoulder blade. A bizarre thing to notice, and he wanted to break the doll in pieces for the trouble it had caused, but she needed it, and the doll was the least of their problems.

He hurried to the back, keeping close to the wall to find his way, because the way was utter darkness. But he remembered seeing a back door on the ground floor. That would give way to a yard. All he needed was a back stair or a window or even a light closet, which would contain a window.

He came to the end of the passage, and his outstretched hand struck plaster. He'd found no door frame on the way. Now his hand met only flat wall.

No. There had to be a way out.

The smoke was thickening, the heat unbearable. Holding fast to Lucie, he slid one hand along the hot wall and struck wood—a window. He didn't even try to wrench it open.

"Hold very tight, sweet," he told Lucie. "Don't look and don't let go, no matter what."

Then he kicked as hard as he could, and glass shattered, and wood, too. He kicked and kicked, knocking out the glass and the crosspieces. The night was dark, and he looked down, dreading what he'd find: a long leap down, for these buildings rarely offered any purchase for climbing. But his luck held, and below, he made out the outline of the yard's back wall. Circling Lucie with his arms, to shield her from sharp ends of glass and wood, he climbed over the sill and dropped to the wall, then down, onto the roof of a privy on the other side of the wall. Though the air was smoky, it was cooler, and he could make out the faint glow of a street lamp through the smoke.

Yes, he said silently. *Thank you.*

His throat closed up and, cradling the child he'd feared he couldn't save, he wept.

Marcelline was sunk so deep in grief that she scarcely noticed anything else.

At some point, though, she became aware of the atmosphere about her lightening, and the clamor abating. The street grew so hushed that she could hear clearly the hiss and gurgle of water streaming into the shop and the voices of the fire company men giving orders.

Even while she listened, their voices subsided, too, and someone cried, "Look! Look there!"

Noise again, but different. Glad noise. Cheering.

She felt hands on her shoulders, pulling. She lifted her head and thought at first it was a dream, a cruel dream.

That could not be Clevedon . . . that great, hulking, blackened and ragged mess . . . carrying . . . carrying a blackened bundle. Little legs dangling out from the edge of a dress . . . rumpled stockings . . . one foot missing a shoe.

Hands were pulling Marcelline to her feet and she

shook her head and closed her eyes and opened them again. But it wasn't a dream.

It was Clevedon, and that was Lucie in his arms.

Alive?

Marcelline couldn't make her feet move. She only stood, swaying and confused, like one come back from the dead.

He walked out of the nightmare—the black monster behind him, flames still flickering in the windows.

He walked toward her, his big hand cradling Lucie's head. She had her arms wrapped about his neck, her face buried in his chest. But as he neared, Marcelline saw the doll dangling from Lucie's hands. She was holding tightly, to him, to the doll.

She was alive.

"Oh," Marcelline said. And that was all she could say.

He came to her and then he looked down at the child he held. Taking his hand away from her head, he said, "It's all right, Erroll. You're the bravest girl there ever was. You can look now."

As he gave her back to her mother he said gruffly, "I made her promise not to look. I thought it best she not see."

He'd seen, though. He'd stared in the face of a fiery death. He'd faced it to save her daughter.

"Thank you," Marcelline said. Two words. Inadequate, beyond inadequate. But there were no words. These were all the language gave her. All else was in her heart, and that could not be said and could never be eradicated.

The shop stood in blackened ruins. The stench drifted over Chancery Lane and Fleet Street.

It might have been far worse, Clevedon heard people say. The wind had not carried the fire east to the shop on the other side of Chancery Lane, and the fire engine had arrived in time to stop it from destroying the shop next door.

He knew it might have been infinitely worse. They might have lost a child.

Lucie rode her mother's hip, and Noirot walked with her, back and forth, back and forth, in the street. Now and again her gaze turned upward, to her shop, in ruins.

Her sisters stood nearby, under a lamp post, standing guard over a paltry pile of belongings they must have grabbed before escaping the house. He watched their gazes swing from the shop to Noirot and back to the shop. The redhead held the doll. Even through the smoky atmosphere choking the gaslight he could read the despair in their faces.

They'd lost all their materials—the most expensive element of their business—along with all their tools and records. They'd lost everything.

But the child was alive.

He was aware of the ink-stained fellows from the various London journals converging on the scene. He ought to make himself scarce. The night was dark, the smoke made it darker, and with any luck, nobody had recognized him.

But he couldn't turn his back on the three women and the little girl, all of them on the street, literally. No shop, no home, no money. He doubted anything could be salvaged from the blackened building.

Still, they had fire insurance, else the engine wouldn't have come. And he knew that Noirot was practical and mercenary to an aggravating degree. She would have money in a bank, or safely invested.

But money in the bank wouldn't put a roof over her this night, and he doubted she could have saved enough to rebuild her business in short order.

He stood for a moment, telling himself he couldn't linger. He'd already dishonored his friendship with Clara and betrayed her love. But only he and Noirot knew that. What Clara didn't know couldn't hurt her, and he wouldn't hurt her for worlds.

Find another way to help them, he counseled himself. There were discreet ways. One could aid those in need without courting notoriety. It was notoriety, furthermore, that would do Noirot no good.

He remembered what the other woman had screeched at her: *Everyone knows you're the duke's whore. Everyone knows you lift your skirts for him, practically under his bride's nose.*

He remembered what Noirot had told him, early on: *What self-respecting lady would patronize a dressmaker who specializes in seducing the lady's menfolk?*

It was time to leave, long past time. The sooner he left, the sooner he could send help.

Marcelline was weary, so weary. What now? Where would they go?

She ought to know what to do, but her brain was numb. She could only hold her daughter and stare at the black ruin of her business, her home, the life she'd built for her family.

"Let me hold her for a bit," Sophy said. "You're tired."

"No, not yet." Lucie still trembled, and she hadn't said a word since Clevedon carried her out.

"Come." Sophy put her hands out. "Erroll, will you come to Aunt Sophy, and let Mama rest for a moment?"

Lucie lifted her head.

"Come," said Sophy.

Lucie reached for her, and Sophy unhitched her from

Marcelline's hip and planted the child on her own. "There," she said. "It's all right, love. We're all safe." She started to walk with her, murmuring comfort.

Leonie said, "We've insurance. We've money in the bank. But above all, we're all alive."

Completely true, Marcelline thought. They were all alive. Lucie was alive, unhurt. Everything else . . .

Oh, but it would be hard. They hadn't enough insurance. They hadn't enough money in the bank. They would have to start over. Again.

Leonie put her arms about her. Marcelline couldn't cry, though she wanted to. It would be a relief to cry. But tears wouldn't come. She could only rest her head on her sister's shoulder. She had her daughter, she told herself. She had her sisters. Right now, that was all that mattered.

All the same, they couldn't stay like this, in the street. She needed to think. She raised her head and moved away and straightened her posture. "We'd better go to an inn," she said. "We can send to Belcher." He was their solicitor.

"Yes, of course," Leonie said. "He'll advance us some money—enough to pay for lodgings, I daresay."

This area of London, where the Inns of Court lay, was the lawyers' domain. Their solicitor's office was only a short distance away. The question was whether they'd find him at his office at this hour.

"We'll find a ticket porter, and send to Belcher," Marcelline said. "Sophy, give Lucie back to me. We need you to talk sweet to one of the reporters, and get a pencil and paper to write a note to Belcher. I think I saw your friend Tom Foxe in the crowd."

While Marcelline took Lucie back, she searched the area for the publisher of *Foxe's Morning Spectacle*.

She became aware of a flurry of motion.

The Duke of Clevedon emerged from the shadows,

Tom Foxe hot on his heels. "Your grace, I know our readers will be eager to hear of your heroic rescue—"

"Foxe!" Sophy cried. "Precisely the man I was looking for."

"But his grace—"

"My dear, you know he won't talk to the likes of you." Sophy led him away.

Clevedon came to Marcelline. "You need to come with me," he said.

"No," she said.

"You can't stay here," he said.

"We're sending for our solicitor," she said.

"You can send for your solicitor tomorrow," he said. "He'll have gone home by now. It must be close to midnight. You all need something to eat and a place to sleep."

"You need to go away," she said, lowering her voice. "Sophy will keep Foxe off for as long as she can, but you've given them a prime story, and he won't be kept off forever."

"In that case, we've not a moment to lose," Clevedon said. He held out his soot-blackened hands to Lucie. "Erroll, would you like to see my house?"

Lucie lifted her head from Marcelline's shoulder. "Is the c-carriage th-there?" Her voice shook, but she was talking.

Relief surged, so powerful that Marcelline swayed a little. She hadn't realized how terrified she'd been, that Lucie would never speak again. For months after recovering from the cholera, she'd had terrible nightmares. It had left her a little more fearful and temperamental than before. Children were resilient; that didn't mean terrible experiences couldn't damage them.

"I've lots of carriages," he said. "But we'll need to take a hackney to get there."

"Are there d-dolls?"

"Yes," he said. "And a dollhouse."

"Y-yes," Lucie said. "I'll c-come."

She practically leapt out of her mother's arms into his.

"Clevedon," Marcelline said. But how could she lecture him, when he'd saved Lucie's life? "Your grace, this isn't wise."

"It isn't convenient, either," he said. "But it must be done."

And he walked away with her daughter.

Chapter Eleven

This gateway cannot possibly be described correctly, as the ornaments are scattered in the utmost profusion, from the base to the attic, which supports a copy of Michael Angelo's celebrated lion. Double ranges of grotesque pilasters inclose eight niches on the sides, and there are a bow window and an open arch above the gate.

Leigh Hunt (describing Northumberland House),
The Town: Its Memorable Characters and Events,
Vol. 1, 1848

*L*ike its present owner, Clevedon House mocked convention. While other noble families had torn down their ancient houses overlooking the river and moved westward into Mayfair, while commercial enterprises took over what the nobles had abandoned, the Earls and Dukes of Clevedon stubbornly remained. One of the last of the palaces that had once lined the Strand, Clevedon House sprawled along the southwestern end of the street, overlooking Charing Cross. It was a great Jacobean pile, complete with turrets and a heavily ornamented gateway topped by a bay window that was topped by an arch upon which a lion stood roaring at the heavens. Marcelline had passed it countless times on her way to one of the many shops and warehouses in the neighborhood.

Within, she found it even larger and more imposing than the street front promised. A marbled vestibule led to an immense entrance hall. At the other end, apparently a mile away, a crimson carpet climbed a great, white marble staircase whose ornate brass balustrades seemed, at this distance, to be made of golden lace. Black, bronze-topped columns adorned the yellow marble walls.

As Marcelline and her family uneasily followed Clevedon past a gaping porter into the entrance hall, a straight-backed, dignified man not dressed in livery appeared, magically, it seemed, from nowhere.

"Ah, here is Halliday," Clevedon said. "My house steward."

Halliday, apparently inured to his grace's erratic habits, did no more than widen his eyes momentarily as he took in the duke's smoky visage, his torn, blackened clothes, and the equally dirty, bedraggled child in his arms.

"There's been a fire," Clevedon said shortly. "These ladies have been driven from their home."

"Yes, your grace."

Lucie still in his arms, Clevedon gestured the house steward aside. They spoke briefly, in low voices. Marcelline couldn't make out what they said. Too stunned and tired to question anything at this point, she left them to it.

Leonie had wandered away a few paces to study the candelabrum that stood on marble bases, one on each side of the bottom of the staircase. When she came back, she reported in a whisper, "They would have paid at least a thousand apiece for each candelabra. Was Warford House like this?"

"This makes Warford House look like a parson's cottage," Marcelline said. "It may even rival Buckingham House."

"No wonder Lady Warford wanted his grace back from France," Sophy said. What if Lady Clara succumbed to another, lesser fellow's lures? *Quelle horreur!*"

Marcelline saw Halliday withdraw, the discussion over. He signaled to a hovering footman, who approached, took his orders, and hurried away. Not two minutes passed before a great tide of servants began flowing into the entrance hall.

Clevedon approached. "Everything is in train," he said. "Halliday and Mrs. Michaels, my housekeeper, will look after you. But I'm obliged, as you no doubt understand, to take myself elsewhere." He relinquished Lucie to her mother, crossed into one of the side rooms on the ground floor, and vanished.

Marcelline hadn't time to wonder at his sudden departure—not that there was anything to wonder at. She understood that he needed to disassociate himself from them. He was merely providing refuge. It was philanthropy, nothing personal.

That explained, she supposed, why the servants treated them so kindly.

As Mrs. Michaels led them up the staircase, she provided the kind of running monologue housekeepers typically offered when taking visitors through a great house. The Noirot family learned that Clevedon House contained a hundred fifty rooms, more or less—"Who can be troubled to count them all?" Sophy whispered to Marcelline—and that it had been renovated and expanded over the centuries. She led them into one of the pair of wings his grace's grandfather had added, which extended into a tree-lined garden.

The staff, Mrs. Michaels assured them, were accustomed to accommodating house guests on short notice. "Lady Adelaide, his grace's aunt, was with us quite recently," she said as she led them into a set of apartments in the north wing overlooking the garden. "Their ladyships his aunts often stay with us, whether his grace is in Town or not, and we pride ourselves on having the north wing always ready for company."

In between pointing out some of the more spectacular furnishings as well as works of art, the housekeeper sent maids and footmen scurrying hither and yon, to make up fires in the rooms and find fresh clothing and draw hot baths.

True, the servants couldn't completely conceal their curiosity about the new houseguests, but they seemed to accept the women calmly enough.

In fact, when Marcelline protested that her assigned bedroom was more than sufficient for them all—it was easily as large as the first floor of her shop—Mrs. Michaels looked shocked.

"We don't want to cause an upheaval," Marcelline said. "It's only for the night." The bed was enormous, and they'd slept all three sisters plus Lucie in a single, far smaller bed more than once.

"His grace's orders were quite specific," Mrs. Michaels said firmly. "The rooms are nearly ready. We're merely seeing to the fires. His grace stressed the dangers of taking a chill after the recent ordeal. And perfectly right he was. Shocks like that are very weakening to the balance of the body. He was worried, in particular, about the little girl. But we've a good blaze now, in the sitting room." She ushered them into one of two slightly smaller rooms adjoining Marcelline's bedroom.

The housekeeper's shrewd gaze went to Lucie, who'd

forgotten her initial shyness and was wandering about the sitting room, gaping at the grandeur about her. "His grace said you would want a nursemaid for the young lady."

Millie had disappeared shortly after Clevedon emerged with Lucie from the burning building. Since the maid was the one who'd let Lucie get away from her, she must have decided not to remain to face the consequences.

"Really, it isn't necessary," Marcelline said. "I can manage."

Mrs. Michaels's eyebrows went up. "Now, madam, I know you've had a dreadful time of it, but here are Mary and Sarah." She beckoned, and two young maids stepped out from among the swarm of servants and curtseyed— quite as though the Noirots were persons of quality. "Very good with children, I assure you. I know you can do with a little rest and quiet while the maids tend to Miss Noirot. And his grace said particularly that the young lady was to see Lady Alice's dollhouse. That was his grace's late sister," she explained in a lower voice to Marcelline. "He said he thought that playing with the dollhouse would take the child's mind off her shocking experience."

She moved to Lucie and, bending down, said gently, "Did his grace not promise you a dollhouse?"

"A dollhouse, yes, he did," Lucie said. She held out the sooty doll, the doll that had nearly killed her, for Mrs. Michaels's inspection. "And Susannah needs a bath."

"And she shall have one," said Mrs. Michaels, not in the least nonplussed. She straightened and put up her hand, and the two young maids drew nearer. "Would you like to have a bath as well? And then a little supper? Would you like to go with Sarah and Mary?"

Lucie looked at Marcelline. "May I go with them, Mama?"

Marcelline looked at the maids. They had eyes for no

one but Lucie, of course. She was recovered enough to be winsome; and bedraggled and dirty though she was, her great blue eyes worked their usual magic on the unsuspecting.

"Yes, you may," Marcelline said.

She would have added, *They are not to indulge your every whim*, but she knew that was a waste of breath. They would pet and spoil Lucie, and she would do as she pleased, and probably drive them mad, as she'd driven Millie mad. It was very difficult to discipline a charming child, even when she was extremely naughty. Lucie, who had the passionate nature and obstinacy of her ancestors, was also gifted with their complete lack of scruples. Being a child, she had not yet learned to get everything she wanted by guile. When her charm didn't work, she threw stupendous temper fits.

Yet she'd had a terrifying time, and the pampering would not go amiss. The dollhouse would draw her mind away from what had happened in the shop. At any rate, it was only for a night, Marcelline told herself while she watched the maids lead Lucie away. And while Lucie played princess, Marcelline would have some quiet time to collect herself and plan what to do next.

It would have been easier if she weren't under Clevedon's roof, if her surroundings didn't remind her of who and what he was . . . apart from being a desirable man who'd belonged to her for a short, short time.

But that was nothing, she told herself. It was lust, no more. From the start, she'd wanted him and he'd wanted her. She'd had him, and that turned out to be more than she'd bargained for.

Still, no matter what she'd bargained for, he was more than simply a desirable man. He was the Duke of Clevedon. She was a shopkeeper. She could never be anything more than a mistress to him. It was a position any of her ancestors would have accepted. But along with the family she had to consider, she had her own aspirations to keep in the front of her mind: the something she'd made of herself, the greater something she meant to be, the work she truly loved.

What was between them was done. It belonged to the past.

She had to think about the future.

They had to find lodgings. They needed a place to work. Sophy would need to deal with the newspapers immediately. Their story was a nine-days' wonder, and Sophy must turn it to account . . . though it might already be too late. Headlines swam in Marcelline's head. The duke's heroics—yes, of course—running into a burning building to save a child—but then the newspapers would speculate about what he was doing there at that hour . . . and why he'd taken the lot of them home with him . . . and what his intended bride would make of it.

"Oh, my God," she said. She clutched her forehead.

"What?" Sophy said. "You're not panicking about Lucie, I hope."

"It's obvious that his grace has ordered his servants to dote on her," Leonie said.

"And what better remedy could she have for her fears than this?" Sophy said with a sweeping gesture at their surroundings. "Nothing but luxury as far as the eye can see. And not one but two maids to slave for her. They'll wash her curst doll, you may depend on it, and style her hair, I don't doubt."

"Not Lucie," Marcelline said. "Lady Clara! Her dress! What on earth are we to do?"

* * *

Pritchett raced to her lodgings, packed, told her land-lady a story about a dying relative, and took a hackney to the Golden Cross Inn at Charing Cross. From there she sent a message to Mrs. Downes, explaining that she intended to board the very next coach to Dover, and if Mrs. Downes wanted any articles from her, she'd better get there quickly. The Royal Mail had left for the General Post Office at half-past seven, but if all went well, Pritchett could hire a post chaise, and would not have to wait for tomorrow's day coach.

Mrs. Downes made her appearance before too long. She made it clear she didn't like being summoned at a late hour to a public inn, and liked still less transacting business in the coach yard. About them, despite the hour, horses were being harnessed, coachmen and postboys fraternized, inn servants came and went, prostitutes tried to lure passengers, and bawds hunted for innocent country lasses.

Ignoring the dressmaker's sour look, Pritchett went straight to the point. "I got more than I expected. Found her portfolio, which they usually keep under lock and key." She took out a drawing.

Mrs. Downes pretended to barely glance at it. "I heard about the fire," she said with a shrug. "She's finished. These are worthless."

Pritchett put the drawing back into the portfolio. "She has insurance and money in the bank. She'll be back in business in a matter of weeks. She's the most determined woman in London. If you don't want these, I'll take them with me. I shouldn't have any trouble doing well with them in the provinces. The patterns are worth their weight in gold, and I know the trick of making them. I can expect to do a great deal better than twenty guineas. Yes, you're quite right. They're more good to me than they are to you."

"You said twenty guineas," Mrs. Downes said.

"That was for the sketchbook," Pritchett said. "And to-night I was in a hurry enough to make it twenty for the portfolio as well. But now you've annoyed me."

"I ought to report you. They hang people for arson."

"I wonder what would happen if I said you put me up to it," Pritchett said. "We'll never know, I suppose. There's my coach." She nodded at a vehicle entering the inn yard. "Fifty guineas. Now or never."

"I don't carry that sort of money with me."

Pritchett tucked the portfolio under her arm, picked up her bag, and started to walk away. She counted under her breath, "One. Two. Three. Four. F—"

"Wait."

Pritchett paused without turning around.

Mrs. Downes walked very quickly toward her. Not a minute later, a very large purse changed hands, and a very short time thereafter, Pritchett stepped into the coaching office to order a post chaise.

Though she and her sisters had made a plan before they collapsed, exhausted, in their beds, Marcelline slept poorly.

She'd watched while one of the maidservants bathed Lucie—and the other one bathed the doll, taking off her filthy little gown and sponging her off—even sponging the soot from her hair—as though it was the most normal thing in the world. They took the doll's dress away to clean, along with Lucie's clothes. Then Lucie had to see the dollhouse. By that time, she had three maidservants wanting to look after her. They moved a dainty little bed into a pretty little room adjoining Marcelline's. And that was where Lucie had wanted to sleep: not with her mother, but in state.

Her child was safe, probably safer than she'd ever been in all her short life. All the same, Marcelline had nightmares. She dreamed that Lucie hadn't escaped the fire, and Marcelline had gone to the mouth of Hell, screaming for her daughter, and she'd heard horrible laughter in answer before the door slammed in her face.

The next morning, when the maid came in with chocolate, Marcelline discovered that she'd slept much later than usual. It was past nine o'clock, she was told, and Lucie was having breakfast with the duke.

She leapt from the bed, rejecting the chocolate. "Where are my sisters?" she said.

They'd agreed to rise by half-past six. The seamstresses had been told to go to the shop at eight. By now they would have arrived and found a charred spot where the shop used to be.

"Mrs. Michaels said we were not to disturb you, Mrs. Noirot," the maid said. "But Miss Lucie was asking for you, and I was told I might wake you."

Noirot didn't burst into the breakfast room, and she didn't seem any more flurried or disordered than usual. Her hair was slightly askew, as always, but in a manner Clevedon felt certain was deliberate, not careless. No matter what happened, she couldn't present herself with anything less than *style*.

Her face was pale, her eyes deeply shadowed. She couldn't have slept well. He hadn't slept well, either, and he'd awakened in low spirits.

But then he'd come down to breakfast and found Lucie, with Joseph the footman's assistance, investigating the sideboard's contents. Seeing her made him smile, and lightened his heart.

Now she sat at his right, enthroned upon a chair piled with pillows. She was happily slathering butter and jam on bread. Her doll sat next to her, on another chair piled with pillows.

"Ah, here is your mother," Clevedon said, while his heart pounded. So stupid it was to pound that way, like a boy's heart upon seeing his first infatuation.

Noirot went to her daughter and kissed her forehead and smoothed her hair.

"Good morning, Mama," Lucie said. "We're going to drive in the carriage after breakfast. There is a very good breakfast on the sideboard. Joseph will help you lift the covers. There are eggs and bacon and all manner of breads and pastries."

"I haven't time for breakfast," Noirot said. "As soon as your aunts come down, we must leave."

Lucie's blue eyes narrowed, and her face set into the hard expression Clevedon had seen before.

"And you will not make a fuss," Noirot said. "You will thank his grace for his kindness—his many kind-nesses—"

"She'll do nothing of the kind," Clevedon said. "We were having an interesting conversation about the doll-house. She's scarcely had time to play with it. She was too sleepy last night. And I promised to drive her in the carriage. I do not see what the great hurry is to be gone."

At this moment, the two sisters entered, looking cross. Doubtless they'd been awakened before they liked, and they were hungry.

"We need to get quickly to the shop and see what can be salvaged," Noirot said. "Someone must be there to meet the seamstresses—if they're there. We should have sent them word last night, but I didn't think of it until this morning. I need them. We need to find a place to work. *We need to make Lady Clara's dress.*"

He ought to wince at the mention of Clara. He ought to feel ashamed, and he did. But not enough to be thrown off the course he'd devised last night, to keep his mind off what had happened in the workroom, and off what he wanted, still, though he'd got what he wanted and was supposed to be done with this woman.

"I dispatched Varley, my man of business, to your shop early this morning, along with a parcel of servants," he said. "They reported that the structure as a whole survived, though the damage is extensive. But the contents that were not reduced to ashes are black, wet, and reeking, as I suspected. We retrieved a set of iron strongboxes, which will be carried up to your rooms as soon as the filth has been cleaned from them."

"Carried up—"

"Varley rescued some account books or some such from wherever you'd hidden them, as well." He gestured at the sideboard. "Everything is in hand. Pray take some breakfast."

"In hand?" she said, and he thought she staggered a bit. But that was his mind, playing tricks. Nothing staggered Noirot.

Yet she sat down hard, in the chair to his left, opposite Lucie.

"Shall I make you a plate, Mama?" Lucie said with a suspicious sweetness. "Joseph will help me." She set down her cutlery, wiped her hands carefully on her napkin, and made to climb down from her throne. The footman Joseph obediently came forward, helped her down, and followed her to the sideboard. She pointed and he dutifully filled the plate according to her directions.

"It's grand to be a duke," the blonde sister said.

"So it is," he said. "I live in a house large enough to accommodate your work without disrupting my own life. I have a good number of servants, all of whom will be happy to do something a little different, if offered. And I possess the resources to assist you, without the least discomfort to myself, in getting your business going again."

Joseph set the filled plate down before Mrs. Noirot, then returned to Lucie, who directed him regarding her aunts' breakfasts.

"Accommodate us?" Noirot said. "You can't be serious."

"I understand that time is of the essence," he said. "You don't wish to lose any more business than can absolutely be helped. I've consulted with Varley on the matter. It's his opinion that a suitable new location can be found within a few days. In the meantime, he agreed that you can do what needs to be done more quickly and easily from here."

"Here," she repeated. "You're suggesting we set up shop in Clevedon House."

"It's the simplest solution," he said.

He knew it was. He'd thought about the problem and little else for most of the night. By concentrating on her business difficulties, he'd kept the other thoughts at bay. "I'm not used to so much drama in my life. I was too excited, you see, to fall asleep. While I lay awake, my mind gnawed on your dilemma."

"It didn't occur to you that your mind might be addled by all the excitement?"

"On the contrary, I believe my mind was sharpened by the experience, in the way that metal is sharpened after being thrust into a fierce flame," he said.

Her dark gaze met his, and then he couldn't block out the memory of their hurried, furious coupling on the worktable: her choked sounds of pleasure, the mad heat and ferocious joy . . .

Business, he told himself. *Stick to business. Order. Logic.*

"Mrs. Michaels can help you organize a proper work space," he said. "You and your sisters may take my vehicles and servants, and purchase what you need to fill the most pressing orders. Your seamstresses may come here, as soon as you like, to start working. If you need additional help, Mrs. Michaels will select the better needlewomen from among the maids."

Her face had gone very white, indeed. Her sisters were watching her. He couldn't tell whether they were alarmed or not. They showed as little of their feelings as she did. But they must have sensed she needed help because the blonde jumped in.

"I like it better than our plan," she said. "Marcelline was going to play cards, to win the money to buy what we needed."

Marcelline.

He was aware of his pulse racing and of the mad excitement that made it race. So ridiculous. Through shipwreck, physical intimacy, catastrophic fire, they'd maintained the polite forms of address. She'd been "Noirot" to him and he was "your grace" or "Clevedon" to her. But now he sat among family members, and they'd revealed who she was to them.

He couldn't say it aloud, but he could feel it on his tongue.

Marcelline. It was a name like a secret, a whisper in the dark.

She was all secrets and guile—and of course she would play cards to get money, he thought.

"We can send for Belcher," the redhead said. "He and your grace's solicitor—Varley, is it?—can draw up papers for a loan."

"Nonsense," Clevedon said. "Whatever your supplies cost can be only a fraction of what we give away to sundry charities every month."

Noirot's—*Marcelline's*—color came and went. "We're not a charity," she said. She leaned toward him, and in a low, choked voice, she added, "I owe you my daughter's life. *Don't make me owe you any more.*"

His heart tightened into a fist, and it beat against his chest. There was a moment of pain so fierce he had to look away and catch his breath.

His gaze went to Lucie, the child he had saved.

Noirot thought it was a debt she owed him, one impossible to repay. She had no way of knowing the value of the gift he'd been given.

He couldn't save Alice. He'd been far away when the accident happened. He knew he could never bring her back. He knew that saving this child could not bring her back.

But he knew, too, that when he'd carried Lucie, alive and unhurt, out of the burning building, he'd felt not only profound relief but a joy greater than anything he could have imagined.

Lucie, with Joseph's help, was settling back upon her throne.

"It isn't the same," he said, scorning to whisper. Let the servants hear, and make what they would of it. "For once, put your pride aside and your need to dominate everybody, and do the sensible thing."

"You're the one who's not being sensible," she said. "Think of the talk."

"My sister is being sensible in that regard, certainly," the redhead said. "We can't accept gifts from you, your grace. We've lost our shop, but we can't lose our reputation."

"We can't give the tittle-tattles ammunition," the blonde said. "Our rivals—"

"We have no rivals," Noirot said, chin up, dark eyes flashing.

He bit back a smile.

"I mean, those who *fancy* themselves our rivals will be sure to tell lurid tales," the blonde said.

He looked at Lucie. "What do you say, Erroll?"

"May I play with the dollhouse?"

"Of course you may, sweetling."

To Noirot he said, "You three drive a hard bargain. A loan it is."

"Thank you," Noirot said. Her sisters echoed her. At her glance, they all rose. "May I leave Lucie in your servants' care, your grace?" she said. "You're all determined to spoil her, and she's not going to discourage you, and I haven't time for a battle of wills. We haven't a minute to lose. We absolutely must have Lady Clara's dress ready by seven o'clock this evening."

He stared at her. "You must be joking," he said. "Your shop burnt down. Surely your customers won't expect you to complete orders *today*."

"You don't understand," Marcelline said. "Lady Clara has nothing to wear to Almack's tonight. I threw out all of her clothes. She must have that dress. I *promised*."

Five o'clock that afternoon

Clevedon House was in a state of what its owner hoped was controlled chaos.

Servants hurried to and fro, some carrying in the

goods the women had shopped for in the morning—what seemed to Clevedon like bales of fabric, along with boxes containing who knew what—while others raced from one part of the house to another, carrying messages or sustenance, fetching this or that from cupboards and closets and even the attics.

A bevy of seamstresses had arrived in the late morning, gaping at their surroundings before they disappeared into the rooms on the first floor set aside for the temporary workplace.

The redhead—Miss Leonie Noirot she turned out to be—at some point assured him that all would settle by tomorrow, once everyone was properly installed and their materials in place. She thanked him more than once for his rescue of the account books and only smiled when he told her that was none of his doing; he wouldn't know a ledger from a book of sermons, never having looked into either item.

The blonde, meanwhile—she was Miss Sophia Noirot—had borrowed paper and pens and ink to write advertising for the newspapers. He'd offered his private study for her use, because Miss Leonie had told him that Sophy needed quiet in which to compose—really, it was like writing a chapter of a novel, she explained—and their work area was too busy, with people coming and going and Marcelline giving orders right and left.

Clevedon had retreated to the library. He could have fled the house altogether, but that seemed irresponsible. He'd started this; he ought to see it through. As it turned out, he was needed more than he'd supposed. Every now and again someone came by with a question only he could answer or a problem only he could solve. Usually, this was one of Noirot's sisters, for madame herself kept scrupulously away, but sometimes it was Mrs. Michaels and occasionally Halliday, regarding one issue or other that puzzled even his omniscience.

The truth was, Clevedon didn't want to flee. He found the enterprise vastly interesting. Every so often, he would stand in the library doorway to watch the hurrying to and fro. He would have liked to watch the women make Clara's dress, but Miss Sophia had tactfully warned him away: The seamstresses would never be able to concentrate with a gentleman about, she said. As it was, the big footmen in their finery threw the women into a flutter.

Clevedon still had doubts they'd be able to finish the dress in time. The materials had not arrived until early afternoon, and what hints he'd caught of the design told him the labor involved would be prodigious.

At present he was scanning a copy of a woman's magazine, *La Belle Assemblée,* that one of his aunts had left behind. Hearing approaching footsteps, he put the magazine down and pushed a heap of invitations on top of it.

The door opened and the footman Thomas announced Lord Longmore, who stormed in close on the servant's heels, black eyes blazing. "Have you taken leave of your senses?" he demanded.

Thomas quietly made himself scarce.

"Good afternoon, Longmore," Clevedon said. "I'm in excellent health, thank you. I regret to say that you seem to be in a state of delirium. I hope it isn't a contagious fever. I've a rather large company in the house at present, and I should hate for them all to come down with whatever is ailing you."

"Don't talk rubbish," Longmore said. "When I read this morning's papers, I thought it was another of their lunatic fantasies—like that nonsense about suicidal scenes with a temperamental dressmaker. And so I attempted to tell my mother, who, as you can well imagine, is in a frenzy."

That brought Clevedon back to earth with a *thud*.

He'd forgotten about Lady Warford. But what difference did it make? He refused to let her nerves and hysterias control his behavior. She was her husband's problem.

"I come here because nothing must do, Mother says, but I must see for myself what my friend is about," Longmore went on. "And what do I discover when I arrive? It turns out that the newspapers, not to mention my mother, have sadly *understated* the case. I find that my friend has settled three unwed women, not in a discreet cottage in Kensington, but in his ancestral home! And along with them another half dozen females—and the servants sweating like coal-carriers, fetching and carrying for *shopkeepers*! With my own eyes I saw Halliday carrying what looked to be a laundry basket. A laundry basket!"

The house steward oversaw the household. He kept his master's books and acted as his secretary. He gave orders. He did not sully his hands with fetching and carrying. If he'd carried a basket, then Halliday was doing it for his own amusement—or as an excuse to appease his curiosity about the strangers in their midst.

Longmore was still ranting. "I know you like to play with convention," he said, "but this— Plague take it, words fail me! Never mind my mother, how am I to look my sister in the eye?"

"Well, that's amusing," Clevedon said.

"Amusing?"

"Considering the women are here still only because of your sister," Clevedon said. "They engaged to make a dress for Clara for this evening, and they seem to believe that nothing—acts of God or man, plague, pestilence, flood, famine, or fire—excuses them from keeping their promise. It is very curious. They seem to view a promise to make a dress in the same uncompromising light you and I would view a debt of honor."

"The dress be damned," Longmore said. "Have you been eating opium? Drinking absinthe? Contracted a fever? The clap, perchance? I understand it goes to the brain. That dressmaker—"

"Which one do you mean?" Clevedon said. "There are three of them."

"Don't play with me," Longmore snapped. "By God, you're enough to try the patience of all the saints and martyrs combined. You'll drive me to call you out. I will not let you make a fool of my sister. You will not—"

He broke off because the door flew open and Miss Sophia hurried into the room. "Your grace, I wonder—"

She stopped short, apparently noticing Longmore belatedly. Or maybe she'd noticed the instant she came through the door, if not before. Clevedon suspected that both sisters were as well supplied with guile as Noirot. For all he knew, Miss Sophia had interrupted on purpose. They'd probably heard Longmore at the other end of the house.

In any case, he would have been hard for her to miss, not only because he was as tall as Clevedon but also because he was standing in her way.

But maybe she'd mistaken him for Clevedon. People did sometimes, from the back or from a distance. They were both large dark-haired men, though Longmore dressed more carelessly.

Whatever the reason, she appeared surprised and stopped short. "I do beg your pardon," she said. "How rude of me to burst in."

"Not at all," Clevedon said. "I told you not to stand

on ceremony with me. We haven't time for ceremony. This is only my friend—or perhaps former friend—Lord Longmore. Longmore, though you don't deserve it, I'll allow you to meet Miss Noirot, one of our esteemed dressmakers."

Longmore, meanwhile, who'd spun around at her abrupt entrance, had not taken his eyes off her. For a moment he appeared dumbstruck. Then he bowed. "Miss Noirot."

"My lord." She curtseyed.

And, oh, it was one of those curtsies, not precisely like Noirot's, but something equally impressive in its own way.

Longmore's black eyes widened.

"What is it, then?" Clevedon said.

Sophia's blue gaze, suspiciously innocent, came back to him. "It's about the notice we're putting in the papers, your grace. I write these all the time, and you would think it'd give me no trouble at all, but I continue to struggle, in spite of having quiet."

She'd heard, Clevedon thought. She'd heard Longmore raging, and she'd stepped in. She was the one who'd written the account for the papers of the famous gown Noirot had worn. She was the one in charge of turning difficulties and scandal to the shop's advantage.

"It's the shock," Clevedon said, playing along. "You can't expect to recover overnight, especially when everything is in a turmoil."

"To be sure, I can't judge my own prose," she said. "Will you give me your opinion?" She shot a glance at Longmore. "If his lordship would pardon the intrusion."

Longmore stalked away and flung himself onto the sofa.

"'Mrs. Noirot begs leave to inform her friends and the public in general,'" she read, "'that she intends re-opening her showrooms very shortly, with a new and elegant assortment of millinery and dresses, in the first style of fashion, on reasonable terms—'"

"Leave out 'reasonable terms,'" Clevedon cut in. "Economies matter to the middling classes. If you want the custom of my friends' ladies, it's better to be unreasonable. If it isn't expensive, they won't value it."

She nodded. "There, you see? Marcelline would have caught that—but I daren't interrupt her. If Lady Clara's dress isn't finished on time, my sister will be devastated."

Clevedon saw Longmore shoot the dressmaker a darkling look from under his thick black eyebrows. "If my mother lets her wear the dress," he muttered.

Blue eyes wide, Sophia turned fully toward him. "Not let her wear the dress? You can't be serious. My sister is *killing herself* to finish that dress."

"My dear girl—" Longmore began.

"Our shop burned down," Sophia said. "My sister's little girl—my niece—the only niece I have—nearly died in that fire. His grace saved her life—he risked his own—he ran into *a burning building.*" Her voice was climbing. "He took us in—he's lent us money to buy supplies—we are all running ourselves ragged to fulfill our obligations to our customers—and you say—you say your mother won't let Lady Clara wear our dr-dress." Her voice shook. Tears shimmered in her blue eyes.

Longmore leapt up from the sofa. "I say," he said. "There's no need to take on."

Sophia drew herself up. "If her ladyship your mother says a word against that dress—against my sister—after what she's endured—I promise you, I shall personally, with my own bare hands, strangle her, marchioness or no."

She threw down the advertisement she'd written and stalked out of the room, slamming the door behind her.

Longmore picked up the piece of paper, opened the door, and went after her.

Clevedon waited until their footsteps had faded. Then he clapped his hands. "Well done, Miss Noirot," he said. "Well done."

Smiling, he quietly closed the door, and returned to perusing *La Belle Assemblée*.

Clevedon had taken the magazine to the writing table. He was making notes when the door opened, only far enough for a bonneted head to make its appearance.

"I'm going," Noirot said. The bonnet withdrew, and she started to close the door.

He rose and started to the door. "Wait."

She stuck her head in again. "I haven't time to wait," she said. "I only wanted you to know the dress is done." She spoke coolly enough, yet he detected the note of triumph in her voice.

He reached the door, and opened it fully.

She had what appeared to be a shrouded body in her arms.

That must be the dress, tucked in among layers of tissue paper, and wrapped, like a mummy, in muslin.

"You're not carrying it yourself," he said. "Where's a footman?" He saw one loitering against the corridor wall. "There. You, Thomas."

"No." She waved Thomas back to his post in the corridor. "I promised to deliver it personally, and it will not leave my hands."

He glanced down at the corpse. "May I see it?" he said.

"Certainly not. I haven't time to unwrap it and wrap it up again. You'll see it tonight, and be astonished, like everybody else. At Almack's."

Almack's. A weight settled upon him. Another Wednesday night with the same people who gathered there every Wednesday night during the Season. The same conversations, enlivened by the latest scandal. That would be him, most likely, tonight. They'd be whispering about him behind their fans, behind their cards. Lady Warford would have plenty to say, and would imagine she expressed herself with the greatest subtlety while she dropped indignant hints as large and unmistakable as elephant dung.

He remembered what Longmore had said about his mother not allowing Clara to wear the dress. "I'd better come with you," he said. "Longmore was here—"

"I know," she said. "Sophy dealt with him. And I'll deal with Lady Warford, if that becomes necessary. I doubt it will. When Lady Clara sees herself in this dress—but never mind, I haven't time to boast, and you'd be bored, in any event."

"No, I wouldn't be bored," he said. He'd been reading *La Belle Assemblée*. He had ideas. "I've been—"

"It's half-past six," she said. "I've still got to get to Warford House."

"Take the curricle," he said.

"I don't know what I'm taking," she said. "Halliday promised I'd have your fastest vehicle. They're waiting for me."

He wanted to go with her. He wanted to see the dress, and Clara's face when she saw it. He wanted them all to see that it was business, and Noirot was not only talented but principled—to a point—when it came to her work, in any case—and honorable—to a point—when it came to her work, in any case . . .

But that, to his shame, wasn't the only reason he wanted to go with her.

He was near enough to breathe her scent, to see the faint wash of color come and go in her cheeks . . . and the pearly glow of her skin where the light caught it . . . and the tendrils of dark hair straying artfully from her bonnet, curling near her ears. He wanted to bring his hand up to cup her face and turn it to his and bring his mouth to hers . . .

Stupid, stupid, stupid.

And ignoble as well, when she was carrying Clara's dress, and he loved Clara and had always loved her and couldn't bear the thought of hurting her.

He'd caused trouble enough. Lady Warford had probably been harassing Clara all day long, blaming her for Clevedon's negligence and misbehavior. The jealous cats who pretended to be their friends would be sure to sharpen their claws on Clara, too.

He stepped back from the door. "I should be a great idiot to keep you, after you've achieved what I could have sworn was impossible."

She stepped back, too. "Let's hope they let me deliver it."

Chapter Twelve

A lady of genius will give a genteel air to her whole dress by a well-fancied suit of knots, as a judicious writer gives a spirit to a whole sentence by a single expression.

John Gay, English poet and dramatist (1685–1732)

Marcelline reached Warford House at five minutes before seven. Though she arrived in Clevedon's carriage, his crest emblazoned on the door, she knew better than to go to the front door. She went round to the tradesmen's entrance, where she was made to wait. It had occurred to her that she might be rebuffed, but she'd refused to entertain doubts. The dress was magnificent. Lady Clara had understood she was in the hands of a master, else she'd have sent Marcelline away the other day, the minute she started tossing out her ladyship's wardrobe.

At last Lady Clara's maid, Davis, appeared and gave her permission to enter. Her expression grim, Davis led Marcelline past the staring servants and up the backstairs.

Her dour look was soon explained. Marcelline found both Lady Clara and her mother in the younger woman's dressing room. Clearly, they'd been quarreling, and it must have been a prodigious row, to make both ladies' faces so red. But when Davis entered and said, "The dressmaker is here, my lady," a silence fell, as heavy and immense as an elephant.

Lady Warford was nearly as tall as Clara, and obviously had been as beautiful once. She by no means looked like the battle-ax she was well known to be. Though a degree bulkier than her daughter, the marchioness was a handsome woman of middle age.

Battle she did, though, going promptly on the attack. "You!" said her ladyship. "How dare you show your face here!"

"Mama, please," Lady Clara said, her gaze darting to the parcel Marcelline carried. "Good heavens, I couldn't believe it when they said you were here with the dress. Your shop—I read that it burnt to the ground."

"It did, your ladyship, but I promised the dress."

"Dress or not, I cannot believe this creature has the effrontery to show her face—"

"You made my dress?" Lady Clara said. "You made it already?"

Marcelline nodded. She set down the parcel on a low table, untied the strings, unwrapped the muslin, and drew the dress out from the tissue paper she and her sisters had carefully tucked among its folds.

She heard three sharp intakes of breath.

"Oh, my goodness," said Lady Clara. "Oh, my goodness."

"This is outrageous," Lady Warford said, though with less assurance than before. "Oh, Clara, how can you bear to take anything from this creature's hands?"

"I've nothing else to wear," Lady Clara said.

"Nothing else! Nothing else!"

But Lady Clara ignored her mother, and signaled her

maid to help her out of her dressing gown. Lady Warford sank onto a chair and glowered over the proceedings as Marcelline and the maid dressed Lady Clara.

Then Lady Clara moved to study herself in the horse-dressing glass.

"Oh," she said. "Oh, my goodness."

The maid stood, her fist to her mouth.

Lady Warford stared.

Marcelline's creation comprised a white crape robe over a white satin under-dress. The neckline, cut very low, displayed Lady Clara's smooth shoulders and bosom to great advantage, and the soft white enhanced the translucency of her complexion. Marcelline had kept the embellishments simple and spare, to better showcase the magnificent cut of the dress and the perfection of the drapery, particularly the graceful folds of the bodice. A few judiciously placed papillon bows adorned the very short, very full sleeves and trimmed the edges of the robe where it opened over the satin under-dress. The robe was delicately embroidered in gold, silver, and black sprigs. The style was not French, but it was just dashing enough to be not completely English.

Most important, though, the dress became the wearer. No, it was more than merely becoming. It made Lady Clara's beauty almost unbearable.

Lady Clara could see that.

Her maid could see that.

Even her mother could see that.

The dressing room's silence was profound.

Marcelline let them stare while she studied her handiwork. Thanks to her fanaticism about measurements, the fit was nearly perfect. She wouldn't have to take the hem up or down. The neckline needed a little work in order to lie perfectly smoothly across the back. The puffs Davis had provided weren't large enough to support the sleeves properly. But these and a few other very minor matters were easily corrected. Marcelline quickly set about making the adjustments.

When the technical work was done, she guided Davis in adding the finishing touches: a silver and gold wreath set just so to frame the plaited knot of her ladyship's hair, heavy gold earrings, a gauze scarf. White silk slippers and white kid gloves embroidered in silver and gold silk finished the ensemble.

All of this took nearly an hour, while Lady Warford grew increasingly impatient, muttering about the time. She gave Marcelline scarcely a minute to admire her masterpiece. She'd made them late for dinner, Lady Warford complained, and swept Lady Clara out of the dressing room without another word.

No thanks, certainly.

Davis admitted gruffly that her mistress looked very well, indeed. Then she ushered Marcelline down the backstairs like a dirty secret, and back to the tradesman's entrance.

As she stepped out into the night, Marcelline told herself she was very, very happy.

She'd done what had to be done. Lady Clara had never looked so beautiful in all her life, and she knew it and her mother knew it. Everyone at Almack's would see that. Clevedon, too. He would fall in love with Lady Clara all over again.

And in the midst of her triumph, Marcelline felt a stab, sharp and deep.

She knew what it was. She was a fine liar, but lying to herself wasn't a useful skill.

The truth was, she wanted to be Lady Clara, or some-one like her: one of his kind. She wanted to be the one he fell in love with, and once would be enough.

Never mind, she told herself. Her daughter was alive. Her sisters were alive. They'd start fresh—and after this night, the ton would be beating a path to their door.

Clevedon had hardly arrived at Almack's before he was calculating how long it would be before he could decently escape. He wouldn't stay as long as he ought to—at least in Lady Warford's opinion—but it wasn't his job to please Lady Warford. He'd come solely on Clara's account, and he doubted Clara expected him to live in her pocket.

He'd arrived as late as he decently could. This didn't improve matters, because Clara had little time for him, there wasn't another interesting female in the place this night, and he was tired of playing cards with the same people. She'd saved only one dance for him. She hadn't been sure he'd turn up at all, she said, and the other gen-tlemen were so pressing.

They certainly did press about her, a greater throng of them than usual. That, he supposed, was as she deserved. She looked very well in the dress Noirot and her women had slaved over. More important, he saw on the London ladies' faces the same expressions he'd noticed on their Parisian counterparts. He wished Noirot could see those faces.

The time dragged on until at last he could claim his one dance. As he led her out, he told Clara she was the most beautiful girl in the place.

"The dress makes more of a difference than I could have guessed," she said. "I couldn't believe Madame Noirot was able to complete it so quickly, after all that had happened."

"She was determined," he said.

She glanced up at him and swiftly away and said, "Your dressmaker is a proud creature, I think."

Proud. Obstinate. Passionate.

"She's your dressmaker, my dear, not mine," he said.

"Everyone says she's yours. She lives in your house, with her family. Have you adopted her?"

"I didn't know what else to do with them on short notice," he said.

There was a pause in the conversation as they began to dance. Then Clara said, "I read once, that if one saves someone's life, the person saved belongs to the rescuer."

"I beg you won't start that ridiculous hero talk, too," he said. "It isn't as though a man has a choice. If your mother had been trapped in that burning shop, I should have hardly stood by, looking on. Longmore would have done exactly what I did, no matter what he says."

"Oh, he had something to say," Clara said. "When he returned to Warford House after visiting you today, he told Mama not to make a fuss over a lot of dictatorial milliners. He said it was just like you to house the provoking creatures. He said they were ridiculous. Their shop had burned down, their child had nearly burnt to death, they had nothing but the clothes on their backs and some rubbishy ledgers, yet all they could think about was making my dress."

"They're dictatorial," he said. "You saw for yourself."

He'd seen, too: Noirot, as imperious as a queen, ordering Clara about.

So sure of herself. So obstinate. So passionate.

"I daresay everyone is shocked at me for having anything to do with her," Clara said.

"*Everyone* is easily shocked," he said.

"But I wanted the dress," she said. "In spite of what

Harry said, Mama didn't want to let Mrs. Noirot in the house. But I made a dreadful fuss, and she gave in. I'm a vain creature, it seems."

"What nonsense," he said. "It's long past time you stopped hiding your light under a bushel. Sometimes I wonder whether your mother—"

He broke off, dismayed at what he'd been about to say, and shocked that he'd only thought of it now: that her vain, proud mother had deliberately dressed her daughter like a dowd. She'd done it in hopes of keeping the other men off, because she was saving Clara for Clevedon.

She'd been saving Clara for a man who loved her but didn't want to be here, didn't want this life, and ached for something else, though he wasn't sure what the *something else* was.

No, he knew what it was.

But it was no use knowing because it was the one thing his power, position, and money couldn't buy.

"What were you about to observe regarding my mother?" Clara said.

"She's protective," he lied. "More than you like, I don't doubt. But you got what you wanted in the end."

He didn't notice the searching gaze Clara sent up at him. His own attention was wandering to the ladies' dresses floating about them. Nearly all wore the latter stages of court mourning: every shade of white, some black, soft shapes against the stark angles of black and white and grey of the men's attire.

The air was warm, and thick with scent, recalling another time and place. But this wasn't like Paris, and the difference wasn't merely the monochromatic colors.

It was the monochromatic mood.

There was no magic.

In Paris, there had been a kind of magic or perhaps

unreality: the absurdity of that ball where Noirot didn't belong, yet made herself belong, where she was the sun, and everyone else became little planets and moons, orbiting about her.

Magic, indeed. What folly! What a fool he was! The most beautiful girl in London was in his arms. Every man in the place envied him.

Yes, he was a fool. The girl he'd always loved was in his arms, and every other man in the ballroom wanted to be in his shoes.

And all he wanted was to get away.

Library of Clevedon House
Friday 1 May

"We have to get away," Marcelline told Clevedon.

She'd seen nothing of him since Wednesday night. She had no idea when he'd come home from Almack's. His private apartments were on the garden front in the main part of the house—the equivalent of streets away.

Now it was ten o'clock on Friday morning. The seamstresses had arrived an hour ago and settled down to work on the most urgent orders. Normally, while they worked, Marcelline and one of her sisters would be in the showroom, attending to customers.

But they had no showroom. And after Lady Clara's triumphant appearance at Almack's, Marcelline could expect customers, a great many. If Maison Noirot didn't quickly seize the opportunity, the ton—not noted for being able to keep its mind on any one thing for any length of time— would forget about Lady Clara's mouth-watering dress.

Her ladyship would have other dresses from Maison Noirot, but the impact would not be quite the same as the first time.

This wasn't the only reason for getting out, but it was the most practical and mercenary one.

Marcelline had been preparing to write him a note when Halliday reported that his grace was in the library, and had asked to see Mrs. Noirot when convenient.

She'd hurried in and found him bent over a table piled with papers and magazines.

She hadn't waited to find out what he wanted to talk to her about.

"We can't stay here," she said. "I don't want to seem ungrateful—you know I'm grateful—but this is very disruptive—of my business, my employees, my family. Lucie in particular. The maids. The footmen. She's starting to think that's *normal*. She's much more difficult to manage than you'd suppose, and I'll need weeks to undo the damage that's been done in a few days by all the pampering and catering to her every . . ."

She trailed off as he lifted his head from his study of the paper in front of him and turned that green gaze on her. Her gaze slid away from those extraordinary eyes and drifted downward over his long, straight nose and paused at his mouth, the sensuous mouth that should have been a woman's and was so purely male.

The room grew too hot. Her mind skittered from one thought to another, trying to avoid the one subject she couldn't afford to dwell on. But the dark longing beat in her heart and sent heat lower, and she took a step back.

"And then there's *that*," she said.

"Yes," he said. "There is that."

"Yes," she said, and added quickly, "I've got Lady Clara, and I should like to keep her. The longer I stay here, the less her mother will love me. I'm not sure how long she can stand up to her mother."

I'm not sure how much longer I can keep away from you.

He looked away and gave a little sigh.

She wanted to touch him. She wanted to lay the palm of her hand against his cheek. She wanted to step into his arms and lay her head on his chest and listen to his heart beat. She wanted to feel the warmth of his body and its strength. She wanted him inside her. She wanted him.

Last night she'd lain awake, imagining: a light footstep in the darkness . . . the sound of the door closing . . . the sound of his breath in and out . . . the motion of the mattress as his weight settled onto it . . . silk whispering as he shrugged off his dressing gown . . . his voice so low . . . his mouth against her ear . . . and then his hands on her, drawing up her gown . . . his hand between her legs . . .

Stop it stop it stop it.

"I've spoken to my sisters, and they agree that we can't stay," she went on. "Leonie and I are going out to find a place to move to."

"That won't be necessary," he said.

"It's *crucial*," she said. "We must seize the moment. You don't understand."

"I understand perfectly," he said. He pushed toward her across the desk the paper he'd been looking at. "Varley has found you a shop. Shall we go see it?"

One of Clevedon's many properties, the building stood on St. James's Street near the corner of Bennet Street. Clevedon told the dressmakers that the previous tenants (a husband and wife) had fallen into dire financial difficulties within months of opening the place. They'd absconded in the dead of night mere days ago, owing three months' back rent. They must have borrowed or stolen a cart, because they'd taken away most of the shop's contents and fixtures.

This was a complete lie.

The truth was, Varney had bribed them to move and sweetened the offer by allowing them to take with them everything that wasn't nailed down.

"What a strange coincidence that this should fall vacant at precisely this time," Miss Leonie said while Varley unlocked the door.

"It's about time we had a strange coincidence in our favor," Miss Sophia said.

While the others filed into the shop, Noirot lingered on the pavement. Clevedon saw her assessing gaze move up over the building, then down and about her to consider the neighborhood. It was certainly prestigious, even though some of the street's establishments were less than savory. Alongside gentlemen's clubs like White's, Boodle's, and Brooks's and some of London's most esteemed shops—Hoby the bootmaker, Lock's the hatters, and Berry Brothers the wine merchants—stood gaming hells and brothels. These, however, tended to be tucked into narrow passages and courts.

"Well?" he said. "Do you approve?"

Her dark gaze shifted to his face then quickly away. "It was in my plans," she said. "From Fleet Street to St. James's. I knew it would happen, but not quite so soon."

With a small, enigmatic smile, she went in. He followed her.

At their entrance, Miss Leonie looked up from her conversation with Varley. "I knew it was too good to be true," she told Noirot. "It's beyond our means. We haven't enough business to cover the everyday expenses, let alone the outlay required to make this usable. We should need two lifetimes to repay his grace."

"Don't be absurd," Clevedon began.

"Don't be absurd," Noirot said at the same time. "The address alone will increase our business prodigiously.

We'll have a proper space in which to work and display our work. We can hire another half dozen seamstresses, and increase our production accordingly. I have so many ideas, and not enough room and people to execute them."

"My love, we need customers," Miss Leonie said. "We should need to double our clientele—"

"Sophy, you must put something in the paper immediately," Noirot cut in impatiently. " 'Mrs. Noirot begs leave to inform her friends and the public in general that she intends opening showrooms on Wednesday, the 6th instant at her new location, No. 56 St. James's Street. With a collection of new and elegant millinery and dresses, which will be found to excel, in point of taste and elegance, collections found in any other house in London. Amongst which are sundry articles for ladies' dress not to be found elsewhere.' etc. etc." She waved her hand. "You know what it must be. But *more*."

"More, indeed," Clevedon said. "You must invent a corset, if you haven't already done so, and be sure to mention it."

The three women turned to look at him.

"I've been reading the fashion periodicals," he said. "There seems to be something irresistible about a new, unique style of corset."

It was the subtlest change in expression. If he hadn't spent so much time with them or paid such close attention to Noirot, he wouldn't have recognized the slight movement of their eyes, a hint of rapid calculations going on inside their conniving skulls.

"He's right," Noirot said. "I'll invent a corset. But for now, Sophy, for advertising purposes, you'll invent a name for it. Something exotic. Remember Mrs. Bell's 'Circassian' corset. But Italian. They want Italian corsets."

"You ought to change the date of opening, too," Clevedon said. "You can't afford to lose another day. Make it tomorrow. You won't have time to paint it exactly as you like, but it was painted only a short time ago for our absconders. With everything cleaned and polished, and with new fixtures, it will look brand-new."

The younger sisters burst out at the same time:

"We can't possibly do this!"

"How on earth can we have everything ready in less than twenty-four hours?"

Noirot put up her hand. The sisters subsided. "We'll need to borrow most of your servants to do it," she told Clevedon. "And carriages again. We'll need materials, yes, beyond what we purchased for the emergency."

"I understand," he said.

"We can't do it without your help," she said.

"I'd planned on helping," he said. "It's a small enough sacrifice to have the lot of you out of Clevedon House forthwith."

That would quiet Lady Warford. And the other cats. For himself, he cared nothing about talk or scandal. But he knew he was making matters very difficult for Clara. He couldn't do as he pleased without causing her embarrassment at the very least.

In any event, he lacked the moral fortitude to resist temptation. The longer Noirot lived under his roof, the greater the likelihood he'd behave in his usual way.

"A *small* sacrifice," Miss Sophia said with a laugh. "Oh, it's good to be a duke."

"It's good to *know* a duke," Miss Leonie said. "This place may give Marcelline's genius scope, but it's going to be deuced expensive to furnish, never mind the materials."

Noirot was already beginning a circuit of what he supposed would be the showroom. "The drawers and counters will do," she said, "but everything must be cleaned and polished within an inch of its life. All else must be purchased. Working our way down from the ceiling—chandeliers, wall sconces, mirrors . . ."

Clevedon took out his little pocket notebook and started making notes.

They had no trouble dividing responsibilities. Marcelline and her sisters had been at this long enough to know who did what best.

Sophia returned to Clevedon House to compose her deathless prose and supervise the seamstresses. Leonie remained at the shop to accept deliveries and supervise the servants and workmen who, they were told, Halliday had already begun organizing, and would be arriving shortly.

Clevedon was to take Marcelline shopping.

She saw no alternative. She needed him. She'd simply have to suppress her lust and longings and other inconvenient feelings and be stoical. She'd had plenty of practice with that.

"If we're to get this done by the end of the day, you must come with me," she told him at the end of her inventory of the place. "I've no time to waste while a clerk dithers or tries to sell me something I don't want. I haven't time for dickering about prices. I need prompt, preferably obsequious attention. Entering with the Duke of Clevedon is a sure way to get that and more."

"I assumed I'd come with you," he said. "Did you not notice how diligently I took notes?"

She had noticed and wondered at it. She held her tongue, though, until they were in his carriage. And then it wasn't the notebook she asked about.

"I thought you loathed shopping with women above all things," she said, remembering what he'd said to Lady Clara.

"That was before," he said. "Now you've made it *interesting,* curse you."

"Interesting?"

"All the bustling about," he said. "All the drama. All that naked ambition coupled with passionate belief in the rightness of your vision. All that . . . purpose. It amuses me to catch the occasional stray bit of purpose by trailing in your wake."

"What nonsense!" she said. "I found a way to make a living that doesn't require me to drudge endlessly for someone else—and one that offers an avenue for advancement as well. If I weren't obliged to work, I shouldn't. I should be happy to have no purpose but to enjoy myself and occasionally bestow some generosity upon lesser mortals."

"You're the one talking nonsense," he said. "You live for what you do. You live and breathe your work. It isn't employment. It's your vocation."

"I look forward to the day when I can live in idleness," she said. "That's my goal."

"The day will never come," he said. "No matter what heights you achieve, you won't be able to stop doing what you do. You can't see yourself. I can. I saw you throw down Clara's dress and kick it aside. It wasn't merely unsatisfactory. In your view, it was *criminal.* You tore those clothes from her hands as though they'd do her grievous bodily harm. You made that dress overnight because it was a matter of life and death to you. It would have killed you if she'd gone to Almack's wearing one of her old dresses."

She looked out of the carriage window. "Talk of

drama," she said. " 'Life and death' . . . 'killed' me." She
was uncomfortable. She'd never thought of herself in that
way. She was stubborn, hardheaded, practical, mercenary. Everything she did was for gain, for ambition. Yet
now he'd said it, she realized he wasn't wrong. And she
had to wonder at his noticing such a thing. She'd thought
he noticed mainly what weakness or unguarded moment
of emotion could get her on her back or against a wall . . .
or onto a worktable.

"Oh, very well," she said. "It wouldn't have killed
me—but it might have made me a little sick."

He laughed.

The carriage stopped. They climbed out, the conversation ended, and the shopping commenced.

It was one of the most hectic days Clevedon had spent in
his life—with the exception of the day he'd raced across
France after her.

They went quickly from one shop to the next: linen
drapers and furniture warehouses, shops specializing in
lighting and shops specializing in mirrors.

He and Noirot received all the prompt, obsequious attention she'd wanted and more. The shop owners
themselves came out to wait upon his grace, the Duke of
Clevedon. They were prepared to move heaven and earth
to get him precisely what he needed and to have it delivered that very day. If they hesitated, he had only to say to
Noirot, "We had better try the next shop—Colter's, is it?"
As soon as a competitor's name was mentioned, what had
been impossible a moment ago became "the easiest thing
in the world, your grace."

Once the shopping began, there was no more personal
conversation. Noirot hadn't time to debate about what
to purchase or wait to be shown the latest this or that.

When she entered a shop, she had to know exactly what she wanted. And so, in those short intervals while they were traveling in the privacy of his carriage, the talk was purely practical, all about furnishings and what size was best, and what colors set off what.

He should have been bored witless. He should have been frantic to get away, to his club, to a card game, to a bottle or two or three with Longmore.

The Duke of Clevedon was so far from bored that he never noticed the time passing. At some point, they'd stopped to eat from a basket his cook had prepared for them. He couldn't say when that was, an hour ago or five.

Then they left a warehouse, and when they reached the pavement she said, "*Mon dieu,* it's done. I think. I hope. That's everything, isn't it?"

He took out his pocket notebook, and it was only when he had to squint at it that he realized evening had fallen. He'd stepped out of the shop and joined the flow of activity on the street without noticing that it had grown dark. He'd been too intent on his own plans and calculations. While she was occupied with choosing articles for her shop, he hadn't been idle.

Now he looked about him at the gaslit streets. The shops would soon be closing, but the streets were busy, the pavements crowded with people passing to and fro, some pausing to look in the shop windows, others going inside—no doubt to the despair of shopkeepers eager for their dinners and the quiet of their hearths. Before long workers would spill from the various establishments, some hurrying home, others to their favorite chop houses and public houses.

What was the last place he'd wanted to hurry to? he wondered. When had he been eager for his own hearth-side?

"If we've forgotten anything, it's minor," he said.

"We'll see soon enough," she said.

He told his coachman to take them back to the shop on St. James's Street.

After what seemed an eternity of crawling through London's streets at a snail's pace, Marcelline climbed down from the carriage and faced a darkened, empty shop.

"I can't believe they're all gone," she said. She heard her voice wobble. She couldn't remember when last she'd felt so deeply disappointed. "I thought—I thought—"

"We were more efficient than we guessed," he said. "I'll wager anything they've gone home—to Clevedon House, I mean—for a well-earned dinner and rest. As we shall do—as soon as we've had a look round." He took out a key and brandished it. "I am the landlord, you know."

Enough light entered from the street to allow them to make their way into the shop without tripping over furniture. After a moment, Clevedon got a gas lamp lit, then another.

Marcelline stood in the middle of the showroom, her hands clasped tightly against her stomach, against the butterflies quivering there—eagerness mixed with anxiety at once. She turned, slowly, taking it in: the gleaming woodwork, the elegant chandeliers, the artfully draped curtains, the furniture arranged as though in a drawing room.

"Does it pass the test?" Clevedon said. "Satisfactory?"

"More than that," she said. "My taste is impeccable, I know—"

"Really, Noirot, you must strive to overcome this excessive humility."

"—but to see it in its proper setting . . ." She paused. "Well, I shall need to rearrange the furniture tomorrow morning. Leonie is very good with numbers and legal gibberish, and her eye for artistic detail is better than most, but she can be a little conventional in her arrangements. The showroom is most important, because that's what our patrons see. The first impression must be of elegance and comfort and the little something else that sets me apart from others."

"The little touches," he said.

"Nothing too obvious," she said.

"The French would say *je ne sais quoi,*" he said. "And so would I, because while I know it's there, I can't for the life of me say what it is."

She let herself look at him, but only for an instant. "You've come a long way from Paris," she said. "Then you claimed not to notice such things."

"I've tried not to notice," he said. "But everywhere I look, there it is. There you are. I'll be glad to be rid of you. When a man sinks to reading fashion journals—no, it's worse than that. When a man finds himself plumbing their depths, seeking arcane knowledge of no use to him whatsoever . . . Oh, it's your corrupting influence. I shall be so glad to see the back of you Noirots, and return to my life."

"It annoys you to be a guardian angel," she said.

"Don't be absurd. I'm nothing of the kind. Come, let's see the rest of the place."

They moved more quickly through the rest of the shop: the offices and work and storage areas. He would be eager to be gone, she thought. For a time the details of setting up a shop, the details of trade might have offered an interesting change of pace for him. But he was no tradesman. Money meant something entirely different to him, insofar as it meant anything. And she supposed he was tired as well of being the subject of tedious gossip, and tired of having his household disrupted.

Little did he know how small a disruption that had been, compared to what her family typically did. Her ancestors had torn whole families apart, lured the precious offspring of noblemen from their luxurious homes to vagabond lives at best, abandonment and ruin at worst.

She had seen all of the new place that mattered, she thought, when he led her, not back the way they'd come, toward the entrance, but to the stairs.

Then it dawned on her what she'd missed. The first floor was to contain work areas: a well lit studio for her, a handsome parlor for private consultations with clients, and private work spaces for Sophia and Leonie.

The second and third floors had been reserved as living quarters.

And that hadn't crossed her mind, not once while she shopped today.

"Good grief, I hope you've a mattress or two you can spare from Clevedon House," she said. "A table and chairs would be useful, too, though not crucial. We've camped before. I can't believe I forgot to buy anything for *us*."

"Let's go up and see what's needed," he said. "Maybe the absconders left something."

He led the way, carrying a lamp.

He didn't pause at the first floor but continued up to the second.

At the top of the stairs, he paused. "Wait here," he said.

He crossed to a door, and opened it. A moment or two later, the faint light of the lamp gave way to soft gaslight.

"Well, well," he said. "Come, look at this."

She went to the door and looked in. Then she stepped inside.

A sofa and chairs and tables. Curtains at the windows. A rug on the floor. None of it would have suited Clevedon House. The furnishings weren't grand at all. But they reminded her of her cousin's apartment in Paris. Quiet elegance. Comfort. Warmth. Not a showplace like the shop below, but a home.

"Oh, my," she said, and it was all she could trust herself to say. Something pressed upon her heart, and it choked her.

From this pretty parlor he led her into a small dining parlor. Then he led her to a nursery, laid out with so much affection and understanding of Lucie that her heart ached. She had her own little table and chairs and a tea set. She had a little set of shelves to hold her books, and a painted chest to hold her toys and treasures.

Thence he led Marcelline to another, larger room.

"I thought you would prefer this room," he said. "If it doesn't suit, you ladies can always rearrange yourselves. But you're the artist, and I thought you should not overlook the busy street but the garden—such as it is—and perhaps catch a glimpse of the Green Park, though you might have to stand on a chair to do it."

She was a Noirot, and self-control was not a family strong suit. But she, like the others, had a formidable control over what she let the world see.

At that moment, it broke. "Oh, Clevedon, what have you done?" she said, and the thing pressing on her heart pushed a sob from her. And then, for the first time in years and years and years, she wept.

Chapter Thirteen

MRS. HUGHES BEGS leave to inform her Friends
and the Public in general that she intends opening
Shew-Rooms on Tuesday, the 4th inst. with a new
and elegant assortment of Millinery and Dresses,
in the first style of fashion . . . Mrs. Hughes takes
this opportunity of returning thanks for the great
patronage she has already received from her numerous friends . . . An Apprentice and Improver
wanted.

Advertisements for January,
Ackermann's Repository, Vol. XI, 1814

Tears had never come easily to her. When she learned
the cholera had taken her parents, she'd ached for
the missed opportunities and for what she'd always hoped
for from them, against all odds and all evidence. When
the disease killed Cousin Emma—who'd taken in Marcelline, Sophy, and Leonie time and again when Mama
and Papa abandoned them—Marcelline had been deeply
saddened. She'd grieved for Charlie, too, for whom she'd
given up all her young girl's heart.

Yet Marcelline hadn't wept like this. She'd never had

time to indulge her grief. Each loss had meant she had to act, right away, to save her family.

She hadn't wept when Lucie had been so very ill, because there wasn't time for tears, only for working as hard as one could to keep her alive. When it seemed the fire had consumed her, the searing shock and pain left Marcelline nothing to cry with.

But now . . . but this . . .

It was the last straw, the very last straw, and she broke down and wept. But no, *wept* was too small a word for the great sobs that seized her, like talons trying to tear her apart. She tried to get free of them, but they were too strong. She could only stand, her face in her hands, and weep helplessly.

"Oh, come," Clevedon said. "Is it truly as ugly as all that? I flattered myself I had a little taste—a very little. One would have thought some of yours would have rubbed off— Dammit, Noirot."

She would have laughed if she could, but a dam had burst inside her. All she could do was stand, her face in her hands, and grieve for she hardly knew what.

"Curse you," he said. "If I'd known you'd make such a fuss, I should have taken you straight back home—I mean, to Clevedon House."

Home. His home. He'd given her a home when she'd lost hers. Then, today, while she thought of nothing but business, he'd made her a home. Another wave of misery churned through her, making her shudder.

"It was supposed to be a pleasant surprise," he said. "You were supposed to say, 'How good of you to think of it, Clevedon.' Then you were to accept it as your due. The way you accept everything as your due. Really, I hope your clients never see you carry on like this. They'll lose all respect for you. And you know it's crucial to cow them. You must rule them with an iron hand, or they'll run roughshod . . ." He gave up. "Devil take it, Noirot. What's the matter?"

You. You're all that's the matter. Only you.

But the storm was subsiding. She took her hands away from her face. To her amazement, they trembled. She found her handkerchief and wiped her face. It was then she saw how he stood, so stiff, his hands fisted at his sides.

He'd wanted to do the natural thing, she supposed. To move to her and put his arms about her and comfort her. But he wouldn't let himself. What had he done? Conjured Lady Clara in his mind, and thought, for once, of her and what he owed her?

Marcelline wanted to laugh then, too. The irony was too rich.

Now, when he'd demolished her defenses at last, he'd found the moral fiber to keep away.

"You d-don't underst-stand," she said.

"You couldn't be more correct," he said.

"No one," she said, and her voice wobbled again. "N-no w-w-one." Another sob racked her chest. She bit her lip and waved the handkerchief at their surroundings. "In all my life. No one. A h-home. You made a h-home."

It was true. No one in all her life had ever made a home for her. Her parents had never stayed in any place for long. There had been lodgings, places to hide, to camp, like gypsies. Never a home, until Cousin Emma had taken them in, and even then, what they had was a place to eat and sleep and work. Nothing in it had belonged to Marcelline and her sisters. Nothing in it was arranged for them. The small rooms on the upper floors of the building on Fleet Street constituted the first true home they'd ever had.

Now this. He'd done all this. He'd done it today, quietly, while she was otherwise occupied. He'd planned a surprise for her.

"Oh, Clevedon, what am I to do?" she said.

"Live in it?" he said.

She looked up at him, into those haunting green eyes, where she'd seen the devil dance, and the heat of desire, and laughter and rage. Oh, and affection, too, for Lucie.

"Someone had to think of it," he said. "You had so much else to do. The shop was—is—the most important thing, of course. Without it, you have nothing. But you only needed me to stand about and look ducal, and I grew bored."

And there was that, too: He understood what her business meant to her. In a few short weeks he'd gone from completely dismissive—no, scornful was more like it—to this. She'd read in novels of people who couldn't speak because their hearts were too full and she'd always thought, *Not my black heart*.

But now she couldn't speak, because it was too much, whatever *it* was. Everything was falling into place, a great puzzle she hadn't realized wanted solving. Now the pieces shifted into place, and she saw.

"It seemed stupid to distract you with ordinary house-hold matters," he went on. "As it was, you were undertaking the impossible. But that's so like you, to undertake the impossible. Clara's gown. Stalking me in Paris. Who on earth would think to do such a thing? Who on earth could imagine she'd succeed? If you had asked my opinion, I should have told you it was a harebrained scheme—"

"And you'd be right," she said. "It was a mad scheme."

"But it succeeded."

"Yes. Yes, it did."

Except for one slight miscalculation. She felt her eyes filling. She blinked and forced a smile. "I'm happy," she said. "I couldn't be happier. Everything I wanted." She gestured. "And more. A fine shop in St. James's Street. Scope for my imagination, my ambition."

He looked about him. "I'm not sure it's big enough. I'm not sure St. Paul's Cathedral would be big enough to contain your ambition. *Are* there bounds to your ambition? Ordinary, mortal bounds, I mean?"

He knew her so well. She laughed. It hurt to laugh, but she did it.

He turned sharply toward her. "Noirot?"

"I was only thinking," she said. "It's all turned out as I'd imagined. No, better than I'd supposed. And yet . . . Oh, what a joke."

She shook her head and moved away and sat on a chair and folded her hands and stared at the floor, at the rug he'd chosen. Crimson poppies intertwined among black tendrils and leaves on a background of pale gold . . . with a subtle pink undertone.

The colors of the dress she'd worn to the Comtesse de Chirac's ball.

Then she realized: This home he'd created for them was his goodbye gift.

How ironic. How fitting.

She'd hunted him and she'd caught him and she'd got what she'd set out to get.

And she'd bollixed it up, after all.

What a joke.

She'd fallen in love.

And he was saying goodbye, in the time-honored fashion of men of his kind, with an extravagant gift.

"Noirot, are you unwell? It's been a very long day, and we're both overwrought, I daresay. It's no small strain, even for you, trying to do the impossible—all this racing from one place to the next, buying, frantically buying.

And I—shopping with a woman—it's possible my sensibilities will never recover from the shock."

She looked up at him.

They had no future.

Given who he was and what he was, she couldn't be anything to him but a mistress. And that she couldn't be. It wasn't because of moral scruples. She barely understood what those were. It was for business reasons, for the business that supported her family, the business she loved, the great passion of her life.

She could keep her feelings to herself. She could suffer in silence. She could say thank you and goodbye, and really, there was nothing else to do.

The trouble was, being who she was and what she was, noble sacrifice was out of the question.

And the real trouble was, she loved him.

And so she made her plan, quickly. She saw it all at once in her mind's eye, the way she saw all of her plans. She saw what she needed to do, the only thing to do.

She stood and walked to the bed and pointed. "I want you to sit there," she said.

"Don't be stupid," he said.

She untied her bonnet ribbons.

"Noirot, maybe you failed to understand why I was in so great a hurry to have you out of my house," he said. "I don't care about talk, if it concerns only me. But you know the talk will hurt someone else."

"You're a man," she said. "Men are readily forgiven what women are not."

"I've promised myself I won't do anything I'll need to be forgiven for," he said.

"You won't be the first man to break a promise," she said.

Still holding the bonnet by the strings, she looked at

him, capturing his gaze. She hid nothing. All her heart was in her eyes and she didn't care if he saw it.

She'd fallen in love, and she'd love for once, openly, without disguise or guile. That was the one last gift she'd give him, and herself.

He came to the bed and sat, his face taut.

She let the ribbons slide through her fingers. The bonnet dropped gently to the rug he'd chosen for her bedroom.

He watched it drop. "Damn you," he said.

"It's all right," she said. "This is goodbye."

"Noir—"

She set her index finger over his lips. "I thank you for all you've done," she said. "I thank you from the very bottom of my cold, black heart. There are some things I can repay but more that I can never repay. I want my gratitude—its depth and breadth—to be clear, perfectly clear . . . because after tonight, you must never come back here. You must never come to my shop. When your lady wife or your mistress comes to Maison Noirot, you'll stay far away. You will not speak to me in the street or anywhere else. After this night, you become the man I always meant you to be, the man whose purse I plunder—and no more than that man. Do you understand?"

His eyes darkened, and she saw heat there: anger and disappointment and who knew what else? He started to rise.

"But for this night," she said, "I love you."

Something flashed in his eyes, and he flushed, and a brief spasm contorted his beautiful face. It was so quick, come and gone in the blink of an eye. But it was hard to mistake sorrow, however brief the glimpse. Then she knew she hadn't made the wrong decision.

She began to undress. It was the same dress she'd been

wearing on the night of the fire. Though his maids had cleaned and ironed it, it was no longer up to her usual standards. However, she and her sisters had agreed that completing their most crucial orders was more important than replenishing their own wardrobes.

This dress fastened up the back, naturally, but that presented no difficulty. She'd been dressing and undressing herself since she was a little girl. She unbuttoned the sleeves. Then she unhooked the hooks at the back of the bodice, from top to bottom. With the hooks undone, the narrow slit below the waist—invisible when the top was fastened—sagged open and the bodice did, too. Under it she wore an embroidered muslin chemisette that tied at the waist. She untied it and took it off, and let it drop from her hand, in the same way she'd dropped the bonnet.

She heard his breathing quicken.

The top undone, she eased her arms from the sleeves. She pulled the dress over her head, and dropped it.

She unfastened the sleeve puffs and dropped them onto the growing heap of clothing at her feet. She stood before him in her chemise, petticoats, corset, stockings, and shoes.

She stood for a moment, letting him drink her in. She couldn't be sure what he felt, apart from what men always felt in such cases, but perhaps, just perhaps, he was trying, as she was, to imprint this moment in his memory.

Then she knelt.

"Marcelline," he said. It was the first time he'd ever uttered her Christian name, and the sound was a caress.

Oh, she'd remember that: his voice, like a caress.

"You made my home," she said. "Let me make our last time together. Leave it to me. Do I not make everything exactly as it ought to be?"

She tugged off one boot, then the other. She stood them neatly next to her heap of clothing.

She rose. She drew nearer now, and she looked down at him, at his black hair, gleaming like silk in the lamplight. He was looking up at her, his eyes dark, his mouth slightly parted, his breathing faster.

She bent over him, and unbuttoned his coat. She eased it off, as smoothly as his valet might have done. She folded it and laid it gently on a chair. She took off his waistcoat in the same way, only pausing for a moment to let her hand slide over the fine silk embroidery. She untied his neckcloth.

His head was at a level with her bosom. She could feel his breath on her skin above the lace of her chemise. She heard him inhale.

"The scent of you," he said so softly. "Heaven help me, the scent of you."

For a moment she paused, her hand trembling on the fine muslin. She remembered the first night, when she'd taken his diamond stickpin and set her pearl pin in its place. She smoothed the muslin lightly before she began to unwrap it from his neck. She slid it away and tossed it onto his coat.

She unfastened the button of his shirt, and it fell open. She laid her palm against his neck and slid it down over the skin bared, over the hard contours of his chest. While her hand rested on his chest, she bent her head, and laid her cheek against his. She remained there for a moment and let herself feel her face touching his while she breathed in the scent of him, the scent of a man, this man, warm and as heady as hot cognac.

Then she stepped back and untied her shoes and stepped out of them. She reached behind and untied the corset string. She quickly drew it through the eyelets, until it was loosened enough to slide down over her hips. Her chemise, released from the corset, slid down from her shoulders, baring one breast. She heard him suck in air. She shed the corset and tossed it aside. She untied her petticoats and let them slide down her legs. She reached under the chemise and untied her drawers and let them fall. She stepped out of them.

She stood now in chemise and stockings. She let him look, let herself enjoy his looking, the heat in his eyes, the pleasure at the sight of her, the excitement.

"You're killing me," he said, his voice rough. "You're killing me."

"You'll die beautifully," she said.

She set her foot on the edge of the bed, near his thigh. She threw back the hem of the chemise, baring her knee. He made a choked sound.

She untied her garter and dropped it on the rug. Then she rolled her stocking down, slowly, over her knee, down her calf to her ankle and down over her instep, and tugged it off. She heard his breath hitch. She dropped the stocking, but she left her leg as it was for a moment. She let him look and let herself watch him look while she planted in her memory the expression on his beautiful face.

Then she drew her leg down and removed the other stocking in the same way. By this time, the chemise had slid nearly to her waist. Only the sleeves, caught in the crook of her elbows, kept it on.

She let her arms relax at her sides and gave a little shake. The chemise slithered down and off her and made a little puddle of muslin on the floor.

That left her with nothing at all, not a stitch.

His breathing was harsh now, his face taut.

"Come here, you wicked girl," he said.

She moved close again, and he groaned and reached for her. Then his mouth was on her, moving over her breasts. When he took her nipple in his mouth, she gave a little cry, and caught her fingers in his hair, grasping his head, and holding him to her. She bent her head and kissed the top of his, and she ached, the flesh-ache of desire, the heart-ache of loving.

She let herself suffer, and she let herself enjoy while he suckled her. But when he started to pull her to him, she pulled back. "I'm not done," she said.

"I hope not," he said.

She pushed his hands out of the way, and unbuttoned his trousers, and tugged his shirt free. "Lift your arms," she said.

He closed his eyes and did as she said.

She pulled his shirt over his head. She grasped the waist of his trousers and pulled, and he leaned back and lifted his hips so that she could pull them down and off. Then, more quickly, came his drawers.

Freed, his cock sprang up from its dark nest, and she couldn't keep herself from clasping it, so warm in her hand, so thick and long and well shaped—like the rest of him.

"Christ, Marcelline," he said.

She smiled and kissed the velvety tip, and he swore.

She would have done more. She could have done more. She wanted to, but she wanted to make this last as long as she could. She released him, and slid her hands down his legs and tugged off his stockings.

She wasn't so steady as before and her pace was not as leisurely. His hands and mouth had set her on fire. He roused her so easily, the way he'd done in Paris, and in her shop—she, who was always in control, who knew all there was to know about men, and felt as though she'd been born knowing it. She went up like tissue paper touched by a flame.

She climbed onto the bed and straddled him. She looked down, and he was reaching up. He set his palms along the sides of her face. For a long moment that was all he did. He held her and looked up at her. She thought he'd say something, but he didn't. Then he brought her mouth to his, and kissed her.

Tender, so tender.

And hungry, deepening in an instant.

She was hungry, too. She kissed him back with all the yearning she'd locked away for weeks and all the dreams and fantasies that had made a turmoil of her nights and all the passion she'd always kept for her work, her great love.

But now there was this man, who'd beat all the odds and made her love him.

He kissed her, and it was deep. His tongue hunted every secret of her mouth and caressed it, and drew her deeper with each caress. His taste and scent were everywhere, a warm sea in which she was floating, sinking, drowning.

She moved her hands over him, over his big shoulders and down over his back. She let herself wallow in skin touch, and in the heady power of feeling his muscles tense under her hands. She stroked over his arms, her palms curving to find the shape of him and imprint it upon her senses, to be conjured again when she wanted him and he wouldn't be there. She moved restlessly, learning every inch of his big, hard chest.

He was hard everywhere, and so powerfully muscled. This wasn't the body of a gentleman. But she'd seen that from the first: the sheer physicality, the size and power, the carnality barely camouflaged by the elegant outer display . . . the beautiful animal lurking under the civilized trappings.

She felt his mouth leave hers, and she could have wept for the loss, but then his lips traced the line of her jaw and trailed over her neck. Then he was kissing her neck, her shoulders. Then his tongue slid over her collarbone, and she moaned, and her head fell back. And he licked her, like a great cat, the panther she'd envisioned, his tongue moving over her skin. Every fiber of her being seemed stretched taut. Her body became a mass of electric sensation, like the air before a great storm. Hot pleasure rippled through her, and settled in the pit of her belly, and sent heat coursing outward again. Then she was trembling for release. His great cock throbbed against her aching belly and her body pulsed with wanting.

She'd wanted to make it last and last and last but her control was slipping. She lifted herself up, and clasped him and guided him in. She made it slow, achingly slow. He made a sound like a laugh and a groan combined. She lifted herself and came down, taking in his full length this time.

"By God," he growled. "By God."

Slow, again, up and down, torturing them both, pleasuring them both. His fingers dug into her hips. "Marcelline, for God's sake."

But she kept on. She'd never get enough but she'd get as much as she could. But as she rose, a mad joy rose, too. It was as strong as a physical blow, knocking her control away, and she cried out, *"Mon dieu!"*

She heard his voice, so low. No words. Growls and gasps and a sound like choked laughter. He grasped her bottom, but he let her set the pace. She tried to slow it again, to make it last and last. But need overrode ev-

erything. Her blood drummed in her veins and it was a
summons, primitive, primal, and it drove her. She was an
animal, too, running hard toward the ending, the something she was meant to find.

She couldn't stop, couldn't slow, couldn't hold back.
She rode him, her body rising and falling, his hips against
her knees, his body lifting to meet hers. He held her, his
fingers digging into her hips, as she rose and fell, and he
was laughing—a raw, hoarse laughter, and she laughed,
too, hoarse and breathless. And whether it was the laughter or the madness that pushed her to the brink, she didn't
know. She knew only fiery exhilaration as her body
clenched and shuddered. A wave of happiness carried her
up, and up, and up, until there was nowhere left to go.
Then it flung her down, like a flimsy craft in a stormy sea,
into a great, drowning darkness.

She lay, spent, on top of him. He lay, shaken, holding her.
It's all right. This is goodbye.

He knew it had to be goodbye. He'd pushed his world's
tolerance to its limit and beyond. He'd pushed Clara's in-
dulgence and understanding far beyond what he ought.
He'd been thoughtless and selfish and unkind to the one
who'd always loved and understood him.

He'd been in the devil's own hurry to get rid of Noirot
and her family because it had to be done. Even he, who
disregarded rules, knew that.

He'd known in his heart that this day had to be goodbye. Giving her a shop and a home were the sop he offered his conscience and his anxieties. They'd be safe.
They'd survive. They'd thrive. Without him.

And he knew that in time he'd forget her.

But for this night, I love you.

He couldn't think about that. He *wouldn't* think about it.
Love wasn't part of the game.

It wasn't in the cards.

And this game was played out. It was time, long past time, they were gone from here.

Yet his hand slid down her back, and he thought nothing in the world was as velvety soft as her skin. Her hair tickled his chin, and he bent his head a little, to feel the soft curls against his face, and to breathe her in.

But for this night, I love you.

She'd said it and he'd heard in blank shock. His mind had stopped and his tongue, too. He'd sat, like an idiot, dumbstruck. At the same moment, he'd believed and refused to believe. He'd felt an instant's shattering grief before he smothered it. He'd told himself he was a fool. He'd argued with himself. He knew what was right and what was wrong. He mustn't stay, no matter what she said. He knew what was going to happen, and he couldn't let it happen again. That would be selfish and thoughtless and unkind and dishonorable.

He'd argued with himself, but there she was, and he wanted her.

And he was weak.

Perhaps not as weak and dissolute as his father, but bad enough.

And so, of course, he lost the battle, that feeble battle with Honor and Kindness and Respect and all the other noble qualities Warford had tried to drum into him.

He could have simply got up from the bed—where he ought not to have sat in the first place . . .

Oh, never mind *could* and *should* and *ought to.*

He'd faced a test of character and he'd failed.

He'd stayed.

He wanted to stay, still.

"We have to leave," she said.

"Yes," he said. "Yes."

It was late. They had to leave. No time to make love again. No time to simply linger, touching her, being touched. No time to bask in lovemaking's afterglow.

This time he helped her dress and she helped him. It didn't take long, not nearly long enough.

The drive back to Clevedon House was far too short.

He hadn't time enough to study her profile as she looked out of the window into the gaslit street. He hadn't time enough to burn the fine contours of her face into his mind. He'd see her again, he supposed. She wanted him to keep away and he knew he must, but he'd see her again, perhaps, by accident. He might see her stepping out of a linen draper's or a wineshop.

But he'd never see her in exactly this way: the play of light and shadow on her face as she looked out onto Pall Mall. He would not, he supposed, ever be close enough again to catch her scent, so tantalizingly light but impossible to overlook. He'd never be close enough to hear the rustle of her clothes when she moved.

He told himself not to be a fool. He'd forget her. He'd forget all the details that at this moment seemed to mean so much.

He'd forget the way he'd stood on the pavement this day, pretending not to look at her ankles while he watched her step down from or up into the carriage. He'd forget the elegant turn of her ankle, the arc of her instep. He'd forget the first time he'd looked at her ankles. He'd forget the first time they'd made love, and the way she'd wrapped her legs about his waist and the choked sounds of pleasure he'd heard when he thrust into her, again and again. He'd forget his own pleasure, so violent that *pleasure* seemed too feeble a word, a word meant for ordinary things.

He'd forget all that, just as he would forget this night.

The memories would linger for a time, but they'd grow dull. The ache he felt now, the frustration and anger and sorrow—all those would fade, too.

She'd given him a night to remember, but of course he'd forget.

Marcelline and her sisters rose early the following day. By half-past eight they were at the shop. The seamstresses arrived shortly thereafter, in a flutter of excitement. But they settled down before the morning had much advanced. At one o'clock in the afternoon, the shop opened for business, as promised in the individual messages Sophy had dispatched and the advertisements she'd published in all the London newspapers.

At a quarter past one, Lady Renfrew and Mrs. Sharp appeared for their fittings. A steady stream of ladies followed them. Some came to shop. Some came to stare. But they kept Marcelline and her sisters busy until closing time.

She was happy, very happy, she told herself.

She'd be a fool to want anything more.

Chapter Fourteen

The rank which English Ladies hold, requires
they should neglect no honourable means of distinction, no becoming Ornament in the Costume.

La Belle Assemblée,
or Bell's Court and Fashionable Magazine,
Advertisements for June 1807

Sunday 3 May

Clevedon House seemed oppressively quiet, even
for a Sunday. The corridors were silent, the servants having reverted to their usual invisibility, blending
in with the furnishings or disappearing through a backstairs door. No one hurried from one room to the next.
No Noirot women appeared abruptly in the doorway of
the library.

Clevedon stood at the library table, which was heaped
with ladies' magazines and the latest scandal sheets. Of the
latter, *Foxe's Morning Spectacle* was the most prominent,
its front page bearing a large advertisement for "Madame
Noirot's newly-invented VENETIAN CORSETS."

He felt a spasm of sorrow and another of anger, and
wondered when it would stop.

He told himself he ought to throw the magazines in the fire, and Foxe's rag along with them. Instead, he went on studying them, making notes, forming ideas.

It staved off boredom, he supposed.

It was more entertaining than attending to the stacks of invitations.

It was a waste of time.

He rang for a footman and told him to send Halliday in.

Three minutes later, Halliday entered the library.

Clevedon pushed to one side the provoking *Spectacle*. "Ah, there you are. I want you to send the dollhouse to Miss Noirot."

There was an infinitesimal pause before Halliday said, "Yes, your grace."

Clevedon looked up. "Is there a problem? The thing can sustain a twenty-minute journey to St. James's Street, can it not? It's old, certainly, but I thought it was in good repair."

"I do beg your pardon, your grace," Halliday said. "Naturally there is no problem whatsoever. I shall see to it immediately."

"But?"

"I beg your pardon, sir?"

"I hear a *but*," Clevedon said. "I distinctly hear an unsaid *but*."

"Not precisely a *but*, your grace," Halliday said. "It is more of an impertinence, for which I do beg your pardon."

When Clevedon only looked at him expectantly, Halliday said, "We had been under the impression that Miss Erroll—that is, Miss Noirot—would be visiting us again."

Clevedon straightened away from the table. "What the devil gave you that impression?"

"Perhaps it was not so much an impression as a hope, sir," Halliday said. "We find her charming."

We meant the staff. Clevedon was surprised. "I should like to know what it is about them. They seem to charm everybody." The housemaid Sarah had gone happily enough to live above a shop and act as interim nursemaid until the Noirots had time to hire a suitable person. Miss Sophia had even disarmed Longmore.

"Indeed, they possess considerable charm," Halliday said. "But Mrs. Michaels and I both remarked their manner. We agreed that it was nothing like what one expected of milliners. Mrs. Michaels believes the women are ladies."

"Ladies!"

"She is persuaded that they are gentlewomen in reduced circumstances."

Clevedon remembered his first impression of Marcelline—his confusion. She'd sounded and behaved like the ladies of his acquaintance. But she wasn't a lady. She'd told him so.

Hadn't she?

"That's romantic," Clevedon said. "Mrs. Michaels is fond of novels, I know."

"I daresay that is the case," Halliday said. "In any event, they were not what one would be led to expect. Mrs. Michaels was greatly shocked when I informed her we had milliners to wait upon. But she told me that she was entirely taken aback when she met them. They did not strike her as milliners at all."

Servants were more sensitive to rank than their employers. They could smell trade at fifty paces. They could detect an imposter a minute after he opened his mouth.

Yet his servants, keenly aware of their position in the employment of a duke, had believed the Noirots were gentlewomen.

Well, it only showed how clever those women were. Charming. Enticing. Three versions of Eve, luring men to . . .

Gad, what the devil was wrong with him? It was reading all the damned magazines, with their serialized sentimental tales.

"You saw them at work," Clevedon said. "They know their trade."

"That is undoubtedly why Mrs. Michaels imagined they were women of rank who'd fallen on hard times," Halliday said. "I must confess that at first I thought it was one of your jokes. I beg you will forgive me, sir, but it did cross my mind that these were some cousins from abroad, and you were testing us. Only for an instant, sir. Naturally, it was obvious there had been a fire, and it was no joke."

The footman Thomas appeared in the doorway. "I beg your pardon, your grace, but Lord Longmore is here to see you, and—"

Longmore pushed past Thomas, strode past Halliday, and marched up to Clevedon.

"You cur!" Longmore said. He drew back his arm, and his fist shot straight at Clevedon's jaw.

Meanwhile, at Maison Noirot

Lucie sat in the window, gazing down into St. James's Street.

She'd been sitting there for hours.

Marcelline knew what she was watching for, and she was dreading what was to come. "It's time for your tea," she said. "Sarah has laid out the tea things on your handsome tea table, and your dolls are in their places, waiting."

Lucie didn't answer.

"Afterward, Sarah will take you to the Green Park. You can see the fine ladies and gentlemen."

"I can't go out," Lucie said. "What if he comes, and I'm not here? He'll be very disappointed."

Marcelline's heart sank.

She moved to sit next to Lucie on the window seat. "My love, his grace is not coming here. He looked after us for a time, but he's very busy—"

"He's not too busy for me."

"We're not his family, sweet."

Lucie's eyes narrowed and her mouth set.

"He made a beautiful home for us," Marcelline said, keeping her voice steady with an effort. "Only look at all the fine things he bought for you. Your own tea set and tea table. Your own little chair and the prettiest bed in the world. But there are others in his life—"

"No!" Lucie jumped down from the window seat. "No!" she screamed. "No! No! No!"

"Lucie Cordelia."

"I'm not Lucie. I'm Erroll. I'll never be Lucie again. He's coming back! He loves me! He loves *Erroll*!"

She threw herself on the rug. She shrieked and sobbed and kicked her feet.

Sophy and Leonie ran into the nursery. Sarah raced in, and stopped short, her expression horrified. This was her first experience of Lucie in a tantrum.

She started toward the raging child.

Marcelline put up a hand, and the maid backed away. "Lucie Cordelia, that is quite enough," she said, keeping her voice calm and firm. "You know ladies do not throw themselves on the floor and scream."

"I'm not a lady! I hate you!"

Sarah gasped.

"Come, Erroll," Sophy said. "You'll only make yourself sick."

"He's coming back!" Lucie shrieked. "He loves me!"

Marcelline squared her shoulders. She moved to Lucie and scooped the child into her arms, in spite of flailing arms and feet and deafening shrieks. She held Lucie tight against her and rocked her, as though she were still the tiny infant she'd been once.

"Stop it," Marcelline said. "Stop it, love. You need to be a big girl."

The kicking and punching stopped, and the screaming softened into weeping. "Why c-can't we st-stay th-there? Why d-doesn't he k-keep me?"

Marcelline carried her to the window seat and held her, rocking her and stroking her back. "If everyone who loved you kept you, where would you live?" she said. "Then where should Mama be? Don't you want to live with Mama and Aunt Sophy and Aunt Leonie? Have you grown too fine for us? Do you want to go away and live in a castle? Is that it? What do you think, Aunt Sophy? Shall we dress Erroll in a princess gown and send her away to live in a castle?"

It was nonsense, most of it, but it quieted Lucie. She tightened her hold of her mother's neck. "I can live here," she said. "Why can't he come?"

"He's a great man, sweetheart," Marcelline said. "He has his own family. Very soon he'll be married and have his own children. You can't have every handsome gentleman who takes your fancy, you know."

Erroll quieted. The motion of her eyes told Marcelline the child was thinking. She was only six, and children had difficulties with logic, but the prospect of being a princess might suffice to distract her.

The tempest over, Sarah said, "I'll tell you what, Miss Erroll. Let's have our tea with the dolls, then we'll take a walk in the Green Park. Perhaps we'll see the Princess Victoria. Do you know who she is, miss? She's the king's niece, and one day she'll be the Queen of England."

"If you do see her," Marceline said, "you must take special note of what she's wearing, and tell us all about it."

While a little girl threw a tantrum on St. James's Street, the Earl of Longmore was throwing his own in the library of Clevedon House.

Clevedon caught hold of his friend's arm. There was some pushing, and a brief scuffle. Then the shouting started.

Halliday had tactfully taken himself out of the room and closed the door. Having failed to break Clevedon's jaw or provoke him into a duel, Longmore was drinking the duke's brandy to sustain him while he paced the room and raged in his usual hotheaded fashion.

Clevedon knew he deserved a dressing down. All the same, it was very hard to bear. It was not as though he was enjoying himself. His life, at the moment, seemed to be utter excrement.

"You don't deserve my sister," Longmore said. "I should never have come to Paris. She raked me over the coals for doing it. She was right. I should have left you there to rot. I should have encouraged her to look elsewhere. I should have told her the leopard doesn't change his spots. But no, I was completely taken in. I wondered why you came back so soon—but I told myself it was because you'd realized how much you missed Clara. Gad, I was a naïve as she is!"

"I don't recall appointing a particular time to return," Clevedon said.

"I told you the end of the month was soon enough," Longmore said. "I knew you weren't done. I only wanted to be able to tell my mother you were coming back. I wish now I'd told her to mark you down in the column under dead losses. I've half a mind to tell her so now."

"If this is about the dressmakers—"

"Who else would it be about?" Longmore snapped. "Who else has been so thoroughly lost to propriety—"

" 'Lost to propriety,' " Clevedon echoed. "I can't believe those words are issuing from your mouth. When did you ever care for propriety? As I recall, your father was happy enough to pack you off to the Continent."

"I've never pretended to be a saint—"

"Good thing, too. No one would believe you."

"But I don't invite *milliners* to sleep in the ancestral home!"

"They were burnt out of their lodgings," Clevedon said. "It was in all the papers. Do you think that was a fabrication? But why the devil do I ask? If you were rational, you wouldn't be here, guzzling my brandy as though it was Almack's lemonade—"

"I never drink the filthy stuff."

"You're not rational. I don't know what's got into you, and I'm not sure I care. But the women are gone. I took them in for only a few days—"

"You couldn't put them up at a hotel?"

"You don't understand a damned thing," Clevedon said. "They have a business to run. They can't afford to lose time. They needed a place to work. They needed help. Bringing them here was the simplest plan. They drove themselves to distraction to finish a dress for Clara—"

"Don't speak of her and them in the same breath, you philandering swine."

"They're gone, you idiot! I had them packed up and out of here in seventy-two hours. They were gone on Saturday morning."

"And you were in bed with the brunette on Friday night," Longmore said.

It was completely unexpected. It was like one of Longmore's lightning blows, coming from the one angle one wasn't prepared for.

For a moment Clevedon saw red, literally: flames danced before his eyes. He clenched his fists, and when he spoke, his voice was deadly calm. "The temptation to knock you down is nearly overwhelming," he said.

"Don't act all nobly outraged with me, as though I've compromised her virtue."

"Only a blackguard would speak of any woman in that way."

"You were with her," Longmore said. "You weren't even discreet. I was at White's when one of the fellows told me he'd seen your carriage in Bennet Street. They started speculating about what you were doing there. I slapped my head and pretended suddenly to remember that you and I had appointed to meet there, and you were waiting for me. I went out of the club and down to Bennet Street. I stood in a doorway and waited for you to come out. And waited. And waited."

"How bored you must have been," Clevedon said, his heart pounding. Not with guilt, the more shame to him. It beat against the turmoil within. It beat with remembering those few miraculous hours.

Longmore tossed back the last of his brandy, stalked to the tray and refilled his glass from the decanter there. He took a long swallow. "You're making yourself a laughingstock," he said. "I've never seen you behave in this way over any woman. The creature has her hooks in you, that's plain enough. If this were the usual thing, I'd merely warn you in no uncertain terms to show a little damned discretion. Plague take it, Clevedon, you might have had the sense to tell the coachman to wait where all of bloody St. James's Street couldn't see him!"

"It didn't occur to me," Clevedon said. "I didn't plan to stay above a quarter hour. I'm sorry you were obliged to wait for so long."

"It was boring," Longmore said. "And damned aggravating. What the devil am I to do? Is this fair to Clara? Should her brother tell her that the man she's been waiting for has well and truly lost his head over a milliner? It'll hurt her, you know. She's always been so tolerant of your foibles. She has a soft spot in her head, I daresay. But this— You know this isn't the usual thing for you."

"It was goodbye," Clevedon said tightly. "It was longer than I'd intended, but it was goodbye. Do you understand? All Mrs. Noirot ever wanted was to dress my duchess. I've never been more than a means to that end. She doesn't care who the duchess is, but I think she prefers Clara because Clara's beauty is up to the beauty of her bedamned brilliant designs. I was infatuated—and you know how I am: Once I set my sights on a woman, I've got to have her. But that's done. It was goodbye, Longmore. And I must ask you, out of regard for Clara, to keep it to yourself. Telling her will only cause her needless pain, and why should she suffer over an episode of stupidity?"

"You swear it's over?" Longmore said.

"I—"

Clevedon broke off as the door opened. Halliday appeared on the threshold. He was holding a small silver tray. This was not a good sign. Halliday never stooped to carrying notes. That was a footman's job.

"I do beg your pardon for disturbing your grace, but I was told that the message could not wait," the house steward said.

Clevedon didn't wait for him but crossed the room in

a few quick strides, snatched the note from the tray, and tore it open.

There was no salutation. Merely six words: "We need your help. Lucie's run away." It was signed *M*.

Clevedon and Longmore reached the shop not twenty minutes later. The child had disappeared sometime after returning home with the nursemaid from the Green Park. Sarah had readied a bath for Lucie, but when she came back into the nursery, where the child had been playing, she was gone. They'd searched the house, every inch of it, Marcelline told him.

"She got out," she said. "She climbed out of an open window at the back of the house. I should never have left a window open if I'd any idea she'd do such a thing."

She must have learned the trick from Clevedon. That was how he'd got her out of the burning house. She'd kept her eyes closed, but she might easily have heard others talk of the rescue. He hadn't talked about it, but anybody might have worked it out, once they saw the broken window.

"Any idea what set her off?" he said. "That might offer a clue—"

"She had a prodigious temper fit," Marcelline said. "But she seemed to calm down afterward. Sarah said she was cheerful enough when they went to the park."

Sarah clapped her hand over her mouth.

"What?" Clevedon said. "If you know something, say it. We haven't a moment to lose."

Sarah began to cry. "I'm sorry," she said. "It was me, madam. I wasn't thinking."

"What, drat you?" Clevedon said.

Sarah hastily wiped her eyes. Her face went a bright red. "When we were in the Green Park. Miss Erroll was asking where your family was. She wanted to know why they didn't live at Clevedon House. I said you didn't have your own family yet. I pointed out Warford House there, overlooking the park. I said a lady lived in the house and everyone said you were going to marry her. She got such a look on her face. I knew I shouldn't have said it. She was that wrought up, before, when she was told you weren't coming."

Clevedon looked at Marcelline.

"She was waiting for you," she said wearily. "I told her you weren't coming. She threw a fit."

The child had been waiting for him. And he wasn't to come, ever again.

This was his fault. He'd given her a doll and she'd cherished it, and it had nearly cost her life. She'd stayed in his house. She'd been petted by the servants and she'd played with the dollhouse. What else was she to think but that he was part of her life now, part of her family?

He'd acted so unthinkingly and selfishly and carelessly. He'd thought only of himself and what pleased him, not of the child and how she might be hurt.

This was how Father had killed Mother and Alice. No thought but for himself.

He was sick, heartsick.

He said, "That simplifies matters. One can assume she decided to hunt me down. That would mean she's headed toward Clevedon House."

"I doubt she knows the way," Marcelline said. "We drove here, recollect. How would she know one street from the next?"

It was easy enough for adults unfamiliar with the area to get lost. She could easily turn into the wrong street.

A six-year-old child, alone in the London streets. In a short time the sun would set. And she might be in any of a hundred places.

"We'll alert the police," he said. "They may have found her already. They would certainly take notice of a well-dressed child alone on the street." He hoped so. Predators would take notice, assuredly.

His fault again. She'd escaped by a method she'd learned from him. She'd run away because of him.

He turned to Longmore. "Send one of the footmen who came with us to the police. But they haven't nearly enough men. I must ask you to muster your servants and mine, and form a search party. We'll comb the streets."

"She's afraid of the dark," Marcelline said. Her voice shook and her eyes were red, but she didn't weep. "She's afraid of the dark." Her sisters went to her and put their arms about her, the way they'd done the night of the fire.

He couldn't pull her into his arms. He couldn't comfort her.

The pain of not doing that was almost as sharp as the fear for Lucie.

"We'll find her before dark," Clevedon said. "I should be a good deal more worried if she'd bolted from your old shop on Fleet Street."

St. James's was safer, he told himself. Much safer. A royal palace was mere steps away. The clubs were there as well. While it wasn't completely respectable, it wasn't the back-slums. And she was a child, on foot. She couldn't go far.

But she could be taken. And then . . .

No. No one would take her. He knew where she was going. And he'd find her.

Half past three o'clock, Monday morning

Nothing.
No sign of her.

Police. Private detectives. Clevedon and Longmore's servants. They'd all searched. They'd knocked on doors and accosted passersby. They'd stopped carriages and hackneys.

No one had seen Lucie.

Clevedon, Longmore, and Marcelline had walked Bennet Street and St. James's Street, parting company to enter clubs and shops, and rejoining to traverse the alleys and courts in the vicinity. They'd combed St. James's Square.

He'd tried to send her home to wait when darkness fell, but she said she couldn't bear to stay home and wait. She walked until she was shivering with fatigue. Even then he had the devil's own time persuading her to get into the carriage, though it was an open one, and she might spot Lucie as easily—perhaps more easily—from its height than from the pavement.

At three o'clock he'd taken her home. "You'll be no good to anybody if you don't get some rest," he told her.

"How can I rest?"

"Lie down. Put your feet up. Take some brandy. I'm going home to do the same thing. The search hasn't stopped. It won't stop. Longmore and I will come back for you in a few hours. When it's light."

"She's afraid of the dark." Her voice wobbled.

"I know," he said.

"What shall I do?" she said.

What shall I do if she's dead?

The unspoken question.

"We'll find her," he said.

The conversation played through his mind again and again while he lay on the library sofa. He closed his eyes but they wouldn't stay closed.

He rose and paced.

He had to think the unthinkable. He had to allow for the possibility she'd been taken. Very well. But all was not lost. A ransom would be sought. Who'd keep a well-dressed child, who spoke with the accents of the gently bred, when money might be made?

Had the police thought of that? He rose and went to his desk. He started making notes and planning strategies while he waited for the sun to rise.

A loud cough woke him.

Clevedon opened his eyes. His mouth tasted gritty and his head ached and he thought at first he'd been on a prime binge. Then he realized his head wasn't on a pillow but on his desk. Then he remembered what had happened.

He jerked his head up from the desk.

Halliday stood on the other side.

"What?" Clevedon said. "What? What time is it?" He looked toward the window. Dawn had broken, but not long ago. Good.

"A quarter past seven, your grace."

"Good. Thank you for waking me. I did not want to oversleep."

"There's someone to see you, sir," said Halliday.

"From the police?" Clevedon said. "Have they found her?"

He saw that Halliday was having difficulty maintaining his composure.

Clevedon leapt up from his chair. There was a great rushing noise in his head. His heart pounded. "What is it? What's happened?"

"If I may, sir."

"May what?"

But Halliday went out.

"Halliday!"

The house steward came back in. He was carrying a very dirty, very wet little girl.

"His majesty presents his compliments, your grace, and requests to know whether this article belongs to you," Halliday said.

The Duke of Clevedon's carriage arrived later than promised. The sun was climbing upward, and Marcelline had already tried and failed to eat the tea and toast her sisters made for her. She hadn't slept a wink. She'd been afraid to.

She was ready and waiting, pacing the closed shop, when the carriage stopped at the front door. She ran out, and nearly collided with Joseph hurrying toward her. "It's all right, Mrs. Noirot," he said. "We've got her safe and sound and his grace sends his compliments and apologizes for not bringing Miss Erroll straightaway, but she wouldn't come. And so I was to come and ask would the mountain please come to Mahomet? That is to say, those were his words exactly, madam."

Marcelline found them in the drawing room—one of the drawing rooms. They were on the rug. Strewn about them were tin soldiers, horses, miniature cannons, and all the other artifacts of war.

Lucie was wearing what appeared to be page's livery, a coat and breeches made for a boy some inches taller. She had on red stockings and no shoes. Her hair had been tied up behind with what seemed to be a man's handkerchief. She was watching Clevedon line up some cavalrymen. He looked up toward the door first, and hastily rose.

Lucie looked up then. "Mama!" she cried.

Marcelline crouched down and opened her arms. Lucie jumped up and ran into them.

"My love, my love," Marcelline said. She nuzzled Lucie's warm neck, and inhaled her familiar scent, mixed with something flowery. Perfumed soap. Her hair was damp.

She held her tight for a long time, until Lucie grew impatient and pulled away. "We're playing soldiers," she said.

Marcelline grasped her shoulders and looked into her vivid blue eyes, her grandmother DeLucey's eyes.

"You ran away," Marcelline said. "You frightened Mama and your aunts to death."

Lucie's lower lip jutted out. "I know," she said. "His grace says I am not to do it again, and ladies do not climb out of windows. But I was *desperate*, Mama."

"And then you wouldn't come home," Marcelline said. "I had to come for you. What next, Miss Lucie Cordelia?"

"I'm Erroll. I had to have a bath. I was very dirty. I hid in the stables when they tried to take me home. I fell in a trough."

Marcelline looked to Clevedon. He'd risen when her daughter ran toward her. He still had a cavalryman in his hand and he was turning it this way and that.

"As near as we can ascertain, she made very good progress toward Clevedon House until she reached Pall Mall East," he said. "It would appear she turned into that street instead of Cockspur Street and wandered in the new construction until she ended up in the Queen's Mews. Naturally, she was soon noticed: Solitary children aren't thick on the ground thereabouts. But by this time, she'd found out where she was, and so, when they kindly asked whether she was lost, and where she lived, she said she was the Princess Erroll of Albania, and she wanted to speak to the Princess Victoria."

"Mon dieu," Marcelline said. "You asked to speak to the princess? You claimed to be a princess?"

"I am Princess Erroll, Mama. You know that."

"Lucie, you know that isn't your proper name," Marcelline said. "That's your play name, your make-believe name."

"Yes, Mama. But her highness wouldn't come to talk to Miss Lucie Cordelia Noirot, would she?"

Marcelline met Clevedon's gaze.

"I wish I could have seen their faces," he said. "They were vastly puzzled what to do. She insisted on speaking to the Princess Victoria. When they told her that her royal highness wasn't at liberty at present, she offered to wait. What could they do? They'd never heard of the Princess Erroll of Albania, but they could see she was quality."

Marcelline rose, her heart skittering. Matters were complicated enough. The last thing she needed was for the world to have any inkling of her background. People would shun her—and her shop—as though she were the cholera itself. "She's no such thing," she said. "It's acting."

He gave her an odd look. "In any event, they couldn't let her wander about London on her own."

"It never occurred to them to contact the police?"

"I'm sure it did, but one doesn't, you know," he said. "For all they knew it was a delicate royal matter, and the police would not be welcome."

She understood what he meant. The Royal Family had not been renowned for chastity. The king had ten children by a former mistress, an actress.

"They tried to sort matters themselves," Clevedon was saying. "Various forms of bribery were tried. But her highness the Princess Erroll of Albania accepted all tribute as her due. Then she fell asleep in one of the royal carriages. They didn't get news of our missing child until early this morning, after they'd sent to the palace for instructions. They had the devil's own time catching her, I understand, once she realized they meant to take her home. A truce was effected when they promised to take her here. She was presented to me some hours after dawn, with royal compliments."

Marcelline didn't know whether to laugh or cry. She feared she'd do both, and fall into hysterics.

The whole absurd story was so typical. It was the sort of thing her parents did all the time: brazenly pretend to be something they weren't. The Countess of This and the Prince of That.

"Well, I'm sorry His Majesty had to be bothered about it," she said as coolly as she could.

"Lucie, your mother and I need to talk privately," Clevedon said. "While we're gone, I recommend you form squares as I explained before, if you hope to repel the French as effectively as the Duke of Wellington did."

Chapter Fifteen

The quadrangle within the gate is in a better style
of building, but rather distinguished by simplicity
than grandeur; and the garden next the Thames,
with many trees, serves to screen the mansion from
those disagreeable objects which generally bound
the shores of the river in this vast trading city.

Leigh Hunt (describing Northumberland House),
The Town: Its Memorable Characters and Events,
Vol. 1, 1848

Clevedon took her into the garden. They were plainly
visible from all the windows facing the quadrangle.
It was the best place for a private conversation. Knowing that curious servants would be watching, he'd keep a
proper distance from her.

Then he wouldn't have her scent in his nostrils, in his
head, weakening his mind and his resolve.

They stood in the center of the quadrangle, where several paths converged.

"I should never have agreed not to see you again," he
said. "I hadn't considered how Lucie would take it."

"Lucie isn't your responsibility," Noirot said.

"She had a shocking experience," he said.

"Children are resilient. She'll throw a few temper tantrums, as she does sometimes when she can't get her way, but she'll recover."

"Does she commonly run away?"

"No, and it won't happen again."

"You can't be sure," he said. "It was a desperate thing to do. I don't think she would have done it if she hadn't been very deeply upset."

"She was deeply upset at being thwarted," Noirot said. "She knows the city streets are dangerous, but she was too furious with us to care about any rules or lectures—and Sarah, unfortunately, doesn't know her well enough to recognize the signs of rebellion."

She was as taut as a bowstring. She was tired, clearly, her face white and drawn. Relieved of fear for Lucie, she was probably feeling the fatigue she'd ignored. He'd better keep this short and to the point. She clearly wanted to be done with this conversation, and with him. She was shutting him out of her life and out of Lucie's.

She was Lucie's mother, but he knew that parents were not always right, and she was wrong to shut him out.

"I don't think that's enough," he said.

"I think you ought to let me be the judge."

He made himself say it. He saw no alternative. "When my mother and sister were killed," he said, "I wanted my father." He had to take a breath before continuing. He'd never spoken of his childhood miseries to anybody, even Clara, and it was harder than he'd supposed to talk of them now. "It was a carriage accident. He was drunk, and he drove them into a ditch. He lived. I was— I didn't know how to cope. I was nine years old at the time. I was grief-stricken, as you'd expect. But terrified, too. Of what, I can't say. I only recall how desperately I wanted him with me. But he sent me to live with my aunts, and he crawled into a bottle and drank himself to death. Everyone knew he was a drunkard. Everyone knew he'd killed my mother and sister. But I was too young to understand anything but that I needed him, and he'd abandoned me."

He took another breath, collecting himself. "Lucie experienced something terrifying, and I don't want her to feel I've abandoned her. I think we must make an exception for her. I think I ought to visit her, say, once a week, on Sunday."

A long, long pause. Then, "No," Noirot said, so calmly. She looked up at him, her pale countenance unreadable.

That was her card-playing countenance. Anger welled up. He'd told her what he'd told no one else, and she shut him out.

"You're right," she said, surprising him. "Lucie does need you. She's frightened. She had a shocking experience. But it up to me to deal with it. You'll visit her on Sundays, you say. For how long? You can't do it forever. The more she sees of you, the more she'll assume you belong to her. And leaving aside Lucie and her delusions, how much more heartache do you mean to cause Lady Clara? How much more public embarrassment? None of this would have happened, *your grace*—none of it—if you had stuck to your own kind."

It was not very different from what he'd already told himself. He'd behaved badly, he knew. But he wanted to make it right. He'd confided in her, to make her understand.

The cold, quiet fury of her answer was the last thing he'd expected. His face burned as though she'd physically struck him.

Stung, he struck back. "You're mighty concerned with Lady Clara's feelings all of a sudden."

She moved away and gave a short laugh. "I'm concerned with her wardrobe, your grace. When will you get that through your thick head?"

What was she saying, what was she saying? She'd turned to him when Lucie disappeared, and they'd searched together, sharing the same hopes and fears. He cared for that child and he cared for her, and she knew it. "Two nights ago you said you loved me," he said.

"What difference does that make?" she said. She turned back to him and lifted her chin and met his gaze straight on. "I still have a shop to run. If you can't get hold of your wits and start acting sensibly, you'll force me to leave England altogether. I'll get nowhere with you causing talk and undermining me at every turn—you and your selfish disregard of everything but your own wants. Think of what you're doing, will you? Think of what you've done, from the time you chased me to London, and the consequences of everything you've done. And think, for once, *your grace,* of someone other than yourself."

She turned away and left him, and he didn't follow her.

He could scarcely see through the red haze in front of his eyes. Rage and shame and grief warred inside him, and he wanted to lash back as viciously and brutally as she'd flayed him.

He only stood and hated her. And himself.

It was a long while he remained standing in the garden, alone. A long time while the anger began by degrees to dissipate. And when it had gone, he was left deeply chilled, because every last, remaining lie he'd told himself had been burned away, and he knew she'd spoken nothing but the plain, bitter truth.

Later that same Monday, the Duke of Clevedon visited the Court jewelers, Rundell and Bridge, and bought the biggest diamond ring he could find, the "prodigious great diamond" Longmore had recommended.

He spent the rest of the day composing his formal offer

of marriage. He wrote it and rewrote it. It had to be perfect. It had to say everything he felt for Clara. It had to make clear that his heart could hold no one else. It had to make plain that he had put all his follies and self-indulgence behind him and meant to be the man she deserved.

Words came easily enough to him when he was writing. He'd always had a knack for an easy, conversational tone, where others would be stiff. When he wrote, thoughts sharpened in his mind as they did not always do when he spoke.

He'd always delighted in writing to Clara, and it wasn't simply for the mental companionship. While sharing his thoughts and experiences with a kindred spirit formed a great part of his enjoyment, there was more to it. In the process of writing to her, he sorted and clarified his thoughts.

But he made heavy going of his marriage proposal. It was very late by the time he finished and memorized it, and by then it was far too late of think to going to Warford House. Clara would have gone out to a ball or a rout or some such.

He'd call tomorrow.

The Duke of Clevedon called at Warford House on Tuesday, naturally, though he knew the family were not at home to visitors—and for once Lady Clara was tempted to be not at home to him.

But when she told her mother she had a headache, Lady Warford said, "Lady Gorrell saw him yesterday leaving Rundell and Bridge. And here he is today when he can have you all to himself, instead of having to make his way through that crowd of bankrupts and mushrooms who hang about you. Surely you can put two and two together—and surely you can postpone indulging your megrims until after you hear what he has to say."

A ring and a proposal was the tally Mama made. She might be correct, but Clara was not in the mood, for him or for her mother. Lady Warford had taken three fits only this morning, complaining that all the world was talking about the Duke of Clevedon and those "she-devils who called themselves milliners, and their wicked child," who had very nearly cost him his life.

Of course, all would be forgiven once he put a ring on Clara's finger, and Mama could lord it over her friends, whose daughters had snared merely earls and viscounts and a lot of Honorable Misters.

Clara would be forgiven, too, for her numerous failings as a daughter. It was her fault Clevedon chased shopkeepers. It was her fault he was so shockingly inattentive and forgot engagements—such as promising to join them for dinner on Saturday night. It was all Clara's fault because she'd failed to fix his interest.

Small wonder, then, that when Clevedon entered the drawing room where she and her mother waited, Lady Clara's smile wasn't her warmest.

After mentioning that Longmore had told them of Sunday's "excitement," Mama asked so very sweetly whether the little girl was well. Clevedon said she was. Though he answered in monosyllables, obviously reluctant to talk about the child, Mama kept on grilling him. Finally, unable to smother her own curiosity, Clara asked, "Is it true she demanded to see the Princess Victoria?"

He laughed. Then he told the whole story. It was the same story Harry had recounted but it was in Clevedon's style, vivid and funny, including a droll imitation of Lucie Noirot explaining that she was the Princess Erroll of Albania.

"And when her mother pointed out that she was not a princess," he said, "Miss Lucie said"—and he raised his voice to a higher, lighter pitch—" 'Yes, Mama, but her highness wouldn't come to talk to Miss Lucie Cordelia Noirot, would she?' It was all I could do to keep a straight face."

And Clara thought, *He loves that child.*

And she thought, *What am I to do?*

"It seems to me that the child gets into dreadful scrapes," Mama said.

"How lucky you are," Clevedon said, "to have three girls who've never given you a moment's anxiety."

"If you think that, you're far out, indeed," said Mama with a titter. "I vow, they give me more anxiety as they grow older, rather than less."

"Yes, Mama is anxious that we shall end up old maids—or worse, married to someone unsuitable."

"Clara has a little headache," Mama said with a warning look at her. "She's a trifle out of sorts."

He looked at her. "You're ill, my dear? I should have realized. You seem not your usual cheerful self."

"It's only a trifling thing," said Mama, glaring at her.

"Trifle or not, you look pale, Clara," Clevedon said. He rose. "I won't weary you. I'll come back at another time."

A moment later he was gone, and in very short order, thanks partly to her mother's badgering and partly to shame and anger and various other emotional turbulence, Clara went to bed with an altogether real headache.

Wednesday afternoon
The Green Park

"You ran away," Marcelline said.

She'd taken Lucie to the park, and Lucie was pushing a child-size baby carriage, one of the numerous presents Clevedon had filled the nursery with. Susannah, who was still the favored doll, sat in it, staring at her surroundings with her wide blue glass eyes.

Marcelline had taken pains to make him hate her forever. Yet in spite of all said, Clevedon had come back.

He'd gone to the shop, and not finding her there, and getting no information from her sisters, he'd insisted on speaking to Sarah. Since the nursemaid was still, officially, his employee, Sophy and Leonie had to let her talk to him, and Sarah had to tell him that Mrs. Noirot had taken Lucie to the Green Park.

He'd come to the park and hunted Marcelline down—to confide his romantic tribulations, of all things!

He was intelligent, caring, and sensitive. He was an artful and passionate lover.

He was obstinate and oblivious, too.

She reminded herself that dukes were not like other men. Getting their own way all their lives damaged their brains.

Her brain was damaged, too, probably from spending so much time with him. No, her heart was what was damaged. In a not-so-secret corner, she was glad that he and Lady Clara were not yet engaged.

But they soon will be, and you'll simply have to live with it.

"You leapt at the first excuse not to propose," Marcelline said. "If you had persevered, I promise you, her headache would have vanished. Your behavior is what pains her, you obtuse man."

"I know I've made a muck of everything," he said. "It was true what you said the other day. But the mess is so horrendous, I'm having the devil's own time finding my way out."

"You're not helping matters, being here," she said.

"You're the expert on everything I do wrong," he said.

"You're the autocratic female who knows exactly what everyone ought to do."

"No, I know how everyone ought to *dress*," she said.

"I'll wager anything she knew why I was there," he said. "I saw Lady Gorrell as I was leaving the jeweler, and she was bound to tell everybody. But I know Clara, and she didn't seem very happy to see me—and when I offered to go, she looked relieved."

"And you have no idea why she'd want you gone?" Marcelline said. "You've neglected her for weeks. You've made a spectacle of yourself with a lot of milliners." Then you go out and buy a ring. And without any warning, you turn up, all braced for matrimony."

"It was hardly like that," he said.

"It was wrong, in any event," she said. "You haven't spent a minute *wooing* her."

"I've known her since she was five years old!"

"Women like to be courted. You know that. What is wrong with you? Have you a blind spot when it comes to Lady Clara?"

He stopped in his tracks and looked at her while a comical look of horror overspread his beautiful face. "Are you telling me I have to chase her and make sheep's eyes at her and hang on her every word the way her sodding idiot beaux do?"

"Don't be thick," Marcelline said. "You of all men know how to cast your lures at a woman. The trouble is, you treat her like a *sister*."

He stiffened, but recovered immediately. In the blink of an eye, he was moving again, walking alongside her in his usual easy, arrogant way, expecting all the world to give way before him. Why shouldn't he demand she solve his romantic difficulties? It was her purpose in life, as it was the purpose of all ordinary beings, to serve him. And wasn't that her job, serving people like him? Not merely her job, but her *ambition*?

It wouldn't occur to him that this was a thoroughly unreasonable way to behave with a woman he'd driven himself mad trying to make love him.

It wouldn't occur to him how painful this was for such a woman.

She reminded herself the pain was nobody's fault but hers for letting herself fall in love with him. She was a Noirot. She of all women ought to know better.

And being a Noirot, she needed to be thinking with her head—and not the soft bit, either.

He had to marry Lady Clara. All Marcelline's plans had one objective: making the Duchess of Clevedon her loyal client. If this marriage didn't take place, who knew how long it would be before he found someone else? It could be days. It could be years. And regardless how much time it took, how many other women in London could provide as splendid a framework for Marcelline's dresses?

Furthermore, that framework wouldn't provide nearly as good advertising were Lady Clara to marry a lesser being than the Duke of Clevedon.

In any case, she'd already cultivated Lady Clara and was grooming her to be a leader of fashion. Marcelline had already won her loyalty. In spite of all the rumors and scandal. In spite of Lady Warford.

In fact, Lady Clara had a fitting this afternoon.

A nursemaid walking with a little girl stopped to admire Lucie's doll. She obligingly stopped the baby carriage and took out Susannah for inspection.

"What a pretty dress!" the little girl exclaimed.

"My mama made it," Lucie said. "She makes dresses for ladies and princesses."

She put Susannah back and the nursemaid led the little girl away. The latter dragged her feet, looking back over her shoulder at Lucie's doll.

"You ought to give Lucie business cards to hand out," Clevedon said. "Have you thought of adding a line of doll dresses?"

"No."

"Think about it."

She had too much to think about as it was. "Lady Clara is coming for a fitting later today," she said. "A dress for Friday night. One of the Season's most important balls, I understand."

"Friday?" He frowned, thinking. "Damn. That must be Lady Brownlow's do. I suppose I'd better attend."

"Of course you'll attend," she said. "It's one of the high points of the Season."

"That doesn't say much for the Season."

"What is the matter with you?" she said. "I know you like to dance."

"In Paris," he said. "In Vienna. In Venice."

"Do you know how many men and women would give a vital organ to be invited to that ball?" she said.

"You?" he said. "Wouldn't you like to be there, showing off one of your creations?" A smile caught at the corner of his mouth and devilment danced in his eyes. "I should like to see you get into that party, uninvited."

She wanted to scream.

"Are you not paying attention?" she said. "You need to court Lady Clara. What you don't need is the woman everybody thinks is your latest liaison calling attention to herself. And what I don't need is to alienate precisely the people I want to come into my shop. How many times must I explain this to you? How can you be so thick?"

He looked away. "I was picturing you at the ball, and

it amused me. Well, I'll imagine it while I'm there. That should allay the tedium."

She could picture herself there, too—not the self she was, but the self she might have been, a gentleman's daughter. But then, if she'd been welcome to that ball, she wouldn't have Lucie. She would never have learned how to make clothes. She would never have truly found herself.

Not to mention she'd look like the rest of them.

Her life wouldn't be so hard but it wouldn't be nearly so much fun. One need only consider how bored he was, the great, spoiled numskull! Lady Brownlow had recently been elected a patroness of Almack's. She was one of Society's premier hostesses. Her parties were famous. And he acted as though he was forced to attend a lecture in calculus or one of those other horrible mathematical things.

"You will attend," she said. "And you will *not* arrive late. You'll make it clear that you want only to see Lady Clara, to be with Lady Clara. You'll act as though no other woman in the place exists for you. You'll act as though you haven't known her for ages, but have only now truly discovered her. It will seem as though she has suddenly appeared to you, like a vision, like Venus rising from the sea."

She wished Sophy were here to offer less clichéd dramatic imagery.

"You'll sweep her off her feet," she went on. "If the weather allows, you'll lure her out onto the terrace or balcony or someplace private, and you'll make it very romantic, and you'll make it impossible for her to say anything but yes. It's a seduction, Clevedon. Do keep that in mind. This isn't your dear friend or your sister. This is a woman, a beautiful, desirable woman, and you are going to *seduce* her into becoming your duchess."

Countess of Brownlow's ball
Friday night

The Duke of Clevedon resolved to do exactly as Noirot advised. He refused to let himself think about what he was doing because, he told himself, there was nothing to think about. He wanted Clara to marry him. She'd always been meant for him. He'd always loved her.

Like a sister.

He crushed the thought the instant it popped into his mind. He went to Lady Brownlow's ball. He followed Noirot's instructions to the letter. He arrived not too early, because that would be gauche, but in good time. And he hunted Clara as he would have hunted a popular demimondaine or a dashing matron.

He exerted himself to amuse her, whispering witty remarks into her shell-shaped ear whenever he could get close enough. She was looking quite handsome this evening, and the sodding idiot beaux couldn't keep away.

Noirot had dressed Clara in rose crepe, one of those robe sort of things. The front opening of this one revealed a white satin under-dress. Some ribbons crisscrossed the deep white V of the bodice, calling attention to her décolletage, while the bodice itself was shaped in diagonal folds that emphasized her voluptuous figure.

The men were almost visibly drooling and the women were almost visibly green.

He led her out to dance, aware that he was the luckiest man at the ball.

And he loved her.

Like a sister.

He strangled the thought while they danced, and it lay lifeless and forgotten in a dark, cobwebbed corner of his mind for the ensuing hours. It still lay dead in the shadows when, as instructed, he led Clara out to the terrace. Others were there, but they'd found their own relatively private corners. No one could be completely private, of course. It wasn't that sort of party. The lights from the ballroom cast a faint glow over the terrace. A sickle moon was sinking behind the trees toward the horizon, but the wispy clouds racing overhead didn't conceal the stars. It was a romantic enough evening.

He made her laugh and he made her blush, and then, when he deemed the moment exactly right, he said, "I have something very important to ask you, my dear."

She smiled up at him. "Do you, indeed?"

"All my happiness depends on it," he said. Was that an amused smile? Mocking? But no, she was probably nervous. He was, certainly.

Time to take her in his arms.

He did it. She didn't push him away.

Good. That was good.

But something was wrong.

No, everything was perfect.

He bent his head to kiss her.

She put her hand up, blocking the route to her mouth.

He lifted his head, and something skittered inside, cool, like relief . . .

But no, that was impossible.

She was looking up at him, still smiling, but now there was a spark in her eyes. He tried to remember when he'd seen that expression before. Then he recalled her eyes sparking in the same way when she snapped at something her mother said.

He wished Noirot were there to shout instructions—or get control of Clara—because he sensed that the situation had taken an unexpected turn, and not a good one, and he wasn't at all sure how to turn it back.

Then he realized what he should have done.

Idiot.

He should have asked first.

He drew back and said, "Forgive me. That was stupid. Presumptuous."

She raised her perfect eyebrows.

His speech, the speech he'd practiced for hours, went straight out of his head. He plunged on. "I meant to ask, first, if you would do me the very great honor of becoming my wife." He started to reach inside his coat for the ring. "I meant—I hardly knew what I meant . . ." Where the devil was it? "You look so beautiful—"

"Stop it," she said. "Stop it. How stupid do you think I am?"

He paused in his searching. "Stupid? Certainly not . . . We've always understood each other, you and I. We've shared jokes. How could I write all those letters to a stupid girl?"

"You stopped writing them," she said. "You stopped writing as soon as you met— But no, that isn't the point. Look at me."

He took his hand away from his coat. "I've been looking all night," he said. "You're the most beautiful girl here. The most beautiful girl in London."

"I'm different!" she said. "I'm completely different. But you haven't noticed. I've changed. I've learned. All the other men notice. But not you. I'm still Clara to you. I'm still your friend. I'm not really a woman to you."

"Don't be absurd. All night—"

"All night you've been *acting*! You practiced this, didn't you? I can tell. There's no *passion*!"

Her voice was climbing and he became aware of other terrace occupiers casually drawing nearer. "Clara, maybe we—"

"I deserve passion," she said. "I deserve to be loved— in *every* way. I deserve a man who'll give his whole heart, not the part he isn't using at the moment, the part he can spare for his *friends*."

"That isn't fair," he said. "I've loved you all my life."

"Like a *sister*!"

The dead thing sprang up from its corner and came running to the front of his mind. He knocked it down again. "It's more than that," he said. "You know it's more than that."

"Is it? Well, I don't care." She tossed her head. Clara actually tossed her head. "It isn't more to me. When you're about, it's the same as if I were with Harry. No, it's worse, because lately you've been a dead bore, and he, obnoxious as he is, is at least entertaining. I know you men are bound to have your outside interests— Oh, why should I bother with euphemisms? We both know we're talking about other women. Mama has drummed that into me. We're supposed to overlook it. Men are born that way and it can't be helped. I was prepared to overlook it."

"Clara, I swear to you—"

"Don't," she said. "I'm long past that. If you can't keep an engagement for dinner, if you can't be bothered to send a message—a few words only: 'Sorry, Clara. Something came up.' But you can't do that much. If this is how it's going to be—you getting all broody and distracted every time you fall in lust with somebody—well, I haven't the stomach for it. I won't put up with it, not for a dukedom. Not for three dukedoms. I deserve better than the role of quietly accepting wife. I'm an interesting woman. I read. I have opinions. I appreciate poetry. I have a sense of humor."

"I know all that. I've always known."

"I deserve to be *loved,* truly loved—mind, body, soul. And in case you haven't noticed, there's a line of men ready to give me all that. Why on earth should I settle for a man who can't give me anything but friendship? Why should I settle for *you*?"

She put up her chin and stormed away.

It was then he became aware that the place had grown quiet.

He looked in the direction she was walking. As many of the guests as could fit had jammed into the open French windows. The crowd gave way as she neared, and let her pass, which she did without hesitation, head high.

From the crowd came scattered bursts of applause.

He heard, from a distance, a shriek. Lady Warford.

Then he heard the buzzing of a crowd excited by scandal. The music started up again, and people drifted back into the ballroom.

He did not.

He made his way across the terrace, past the couples returning to their shadowy corners. He walked out into the garden, through the garden gate, on through a passage, and into the street.

Then, finally, he paused and looked about him. That was when he realized he was shaking.

He lifted his hands and stared at them, wondering.

The thing inside, the thing he'd strangled and knocked down, bounded up again, and danced happily about.

The Duke of Clevedon stood, dragging in great lungfuls of the cool night air, as though . . . as though . . .

Then he realized why he trembled.

He felt like a man who'd climbed the steps to the gallows, felt the rope dropping over his head and onto his shoulders, heard the parson pray for his soul, felt the hood pulled over his head—

—and at the last minute, the very last minute, the reprieve had come.

It was near dawn before Sophy came home.

Marcelline, who'd been lying in her bed staring into the darkness, got up when she heard her come up the stairs.

Sophy had gone to the ball. Clevedon was going to propose, and the world needed to know exactly what Lady Clara was wearing, along with who had made it. Sophy hadn't gone to find out what Lady Clara was wearing, of course. They already knew every detail, not only of the dress but of the accessories as well. Sophy had gone because, in exchange for the large amount of column space she wanted in tomorrow's—today's, actually—*Morning Spectacle*, Tom Foxe would want inside information. From an eyewitness.

It was by no means the first time Sophy had entered a great house for this purpose. Hosts often needed to hire additional staff for larger events. Reputable agencies existed to meet the need. Sophy was registered, under another name, of course, with all of the agencies. She knew how to wait on her betters. She'd been doing it since she was Lucie's age. And she knew how to blend in. She was a Noirot, after all.

"It's all right," Sophy said as she took off her cloak. "It didn't go exactly as planned, but I've taken care of it."

"Didn't go exactly as planned," Marcelline repeated.

"She refused him."

"*Mon dieu.*" Marcelline's chest felt tight. It was hard to breathe. She was in knots. Relief. Despair.

"What?" came Leonie's voice from behind her.

Marcelline and Sophy turned that way. Leonie stood in the open doorway of her bedroom. She hadn't bothered to pull on a dressing gown, and her nightcap—a wonderful froth of ribbons and lace—hung tipsily to one side of her head. She had the owlish look of one barely awake.

At least someone had slept this night.

"Lady Clara refused him," Sophy said. "I saw it all. He wooed her so beautifully. It was as though he was seeing her for the first time and he couldn't see anybody else. It was so romantic, like something in a novel—really, because we all know that men, generally speaking, are not very romantic."

"But what happened?" Leonie said. "It sounds perfect."

"It looked perfect. I was in a prime position, by the open French windows, and the wind carried their voices beautifully. When she said no, I vow, my mouth actually fell open. I don't know where she found the strength to refuse him, but she did, in no uncertain terms. They all heard it. The music had happened to stop at that moment, and others near the terrace heard, and word spread at a stunning rate. In a moment, you could have heard the proverbial pin drop. Everyone was straining to hear—and some of them were shoving to get to the windows."

Marcelline's shoulders sagged. "Oh, no."

"No need to worry," Sophy said briskly. "I saw at once what to do, and I've done it, and everything will work out very well. Please go back to bed. There's nothing on earth to fret about. I expect to have proof in the morning, and then you can see for yourselves. But for now, my loves, I must have some sleep. I'm ready to drop."

Chapter Sixteen

If, some years ago, our neighbours in sneer, called us a nation of shopkeepers, we think that they must now give us the credit of being shopkeepers of taste: we apprehend, no place in the world affords so great a variety of elegant amusement to the eye, as London in its various shops.

The Book of English Trades,
and Library of the Useful Arts, 1818

Eight o'clock, Saturday morning

Despite having gone to bed only a short time before, Sophy hurried in to breakfast only minutes after her sisters. She had a copy of the latest edition of *Foxe's Morning Spectacle* in her hand, and she was grinning.

"I told you I did it," she said. "Column inch after column inch, all about the gown Lady Clara Fairfax—or 'Lady C' as Foxe so delicately puts it—wore to the Brownlows' ball." She sat down and read aloud, " 'A white satin or *poult de soie* under-dress, a low *corsage,* the front square.' "

Marcelline paused, her coffee cup halfway to her lips. She needed coffee. She hadn't slept. "Clearly you gave Tom Foxe what he wanted."

"And he gave me columns of space," Sophy said triumphantly.

Leonie snatched the paper from her. "Let me see. 'Open robe of *rose noisette* crepe . . . *corsage* . . . descends in longitudinal folds on each side.'" She looked at Marcelline. "It goes on and on, like a fashion plate description. Down to the shoes. Good grief, what on earth did you do for him, Sophy? No, never mind. It's none of our business."

"I told you I'd take care of everything," Sophy said. "Never mind the rest of the description. You know what she was wearing." She pointed. "Start there."

Leonie read, "'The reader will wonder at our entering into minute detail regarding the fair attendee's attire. But no lesser tribute, we feel, would suffice for a dress that inspired its wearer not only with the confidence to decline the addresses of a *duke* but with the fire of poetry, for no lesser description could properly characterize the speech with which she so unequivocally rejected his offer of matrimony.'"

Thence followed Lady Clara's rejection speech. In this context it read like a scene from one of Lady Morgan's novels.

Marcelline put down her coffee cup and rubbed her head. "He's the Duke of Clevedon. She loves him. He's the world's foremost seducer of women—and he botched it. Well, goodbye Duchess of Clevedon."

"Goodbye to the duchess, perhaps," Sophy said. "It may take him a while to find another. But look on the bright side. Lady Clara will come back to Maison Noirot. She understands what we do for her. You read what she said to him. *'I'm different.'*"

"Her friends will come, too," Leonie said. "Every woman who was at that ball will want to see the creations that could give a woman confidence enough to reject a duke. Sophy, my love, you've outdone yourself."

"Leonie's right," Marcelline said. "Excellent work, love. Brilliant, actually. I would have stood there with my mouth hanging open and my mind completely blank. But you saw how to turn it to account, as you always do."

"Your mind never goes blank," Sophy said. "We've all mastered the art of quick thinking. And this was the easiest thing in the world. But now we've got to give them something to see. What dress shall we put out?"

"Leave it to me and Marcelline," Leonie said. "You need to get more rest. The ton will be all atwitter about last night, and the other scandal sheets will rush to copy this piece. It'll be all over London by afternoon. It's going to be a busy day, and you've had only a few hours' sleep."

Marcelline had had no sleep, but they didn't need to know that. She'd been lying awake in her bed, reminding herself she'd done the right thing, the only thing. If there had been an alternative, she would have jumped at it. But there wasn't: She and her sisters had devoted themselves to winning Lady Clara's loyalty. They'd given their utmost to make more of her than she realized she was.

Clevedon had to marry *her*. That was the whole point.

That was why Marcelline had pursued him in Paris, mad scheme that it was. The Duchess of Clevedon was their direct route to success. She'd end Dowdy's dominance. Then the perverse incompetent who called herself a dressmaker would no longer have the power to undermine them.

That was the plan. The Duchess of Clevedon had been the main objective.

Lady Clara was not going to be the Duchess of Clevedon—not after that speech, in front of an audience. But Sophy had rescued them, which meant that the essential plan, of dominating London's dressmaking trade, remained.

Marcelline's feelings didn't come into it. Her feelings were her problem.

Sophy, on the other hand, had spent the night on her feet, working, after a long day in the shop spent mainly on her feet, working.

"I'll admit I met with a bit more excitement than I'd expected," Sophy said. "I told you I'd maneuvered to a prime position near the French windows, where I could hear every word. No one noticed me. No one notices servants. Then, when I was coming away, I ran into Lord Longmore."

Both Marcelline and Leonie looked at her, eyebrows aloft.

"Not literally," Sophy said. "But there he was. I expected he'd look right through me and continue on his way the way they all do, as though nobody was there. Servants, like shopkeepers, *are* nobody, after all. But he stopped dead and said, 'What are *you* doing here?' You could have knocked me over with a feather, but I never blinked. 'Working, sir,' said I in my best maidservant voice—you know, the one with the hint of the Lancashire country girl. 'What, did they turn you off from the shop?' said he. 'What shop?' said I. And then, as deferential as you please, I suggested he'd mixed me up with another girl. But he wasn't having any of it. He gave me a hard look, and I was sure he'd keep at the interrogation, and give me away, but then his mother started shrieking, and he rolled his eyes and went that way."

"You'd better watch out for him," Marcelline said sharply. "He's not the fool he makes out to be, and the last thing we need is another one of us getting mixed up with an aristocrat."

"I don't think he wants to get mixed up with me," Sophy said. "I think he wishes us all at the devil. I think he may even believe we *are* the devil."

"Let's hope the ladies of the beau monde don't feel the same way," Leonie said.

"They won't," Sophy said. She got up and started for the door. "I believe I will go back to bed. But don't let me sleep for too long. I don't want to miss the fun. Oh, and if I were you, I'd put out the grey dress."

Downes's shop, later that same day

Mrs. Downes grimly regarded the dress lying on the counter. "How many does this make?" she asked her forewoman Oakes.

"Six," said Oakes.

"Lady Gorrell threw it at me," said Mrs. Downes.

"Shocking, madam." Oakes, who'd witnessed the event, wasn't at all shocked. Had she been the one to learn she'd paid a premium price for a dress exactly like one her friends had seen at Covent Garden Theater last year, she'd have reacted the same way.

Oakes had warned her employer. The sleeves, she'd pointed out when she saw the patterns—allegedly sent by Madam's associate in Paris—were in last years' style. Mrs. Downes had assumed either that Oakes was an idiot or her customers wouldn't notice. Many of them, accustomed to trusting her implicitly, didn't. At first. But they were quickly set straight.

Only one dressmaker in London made such memorable attire for ladies, and that dressmaker was not Mrs. Downes. Her customers' eyes were soon opened by their more observant friends and relatives, who recalled seeing such and such a dress at a banquet, the theater, Hyde

Park, and so on. Of a dozen orders so far, six owners had returned their purchases, furious about having paid high sums for not merely copies, but copies of *last years'* fashion. Mrs. Downes had been hoaxed, beyond a doubt, beautifully hoaxed.

Oakes wondered how much her employer had paid for old patterns, and how many customers she'd lose as word got about.

It was time, the forewoman thought, to find a new position.

As Clevedon had expected, the shop was mobbed that day.

He passed it on his way to White's Club and again on his way to the boot makers, the hat makers, the wine merchant, and others. He'd shopped for things he didn't need, simply to keep in St. James's Street. He was waiting for Maison Noirot's eager throngs to melt away.

He'd read the *Morning Spectacle*, as had most of the Beau Monde, apparently. He wasn't amazed at Foxe's having got hold of the story. The man was noted for that. The detail was another matter. Clearly, Foxe had planted a spy in their midst.

The spy could be none other than Miss Sophia. The story—entirely about the dress, lovingly described, with the dressmaking establishment prominently mentioned—was in her dramatic style. To have done all that in time for today's edition, she had to have been on the spot.

That, actually, was a relief.

His one great worry was that last night's debacle would mark the end of Maison Noirot. The ton would blame Mrs. Noirot for leading him astray, and they'd shun her, as she'd warned him time and again. Clara would never return to the shop, and Mrs. Noirot would be marked down as a temptress and a harlot. Henceforth the ladies would have nothing to do with her.

But the ladies came today in an endless parade, stepping down from their carriages and peeping into the shop windows before going in. At this rate, they'd wear out the shop bell.

. . . a dress that inspired its wearer not only with the confidence to decline the addresses of a duke but with the fire of poetry . . .

The impudence of it passed all bounds.

Typical. The impudence of those Noirot women was beyond anything. And like all else they did, the article was well done, indeed. He would have liked to hug Sophia for it, but Sophia wasn't the first person on his mind.

It wasn't Sophia who'd kept him awake all night.

It wasn't Sophia who'd got him up to pace and argue with himself. A futile argument.

From the time he'd escaped the party, from the time he'd stood on the pavement and realized why he was shaking, he'd seen there was only one way to put an end to this farce.

And so he waited until the afternoon waned and the ladies had gone home to dress for the ritual promenade in Hyde Park.

Then he crossed to the other side of St. James's Street and entered Maison Noirot.

The shop bell tinkled, and Marcelline thought, *Will they never go home?*

She was happy, of course. This had been a day like no other—not even the day after she'd returned from Paris and the ladies had come to stare at the *poussière* dress. Today, though, herds of women had come. Their old shop could never have contained them all. As it was, she needed to find at least six more seamstresses in no time at all, otherwise they would never complete all the orders by the dates promised.

All this went through her head in the instant before she lifted her gaze from the tray of ribbons she was sorting, and looked toward the door.

Her heart beat painfully.

The gentleman stepped inside, and stopped and looked about. He did it exactly in the way all gentleman did when entering a shop for the first time: gazing coolly about them, evaluating what they saw, deciding whether it was worth their notice, and taking no notice of the lowly shop-keeper behind the counter.

But this wasn't the first time he'd been here and this wasn't any gentleman.

This was Clevedon, tall and arrogant, his hat tipped precisely so, his black hair curling under the brim. He carried a gold-tipped walking stick, and as he paused to examine the shop, he set both hands on it. His tan gloves fit like skin. She could see the outlines of his knuckles.

His hands, his hands.

She remembered his hand stroking down her back. Cupping her face. Sliding over her breast. Gliding between her legs.

Had this been any other gentleman, any shopkeeper would have stepped out from behind the counter, prepared to give him personal and exclusive attention.

She stayed where she was, bracing her hands on the counter. "Good afternoon, your grace," she said.

"Good afternoon, Mrs. Noirot." He took off his hat and bowed.

She dipped a quick curtsey.

He set his hat on a chair, then walked to the manne-quin and inspected her dress.

It was a dark grey tulle, a color called "London Smoke," which the lavish pink satin bodice trim set off beautifully. Richly embroidered roses and twining leaves adorned the skirt.

"That looks very . . . French," he said.

"I always dress the mannequin more dashingly and flamboyantly than I would dress my customers," she said. "After seeing what the mannequin is wearing, they're less likely to become hysterical when I propose something rather more exciting than they're accustomed to."

He smiled a little and came to the counter. "How fitting," he said. "*You* are something rather more exciting than some of us are accustomed to."

"Not *some*," she said. "All of you. Maison Noirot is not the usual thing."

"I couldn't agree more," he said. "I was glad to see that Miss Sophia turned last night's debacle to good account. But of course, I should have expected no less."

"I expected a good deal more from you," Marcelline said. "You bungled it."

"Yes," he said. "What else could I do? I was asking the wrong woman to marry me."

Her heart seemed to stop beating altogether. She felt dizzy.

He moved to the door and turned the sign to Closed.

"We are not closed," she said. Her voice seemed to come from miles away.

"You've had enough business for one day," he said.

"You do not determine how much business is enough," she said.

He came back to the counter. "Come out from behind there," he said.

"Absolutely not."

He smiled. That was all he did. But to say *smile* conveyed nothing. Anybody could smile. What he did—only Sophy could have words for it.

His beautiful mouth turned up, a little crookedly, and his green eyes regarded her with an amused affection that went straight to her pounding heart, and left her disarmed and weak and wanting.

"I need all the customers I can get," she said. "I'm not at all sure that Lady Clara will return—"

"You know she will. For more dresses to give her the strength to contend with stupid men."

"—and since there's to be no Duchess of Clevedon in the immediate future, I'll have to make up for it with lesser mortals."

"I was thinking," he said, "that you ought to be the Duchess of Clevedon."

She stood for a moment, speechless for once in her life, though she'd sensed trouble coming. Even so, as fine-tuned as her instincts were, she couldn't take it in. She thought her ears must be playing tricks. Or he was playing tricks.

She was tired. It had been a long, very busy day, after a sleepless, wretched night—after hearing the news from Sophy and not knowing whether to laugh with relief or weep with despair, for all her plans and all she'd borne. All for nothing. She'd done her best, and she'd paid a price higher than she'd ever imagined. Then, when Sophy came home and told them what had happened, Marcelline had looked around at all her hopes and dreams for their future, smashed to pieces.

She took a steadying breath. Breathing wasn't enough. She needed to sit down. She needed a strong drink.

She said, "Have you lost your mind?"

He said, "I don't know about my mind. My heart, yes."

She scrambled for her wits. "I know what this is. You had a shock to your sensibilities. There was that beautiful girl, the one you've loved all your life—"

"Like a *sister*. She was right. You were right."

"You're still in shock," she said. "Angry, I dare say. She humiliated you. In front of everybody. People applauded her, I understand."

"Did Miss Sophia tell you that? I deduced, from today's *Morning Spectacle,* that she'd been there. Her style is unmistakable."

She couldn't let him distract her. "The point is, you're striking back."

"At Clara? Don't be absurd. She was absolutely right. She knew my heart wasn't in it. She knew I was acting. I followed your instructions to the letter. Exactly as one follows instructions. That isn't how it ought to be. It ought to happen of itself, because nothing else is bearable."

"Stop," she said. "Stop right now." She needed to run far away, the way her forebears ran from difficulties. She needed to run because with every fiber of her being she longed to say yes. And that was a quick route to self-destruction.

"When I left that party, I was shaking," he said. He looked down at his hands, at the beautiful tan gloves. He set them on the counter. Her hands, still braced on the counter, were not so very far away. She had only to reach a very little way to touch him. She kept her hands where they were.

"I realized it was because I'd been on the brink of the worst mistake of my life," he said. "A mistake that would have ruined two lives. I realized that Clara had spared me. She'd saved us both. She was right. I could never be the husband she deserves. For me there can't be anyone but you."

Don't do this don't do this don't do this.

There was a weight on her chest. It hurt to breathe. "Don't be an idiot," she said.

"Listen to me," he said.

"No, because you're not thinking."

"I've done nothing but think," he said. "Last night, all this day, while I wandered up and down St. James's Street, waiting for the mobs to leave, so that I could talk to you. I've had plenty of time for second thoughts, and I haven't any. The opposite, in fact. The more time I've had, the surer I've felt. I love you, Marcelline." He paused. "You said you loved me."

He wasn't going to stop. He wasn't going to give up. He was obstinate. Hadn't she already learned that, over and over again? When he wanted something, he went after it, single-mindedly, and he was not over-scrupulous in his methods.

He was like her, in other words.

The irony was too rich.

She slid her hands from the counter and folded her arms, protecting herself. "I told you that doesn't matter," she said. "You can't marry me. I'm a *shopkeeper*. You can't marry a shopkeeper."

"Noblemen have married courtesans," he said. "They've married their housekeepers and their dairymaids."

"And it never turns out well," she said. When gentlemen married far beneath them, their wives and children paid for it. They became outcasts. They lived in limbo, unable to return to their old world and shunned in their new one. "I can't believe you think this is sane."

"You know it's the only sane thing," he said. "I love you. I want to give you everything. I want to give Lucie everything she needs—not merely dolls and fine clothes and schooling, but a father. I lost a family, and I know how precious it is. I want you and I want your family and I want to be part of your lives."

She heard the desperation in his voice, the urgency, and she wanted to weep.

"I know the shop is your passion," he said, "and it would kill you to give it up—but you don't have to. I thought about that, too. In fact, I've been thinking about your shop for weeks."

She didn't doubt it. She didn't doubt that he meant every word.

"I have ideas," he went on eagerly. "We can do this together. Other noblemen have business interests. I can write, and I've the resources to create a magazine. Like *La Belle Assemblée,* but better. I've other ideas about expanding the business. You said you were the greatest modiste in the world. I can help you make all the world realize it. Marry me, Marcelline."

It wasn't fair.

She was a dreamer, yes. All of her kind were. They dreamed impossible dreams. Yet she and her sisters had made some of them come true.

It was a beautiful dream he offered. But he saw only the beautiful part.

"Other noblemen's business interests have to do with property," she said. "And great schemes. They own mines and invest in canals and the new railways. They do not open little shops and sell ladies' apparel. The Great World will never forgive you. These aren't the old days, Clevedon. These aren't the days of the Prince Regent and his loose-living set. Society isn't as tolerant as it used to be."

"Then Society is a great bore," he said. "I don't care whether they approve of my going into trade. I believe in you and in what you do. I want to be part of it."

He didn't know what he was saying. He didn't understand what it meant to lose Society's regard and his friends' respect, to be barred from the world to which one ought to belong. She knew all too well.

Even if he could understand that and accept it, there remained the nasty little business of who she really was.

She had no choice. She had to be the sane one. This was one dream she couldn't dream. He was watching her, waiting.

She unfolded her arms.

She put her hands together, like one offering a prayer, and said, "Thank you. This is kind and generous, and, truly, you do me a great honor—I know that's what one is supposed to say, but I mean it, truly—"

"Marcelline, don't—"

"But no, your grace, no. I can never marry you."

She saw his face go white, and she turned away, quickly, before she could weaken. She walked to the door that led to the back rooms, and opened it, and walked through, and closed it, very, very gently, behind her.

Clevedon walked blindly from the shop, down St. James's Street. At the bottom of the street he paused, and gazed blankly at St. James's Palace. There was a noise in his head, a horrible noise. He was aware of misery and pain and rage and the devil knew what else. He hadn't the wherewithal to take it apart and name its components. It was a kind of hell-brew of feelings, and it consumed him. He didn't hear the shout. He couldn't hear above the noise in his head.

"What the devil is wrong with you, Clevedon? I've been shouting myself hoarse, running down the street like a damn fool. One damn fool after another, obviously. I saw you come out of that shop, you moron."

Clevedon turned and looked at Longmore. "I recommend you not provoke me," he said coldly. "I'm in a mood to knock someone down, and you'll do very well."

"Don't tell me," Longmore said. "The dressmaker doesn't want you, either. By gad, this isn't your day, is it? Not your week, rather."

The urge to throw Longmore against a lamp post or a fence or straight into the gutter was overpowering. The guards would probably rush out from the palace gates—and there Clevedon would be, in the newspapers again, the name on every scandalmonger's lips.

Hell, what was one more scandal?

He dropped his walking stick and grasped Longmore by the shoulders and shoved him hard. With an oath, Longmore shoved back. "Fight me like a man, you swine," he said. "I dare you."

A moment later, they'd torn off their coats. In the next instant, their fists flew, as they tried, steadily and viciously, to pummel each other to death.

Marcelline sent Sophy out into the showroom to close the shop.

Though she was so tired, tired to death and heartsick, she knew better than to go to bed. Lucie would think she was ill, and she'd get panicky—and very possibly do something rash again.

In any case, Marcelline knew she wouldn't be able to sleep. She needed to focus on making beautiful clothes. That would calm her.

She was trying to redesign the fastening for a pelisse when Sophy came in. Leonie trailed after her. Sophy hadn't said anything before, but she'd given Marcelline a searching look. Even wearing a card-playing face, it was hard to hide one's emotions from one's own kind.

The two younger sisters had come to find out the trouble and comfort her as they always did.

"What happened?" Sophy said. "What's wrong?"

"Clevedon," Marcelline said. She jammed her pencil into the paper. The pencil broke. "Oh, it's ridiculous. I ought to laugh. But I can't. You won't believe it."

"Of course we will," Sophy said.

"He offered you carte blanche," Leonie said.

"No, he asked me to marry him."

There was a short, stunned silence.

Then, "I reckon he's in a marrying mood," Sophy said.

Marcelline laughed. Then she started to sob.

But before she could fall to pieces, Selina Jeffreys came to the door. "Oh, madame, I beg your pardon. But I was just out—I went to get the ribbons from Mr. Adkins down the bottom of the street—and when I came out of his shop, there were the two gentleman fighting down at the palace, and people coming out of every shop and club, and running to watch the fight."

"Two *gentlemen*?" Leonie said. "Two ruffians, you mean."

"No, Miss Leonie. It's his grace the Duke of Clevedon and his friend, the other tall, dark gentleman."

"Lord Longmore?" Sophy said. "He was here only a little while ago."

"Yes, miss, that's the one. They're trying to kill each other, I vow! I couldn't stand to watch—and besides, there was all sorts of men coming along to see. It wasn't any place for a girl on her own."

Sophy and Leonie didn't have Jeffreys's delicate scruples. They ran out to watch the fight. They didn't notice that their older sister didn't follow.

* * *

Sophy and Leonie returned not very long after they'd gone out.

Marcelline had given up trying to create something beautiful. She wasn't in the mood. She looked in on the seamstresses, then she went upstairs and looked in on Lucie, who was reading to Susannah from one of the books Clevedon had bought.

After the visit to the nursery, Marcelline went into their sitting room and poured herself a glass of brandy.

She'd taken only a few sips before her sisters returned, looking windblown and sounding a little out of breath, but otherwise undamaged.

They poured brandy, too, and reported.

"It was delicious," Sophy said. "They must practice at the boxing salons, because they're very good."

"It didn't look like practice to me," Leone said. "It looked like they were trying to kill each other."

"It was wonderfully ferocious," Sophy said. "Their hats were off, and their coats, too, and they were trampling their neckcloths. Their hair was wild and they had blood on their clothes." She fanned herself with her hand. "I vow, it was enough to make a girl swoon."

"It put me in mind of the Roman mobs at the Coliseum," Leonie said. "Half of White's must have been there—all those fine gentlemen, and all of them shouting and betting on the outcome and egging them on."

"Leonie's right," Sophy said. "It did look to be getting out of hand, and I was thinking we ought to find a safer place to watch from. But then the Earl of Hargate came out of St. James's Palace with some other men."

"Straight through the crowd of men he came, pushing them out of his way—and he must be sixty if he's a day," Leonie said.

"But he carries himself like Zeus," Sophy said. "And the men gave way, and he ordered his grace and his lordship to stop making damned fools of themselves."

"They weren't listening," Leonie said.

"It was the bloodlust," Sophy said. "They were like wolves."

"None of the other men had dared to try to break it up," Leonie said.

"But Lord Hargate waded right into the fight," Sophy said. "And he got in the way of Longmore's fist. But the earl dodged the blow—oh, Marcelline, I wish you'd seen it—and then he grabbed Longmore's arm and pulled him away from Clevedon. And one of the gentleman with him—it had to be one of his sons—the same features, build, and coloring. Whichever one it was, he took hold of Clevedon."

"And then the earl and his son dragged them away."

"And one of the other gentlemen was threatening to read the Riot Act, and so we came away." Sophy drank her brandy and poured some more.

"I'm sure we needn't wonder what it was about," Marcelline said. "Longmore avenging his sister's honor, or some such."

"Why should he need to?" Sophy said. "Everyone thought Lady Clara avenged her own honor very well. Anything Longmore did would be anticlimactic, don't you think?"

"Then what provoked fisticuffs in St. James's Street?" Leonie said.

"Don't be thick," Sophy said. "It's not as though men need a sane reason. They were both in a bad mood. One of them picked a fight. And I'll wager anything that now it's over, they'll be getting drunk together."

"Why was Longmore in a bad mood, Sophy?" Marcelline said. "You said he'd been here, after Clevedon left."

"He came to plague me about the ball and call me a traitor for spying for Tom Foxe on his sister and friend. I pretended not to know what he was talking about. Oh, Lord." Her pretty countenance turned repentant. "Oh, Marcelline, what horrid sisters we are. We hear of a fight, and off we go, little bloodthirsty cats, and there you are, your heart breaking—"

"Don't be ridiculous," Marcelline said. "Save the drama for the newspapers."

"But what happened, dearest?" Sophy set down her glass and knelt by Marcelline and took her hand. "What did Clevedon say and what did you say—and why are you pretending your heart isn't broken?"

Clevedon House
Sunday 10 May, three o'clock in the morning

The house was dark, everyone abed but one. In the library, a single candle flickered over a solitary figure in a dressing gown whose pen scratched rapidly across the paper.

The Duke of Clevedon had done his best to beat Longmore to a bloody pulp. Afterward they'd emptied one bottle after another. Yet he'd come home all too sober. It seemed there wasn't enough drink in all the world to dull the ache in his heart or quiet his conscience and let him sleep.

Nothing to be done about the heartache but endure.

His conscience was another matter.

It drove him to the library. Then, even before he took up his pen to write to Clara, he knew how it must begin:

Be not alarmed, madam, on receiving this letter, by the apprehension of its containing any repetition of those sentiments, or renewal of those offers, which were last night so disgusting to you.

It was the start of Mr. Darcy's letter to Elizabeth Bennett in *Pride and Prejudice*, Clara's favorite novel. He could easily imagine her reluctant smile when she read it. He continued in his own words:

I was wrong to make an offer, and you were right in all you said, but you said not half enough. Our listeners should have heard the thousand ways I've taken you for granted and tried your good nature and the ways I've thought only of myself and never of you. You've been true to me for all the time I've known you, and for all that time I, too, have been true only to me. When you were grieving for the grandmother I knew you dearly loved, I abandoned you to jaunt about the Continent. I expected you to wait for me, and you did. How, then, did I return your patience and loyalty? I was neglectful, insensitive, and false.

He wrote on, of the many ways he'd wronged her. She'd brought joy and light into his life when he was a lonely, heartbroken boy. Her letters had brightened his days. She was dear to him, and always would be, but they were friends and no more. Surely he'd known in his heart this wasn't enough for marriage, but it was the easy way and he took it. He'd been false to her and false to himself, because he'd been a coward, afraid to risk his heart.

He acknowledged all his thoughtless and unkind acts, and concluded:

I'm sorry, my dear, so deeply sorry. I hope in time you'll forgive me—though I can't at the moment suggest a reason to do so. With all my heart I wish you the happiness I ought to have been able to give you and a hundred times more.

He wrote his usual affectionate closing, and signed with his initial, as he always did.

He folded up the letter, addressed it, and left it in the tray for the servant to take out with the morning mail.

Then, only the heartache remained.

Chapter Seventeen

Experience, the mother of true wisdom, has long since convinced me, that real beauty is best discerned by real judges; and the addresses of a sensible lover imply the best compliment to a woman of understanding.

La Belle Assemblée,
or Bell's Court and Fashionable Magazine,
Advertisements for June 1807

Early afternoon, Sunday 10 May

The Duke of Clevedon blinked at the excessively bright light. Saunders, the sadist, stood looking down at him. He'd opened the curtains, and the sun was as bright as lightning bolts. When Clevedon moved his head, thunder cracked, right against his skull.

"I'm so sorry to disturb you, your grace."

"No, you're not," Clevedon croaked.

"Mr. Halliday was most insistent," Saunders said. "He said you would wish to be wakened. Mrs. Noirot is here."

Clevedon sat up abruptly. His brain thumped painfully against something hard and sharp. The interior of his skull had grown thorns. "Lucie," he said. "Is she ill?

Lost? Damn, I told her that child needed . . ." The sentence trailed off as his drink-poisoned brain caught up with his tongue.

"Mrs. Noirot said we were to assure your grace that the Princess Erroll of Albania is well and safely at home doing sums with her aunt. Mr. Halliday has taken the liberty of asking Mrs. Noirot to wait in the library. Being aware that you would need time to dress, he saw to it that refreshment was brought to her. I have brought your coffee, sir."

Now Clevedon's heart was pounding, too, along with his brain, but not at the same tempo.

He did not leap from his bed, but he got out more quickly than was altogether comfortable for a man in his condition. He hastily swallowed the coffee. He washed and dressed in record time, though it seemed an age to him, even though he decided not to bother with the nicety of shaving.

A glance in the mirror told him shaving wouldn't do much to improve his appearance. He looked like an animated corpse. He tied his neckcloth in a haphazard knot, shrugged into his coat, and hurried out of the room, still buttoning it.

When he came in, smoothing his neckcloth like a nervous schoolboy called on to recite from the *Iliad,* he found Noirot bent over the library table.

She was perfect, as usual, in one of her more dashing creations, a heavy white silk embroidered all over with red and yellow flowers. The double-layered short cape, its edges gored and trimmed in black lace, was made of the same material. It extended out over her shoulders and over the big sleeves of her dress. Round her neck she'd tied a black lace something or other. Her hat sat well back on her head, so that its brim framed her face, and that inner brim was adorned with lace and ribbons. More ribbon and lace trimmed the back, where a tall plume of feathers sprouted.

He, clearly, did not make nearly as pretty a picture. At his entrance she looked up, and her hand went to her bosom. "Oh, no," she said. Then she collected herself and said, in cooler tones, "I heard about the fight."

"It's not as bad as all that," he said, though he knew it was. "I know how to dodge a blow to the face. You ought to see Longmore. At any rate, this is the way I always look after an excessively convivial night with a man who tried to kill me. Why are you here?"

He was careful to keep any hope from his face as well as his voice. It was harder to keep it from his heart. He didn't want to let himself hope she'd changed her mind. He was fully awake and sober now and wishing he were drunk again.

He could truly understand at last, not only in his mind but in his gut as well, why his father had crawled into a bottle. Drink dulled the pain. Physical pain dulled it, too. While fighting with Longmore he'd felt nothing. Now he remembered every word he'd said to her, the way he'd opened his heart, concealing nothing. It hadn't been enough. *He* wasn't enough.

She gestured at the table. "I was looking at the magazines," she said. "I'm unscrupulous. I looked at your notes, too. But I can't read your writing. You said you had ideas. About my business."

"Is that why you've come?" he said tightly. "For the ideas for your shop—the ideas to make you the greatest modiste in the world."

"I *am* the greatest modiste in the world," she said.

Dear God how he loved her! Her self-confidence, her

unscrupulousness, her determination, her strength, her genius. Her passion.

He allowed himself a smile, and hoped it didn't look too sickeningly infatuated. "I beg your pardon," he said. "How could I forget? You *are* the greatest modiste in the world."

"But I'm someone else as well," she said.

She moved away from the table and walked to the window and looked out into the garden.

He waited. Had he any choice?

"I was tired yesterday," she said, still looking out. "Very tired. It was a shockingly busy day, and we were run off our feet, and I was in a state, trying not to fall apart." She turned away from the window and met his gaze. "I was trying so hard that I was unkind and unfair to you."

"On the contrary, you declined my offer quite gently," he said. "You told me I was kind and generous." He couldn't altogether keep the bitterness from his voice. It was the same as telling a man, *We can still be friends.* He couldn't be her friend. That wasn't enough. He understood now, not merely in his mind but with every cell of his being, why Clara had told him it wasn't enough.

"You were kind and generous enough to deserve the truth," she said. "About me."

Then he remembered the stray thought he'd had after he'd seen Lucie for the first time. "Damn it to hell, Noirot, you're already married. I thought of that, but I forgot. That is, Lucie had to have a father. But he wasn't in view. You were on your own."

"He's dead."

Relief made him dizzy. He moved to stand at the chimneypiece. He pretended to lean casually against it. His hands were shaking. Again. He was in a very bad way.

"Your grace, you look very ill," she said. "Please sit down."

"No, I'm well."

"No, sit, please, I beg you. I'm a wretched mass of nerves as it is. Waiting for you to swoon isn't making this easier."

"I never swoon!" he said indignantly. But he took his wreck of a body to the sofa and sat.

She walked back to the library table and took up a cup from the tray resting there. She brought it to him. "It's gone cold," she said, "but you need it."

He took it from her and drank. It was cold, but it helped.

She sat in the nearest chair. A few, very few feet of carpet lay between them. All the world lay between them.

She folded her hands in her lap. "My husband's name was Charles Noirot. He was a distant cousin. He died in France in the cholera epidemic a few years ago. Most of my relatives died then. Lucie fell gravely ill."

Her husband dead. Her relatives dead. Her child on the brink of death.

He tried to imagine what that had been like and his imagination failed. He and Longmore had been on the Continent when the cholera struck. They'd survived, and that, as far as he could make out, had been a miracle. Most victims died within hours.

"I'm sorry," he said. "I had no idea."

"Why should you?" she said. "The point of all this is my family, and who I am."

"Then your name really is Noirot," he said. "I'd wondered if it was simply a Frenchified name you three had adopted for the shop."

Her smile was taut. "That was the name my paternal grandfather adopted when he fled France during the Revolution. He got his wife and children out, and some aunts and cousins. Others of his family were not so lucky. His older brother, the Comte de Rivenoir, was caught trying to escape Paris. After he and his family went to the guillotine, my grandfather inherited the title. He saw the folly of trying to make use of it. His family, the Robillon family, had a bad name in France. You know the character, the Vicomte de Valmont, in the book by Laclos, *Les Liaisons Dangereuses*?"

He nodded. It was one of a number of books Lord Warford had declared unfit for decent people to read. Naturally, when they were boys, Longmore had got hold of a copy and he and Clevedon had read it.

"The Robillon men were that sort of French aristocrat," she said. "Libertines and gamblers who used people like pawns or toys. They weren't popular at that time, and they're still not remembered affectionately in France. Since he wanted to be able to move about freely, Grandfather took a name as common as dirt. Noirot. Or, in English, Black. He and his offspring used one or the other name, depending on the seduction or swindle or ruse in hand at the moment."

He was leaning forward now, listening intently. Pieces were falling into place: the way she spoke, her smooth French and her aristocratic accent . . . but she'd told him she was English. Well, then, she'd lied about that, too.

"I knew you weren't quite what you appeared to be," he said. "My servants took you for quality, and servants are rarely taken in."

"Oh, we can take in anybody," she said. "We're born that way. The family never forgot they were aristocrats. They never gave up their extravagant ways. They were expert seducers, and they used the skill to find wealthy spouses. Being more romantic and less practical than their Continental counterparts, the men had great luck with highborn Englishwomen."

"That must hold true for English *men* as well," he said.

Her dark gaze met his. "It does. But I never set out to get a spouse. I've lied and cheated—you don't know the half of it—but it was all for the purpose I explained early in our acquaintance."

"I know you cheat at cards," he said.

"I didn't cheat during our last game of Vingt et Un," she said. "I merely played as though my life depended on it. People in my family often find themselves in that position: playing a game on which their life depends. But cheating at cards is nothing. I forged names on our passports to get out of France quickly. My family often finds it necessary to leave a country suddenly. My sisters and I were taught the skill, and we practiced diligently, because we never knew when we'd need it. We were well educated in the normal ways as well. We had lessons in deportment as well as mathematics and geography. Whatever else we Noirots were—and it wasn't pretty—we were aristocrats, and that was our most valuable commodity. To speak and carry ourselves as ladies and gentlemen do—you can imagine the fears it allays, the doors it opens."

"I can see that it would be much easier to seduce an aristocratic English girl if you don't sound like a clerk from the City or a linen draper," he said. "But you married a cousin. You have a shop. You didn't follow the same path."

She got up abruptly from her chair and moved away in a rustle of petticoats. He rose, too, unsteadily, and he couldn't tell whether that was the aftereffects of fighting and drinking or the hope warring with the certainty he'd lost her.

She walked to the library table and took up his notes. "Your handwriting is deplorable," she said. She put them down and, turning back to him, said, "I haven't told you about my mother."

"An English aristocrat, yes? Or something else?"

She gave a short laugh. "Both."

She returned to her chair, and he sat, too. His heart thudded. Something was coming, and it wasn't good. He was sure of that. He was leaning forward, waiting. He was wanting it to be over with and hoping against hope it would be good news. But it couldn't be good, else she wouldn't be so ill at ease, she who was never ill at ease, mistress of every situation.

And what was wrong with him? She'd admitted to forgery! She'd told him she came from a line of blue-blooded French criminals!

"My mother was Catherine DeLucey," she said.

He recognized the surname, but it took a moment for him to place it. Then he saw it: blue, vivid blue.

"Lucie's eyes," he said. "Those remarkable blue eyes. Miss Sophia, too. And Miss Leonie. I knew there was something familiar about them. They're unforgettable. The DeLuceys—the Earl of Mandeville's family."

Her color came and went. She folded her hands tightly in her lap.

He remembered then. Some old scandal to do with one of Lord Hargate's sons. Not the one who'd manhandled him yesterday, though. Which one? He couldn't remember. His brain was slow and thick and aching.

She said, "Not those DeLuceys. Not the good ones with the handsome property near Bristol. My mother was one of the other ones."

* * *

He'd been leaning toward her so eagerly, and she'd seen the hope in his eyes, and the uncertainty.

Then she saw the truth dawn. His head went back, and his posture stiffened, and he looked away, unable to meet her gaze.

Sophy and Leonie had told her he didn't need to know. They'd said she'd only heap coals on her own head, and since when had she taken on the role of martyr?

But they didn't know what it was to love a man, and so they didn't know what it was to hurt at causing him pain. He'd opened his heart to her. He'd offered her the moon and the stars, knowing nothing about her. And she hadn't had the courage to offer what she could in fair return: the truth.

She'd reminded him again and again of her trade, because she could cope with his coming to his senses and rejecting her because of what she did for a living. But to tell him who she *was,* then see his face change as he shut her out . . . That would hurt more than she could bear.

She saw it now, and it hurt more than she'd imagined. But the worst was over. She'd live.

She went on quickly, eager to have her sordid tale done. "My mother was a blueblood, but she wasn't like the other Noirot wives. She hadn't any money. They married each other for fortunes that turned out not to exist. They didn't learn the truth until the marriage night, and then they thought it a great joke. She and Father led a nomadic life, from one swindle to the next. They would run up debts in one place, then leave in the dead of night for another. We children were inconvenient baggage. They left us with this relative or that one. Then, when I was nine years old, we ended up with a woman who'd married one of my father's cousins. She was a fashionable dressmaker in Paris. She trained us to the trade, and she saw to our education. We were attractive girls, and Cousin Emma made sure we learned refinement. That was good for business. And of course, a pretty girl with good manners might attract a husband of wealth and quality."

She looked up to gauge his reaction, but he seemed to be studying the carpet. His thick black lashes, so stark against the pallor of his skin, veiled his eyes.

But she didn't need to read the expression in his eyes to know what was there: a wall.

A sense of loss swept over her, and it was like a sickness. She felt so weary. She swallowed and went on, "But I fell in love with Cousin Emma's nephew Charlie, and he had no money. I had to continue working. Then the cholera came to Paris." She made a sweeping gesture. "They all died. We had to close our shop—not that I would have stayed. I was terrified I'd take sick. Then who'd look after my daughter and sisters? I felt we'd be safer in London, though we were nearly penniless. But I went to the gaming hells and played cards. You saw how I won in Paris. That was how I fed and housed my family when we first came to London, three years ago. That was how I started my shop. I won the money at cards."

She stood. "There it is. You know everything. Your friend Longmore thinks we're the devil, and he's not far wrong. You couldn't ally yourself with a worse family. We seduce and swindle, lie and cheat. We have no scruples, no morals, no ethics. We don't even understand what those things are. I did you the greatest favor in the world when I said no. No one in my family would understand why I did it."

She started for the door, still talking, unable to help herself. It was the last time, perhaps, they'd ever speak.

"They'd see you only as a pigeon ripe for plucking," she said. "But you needn't believe I was being noble and self-sacrificing in declining your proposal. It was pure selfishness. I'm too proud to endure being snubbed by your fine friends."

"You could endure it." His low voice came from behind her.

She hadn't heard him rise from the sofa. She'd been deaf and blind to all but despair, and too busy trying not to fall apart. She wouldn't turn around. Nothing he said could make any difference now. He was trying to be kind, probably. She couldn't bear kindness. She continued toward the door.

"You can stomach the obnoxious women and their demands and their treating you like a slave," he said. "You have no trouble handling them. You have Lady Clara eating out of your hand."

Hope was trying to claw its way up out of the dark place where she'd buried it. She stomped it down. "That's business," she said without turning her head. "That's part of the guile and manipulation. My shop is my castle. But the beau monde is another world altogether."

"It's Lucie you're protecting, not yourself," he said. "You insist you have no redeeming qualities, but you love your daughter. You're not like your mother. Your child is not an inconvenience."

She paused, her hand on the door handle. Her chest was tight, a sob welling there, threatening to get out.

"Perhaps you don't own the usual set of scruples and morals and ethics and such," he said, "but you don't cheat your customers."

"I manipulate them," she said. "I want their money."

"And in return, you give them your utmost. You make them better than they think they can be. You gave Clara the courage to stand up to her mother and to me."

"Oh, Clevedon, you're such a fool. You're blinded by love." She turned to him then. "Do you think, because you can find a redeeming quality or two in my black heart, that all of the ton will see the same? They won't. They'll see that you married a Dreadful DeLucey—"

"The Earl of Hargate's son married one, and her daughter married an earl."

"I've heard that old story," Marcelline said. "You're talking about Bathsheba DeLucey. She brought Lord Rathbourne a great fortune. What do I bring? A shop. And Rathbourne's father, Lord Hargate, is a powerful man. You may stand higher in rank, but you've nothing like his power. Yesterday he walked into a crowd of bloodthirsty men as though you were a lot of schoolboys. The world respects and fears him. You're not like that, and you've no one like that to throw his weight around on your behalf. You've lived on the Continent and in the fringe world of London where idle aristocrats play. You've no political power. You haven't cultivated social power. You can't make your world accept me. You can't make them welcome and love Lucie."

"If you can't be welcome in my world," he said, "I'd rather not live there."

The horrid sob was building in her chest.

"I love you," he said. "I think I've loved you from the moment I first saw you at the opera—or, if not then, from the time you took my diamond stickpin. I'll admit that matters are sticky—"

"Sticky!"

"But it was a mad scheme to come to Paris and attract

my attention, in hopes of getting your hooks into my duchess," he said. "It was a mad, brave scheme to come to London in the first place, with a small child and two younger sisters and a few coins. It was mad to think you could set up a dressmaking shop by winning money at cards. But you did that before you knew me, before you'd ever thought about the Duchess of Clevedon. And so I'm very, very sure that you'll devise a mad scheme to solve our present problems, especially with my brilliant mind assisting you."

She was looking up at him, into those dangerous green eyes, and all she saw there was love. His beautiful mouth curved into the smile that could so easily warm a woman's heart, and lower down.

He truly did love her. After all she'd told him. He truly believed she could do anything.

"And if I don't?" she said. "If this sticky little matter proves too much even for my guile and imagination—"

"We'll live with it," he said. "Life isn't perfect. But I had much rather live it imperfectly with you."

"Th-that is a very f-fine s-sentiment." The sob was filling her chest.

"I didn't practice it at all," he said.

"Oh, Clevedon," she said.

He opened his arms. She walked into them. There was no choice, no choice at all. His arms closed about her and she wept, stupidly, but it was days and nights' worth of bottled-up fear and worry and sorrow and anger and hope.

Against all odds, hope. Because she was a dreamer and a schemer, and one didn't dream and scheme without hope.

"Does this mean I've won?" he said. Tears were all very well, but he needed to be absolutely sure.

"Yes," she said, her voice muffled against his waistcoat. "Although some might argue that you've lost."

"Will you marry me?"

A long pause.

His grip of her tightened. "Marcelline."

"Yes. I'm simply not noble enough to say no."

"Don't be noble, I beg you," he said. "I think nobleness of spirit . . . and morals . . . and ethics . . . and scruples . . . those sorts of things are all very well in their place. To a point, you know. But beyond a certain point, I think they make me bilious."

She looked up at him. Tears shimmered in her eyes but there was laughter as well, and it curved the corners of her beautiful mouth.

"It doesn't agree with me," he said. "I tried to be good. I tried not to be my father. I tried to live up to Lord Warford's standards. Then one day I realized it was pointless, and I'd had enough. That's when I set out with Longmore on a Grand Tour. But when he decided he'd had enough of the Continent, and wanted to come home, I didn't think I could stand coming back. Then you came into my life and everything changed. Because you were right. For me. Are. Right. For me." He slid his hand down her back. He heard her breath hitch.

That was all it wanted. That little sound. He had waited for so long. He'd suffered the tortures of the damned.

He tipped up her chin and untied her bonnet. He tossed it aside.

She winced. "That was my best bonnet. It took me forever to decide which one to wear."

"You? But you always know what to wear."

"I never had to confess to anybody before," she said. "That's my confession bonnet. I even trimmed it special—and you toss it aside like a soiled handkerchief."

"You confessed," he said. "It was beautifully done.

Like everything you do." He quickly untied the black lace thing around her neck.

She caught his hand before he could throw that down. "Clevedon, what do you think you're doing?"

They'd waited long enough. They'd made each other miserable for long enough. It was time for happiness.

"You know very well what I'm doing," he said.

"You didn't even lock the door," she said.

"Right."

He let go of her hand, picked up the nearest chair, and pushed it under the doorknob.

Then he led her to the sofa. He draped the lace thing over the back, and brought his hands to the fastenings of the layered cape.

"You can't undress me," she said.

He looked down at the layered cape and the great puffed sleeves and the belt, and he remembered what was underneath, layer upon layer. He remembered watching her undress herself. He remembered the way she'd set her leg on the bed, against his hip, and rolled down her stocking.

For a moment he couldn't breathe. His heart was pumping too fast and his breathing was too quick and that was nothing to the excitement stirring down low.

"Right," he said. "Another time." He drew her down onto the sofa and gathered her in his arms. He kissed her until her body went all soft and yielding and her arms wrapped about his neck, and she kissed him back in the same fierce way.

He lifted his mouth an inch from hers. "I've been wretched," he said.

"I've been wretched, too," she said. "I'm no good at being good."

"I don't want you to be good," he said. "I want you to be you. Marcelline. The woman I love."

She caught hold of his head and brought his mouth to hers.

It was a long, searching kiss, and a lifetime seemed to pass in that kiss, and a lifetime opened up before them. He'd very nearly ruined his life and hers, but they'd found their way at last.

He eased his mouth from hers and said against her cheek, "One of these days—soon—we'll have time for leisurely lovemaking. I'll spend a delicious forever taking off your beautiful clothes. "But for now . . ." He found the bodice fastening under the cape and he unhooked enough of the bodice to get to her corset and chemise, exposing a few inches of her velvety skin. He kissed the hollow of her throat, and the smooth curve of her neck, and she sighed, and arced back, like a cat stretching simply for the pleasure of it.

She still had one hand tangled in his hair while she moved the other over him, taking possession of him the way he took possession of her, so easily and naturally, with a touch. He heard the brush of her fingers over the wool of his coat sleeve and the rustle of his starched neckcloth as her hand moved downward. When she came to the waist of his trousers, he caught his breath.

She slid her hand down, and his cock swelled and rose at the touch, and "Mine," she said softly. "All this manly beauty. All mine."

He caught hold of her dress, the embroidered flowers feeling almost alive under his hand. He dragged it up by fistfuls, a great mass of dress and petticoats that billowed over his arm. He stroked over her drawers, upward over her thighs and between her legs to the opening of her drawers. He cupped her and she shivered. "Mine," he said. "All this feminine perfection. Mine."

His mouth found hers again and he kissed her and drank in the taste of her and the feel of her mouth and her tongue, and he took it all in like a man starved. And while he kissed her, he slid his fingers into the soft cleft between her legs. She was wet there, and her legs trembled as he stroked her, and then he was trembling, too. So much happiness.

"What a lucky man I am," he said.

She let out a throaty laugh. "You're about to get luckier."

She unfastened his trousers fully and grasped him. "I want you," she said softly. "I want you inside me. I want you to be mine and I'll be yours."

"Yes, yes, yes, whatever you say." He pushed into her, and he seemed to fly up into the heavens. He saw stars, and "Oh," she said. "Your *grace.*"

"Gervase," he said.

"Gervase," she said, and she made it a whisper, and the sound made him shiver. "*Mon amour.*"

Then in French: murmured words of nonsense and love and pleasure while they made slow love, then faster love, until there was nowhere farther to go, and they seemed to leap to a blinding happiness, like flying to the sun. Release came in a cascade of sweetness. Then he was sinking onto her, burying his face in her neck, and murmuring her name.

For a time they simply lay together.

Quietly. At peace.

So hard to believe, after so much turmoil. But here he was, in her arms, and there was her heart beating steadily in her chest and filled with happiness.

She held him, relishing his weight and the feel of his silky hair against her skin and the scent of him, while her breathing quieted, and the world came back.

"That was much more fun than self-sacrifice," he muttered.

She laughed. "Yes, *cheri*, it was."

He raised himself up to look at her. *"Cheri,"* he repeated. "Why does it sound so delicious when you say it?"

"Because I'm delicious," she said.

"The delicious Duchess of Clevedon," he said. "I like the sound of that. I like the feel of her better," he said. "And the scent of her. And the sound of her voice. And the way she moves. I love her madly. I would like to stay here, and count all the ways I love her, and show her all the ways I love her. But the world calls. Life calls." He kissed her, so tenderly, on her forehead. "We have to put our clothes on."

It took only a minute or two, since they hadn't taken very much off. For her, a slight rearrangement of her undergarments, a few hooks to fasten, a stocking to pull up, a garter to tie. For him, a quick business of pulling up his drawers and trousers, tucking his shirt in, and buttoning a handful of buttons.

He found her black lace fichu, and she tied it.

He collected her hat from the corner it had bounced to. He brushed it off, and attempted to straighten the plumes.

She watched him for a moment, then laughed. "Oh, Clevedon, you're the dearest man," she said. "Give me that thing. You've no idea what to do with it, but I do love you for trying."

He stilled briefly. Then he looked down at the hat and back at her. "Isn't that it?" he said. "Trying? If we try with all our hearts, do you not think we can make a go of this—of us? And then, even if it doesn't come out quite as we wish, at least we'll know we tried wholeheart-edly. That's the way you do everything, is it not? With all your heart. And look how far you've come and all you've achieved. Only think what we can do together."

"Well, there's that," she said, gesturing with her hat at the sofa. "We did that very well. Together."

He laughed. "Yes. And don't you think that a man who could do that—after a fight and a night of maudlin drinking—don't you think he could take on the ton? I may not be much of a duke, but I haven't given any time to the job. Only think what I might do, once I set my mind to it—with madame la duchesse at my side." He grinned and added, "And under me or on top of me or behind me as the case may be."

She lifted her eyebrows. "*Behind* you, your grace?"

"I see that you still have some things to learn," he said. He straightened his waistcoat.

"I was married very young, for a very short time," she said. "I'm practically a virgin."

He laughed again, and the sound was so sweet to her ears. He was happy, and so was she. And so she dared to hope, and dream, as she always did. And she dared to believe, that it would all come out as it ought, somehow, eventually.

He took her into his arms, crushing the hat.

She didn't care.

"I have a plan," he said.

"Yes," she said.

"Let's get married," he said.

"Yes," she said.

"Let's conquer the world," he said.

"Yes," she said. No one in her family had ever been accused of dreaming small.

"Let's bring the beau monde to its knees."

"Yes."

"Let's make them beg for your creations."

"Yes," she said. "Yes, yes, yes."

"Is tomorrow too soon?" he said.

"No," she said. "We've a great deal to do, you and I, conquering the world. We must start at once. We've not a minute to lose."

"I love hearing you say that," he said.

He kissed her. It lasted a long time.

And they would last, she was sure, a lifetime. On that she'd wager anything.

Epilogue

The dresses were brilliant in the extreme; and it afforded us much gratification to notice that those worn by her Majesty and the Royal Family, as well as many others, were chiefly composed of British manufacture.

The Court Journal, Saturday 30 May 1835

The Duke of Clevedon married Mrs. Charles Noirot at Clevedon House on Saturday the 16th of May. In attendance were her sisters, his aunts, Lord Longford, and Lady Clara Fairfax.

The two latter appeared in defiance of their parents—but Longford had never been noted for filial obedience, and Lady Clara had lately developed an invigorating habit of defying her mother. She'd worn a Noirot creation to the Queen's Drawing Room the previous Thursday, which caused a most gratifying stir.

When her brother had taxed her with aiding and abetting Clevedon's lunacy, she said, "He's still my friend, and I scorn to hold a grudge. I certainly shan't cut off my nose to spite my face. You know that no one has ever or will ever make me look as well as Mrs. Noirot does. Do stop acting like Mama."

That last remark brought Longmore around.

The duke's aunts presented a more formidable challenge. As soon as they received his message regarding his impending nuptials, they hurried to Town and took possession of Clevedon House, determined to bring him to his senses. On Wednesday afternoon, they'd settled down for a bout of tea drinking and bullying their nephew when Halliday ushered in his grace's prospective wife and in-laws and, as heavy artillery, Lucie. The aunts might have withstood the Noirot charm alone, but charm combined with mouth-watering dresses weakened their defenses, and Lucie, at her winsome best, routed them utterly.

On the Monday following the wedding, the youngest aunt, Lady Adelaide Ludley, visited the queen, with whom she shared a given name and was on warm terms. Her ladyship extolled the new duchess's deportment and taste. On learning that the queen had admired Lady Clara Fairfax's dress, Lady Adelaide pointed out that Maison Noirot patronized British tradesmen almost exclusively—a cause dear to Their Majesties' hearts. She mentioned that the Noirot sisters were founders of the Milliners' Society for the Education of Indigent Females—another point in their favor.

Lady Adelaide agreed with the queen that the Duchess of Clevedon, in intending to keep up her shop, presented the Court with a social dilemma. On the other hand, said her ladyship, the duchess acted on good moral principle in being unwilling to abandon either her customers or the young women she was training as seamstresses. In any event, as the duke had pointed out to his aunts, one could not expect an artist to give up her art.

In the end, Lady Adelaide received permission to present the new duchess to the queen. She did so at the Drawing Room held in honor of the King's Birthday, commemorated on the 28th of May. At one point during the festivities, the king summoned Clevedon, and spoke to him privately. His Majesty was heard to laugh.

When Clevedon returned to his wife's side, she said, "What was that about?"

"The Princess Erroll of Albania," Clevedon said. "He asked after her." His smile was conspiratorial. "I think we've done it. They've decided I'm eccentric and you're irresistible."

"Or the other way about," she said.

"Does it matter?" he said.

"No," she said. She bent her head, and the sound was soft, but he recognized it. "Duchess," he said, "are you giggling?"

She looked up, laughter dancing in her dark eyes. "I was only thinking: This has to be the greatest trick any Noirot or DeLucey has ever brought off."

"And to think," he said, "this is only the beginning."

Not many days thereafter, in the course of a promenade in St. James's Park, Miss Lucie Cordelia Noirot allowed the Princess Victoria to admire Susannah. The doll, as would be expected, was dressed for the occasion, in a lilac pelisse and a bonnet of *paille de riz,* trimmed with white ribbons and two white feathers.

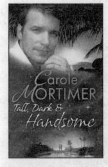
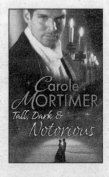
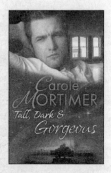
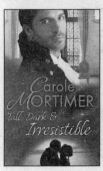

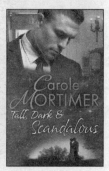

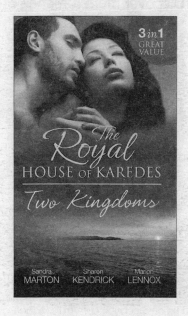

Discover more romance at

www.millsandboon.co.uk